The Secret Holy
War of Santiago de Chile

The Secret Holy War of Santiago de Chile

MARCO ANTONIO DE LA PARRA

A NOVEL

**translated by
Charles Philip Thomas**

INTERLINK BOOKS
An imprint of Interlink Publishing Group, Inc.
NEW YORK

To my father, Raúl Ruiz, and José Donoso, *indispensables*.

First published in English 1994 by

INTERLINK BOOKS
An imprint of Interlink Publishing Group, Inc.
99 Seventh Avenue
Brooklyn, New York 11215

English translation copyright © Charles Philip Thomas, 1994
Original Spanish copyright © Marco Antonio de la Parra, 1989

Originally published in Spanish as
La Secreta Guerra Santa de Santiago de Chile by
Editorial Planeta Chilena S.A., 1989

Library of Congress Cataloging-in-Publication Data

Parra, Marco Antonio de la.
    [Secreta guerra santa de Santiago de Chile. English]
    The secret holy war of Santiago de Chile / by Marco Antonio de la
Parra; translated by Charles P. Thomas.
        p.   cm. — (Emerging voices)
    ISBN 1–56656–127–2—ISBN 1–56656–123–X (pbk.)
    I. Title. II. Series.
PQ8098.26.A67S43 1994
863–dc20   93–19641
                                                                  CIP

Printed and bound in the United States of America
10 9 8 7 6 5 4 3 2 1

Contents

1

The Hidden Side of the Virgin of Peñablanca

The week immediately preceding the beginning of this story, Tito Livio had a dream: he was running through a long passageway full of doors, which upon opening submerged him in other corridors which were darker and darker, with the walls covered by distorted mirrors like those in amusement parks. He woke up anguished. Its theme seemed to come more from *Yellow Submarine*, which he had seen on video recently, or from Lewis Carroll, whom they had discussed in the office for the purpose of a commercial. But in spite of the dream which kept repeating itself all night, he didn't hesitate to brush it aside and attribute it to having had one too many, his pounding brain, or the sea-bass Chambourd which, although splendid, suffered from acidity.

Because of this, for him, Tito Livio, everything began just a couple of days before finding his father's body, when he left to take notes on the miracle of the Virgin of Peñablanca.

In a greasy spoon restaurant in Villa Alemana, that small city which no one remembered much about until the news of the supposed

1

apparitions of the Virgin, on an exceptionally bright sunny day for the month of November, Tito Livio began to talk to a photographer friend in a very loud voice. The table was full of beer bottles.

"You know that in an advertising agency the only thing that's important is to be outstanding. Do you hear? A genius! There's no middle ground! To be a genius that day according to the daily brief was nothing less than to come up with a video ad with a presentation for hair coloring by Julio Iglesias. Can you imagine what it's like for a sensitive man, a free spirit, preoccupied with art, the avant-garde, culture, to even think of working with Julio Iglesias?"

"You've worked on worse things," the other guy said to him, fiddling with the telephoto lens on his Nikkon.

"Five years, five years of my creative life dedicated to wasting my creative talent as a creative editor and then creative director. And that creative day writing a creative script for that goofball Julio Iglesias and the boss of the creative department asking me: Do you like Julio Iglesias? And how about your wife? He's asking *me* this, I'm not asking you. And I'm thinking about my *mina*, my gold mine, my honey. In the Gente discotheque watching a video of Julio Iglesias in the Bahamas. In the Bahamas, the motherfucker! And this *mina* drinking an Old Fashioned and another Old Fashioned and telling me that yes, that she likes Julio Iglesias and another Old Fashioned and one more because my *mina* has a thick skull, and then I short circuit, the gringo Mac-Pherson, my *mina*, Pinochet, the dictatorship, Fatty Aspillaga, the clients calling me, the same old shit, and I'm saying to her, Mina, hey, I'm going to the can . . ."

"Your *mina*'s name is Mina? That's fuckin' funny."

"Yeah, she's Italian. Her name is Mina. Well, what's important is that I leave in my car like a bat out o' hell, and I get into her apartment and pack my suitcase and scribble down a few stupid lines to Mina. And I came right here. To Villa Alemana."

"Do you believe all this stuff about the miracle?"

"Look, I don't really care one way or the other. What I came for was to write a book. A sensational book, nothing mediocre. Creative nonfiction. Do you hear, Arturito? *A la americana.*"

"It's not gonna fly, Tito, it's a bad idea. It's not gonna get you anywhere."

"If it falls flat, it falls flat. I could care. Have you even noticed the people that are coming here? Don't you think this miracle thing is pretty weird? What are these little daddy's girls doing on their knees praying to the Virgin, seeing fish in the clouds, burning out their eyes looking straight up at the sun? What are all these people who've already got more than they need asking for anyway? Why are they listening to that mental midget of a pimp who thinks he's Saint Bernadette of Lourdes? What's gonna happen when the whole mess comes crashing down? And the poorer people. Do they really think they're gonna get something useful out of this Virgin? Why are they saying that she spoke out against the church in Chile? The whole thing's really weird. Sure. That's exactly why I've gotten into it. Remember that in my first novel . . ."

"The only one . . ."

"The only one, right, the only one. You have to keep reminding me. Look, my novel was a shot in the dark. And you know why? Because they banned it, because I said what you weren't supposed to say, because it was against the law. I insulted any jerk that got in my way. I didn't leave any prisoners."

"You mean you didn't 'take any prisoners.'"

"Oh, yeah. Beer is the cancer of literature. Let's have a toast, Arturo, grab yourself one. To the return of Tito Livio Triviño to the world of Chilean letters! Tito Triviño!"

He savored his thoughts before continuing.

"*The Hidden Side of the Virgin of Peñablanca.* Doesn't it sound suggestive enough? Ambiguous enough?"

"You're gonna get in trouble with the church, and you know what that means in Chile today."

"So I get in trouble with them. There shouldn't be any untouchables in Chile. No hierarchy above the truth. That's what's got us where we are. I'm gonna give it to all of 'em, to the secret police, to the Democratic Alliance, to the soap stars who think they're such artists . . ."

"The same as you."

"If it's all about selling out, we've all sold out. You're not a very good buddy, Arturito Estevez. It must be the beer. A lot o' beer. And you know what else? I'm gonna have to find the head because nature is calling." He stood up pompously. "There hasn't been enough written on the diuretic effects of these beverages, a physiological affront to the free flow of conversation."

"Don't leave me hanging like your *mina*, huh? I don't plan on paying for the whole dozen beers."

Tito laughed. He threw a thousand peso bill on the table.

"We publicists are just more expensive whores than photographers. There you go so you'll go away happy. See you at the miracle."

"You got it."

Tito went to find the urinals. Between the stacks of cases of bottles he saw a door that looked promising. He hurriedly went in, his bladder about to burst, but there was only a dirt patio with a filthy grill, a dry trough and more cases of bottles, empty this time. He thought they must have stocked up for the miracle. Maybe that was the reason for this real labyrinth. He was going to jot down the image but his bladder emergency got first priority. Without turning around again he took out his member, ready to make his personal mark on the adobe wall. He laughed at himself. From his foggy, slightly woozy beer-soaked brain, he toasted the Virgin. He was shaking it off, amused by his sophomoric blasphemies, when he felt he was being watched.

He turned around. An average sized guy, with glasses, blond, with frizzy hair, balding, in his fifties. His thick tortoiseshell eyeglasses were refracting this Thursday's bright Villa Alemanian sun.

"What are you looking at?"

A pervert? A bisexual voyeur? The owner of the place coming to give me shit for pissing on his wall? The Minotaur from this labyrinth of cases and bottles?

"We're waiting for you."

"Waiting? What for?"

The guy smiled at Tito. Politely, one would say.

"For you to come with us."

Directly behind him another man appeared, thinner, taller. Both wore three-piece suits that were somewhere between sky gray and olive green, having lost their original color through great use as revealed by the shiny sleeves and trouser legs. They had on nondescript woven ties, super-thin, very wrinkled, and were wearing hats.

4

THE SECRET HOLY WAR OF SANTIAGO DE CHILE

The first thing that Tito thought about was his father taking him, as a child, to Santa Laura Stadium, downtown, to Cousino Park. Without understanding why he remembered the Café Jamaica, the Quick Lunch Bahamondes, the great Ravera pizzas with oil dripping over the edges. Be careful not to get stains, his father's voice. His mother wiping the oil off his skin with a handkerchief.

"We want you to come with us."

Tito Livio was crapping his pants. He thought they were from the secret police. Finally the famous and terrifying CNI in front of him, the highly feared monster from the national collective unconscious in front of him. After so much raving from inoffensive platforms: the office, bed, in taxis, some bookstores, the bar. Now they were coming, they were grabbing him, they were putting him through infinite tortures and proving what was an absolute certainty: Tito Triviño was a coward. He would inform on Fatty Aspillaga, however many friends or enemies he met in his varied university studies: medicine, theatre, sociology. Half of them were in exile. Like his brother Gustavo, now living in Madrid. He would also denounce him. Mina had to have turned him in. She was capable of anything. A traitor.

"It's because of your father that we're looking for you."

Oh, because of Alberto Triviño, his father. The original Tito, he knew it, the academician and professor of biology at the illustrious National Institute. How long had it been since they had talked about him? He became calm for a few seconds but then remembered that his father had been fairly radical, socialistic, much like Aguirre Cerda, voting for Allende like a stubborn mule until he won, a supporter of the Popular Front, champion of the people of Chile. They were from the CNI, there was no doubt. It was certain that the old guy was involved in the outlawed Communist Party.

"Why don't you come with us?" said the other guy, the thin one. He was overly friendly, almost suave, which was very unsettling. His voice was sharp, like a beverage vendor at the National Stadium. A pencil-thin mustache like a bolero singer. Like Javier Solís, thought Tito.

"Listen, I'm not going anywhere," he boasted. "You guys don't have any IDs or any court order, and you can't make me and that's that."

The two of them looked at each other. The shorter one shrugged his shoulders and the skinny one clicked his tongue. They touched the brim of their hats almost at the same time and turned halfway around: ciao. Tito felt even more confused. What was going to happen now? Were they trying to get their courage up to beat the hell out him? Were they going for reinforcements? He looked at the walls of the small patio. A door, a door, for the love of God. He looked at the sky searching for the Virgin, asking her to take him out of there. His bladder swelled up again: fear. Or was it punishment from heaven for having blasphemed? One door, he saw it, a blue door. Some unbelievably idiotic chickens got in his way. A lot of squawking: stepping in chicken shit, chickens pecking at him, he opened the door and went out into an alley that he didn't recognize. Nobody. He began to jog. Tito Livio Triviño, alias the coward, the son of Alberto Triviño, alias Tito Puente for his mambo dancing ability in his younger days. He was running and he was beginning to repent: What the hell am I doing here? Why didn't I become a doctor like my mother wanted? Why did I stay with her when the old couple separated? Why did I take off? Why did I leave the little girls alone with Ana María? Why did I get mixed up with Graciela, and with Isabel, and Nicole, and with Mina? Above all, how the hell did I get mixed up with Mina?

Tito was running, believing he was moving out of danger, without knowing that he was only beginning a series of troubled days and that he was kicking up more ground than he was covering. A dirt road, sure it is. He took a look at his dirty pants and awkwardly shook them off.

"Where are you going in such a hurry?"

It was the sweetest sound in the world. He felt her shining and soft to his right. It was a mixture of his older daughter's speech when she recently mentioned him by name, with the same phrasing as his beloved ex-wife, always beloved, always more in love than he.

"Where are you going?"

An incredibly beautiful woman, translucent, clear eyes unlike any human eye he could have ever seen, transparent skin as if tropical fish could float inside her, seawater, flowing. Her voice was coming out to him like a dissipating cloud, a most friendly and hypnotic fairytale. The heat was disappearing as if it had only been a bitter memory, a bad joke that's easier to forget. Tito's mouth fell open: we've only come this far, what a beautiful woman. And the strangest thing: he didn't have any desire to try a line on her, nor to whistle at her, or to try to pick her up.

He remained enchanted, studying her. The woman pointed directly through him (what beautiful fingers, white, long, a pearl-colored fingernail which reflected the above-mentioned sun) and Tito turned around.

"What's my car doing here?"

She laid her head on her shoulder and covered herself with a mantilla, her long softly flowing hair. What color was it? A color that none of those dyes for which he wrote promotional and strategical sales copy could ever match. Her hair was beyond anything having to do with chemicals, I swear to you, I swear to you, the most incredible hair and me, Tito Livio, looking at my car, looking at her, I understood what she was telling me, without her telling me, to go away, that it was good for me, that it would be the best thing that could happen to me. So I jump into my car and it starts immediately with the faithful hum of the Toyota, blessed motor, thank God.

Then she comes up to the car and Tito doesn't know if she's skating or walking on water, sliding over the ether. The fact of the matter is she's not stirring up one speck of dust. She's approaching like a small yacht, like skiing over a frozen lake and bending like a ship's mast. It's not overdone! I swear to you! That's what she was like! And she says to me: "It's better for you to go with them when they ask you to. Then you'll see that they don't have bad intentions."

Tito was barely listening, or not listening, or half listening or is charmed and he leaves like a shot and begins to recover when he's already on the highway and thinks: Who was she? And he tries hard to figure out who she could be. He's seen her somewhere but he doesn't believe in the Virgin or in Christ Our Lord, nor in the resurrection of the dead nor in everlasting life, nor amen.

He is pensive, driving slowly, too slow for his vain Toyota Celica, imposing.

Who was she? The question is not getting any clearer. A small Citroen shows up in his rearview mirror, which wouldn't mean anything if there weren't two men with hats manning it. Those guys. He gets restless but then puts on an arrogant smile. How long has it been since he's seen Citroens of that type, the French miracle, the dream of the Chilean middle class of the sixties? Ridiculous, he says.

He accelerates in the middle of a loud laugh but the Citroen follows, stuck in his mirror as if it had been drawn on the back windshield. Impeccable, dauntless. People coming in the opposite direction are staring at it. The only thing that Tito Livio wants is to get to Santiago, but first he has to lose that damned Citroen. He accelerates, pushes it to the floor. He's thinking about the police and their radar guns. He has to avoid them. There's no doubt that if they grab him for speeding they'll hand him over to the guys in the Citroen: they're all in it together. He lays off on the gas, noticing that they aren't interested in cutting him off. They're keeping their distance. Oh my God, who are they? He surprises himself by saying *my God*. His mother, praying her fucking brains out. A veritable museum of plaster saints through the whole house. Especially since she started living alone. A Virgin in her bedroom who she would always ask for things, and ask, and ask, and then ask for more. Tito would watch her from his nearby bedroom and they would put scapularies on her and he accompanied her to the offerings from San Cristóbal Hill. "She's a Virgin who can do more, don't you see that she's higher up?" Complaining against the Virgin of Lourdes de la Quinta Normal. Don't you see that it's a copy and not the original? But what did he get from praying if they were still following him. He looked in the rearview mirror. It can't be. No one. They weren't following him now.

He stopped to look. In Llay-llay he had a drink right next to the highway, waiting to see them pass. Nothing. He got back into the car and left for Santiago, the capital of Chile. He was not at all calmed down.

2

You're harassing me in my dreams, Mother

Santiago was sunny and deadly as only Santiago can be. Humidity and hard cement. Tito Livio got on lower Alameda. He thought about going to MacPherson but he decided to take the day off instead. They've probably tried the apartment, and Mina answered, furious after reading his note. Fatty Aspillaga, like the voice of a guardian angel, explaining to Mina that it's a good idea that she take care of him, that she watch out for him, you know what Tito is like. No, no one knows what Tito is like. Nobody knows what I'm like and it's better that way. He thought about going to see his mother in her apartment near the Chacabuco Plaza. As he was directing the course of his Japanese ship, he remembered the infinite craftiness of his forbearer who didn't want to separate herself from the church of Nuestra Señora de la Estampa where he and his brother had taken their first communion. The first and last, like his novel. That damned Estevez, photographer for *La Nación*, had to remind him of that fact. Who in hell gave him a license to preach? Arturo Estevez, the photographer that the Chilean movie scene needed, his camera work, his brilliance, the man God the Father would have asked to

9

photograph the creation of the world? What is someone like you, the envy of Alekian, Almendros, and Hamilton, doing working for a dying, government-serving paper like *La Nación*? And what are you doing, Mister Tito Livio, writing drivel, barely convincing yourself that granulated coffee has important advantages over toothpaste or gel with flouride, or absorbent paper towels with bubbles, or beer with saccharine? Because of that we understand each other, unbelievers, traitors. That's the essential question: What's a guy like me doing in a place like this? Pure metaphysics. The existential definition of *Dasein*, the being-there, the being-for-purely-being, the being-for-being. No, much less frivolous. Mercenaries, that's it.

He was coming up on Independence Street, ugly as sin, a filthy mess. He would never use it as a location for any commercial. Who would buy anything that they liked there? Right away, pow!, a big billboard with Everybody's Soap. His unmistakable trademark that had make him famous, rich and famous but alone and poor in spirit, unknown in all true artistic and literary circles. Invitations still came: some galleries, a book promotion. His name was still on the computers. He gave them to his mother who collected them. She was proud, she always told him: They talked about you, they quoted you. What for? Because you haven't written anything else, with your talent, a gift from heaven, I know full well.

Independence Street made him more depressed and hurt. He thought about his father telling him for the nth time about what Gomez Millas wanted when he was Rector of the University of Chile, to construct a great university city on the Central Plain, taking the womb and intestines of the capital with it, futher north. Can you imagine how the neighborhood would have grown? Waiting for this, they had stayed on the outskirts of the plaza. In the beginning, a small house on some land, afterwards the separation and the apartment near the hospital: In case I die, said his mother, who spoke out so much against the neighborhood, and who, at the end, refused to leave. Concrete piece of land, asphalt heart.

What did they say about me? About why you weren't writing again, about if you were a lost talent, about if yours was only a fleeting attempt like so many in this country who get frustrated and have to leave for foreign countries. Like José Donoso, sure. It made him so mad that

10

they were quoting him. What were they saying about me? His mother always said to him: I want to have a famous son. Gustavo only writes for parties. You know what he's like.

If anyone didn't say anything to him it was his father. He limited himself to running his hand over his face when they would have lunch together at the Chez Henry or at the Faisan d'or, across from the Plaza de Armas which he seemed to idolize for its persistence, and which Tito hated. (The sickening docility of its pigeons, the limitations of a small town plaza, the unkempt look of the cathedral, the retired people who put pro-Pinochet insignias on their lapels, the smell of hair-dye which emanated from the old variety-show artists who offered themselves for a few quick pesos while standing in front of the Vicarage of Solidarity, the van full of policemen, the loud gruff voice of a deranged preacher who insisted that the end of the world was just around the corner.) His father would say to him invariably: I'm old, but if you need anything ask me for it. And he didn't have anything to give him. Tito himself paid the room and board for him, almost took care of the elder Triviño by himself, also retired, but one of those without an insignia, one of the ones who at least did not show their old age. Only once in a while a package would come for him from Spain. Tobacco, a bottle of brandy, magazines. Every time, together with dessert, he would announce his impending death from a heart attack in the middle of the Chile Hippodrome, on Wednesday or on Saturday, in the middle of the electronic scoreboard, in the middle of the final race, with the horses giving it all they had straight ahead on the track, with Last Chance on the rail, Father Smurf in the center, Calamity Jane out front and Grace Jones half a head behind. There, Alberto Triviño would fall, face down in the dirt, babbling, grasping in the air in search of an invisible helping hand. Where are you now, verbose father? Where?

"Hello."

His mother opened the door for him. Her face was stained by a blotched lupus which changed her into an abashed complainer. She used to go out on the street with her parasol and Tito thought: This is the Madwoman of Chaillot. But she felt happy. When Tito came in she opened the windows so light would come in with her son, light of my life, and Tito would say to her: "Mom, sun is bad for your skin," he always told her.

But this time his mother did not follow her ritual. She stayed where she was, just looking at him, asked him if he came alone. Tito nodded and she let him in. The house was dark, as it always was. She turned on a flickering light, less than 25 watts. Wooden and plaster saints filled the walls. She had rearranged all the furniture, rugs, and house plants again.

"Do you like them? I'm going to buy a red flowering rubber plant, and a yellow one. They don't cost very much."

He also provided the houseplant money. How did they ever survive in the darkness? When could they possibly find enough light to keep growing? Finding any in here was impossible. Some spider plants were drooping over a bloody San Sebastián, punctured with arrows, the ferns were reaching higher, the shamrock was reaching out its shoots, half covering the tortured nakedness of the leaf of a dwarf philodendron, too big for its age. He thought about the other name for spider plants: bad mother. They threw their children out of the nest, but without cutting the cord. An intimate friend of his, whom he couldn't remember now, had pointed this out to him. Exiled, for a change.

"Mina called me, asking for you. You had a fight with her."

Asking without asking, that's my mother's strategy. She's so happy every time I finish or start a relationship. If it lasts a long time she gets nervous. One time I dreamed she was chasing me with an electric saw. That was before I met Mina and left Nicole. Obviously, I left Nicole and I was calm, finally at peace.

"You're harassing me in my dreams, Mother."

"They aren't those erotic dreams, are they?" and she fixed her wig coquettishly. She's lost her hair from the medicine. The corticoids have made her put on weight.

"I broke up with Mina."

"What do you want me to say, I'm happy. I thought she was pretty average and a little chubby. Those Italian girls get fat a lot and Mina never takes care of herself. Do you want a glass of orange juice? I've got a new juice that just came out and turkey-ham that you love, and some cans of Spanish sardines that you just won't believe, but they were selling them on the street and they're so good."

Tito's stomach was getting tense just thinking about what was coming. However, he noticed a contradictory feeling of peace, of refuge, in spite of all the tension that was there.

"How come you didn't open the windows?"

"The sun is bad for me. That's what you always tell me."

A glass of rancid orangeade, and ham that had been in the refrigerator so long it almost had freezer burn. Under no circumstances would there be any unfavorable comments about what he was being offered. The table was full of food. She was on a diet because of the lupus. Everything for him, everything for you. Who takes care of you like I do? Your damned mother, as every one of his partners would say. No one like her. French pastries, homemade mayonnaise, little hot sausages sizzling in oil in the frying pan, the rattling of the outside ventilation fan making the suffocating atmosphere of the apartment vibrate.

Gustavo had said to him: At least in Madrid I save myself from Mom's big feasts; and then: Why don't you come over? Tito hadn't answered him. He gave the argument about a rising career, commitments in the country. You should come back, he scolded him. You don't even have a reason for being in exile. You should be fighting to get democracy back in Chile. Etcetera. A bunch of bull. Gustavo had smiled to himself. The fact of the matter is, you have to take care of Mom. And Dad, and everyone, and myself too.

"Why are they following you, son?"

If this had been a gangster film, Tito would have squeezed the glass of whisky and the ice cubes would have doubled from the absolute cold he felt. Crack! His false front broke into pieces. She had him, and he had to put on a fake smile. He thought about the half fallen down roadside signs for Pepsodent: That kid's got *pep*, this kid's got *fear*.

"Where'd you get that idea?"

"They were here," she was talking to him from the kitchen, wandering in and out without looking at him. That's what she was always like with the hottest topics. Checks? I prayed for you. Women? You know that I know of a few midwives and we pray to San Ramón Nonato so that . . .

Tito jerked around. Through the slats in the venetian blinds he made out a small Citroen going slowly past, very slowly, in front of the building.

"Is it them?" Tito pointed with his finger.

"Who? No, it was a big car, sleek. It scared me quite a bit, what else can I say? A silver car. Very nice people. They said that it didn't have anything to do with anything bad, but it came to me like a premonition, a strange feeling. And it's not like you either, to come around here at this time of day, in the middle of the week. You don't think about your mother very much. Sometimes it's like I didn't even exist. I could die and nobody would ever know. You two never ask about me. You're just like your miserable father. You never take me to see my grandchildren. Never."

Tito had heard this song before. He thought, without listening, about the fact that there were now others who were after him, maybe the same ones. No, the ones your mother saw were "good looking guys, tall like you, Tito, handsome, around forty. There were three of them and very much the gentlemen. But they were intimidating, what should I say, a strange look, I don't know."

"Look, Mom, a lot of strange things go on in this country. Don't pay any attention to it."

"Sure. And above all to you, who's a well-known intellectual. Are you writing? Really? What's it about?" Tito cleared his throat. The interrogation was beginning.

"It's about the Virgin."

"I hope you won't be too hard on her," his mother interrupted. "It's a very delicate situation. They'll take you to jail right away. They might do something to you."

"No, it's a very sensitive homage to the figure of Mary," lied Tito Livio.

He was sick of nibbling sausages, canned seafood, quail eggs. Later on his mother would give him a tranquilizer and a muscle relaxer. It was the same as always. With an envelope of Enobrand fruit-flavored powdered bicarbonate of soda, or whatever was on sale in the pharmacy on the first floor. Thanks Mommy, without you I'm nothing.

"Do you want to stay here?" Why was she asking that? Had everything frightened her that much?

"Look, Mom, the fact is I'm not writing anything, that's the truth. I'm tired of writing stupid things for a supposedly high salary that gets less every day and harder to take because of the stupid sleazy work."

"I really liked the lotion commercial. It makes you think, you know?"

14

"Mama, it's all taken from an Australian ad campaign. You're not listening to me. I'm worse off than ever. I broke off with everything. I would like to write again but I've got a block. I'd like to go back, begin all over again. Do you understand?"

"You're exaggerating. Besides, it's not good for you to weigh yourself down with so many depressing thoughts. You know that bad vibrations attract bad things. There's always been some catastrophe ever since you were young. You should go see Gonzalo."

Tito put the glass on the table with a brusque movement. An orangeade storm. Crush.

"I can't spend my whole life in the psychologist's office! I've been going to see him since I was ten years old."

"You were affected a lot by the separation. You're more sensitive and more intelligent than boys your age."

The word *boy* didn't even affect him now. It was old hat, inevitable in his mother's vision of the world. His brother Gustavo was the only survivor. He had dedicated himself to teaching and then to research. A worthy successor to his father, a corrected and augmented version one could say. In Madrid, married with children, walking on Isaac Peral Street towards Complutense. A good guy, he deserved it.

He looked at the plaster Virgin in the bedroom while he walked back and forth listening to his mother's droning. Underneath the image was a pile of medicines with which, over a span of time, she was trying to kill herself. He congratulated himself for having prevented it in the past five years, thanks to periodic visits and opportune attention. According to Gonzalo, thanks to their separation. But that was a whole different story. He looked at the Virgin and it seemed to him that she moved. He got scared.

"If you believed more, if you had more faith, only God knows what you could end up being. Pay attention to me, pay attention to me. Don't listen to that Mason of a father of yours."

"Don't talk to me about him."

She focused in on another favorite topic: raving against Alberto Triviño who never gave you anything, who ran away abandoning his family, two children, making them suffer. The dubious sexuality of her ex-husband, his stinginess, the contempt he always had for his offspring, a womanizer, hypochondriac, a liar.

Tito thought that it was time to leave. From the age of seven on, according to his calculations, he had been listening to this long list of his father's unpardonable defects. Señor Triviño, your son wants to talk to you, Tito Livio. And his father would break into a smile and hug him in the middle of the school corridor. He would get sad afterwards, before saying goodbye, and would relentlessly run his hand over his face.

The Virgin's face. He stared at it. The pretty Virgin.

"Where can I go now?" thought Tito. His mother had stopped her diatribe.

"Take a siesta," she said.

He stretched out on the sofa. He heard her shut her bedroom door and begin to pray the rosary. He got up on tiptoe and left, closing the door carefully. He was an expert at escapes. Before he left he wrote her some sweet, trivial line that she would feel was unforgettable. Outside, the sun continued to beat down on the city. He got into his car, which was like an oven, and it started on the first try.

Where do I go now?

3

I'm lost, there's no hope for me

So that's how Tito decided to go to the agency. He would make up some vague story about an accident which would permit him to make an honorable return to his home base of MacPherson Advertising, and he was ready. When he was driving the Toyota into the noble agency's parking lot, he noticed the empty space in the manager's slot. A good sign. The stars are with you, my friend. He was getting out of his car when he spotted Barbara. That knockout Barbara, who, as soon as she noticed Tito Livio staring at her, shook her hips and threw back her long blonde Amazon mane. Some day you'll be mine. How many times had he vowed the same thing. She had even appeared in one of his masturbatory fantasies. Are you still beating off, Tito Livio? Still. And why do you think that is? Because I was born pulling my pud, and because whacking it is my vocation, my purpose. What else but masturbating is my way to face the world, almost an ideology, an ethic of self-sufficiency, a stance in front of the world. Is there anyone who thinks differently? No one. Except Steiner, the heavy-breathing account executive who is coming limping through the reception area. There was a framed poster from the Lipton campaign behind him, and Tito looked at himself in the glass: *I'm a Lipton fanatic*. His apparent namesake: Tito Fouilloux, inflexible, in the Chilean copy of the international campaign with Don Meredith. *The exact copy of Eden*. We've even been blaming ourselves in the words from the national anthem: copycats.

"Tito, we're waiting for you upstairs. It's time for the kick-off," said Steiner with a twinkle in his eye. A kick-off! It had the air of a worldwide event. Here, the course of events of human destiny will be changed.

Tito Livio doesn't pay much attention, he climbs the stairs and hurries through the Creative Department. Fatty Aspillaga, where did you go, Fatty Boy?

"There's a meeting this afternoon about the filming in Fallabella," they say to him in passing.

Yeah, yeah, shooting in the daylight, pretending it's night. *La nuit americaine*.

"Outstanding, Tito, it's gonna come out fantastic, you gotta see the takes, they gotta be edited before six." Once again. Okay, okay.

Outstanding, outstanding. Wasn't Arturito Estevez telling you that? You're outstanding, Tito Livio. Yeah, yeah, I know it. Fatty shows up and he's got wicked garlic breath. They were eating with some clients at the Catalá. No doubt about it. Fatty loves garlic and he eats it without being one bit shy, as if it were gum. Then he eats some mints. An illusion: garlic and mints, the new essence from Limara, the *parfum dea*.

"They're looking for you."

Fatty greets him with this sentence, up close. The door to the office is closed. Coca-Cola: an advertising classic along the entire wall.

"They're looking for you, Tito."

Naively, he thought about Harry MacPherson, the Tito himself. Then all of a sudden it hit him, it came down on his body like a ton of bricks, more like blocks of ice from an igloo, a cold chill down his spine: a cold sweat melting away any chance for a moment of safety, at home, or at the office.

"They came by this morning. What kind of mess have you gotten yourself into? Besides that, Mina called at least five times. Five times! Does it have to do with her? Or do you want me to take a guess?

Money? the Celica GT? You bought yourself the new Celica? Fantastic! Just what you needed, they'll be hauling your ass off to the poorhouse."

"No, I don't owe money and I didn't buy the GT . . ."

"Well, then?"

Tito closed the blinds. It was beginning to get hot. Soon it would be impossible to work without the air conditioner running full blast. There was a bumper sticker from the Christian Democrat party stuck to the window: the Moeiera kid is overdoing it with the propaganda. We don't allow political ads here, the gringo would say, and that would start a fruitless debate about the politics of supposedly non-political advertising.

"So, then, what the hell's going on?"

Fatty adopted him. Every time there was a disaster, Fatty would designate him as his adopted son. He transformed himself into father godfather overseer older brother Mary Poppins Salvation Army Saint Bernard. In deep shit up to his eyeballs: Aspillaga appeared.

"I don't know why they're following me, Fat One."

"That can't be right. Some big guys that look like they're CIA agents?

"Oh, those guys. My mom told me about them."

"I'm fed up with hearing about your mother."

Steiner opened the door. Another blast of garlic. Now I understand everything.

"Brainstorming!"

The worst thing was Steiner's English, and the garlic on top of that. To the conference room. Red alert! Some injustice was reputedly being carried out against Skinny Scott or Blacky Mendoza. We've got a leak, get ready for action.

Before leaving the office, Aspillaga took Tito by the arm as only an ex-university boxer can.

"Let go of me, Fatty."

"I want you to explain to me what's happening."

"Yes, Daddy."

"You're getting yourself into a real mess. For the first time in your life, listen to someone who knows more than you. A big hassle, I can smell it."

More garlic breath.

"I can smell it too."

"Oh, I'm sorry . . . it's just that we went to the Catalá."

"Yes, Father."

They left. What Aspillaga wanted was a confession. Isn't that right, Tito? You should get on your knees and pray, force yourself, cross yourself like you've never done before. You should feel remorse from your guts and accept the fact that you're a wimp, disloyal, full of arrogance about everything, vile, cunning, despicable. God, I'm not worthy of you coming into my body, but only one word.

Ego te absolvo.

The room was full. Milton was hanging up all the fold-out pages from an exhausted newspaper campaign for a model of a car that no one would buy in a country that was always on the brink of going down the tubes, always getting the ball right before it goes out of bounds, or tying by a penalty shot at the last moment. But there would always be fearless and daring people. Humility is the enemy of the profession, MacPherson used to say. There he was, ironically walking by right next to Tito.

"Where did you go? You know how important it is to have the agency's genius here, don't you?"

Tito found himself drifting away. The image of his father was coming to him incessantly. What the hell was happening?

"Let's see what our ace says."

Everyone stares at Super Tito, in you we trust, give us peace and unity, open your golden mouth and grant us the power of your word.

One of your words is enough to heal us.

Should I say what I'm thinking? I say that we're fabricating a royal farce selling something that is not of interest if they do buy it, that we're only destroying values, culture, language, customs, that it is frankly immoral to succeed in selling?

No, it's not worth the trouble, Tito. Don't take it to heart so much. They're not to blame. Neither MacPherson nor Nissan. Calm down.

"I feel real sick. Please excuse me . . ."

He stood up to leave. As if to dramatize the situation, he ran into Willy, who was bringing in cups of coffee, mineral water and cookies. Everything ended up on the floor. Both of them were soaked, everything was soaked: the door, the wall hanging, the papers. A close up of Tito picking up the cups which were rolling on the thick rug towards Sandra's legs. He grabs them and Sandra's look grabs him. Come to see me tonight. The soft voice, melodious when she wants, of the Titan of the Creative Department. What do you want from me, Moorish queen? Sweet Moorish woman, so fine. Come to see me, I'll treat you well. Queen mother whore mother, what do you want from me? Nothing, I'll give you what you want. Error. Tito is leaving. Error, you're wrong, Sandra. The muscles of the infamous one become excited in the air, intertwining themselves, to the right, to the left: between my legs is tranquility, the final rest, calm, the place where mammals die.

Tito leaves.

"They're looking for you."

To the bathroom, run to the bathroom. In the reflection from a framed poster, in the face of a beautiful model, very maternal, he sees the images of two guys with hats in the reception area. To the bathroom.

Closing the door, opening the window which looks over the parking lot. He will hang out the window like one of Dumas' musketeers in the Richard Lester version, and he will drop to the ground, the assistant accountants will stare at him, gringo MacPherson and his whole court will watch him. To the car: started up and sounding like a percolator, he backs up like a shot, changes gears and is getting out of there. He sees the beat-up little green Citroen next to the door. He's leaving when he sees them in the rearview mirror. They don't seem to be in a hurry, they put their hats on very calmly, and with the mildness of those who are in power, they come towards the exit. They're coming. Tito.

Then Triviño Junior does one of those things which cost one so dearly in life. Without thinking twice, he slams his Toyota full force into the Citroen and smashes out a headlight. He backs up and attacks again. The battering ram of the Huascar going into the fragile Esmeralda. Sink, sink. He crushes it to pieces. The workers are watching him from the agency's windows. Tito Livio Triviño is sick, very sick. Fatty Aspillaga will begin to cry. Sandra will feel that she didn't do enough. Harry Mac will say that he should have looked for another editor, another, any other except the jackal from Lyon street. The Citroen is smashed to smithereens and Tito Livio accelerates and leaves rubber, and he runs red lights, very red, and streaks like a comet to Costanera Avenue, and from there to Vitacura and the apartment. If Mina is there he'll let her have it, if she isn't, he'll think about how he's going to do it later on. He'll take a shower, and change clothes, he'll throw a tantrum, want to be a child, have a mom and dad who can say to him, what's wrong, what's the matter?

"I'm lost, there's no hope for me," he says to himself, like in the comics. He still feels the twisted bones of the French miracle grating in his mind. The dented Toyota cruises along Nueva Costanera. He slams on the brakes. The open window tells him that Mina is there, she's there, she's there.

He opens the door which is ajar. A soft melody is coming from the radio. American folk music.

"You're forgetting that nowadays I can hurt you if I decide to."

Mina's voice, loud, flaming scraggly hair, raging eyes, originally green but now irate: blazing.

"Who the hell do you think you are? Doing something like that to me. How is it possible? You think people are on this earth to wait on you."

Nothing new, the same as always. Tito knows this goodbye scene by memory. His ex-wife, his lovers, they're all taking turns. But Tito's fed up, Mina. You should consider that you don't fuck with a man who's reached his limit. Tito goes over and slaps her. I told you, Mina.

But she's to be reckoned with. She takes a blow and gives him a kick you-know-where.

Poor Tito.

One of your words won't be enough to heal yourself.

Another kick in the face. A kick of admirable precision.

Half bleeding, his jaw half broken, Tito glimpses the noble and ancient sequence of kung fu movements. He tries to avoid her and throws himself forward to try to tackle the very dangerous and maligned woman named Mina. As he does this he notices that the FM station is playing Phil Woods' version of *Cheek to Cheek*.

On the floor, shit, fingernails. She's a cat now, she's making mincemeat out of every piece of skin possible. Let her go, Tito. She's on her feet. Another flying kick, like a swordfish, like a torpedo, like a boomerang. His ribs sound like a piano crushed by another piano. Sometime you'll have to find out, Tito, crime always pays. All of a sudden, silence. The only thing he hears is the static crackling in the speakers as that woman turns off the receiver, and goes swaying by with her clothes in her arms, dragging her keys over the glass table. Afterwards, silence and, softly, the flowing of blood from his nose on to the carpet.

Virgin of Villa Alemana, help me to stay unconscious, so I can die today, so everything will stay dark, so no one will find out anything.

Last one out, turn out the lights.

Virgin of Villa Alemana, who doesn't know my name, if there's any life left in me, because I can't breathe, and because my head hurts so much, as if there were a theatre inside, and everyone were struggling to leave down the stairs in my nose. All my life's blood is running out onto the carpet.

My sweet Virgin, keep me unconscious, submerged, innocent in body and soul.

Thank you, my sweet Virgin.

Thank you.

For the favor you have granted.

4

They're going around looking for you, son.

He woke up to the noise of the telephone ringing. It was getting dark, and the light from the streetlamps was leaving its mark among the shadows from the bookshelves, the small African idol next to the window, and the armchair which was facing the terrace.

The telephone was on the carpet, next to the large chair upholstered in green chintz with bamboo prints. Tito opened one eye and realized the limits imposed by the swelling, the edema, certainly the hematoma, an unmistakable sign from the attack he had suffered. A crust of dried blood was sticking him to the fabric of the dark brown wall-to-wall carpet, now old coffee-colored blood. The telephone was ringing and ringing: Who? He crawled forward and felt the crunching of his ribs. He thought vaguely about a punctured lung, a quick run-through of his medical school knowledge, a foul suffered on a soccer field in the Providencia league. He thought he was going to throw up blood. He coughed and it hurt again.

The phone stopped ringing.

He took a deep breath. The pain was going away. A fracture? He didn't dare touch himself to search for the source of the intense pain. It didn't seem broken. He was breathing okay. He wiped the dried blood from his face. Shit, it started bleeding again, but only a little. The handkerchief held back the blood and the feared hemorrhaging stopped.

What happened to me? Mina: the feared goddess of death dancing her macabre dance in the middle of the room, kicking in the air, catching the small devil in the middle of her unmistakable dance of Shiva.

A suspicious little Hindu statue on the coffee table: the aforementioned goddess making sacred movements, multiple arms blending together into celestial designs.

Who thinks up a woman like that?

The phone rang again. He stretched out his arm, hallelujah: his hand on the receiver.

"Hello? Dad?"

Caroline's voice, the oldest of his daughters.

"Dad?"

How old are you now, Caroline? Eight? Seven? Are you still playing with dolls? Or, do you drink whisky that your father advertises? Or, do you use sanitary napkins that your father launched in a spectacular promotion for all the bleeding uteruses of Santiago high society? Do you take the pill now? Well done.

"Daddy?"

"Caroline. Hi, Caroline."

His voice was like a worn-out hurricane. He was coming home from all wars. His words began to straighten out and fall into haphazard order, as if they were not listening to the brain's wake-up call at the same time.

"Are you okay?"

"Sure, my love," said the champion of deceit and cunning. "Why should I not be okay?"

"I was worried. I dreamed some devils were chasing you."

"Some devils?" laughed Tito.

"Yes, Daddy." Caroline's laugh began to calm down Tito's false front. "How funny! Some little devils with horns and tails. Hee, hee, hee."

25

He liked Caroline's laugh, from the beginning. He missed her more than one night a week, whoever was at his side. There must have been an indissoluble Electra complex to have continued the marriage with Anita María. I love that rattle you have, Caroline. Hello Caroline. You're my life, my happiness, my desire. All the love songs for you, all of them.

"Mom was worried, too."

Silence. What was that woman doing butting into his life? Weren't seven years together enough to keep adopting you, taking care of you, watching over you, dressing you?

"She wants to talk to you, Daddy."

Not me, thought Tito.

"Okay, tell her to get on the line."

"Hello? Tito?"

"Hello, Anita."

"Are you okay?

"Yes, real good . . . And you?"

"Busy. You must know why."

Me? Know why? What am I supposed to know?

"I don't know what you're talking about."

The sentence sounded to him as if it had been taken from any of the numerous television programs that he devoured in his bouts with insomnia, before setting about to read Stendhal, Conrad, an untimely Proust, infallibly hypnotic. Always untimely, always hypnotic, always untimely, always hypnotic.

"But they've asked about you at the office."

Fatty Aspillaga told you that, no doubt, sure. That bunch of fake mothers and fathers can all take a flying leap. I'm not anyone's son. When are they going to get it straight?

Tito was beginning to lose his patience.

"Well, it doesn't matter." Ana María's infinite sigh of tolerance, always courteous, immaculate, discreet: "Remember that the kids and I are thinking about you, and we love you."

Tito felt very angry. I should slam the phone down and hang up on her, he thought. As if that were an insult.

"Thanks. Ciao, Anita."

"Ciao."

Tito hung up and kept listening into the receiver. The soft and continuous miaow of the empty line, the sound which replaced the silence: a humming from nothingness. Thanks, Anita María.

He was going to get up, but the pulling on his body reminded him of his wounds and bruises. Christ my Lord, have pity on me.

Lamb of God who taketh away the sins of the world.

The half-opened door.

That fucking bitch of a woman Mina, who's dangerous down to her soul, limitlessly harmful. They should all see me thrown on the floor, like a drunk, so that thief of a concierge and his greedy family of rats then get scared and yell for help.

The half-opened door.

There wasn't enough light and it didn't reach the doorway.

Fear, Tito was afraid.

Lamb of God who takes away the sins of the world, what have you gotten yourself into?

A shadow was outlined against the subdued lighting in the hall. A hat, he's wearing a hat.

Guardian angel, my dear companion, don't ever forsake me.

He saw the revolver and saw the shot, and saw his body slumping against the white wall which he had leaned against.

No, there was no such a shot.

The man, well it was a man, took off his hat.

Tito was extremely terrified.

"They're going around looking for you, son."

It was his dad. Not his father, his dad. Tito trembled, his forehead tightened, his chin, his stomach. He got a lump in his throat.

"Dad."

Where have you been, Daddy?

He saw himself as a five-year-old, six, seven. He saw himself watching his father leave, with the same gray hat, for the Independence afternoon, with his mother triumphant and throwing him out. Daddy, where are you going, Daddy?

His father had closed the door, and the light from the lamp next to the goddess Shiva was inundating the room.

He thought it absurd but he wanted to cry. The storm was passing and the fresh air was filling his nostrils again. It's absurd to cry in front

27

of my father, ridiculous to have felt that infantile torrent.

No, Dad, I'm okay.

"I see they've beaten you up."

Dad, first aid professor.

"No, it's nothing, I fell down."

Since when do you steal lines from TV, Tito?

"Let me see."

Alberto Triviño's fingers ran their way over Tito's bruised face.

"Someone who knows what they're doing hit you. All traces will be gone soon. They're expert hits. Security people?"

Do I tell him it's a *mina*? A *mina* named Mina.

"A woman, it was a woman."

Tito Senior didn't say anything. He shook his head and let himself fall into the chintz-covered sofa.

"You don't need medicine or a doctor. People like that know how to do damage without leaving any traces. You couldn't even sue her for damages."

"And if it were me who had hit her?"

"With someone who knows how to hit like that, you don't have time to do anything . . . Nothing."

Did you hear, Tito?

He hated Mina, he had met his match. Bathed in Old Fashioneds, she undid all his training. What luck that she didn't bring her lynching rope, what a stroke of luck.

There was a pause. Tito felt some pain again, but he also felt there was no way to show it. Nor how to tell him how good it was that he had come, nor anything else.

"Where have you been all this time?"

"In a small hotel, downtown. I came because it's a good idea for you to know what's going on."

Careful, Tito. He's trying to tell you something, pay attention. Tito, they're talking to you.

"Some friends of mine want to talk to you," continued Triviño Senior.

Lamb of God, guardian angle, angels and archangels, apostles, cherubs, angelic powers and whatever else there is in heaven, come and help me.

"And my enemies are looking for you, too . . ."

"Explain yourself, Dad."

Alberto Senior smiled. He liked to hear that.

"There are some things about me that you don't know, Tito."

The terrible things your mother used to tell you? The perversions and tortures he was implicated in? Being hooked on drugs? Alcoholism?

"Some real secret things which I didn't think it would ever be necessary to tell you. I'm retired, you'll see."

"Retired from what? You're still giving classes."

"Let's see . . . How should I tell you? I've been . . ."

Alberto Senior got quiet all of a sudden. His pupils swung towards the door.

"What's the matter?"

"Someone's coming up in the elevator . . . Is there another way out?"

Tito was left perplexed. He hadn't heard anything.

"What's going on, old man?"

"Can I jump to the terrace?"

"Yes, but be careful. At your age."

He didn't pay attention. Alberto Senior opened the large window and walked out on the balcony. Before he jumped, he turned back towards Tito Livio, Triviño's son.

"Have faith in my friends, they're good people and their cause is just. They'll explain it all to you. And be careful."

"Of what? Who should I be careful of?"

The doorbell rang, a harmonious and delicate ring. It rang again.

"Of them, Tito."

Alberto Triviño, after saying this, lost himself in the night. Tito Junior managed to hear his steps in the garden which surrounded the building. The doorbell rang over and over again.

Tito went to the door.

When he passed in front of a picture, he saw himself reflected in the glass: the wounds weren't noticeable. Experts, yes sir.

He moved close to the peephole before opening the door.

5

Hello, Rolando

B ut what are you going to do, Tito Livio? What question is going around in your hard, hollow head when your eye approaches the little peephole where you'll spy on the face of I don't know who rang the bell, I don't know who your father pointed out as the imminent danger? Who are you afraid it might be, Tito Livio?

Afraid, I imagine two very elegantly dressed men, two hired goons who grab me by my arms and carry me, feet dangling, to a Chevrolet Opala that's waiting at the front sidewalk and no one admits to seeing me, nobody thinks about recognizing my voice, my shadow, my hopelessness, no one thinks they'll torture me, harass me, trap me, I'm disappearing.

Or, I imagine that it's Mina who's coming softly, rhythmically, daintily, to ask me to forgive her, the fucking bitch, to tell me she overdid it, the woman from Milan telling me the truth, the mother of the lamb, the fucking mother of the fucking lamb who doesn't take the fucking sins away from the fucking world even one fucking time and has all of us here, fucked up.

Or, I imagine I'm afraid and I'm going towards my death, I don't know why I think that, that I'm heading for an imminent death. I can't quit thinking about that and then, sure it's then, I hesitate and I look towards the balcony, towards the curtain that's still open and moving back and forth and I decide to straighten it out because it's a clue, it's a trace, it's a signal of Papa Triviño's presence, emerged from nothing, and it makes me want to run after him, and I'm amazed at not hearing his footsteps when he's running on the pavement nor a car that's shifting gears and leaving nor his breathing among the shrubs nor his body floating face down in the river still lifeless lost forever.

And the doorbell rings again and I ask myself: Father, why have you abandoned me?

Then he opens the door and no one's there. Nobody. He listens carefully and hears footsteps going down the stairs. It's not a real second floor, let's remember that, and whoever it was that was there behind the door was not a woman, nor was it only one person. There are a few people and now they've stopped, they've listened to the door opening and they're retracing their steps.

"Tito?"

Rolando Donkavian in person. What is he doing in my apartment? What is the director himself of the Tempora Agency doing here? What is he doing coming into my space, I'm asking myself?

"You're probably wondering about my visit, my friend," and he extends his friendly gauntlet and his fine catlike behavior and advances wrapped in his light beige linen suit, canvas shoes, the kind of guy who comes off the plane that brought him from Nassau, or Florida, or Tahiti, the type of guy who you run into in Bahia when you're working and he isn't. He, who never appears to be doing anything which takes an effort, he walks in slow motion with Carrera Porsche lenses dangling in his left hand, or the keys to an Alfa Romeo selected for him by Schmauck, made to order one would say. The type of guy who sells anything to anyone at any price, eternally suntanned, a mixture of the beach sun and the sun reflected off the eternal snows, sent to create à la Fuji to better show off the perfect color that any movie star would want for themselves. A bronze bracelet on his wrist shows his confidence in esoteric medicine. Rolando Donkavian squints his wrinkle-filled eyes, two heavenly buttonholes in the middle of his skin's perfect golden brown tan.

"Hello, Rolando."

Behind him were the two henchmen whom Tito feared, elegant but less so than in his imagination, and behind. Which is how life goes, up against the wall, cunning but arrogant, looking down at him from above as if Tito had shrunk about half a foot and she had grown taller than her 5'8", Mina herself stared at him: her teased hair, sweet and frightful.

"Hello, Tito."

Rolando mumbled some introductions. Tito doesn't realize how, but they're already seated in his Landea furniture. Donkavian is in his Cruz Valdés armchair, and they have served what seems to be gin and tonic and Mina, take a guess, is drinking an Old Fashioned, topped with a maraschino cherry floating over the ice and a wedge of pineapple. Not Tito, he has a glass of Coca-Cola. Not Tito, Tito is hanging in there. His father's words are going around in his brain and are converting his attitude into fear, into caution, into vigilance.

"Tito." Rolando's a wildcat, but a cat, he purrs, rubbing himself against the sheepskin in the armchair, over the velvet covered sofa, over the fire without burning himself. "I ran into Mina and we were having a drink."

An Old Fashioned, guesses Tito.

"She was coming over here and I saw her," Donkavian continues and looks at her, and the stupid whore laughs and laughs. "You're marvelous, Mina." The henchmen laugh and everyone looks at Tito, the center of attention again, a common target, public enemy number one at this moment. "And I told her what we have for you . . . Do you know who's in Santiago?"

Rolando remains silent, like making a goal shot after having made a header with the ball towards the goalie, a silence so that Tito might let a *Who?* escape, like a balloon that fills the room and leaves a mark on the cork-bark wallpaper, on the silent pier where all ideas moor, all protests, all noise. But Tito doesn't say anything, he only raises an eyebrow, imperturbable. He knows what's going on.

"Rubem . . . Riveiro. Do you realize?" says Donkavian who now makes another header and is now dominating at the goal line, eluding defenses on the tile floor, dodging the referee and the photographers if it's necessary, anything provided he gets the attention of this un-affected audience which Tito turns out to be. The sound of ice cracking in Mina's glass is heard. Tito says nothing, nothing. His head is in another secret place. First he thought the pause about Ruben Fonseca was to blame. He had felt himself such a writer in the last few days, but then, click!, Rubem Riveiro, movie director, also Brazilian, winner of as many advertising agent Clios as he desires. Everyone in Cannes is sucking up to him.

"We want you to work with him. In São Paulo. A short, but important freelance for good pay. One month in São Paulo. It's the right weather for it. Leaving Chile is a good idea, this country is screwed up; to create real movies. Another thing. You'll be arranging it with MacPherson. Tell him that you're sick, that you have to write a book, that your father's died. He'll understand in the end. It will be prestigious for his agency. Besides, the gringo appreciates you. What's the matter, Tito?"

The one alluded to doesn't respond. He thinks, I think. That my father is dead. And he sees him face down on the floor of his hotel, and he sees the mark of a bullet in his back, the projectile's entrance or exit, but he's face down. And he knows that it's not his imagination, it's another plane. And he understands that Rolando knows he was in Villa Alemana and he understands that they didn't have any reason to come to his home, and least of all run into Mina. They're professionals, his dad had said.

"You've got until tomorrow to think it over. But don't wait. That's why we came to talk to you personally. You're the best and you have to take care of yourself. It wasn't a good idea to look for you at the agency, you understand."

Tito sips from his glass of Coca-Cola. The bubbles fizz against his lips.

"Sure I accept," he says and the smiles from the whole group are more than tremendous. If the truth be known, the image of the Clio he can get when working with Riveiro makes his heart beat fast, it whets his appetite, it makes his mouth water, it fills him with emotion. You're the best, he said to him.

Mina approaches him and kisses him on the lips. Tito feels her tongue poking against his tonsils and he imagines that the tongue has eyes and a mouth and a forked tongue that vibrates in there. Don't move, Tito. Rolando stands up. Mina goes back to her corner and the henchmen open the door.

"Good. I knew we could count on you. But you should come over to my house today to talk to him," says Donkavian.

"Now?"

Donkavian approves. Uh huh, now. Mina approves. Everyone approves. The image of reconciliation, goodness, agreement, the end of bad feelings. Happiness has knocked on your door, Tito.

"You're the best," that woman, the same one, repeats to him. Everyone laughs, even Tito who already sees himself in Cannes, with the Clio in hand, embracing Riveiro, and a photo on top of his messy ad agent's desk.

He sees Rolando Donkavian's business card fall on the old oak table. An old door transformed into a table, as is the custom.

Bye bye, ciao ciao.

The soft closing of the door leading to the street surprises him, he smiles and throws down a glass of Chivas Regal in order to begin to get loaded. To hell with the Virgin of Villa Alemana. He looks through the picture window and sees the cars leaving all at once, the chrome stripping shining under the light of a plate-like moon, and the harsh melody of the motors caresses his soul, and he decides to tell his father to fuck off, along with anything else that has to do with him. My mom's going to like this, he says to himself, and he goes over to the phone, but when he lifts up the receiver there's no dial tone, nothing. It remains deaf and dumb in his hand.

After all, she'll find out later anyway.

What a screwed up country, more fucked up every day, he says to himself and hangs up the useless apparatus. He reads the card. What does a phenomenon like him do in this country? He'll be too big for *Cosas* magazine, pure Concorde set, pure gold and diamonds. He thinks about his middle-class ancestry, surpassed forever. Now he'll see how to get rid of Mina. Right away, yes that's it, his father's image comes to him like salt on a wound.

Old radical bastard, spoiled and hedonistic, what do you know about what my life is going to be like, indignant pseudo-socialist, where did you go, you left me there, you never talked to me, you never showed me the galaxies, the Milky Way, the Southern Cross, the North Star, I had to learn it all by myself. Where were you when I needed you most?

And he took his best jacket out, new, almost new, impeccable coarse white linen, wide, with shoulder pads, and singing, he turned on the shower.

He asked himself if today would be the real beginning of a new life. He always asked himself that with every woman, with every job change, new studies, car. But this time he was serious. His mother was right, he was destined for great things.

A light coming through the window bothered him. He was naked and covered himself with a towel. He thought about a UFO but it was only some kind of signal light. Vaguely recalling the Morse code he learned as a child, he translated it, with difficulty. S-E-A-R-C-H-F-O-R-G-O-D-T-H-E-F-A-T-H-E-R. Then the series of letters was repeated over and over. Furious, he looked among his sweaters for a heavy Walter PPK that he kept hidden. He was just about to shoot when the light went out.

He put down the revolver. The shower was dancing in the background, behind him, it was the only noise.

He sat down on the bed and played with the loaded pistol. It was always loaded. What for? He had never used it. He was a little afraid at having been on the verge of pulling the trigger.

Something in some remote part of his brain full of golden dreams suggested to him that the Walter would look real good in his shoulder holster. The idea was almost calming.

Already dressed, newly shaved with his Vetiver de Puig, and almost as elegant as a pale version of Donkavian, he felt the pistol under his left armpit. Without exhibitionist fanfare he took it out, he put it back, he pulled it out, he put it back. He put it against his temple like Trintignant in Bertolucci's film. He hid it away again.

He left carrying the card in his hand.

35

6

Why don't you go away and leave me in peace?

Papa, what the hell are you doing there, Papa, what in hell has gotten into you? Don't you realize I'm coming as fast as I can? Your son is racing there as fast as he can, your magnificent son racing headlong towards the trophy he deserves, towards seventh heaven, elevated, included in the quagmire of Latin America to be raised to advertising glory, cinematography, the seventh art, the silver screen of all the scenarios of the great theater of the world.

Father, why haven't you abandoned me?

"Tito, I want to explain some things to you."

Explain them, you old bastard, explain them.

"Open the car door."

He got in. Tito stayed seated inside the Toyota, inside the parking garage, inside the building. The neon lights rebounded from the hood to the windshield towards them, the two of them weren't touched, as the windows were polarized, completely polarized. The sun doesn't touch me, it will never stain my skin, my retina will never see itself wounded by the sun.

"What do you want?"

"Start driving and I'll tell you."

The motor made its usual purr, faithful as a samurai it obeyed the shift and smoothly headed towards the gate. The electric garage door opener was slowly opening to the night. The moon shone into the tunnel-way. Tito Senior did not speak until the car appeared under the lights and stars, blended into the night sky, the lighted advertisements, the distant traffic lights all along Nueva Costanera Avenue.

"Whether you like it or not, son, you're involved in a war."

"Oh?"

Tito mentally searched every corner of his mind before allowing so important a phrase to nestle there.

"In the holy war of Santiago de Chile. And it's my fault."

The street was going by as if it had no importance, as if asphalt were a silent rail. Only the tick tock from the clock, like in the Rolls Royce in the commercial that Ogilvy wrote. But the fact is the silence now isn't like it was, not now. You only have to look at the quartz clock: stopped.

"Some guys are going to come looking for you," continued Tito Senior, uncommunicative and gray. "It's a dubious inheritance I'm leaving you. It cost us my marriage with your mother. I wouldn't have wanted it to affect you. Not you, or Gustavo, or her. But things speeded up. I'm going to disappear . . . I have to do it."

Tito put on the brakes, flipped on the flashers and kept staring at his father's face, badly illuminated by the flashes of light filtered in from the street.

"Are you mixed up with spying?"

"No."

"With the communists?"

"No, it's not just a question of politics. It's the struggle between good and evil, my son."

Cut the bullshit, you old bastard. Right now, the midnight sermon, just what I needed, right when I'm going to an interview from where I can leave by plane to São Paulo, and from there to Cannes to put a Clio in my pocket. No one in Chile has ever gotten a Clio. Do you know what a Clio is, Dad? Do you know what that is? It's the Oscar of advertising! The ultimate aspiration in this business full of whores, mercenaries and pimp salesmen! And from there it's just a jump to real cinema. Like Ridley Scott, like Alan Parker, like Adrian Lynne. Do you hear? So just tell me where I can let you out and . . .

"You're possessed. It can't be. They can't do this to you. Do you know who Donkavian is?"

"Don't tell me you stayed there spying."

"He's an agent for evil. He works for them."

"Now you're telling me he's the bogeyman, the grim reaper . . . Why don't you go away and leave me in peace?"

He thought about his wife and her sickening sweetness, her presents, her advice. He thought about Gustavo who was equally as tranquilizing as his father, in the mass of bureaucratic professors, just like the one who was facing him. And the only thing they did was to poison the little bit of spark that the Chileans had in weak, decrepit classes, devoid of life.

"Be careful, Tito Livio. I really love you and I'm sorry you happen to be involved in all this."

"What do I have to be careful of? Can I know? That the devil with horns and a tail might be coming to get me?"

"Something like that. Without the horns and tail."

Caroline's dream. His forehead, which had been burning up in the heat, suddenly got cold. Something hit him real hard inside. His father took him by the shoulder. Take your hand off me, old man, okay?

"I can't tell you anything more. It's dangerous for me to say anything to you, so goodbye. If they find me here I've had it."

Triviño Senior got out. A soft breeze comes in and wakes Triviño Junior up, who stays watching Papa Triviño's shape crossing the Plaza del Hoyo. A shape lost in the background like in a Delvaux painting. So correct, so insignificant. His bumbling meddling professor father on the road to nowhere. To his dirty hotel, his boardinghouse room where he'll sink his spoon into his soup to taste a loneliness of useless years, barely visited by widowers or veterans of various passionate wars who don't even receive a pension.

"You old asshole," murmured Tito, but without anger. It was like showing affection for someone with a fake slap. Ambiguous as always, he got a chill and assumed his old fondness for relishing horror movies, cheap books on satanism, tales of the fantastic read in the middle of his university staff meetings.

"Tomorrow I'm going to see him," he promised himself, but he did not stay calm. I should do something more, something more.

Hour, the hour, the appointed hour, the promised land. He starts the motor running, absentminded Tito. Maybe you don't even know what time it's taking place? Donkavian's address. Turning off on Las Condes Avenue, the road to Arrayan, Kennedy Avenue.

He rolled down the windows, summer was becoming hot as hell. The music: a Spaniard was asking his lover about a lie. Queer, I'm sure he's a faggot. Later, a woman was complaining about her cheating husband getting home late: things aren't what they used to be. As he was coming to Estoril, a separated woman was singing to her children about her secret encounters at a questionable hotel. The poor dears. Poor Caroline. Poor Janine. I wonder if Anita María is frolicking in some hotel with some guy? Why was he worrying about that now? Can I find out?

Further on, Tito. And he stopped near the Clínica Las Condes, that miniature North American hospital where you can run into your classmates from your university days, now arrogant, wise, successful physicians.

Celedón lives around here, he thought, remembering the macho stud of advertising abusively switching topics on his guests. He had copied that ranting from him in order to throw his clients off guard. Friendly and resourceful at the same time. Celedón made him laugh, imitating him also made people laugh.

Laughter loosened him up a little, but only a little. He kept going with a knot in his stomach, a case of butterflies that had mutated, undergone metamorphosis, and began to break open and threatened to become an enormous bird, a bird of prey that would tear you apart with its claws if it got the jump on you. Accelerate, so it won't get you.

Donkavian's house: the painted number barely visible on a rock, a rustic touch allowed only for the most refined. The number made him laugh again: six six six. The number of the Antichrist. He remembered it from an awful horror movie which he had seen a little while after separating from Anita María. Who did he go with? He didn't even remember. It was some promoter from Jumbo, pretty and dumb as only she could be. Right in the middle of her horrified scream he had grabbed her by a tit, two tits, her crotch. She, solicitous priestess of the black mass, grabbed him by his erect phallus as if she were grabbing one of the horns of the Beast himself.

The bird of prey began to flap its wings again when he turned off the motor. The FM announcer's voice faded among the crickets: a Santiago night.

Celedón had told him that the customs station for the road to Argentina was somewhere around here.

The house: white, large, a senator's house if there were any, a movie star's house if we had any movies. It had an old English air, maybe it was, finished with a mixture of typical folklore and sophistication. Lighted up like scenery in an opera.

He listened to the sound of voices, drinks, soft music. It was like a prepared sound tape that they use in some radio commercials: a party.

That relaxed him, familiar territory, a church, a rural chapel converted into a luxurious dwelling. He smelled the Vetiver de Puig but it had mingled with the smell of fear, the one that dogs smell. A Russian greyhound growled at him from behind the wrought iron gate. No, there were two of them.

He went under a wooden eave looking for a doorbell, a door knocker, anything. He found a small bronze devil, in a prancing motion. He was going to try it when the door, enormous, two solid slabs, with heavy plating exuding antiquity, opened without a single creak.

"Come in."

No less than Donkavian himself.

"Come on in, Tito."

7

An unforgettable party

D onkavian was dressed in blue on blue, wearing a stylized sky blue Huaso suit. A sailboat cutting through the murmur of conversations. Here I go: Tito Livio dressed in white, going through the great hall where the white piano floats like a portion of the last glacier, at which an effeminate instrumentalist with silver hair plays a jazz tune by Gilberto Gil which Tito knows but doesn't recall its name.

He has crossed a garden inundated with the floating perfume from the wisteria. Through the lights he discovers a pair of tall larch trees which preside over a Chilean-style garden, flower beds of hydrangea and red and orange water plants underneath the bunches of an enormous bougainvillea which give it the air of a plaza in Viña del Mar. In the center there is a paved path (which could almost be said to be yellow brick) which ascends around a slight incline towards a mahogany and beveled glass door which, like a music box, seals the sound which now surrounds him.

People were smiling at him as if he were wearing the principal product from an unacceptably priced ad on his face. He recognizes

41

people from television, women whom he's seen out of the corner of his eye when he was switching from channel to channel together with Mina, the two of them naked on top of a waterbed in a five-star motel. They were there, dressed in brilliant coveralls, sprinkled with lamé, killer ascots, punk singer make-up, a purple streak that crosses their long hair like a bolt of lightning. A woman who looks like a man, wearing a lilac smoking jacket, approaches to say hello to him. Her hair is slicked back on her head, a smile like the Joker in *Batman*, her thin hand which grabs his. She has gloves, just one on her left hand. My pleasure. *Glad to meet you.* I swear to you, they are greeting me in English, I swear, they're kissing my cheeks and there are aromas of oriental essences. An occasional lapis lazuli earring on the earlobe of some marketing manager. They're beautiful, I promise you, beautiful and seductive. The drinks shine in their hands like gems, the music is splendid. A Gershwin adaptation, now in jazz, never in swing, rhythmical.

Didn't you always dream about a party like that, Tito? Didn't you dream about being on a page in the Social section, with a color photograph of you and those stars from *Ecran Criollo*? Bo Derek dressed like a nun, Pinochet hugging Gabriel Valdés, Caroline of Monaco announcing her divorce, Bjorn Borg holding hands with Rose of Luxembourg, some European prince shooting up heroin underneath a marble staircase with golden banisters? And you, Tito Livio, presiding over the magazine's blender that mixes everything, nullifies time and space, ideas and values, creating that beautiful young woman, culture puree, history made into juice.

"Prepare yourself," says Rolando in soft blue, a bright sky blue shirt in which you can recognize very fine filigrees and arabesques in relief, and whose color makes his Doc Savage-type tan more smooth and beautiful. "I'm going to introduce you to Riveiro."

He's going to cross the room with the perfect parquet floor, vitrified like a mirror they use for advertising wax, when he sees her.

As soon as he sees her he succumbs.

It's a certainty, love at first sight, just one quick look and see you later guys.

You can't even imagine what she's like, he'll say at the agency, wild, a fantastic woman, you won't believe it but I'd seen her before, at the

Almac in Arauco Park, that monument to imprudence, to stupidity, to dementia. He had seen her dressed in a t-shirt and short shorts, English style. He had seen how she caused a disturbance among all the guys with their carts full of merchandise, he listened as bottles broke as she walked by, canned goods rolled around, they forgot about everything just looking at her. Breasts like twin temples, her ass like a glorious curve that any architect would be proud of, legs as impressive as the most celebrated of feasts, the most secret of the temples. The stupid woman, challenging the world that time with her hair frizzed up by the shower, without make-up, hoisting a flag so every red-blooded man would mentally fuck her. What are you going to do? You had to love her or kill her, I swear to you, guys.

Tito didn't manage to say any of that. His jaw fell wide open and he let go of a whisky sour which they were offering him. "There she is," he mumbled, but it was inaudible.

"Who is she?" he dared to ask when he could.

The woman, the terrible one, blazing in the middle of a dress, thin cut, short. Legs: legs. The goddess Kali has eight arms, this one does just fine with those two legs. Thin on top of that, and curly hair that crests in waves that would drown shipwrecked fingers, leaving all the testicles of the planet dry.

"Who?" half smiles Donkavian who is playing stupid.

"Her."

"Ah . . ." A satisfied smile of a completed mission. "She's la Maga."

"La what?"

"La Maga. Didn't you read *Hopscotch*?" A pull from Donkavian brought him out of his ecstasy. The Brazilian boy, Rubem Riveiro, right in front of him. A kind of thin Demis Rousos: bald on top, long hair and an even longer beard, dressed in a tunic making some samba-like movements. *The rhythm is in their blood*, Julio Martinez would point out on television as he always does, national champion of the cliché. His trademark.

Rubem Riveiro said something in a mixture of Spanish and Portuguese, but Tito was off somewhere else.

"The fact is he's in love," explained Rolando.

They were dancing, they were dancing alone. La Maga was dancing, la Maga à la Isadora Duncan, the magic woman raising the hem of her

43

short skirt. Legs. I already said it: legs. But this woman is at least sixty years old, thought Tito, and he kept looking at her. He's pulling my leg. And he was admiring her. It can't be her, the original, she must be her daughter, her little sister. She has to be eternal. And he was staring at her. And the other one was dancing.

"She's dancing for you, don't you realize?"

Rolando's voice: fuel on the fire. Rubem Riveiro's voice. A voice just like any other in the crowd.

"Who's the party for?"

"For you, Tito."

"But . . . why?"

"Because you're a prodigious man, a brilliant talent."

You always wanted to hear that, Tito. Your whole life. Your mother used to say it, but just the same, you used to shake when you spoke in public. All through your complicated adolescence, not being intelligent enough, handsome enough, athletic enough, seductive enough.

Be careful with your dreams when you're young because they just might come true later on. The quote is from Goethe, changed several times through the abuse of forgetfulness, not to mention reading it misquoted coming from the mouth of one of the characters in Joyce's *Ulysses.* The years which ill-treat the syntax, the words, the original idea. There's la Maga. How old were you when you wanted her? You weren't even twenty. You read *Hopscotch* so precociously? In the first *Sudamericana* edition. The black book, the cover with the chalk lines. *Tierra Cielo.* Of course I remember. Are you sure it's the same one? Would it matter at this point? It's as if it were. So that's what Tito Livio was like. Enchanted with la Maga in his eyes, like a teenager. Promising himself that he would attach her like a butterfly in an insect collection. Or is she a spider? A black widow? A *Latrodectus Mactans*? A *Loxosceles Laeta*?

"Does she bite?"

Donkavian laughed. People were dancing.

"Are you going to São Paulo, or not?"

"I don't know."

"I know that you are."

Buffet: lots of surprising salads, cheeses, radishes, bread sticks, anchovies with lettuce, chestnuts, a varied assortment of finely cut vegetables. Red and white cold cuts. Plums wrapped in bacon. People were dancing, drinking, and talking.

Tito couldn't manage to concentrate: la Maga.

All of a sudden the thought passed through his mind that probably maybe perhaps everything might have been poisoned.

La Maga was alone.

Right away, there, within reach, stealing a turkey canapé.

The protagonist turned towards her and felt the weight of the Walter in his armpit: his father, getting further away from him in a Delvaux painting that is disappearing.

"Hello."

She spoke with the timbre of a voice from a radio commercial. A slight River Plate area accent. Smooth, it was noticeable when she pronounced the *y*'s and double *l*'s. It was more like from Montevideo than from Buenos Aires.

She's a Frankenstein monster, Rubem Riveiro's mechanical doll, too much to be human.

"They've told me about you, you know? Wonderful things."

Marvelous things. He notices the Pocitos spirit, the Café Sorocabana, Carrasco, an aftertaste of Candombe. Remarkable.

What? What's that? I'm nothing, I'm nobody, I float around sad, alone and abandoned.

"I've heard a lot about you, really."

The way she pronounced this was distinct too, direct. Like the crack of a whip, a whiplash.

"A lot," insisted the frightful demigoddess.

Tito spoke without knowing what he was saying. His voice was coming to him by accident, as if a ghost were talking for him, as if his body were there by chance. He was afraid of falling apart from one instant to the next, that his muscles would all give out, his skin would fall to the floor like a plastic bag, that a slight breeze would be enough to spread his bones over the grass in the back patio, which seemed like a golf course with small perfect hills, like adolescent breasts. He was afraid that la Maga might gather him up and put him back together at her whim, afraid that she might carry a phalanx of his forever, hung around her neck: a talisman, a lucky charm, his head shrunk for a key chain.

Like Riveiro's little hand.

"He says he wants to work with you, that he's seen your work and he's been very impressed," Rolando interpreted unnecessarily.

In the middle of a sudden feeling of nausea, Tito thought about which work he was talking about. He had only adapted some German campaigns lately, plagiarizing Yankee advertising, every now and then getting a crazy idea which was always rejected by the client, media experts, or the budget director. Or misrepresented by the production staff. His nausea was getting worse. He switched drinks. A diligent waiter who seemed to be hanging on his every movement came up to him, putting the idea of some bittersweet hors d'oeuvres in his head.

The guests were laughing. He felt himself the smallest, shyest, least expert, least daring person.

He squeezed his pistol with his arm to give himself some courage.

But he was sick. More so every minute: spirals, the world is spinning around me.

"What's the matter?"

"I don't know, the drink."

"The food."

"The smoke."

They were laughing.

"The poor guy."

"The poor dear."

"Tito."

That's the last he remembered.

8

La Maga

When he woke up he was lying down on the fluffy mattress in a bed in an unfamiliar immense second floor bedroom. Wooden beams crossed the very high ceiling, creating the same mixture of sophistication and rural air of the Chilean Central Zone which the whole house possessed. A balcony looked over the lighted garden: the bougainvillea shoots. The members of the household were gossiping, they were laughing, they were singing along with a harp and a guitar to what seemed to be songs from *Los Huasos Quincheros*. More laughter, bubbles floating in the crystal night at Donkavian's house. The low light in the room didn't permit him to see until all of a sudden he recognized a face.

"Maga!"

"Of course I'm here."

She speaks like a goddess. She is one.

"Thanks."

A glass of water. He drank.

"Did I faint?"

47

La Maga confirmed the diagnosis. She was seated on the edge of the bed. She stood up and took a few steps around the room until she stopped in front of the window. She looked at Tito, or we suppose she did. The light only permitted a guess, not certainty.

"You shouldn't carry a pistol, Tito."

Chills: They're on to me.

"It's a habit of mine. Did they take it away from me?"

Where does our hero get that type of answer? That hired arrogance in *Death Wish*, that archetypical nighttime antihero? Drunk, he always comes back.

Or so it seems.

"It's under your armpit. Don't you trust us?"

Us?

"I always carry it."

La Maga sits down to his side, on the bed again. Tito thinks about those Hollywood-style movies where the heroines throw themselves at the heroes, where they're so indiscriminate and excitingly malicious. Mae West. He imagines himself Bond, Flint, Cary Grant with Eva Marie-Saint in a Hitchcock film.

But she scares him.

"I have to go."

Where is this panic coming from? From the kick the other *mina*, Mina, treated him to? From so many strange things? From the shine coming from la Maga's eyes in the darkness?

"What's your name? It isn't Maga? Right?"

"I can call myself whatever you want."

"Uh huh."

A pause. A breeze passes between them. The curtain moves gracefully.

But it's known that fear cools down any storm, heats up rebellious hormones, returns the entire jungle to its natural state.

"I'm going, Maga."

He gets up and leaves the room. He's still nauseous.

But it's known that sometimes fear helps, increases tension, makes your pulse better, gets the sleepy moving, wakes the dead. Adrenalin.

Tito is going down the stairs, la Maga right behind, and Donkavian is below in his short jacket, styled in a Huaso boss pattern, ranch owner style, which he's never been. Old folklore by Marcos Correa, *very sophisticated.*

"Are you leaving?"

"Sure."

"Won't it be better if I take you?"

"No, I can drive."

That's not true, Tito, look at how you're staggering. If you close your eyes and put your feet together you'll fall over for sure. Romberg positive.

He wavers, he's afraid he has a sprain, he's afraid he has an ankle sprain in his very soul. Something like that.

"I'm driving, Tito."

La Maga was the one who spoke to him. Who else?

"Okay."

"I need you to leave for São Paulo no later than Saturday."

Rubem Riveiro appears out of the crowd. They say goodbye, he says something to him.

"He's very excited about you," continues Donkavian, and Tito nods. Uncomfortable, thankless body that's acting real strange.

La Maga is waiting in the car. Who took my keys from me? You should be thankful, Tito, that they only took your keys. Maybe you're missing something else, or maybe you've got more than enough.

"And how are you going to get back?"

She smiles. Those who know la Maga will know what that means.

"Who said I was coming back?"

Tito understands, although it takes an effort, although it scares him, although it pleases him. Even though he's dying of fright, and desire. Although . . .

Good luck, Tito.

9

In the name of the Father

The man with the frizzy copper-colored hair was losing his patience. When he saw Tito Triviño's car being guided by that woman, he hit the blinds with his fist. He was peering between his thumb and index finger, like the lips of a dead person they stayed shut: metallic eyelids, without lashes.

"Don't make so much noise, boss."

The other one, the thin man with a mustache like a bolero singer, was just singing *Dos Almas* when he felt the curly haired guy's slap, the short guy.

"What happened now, boss?"

"We're wasting time, Donkavian grabbed him."

"Do you think so?"

The shoddy Javier Solís, rather rangy and tall, went back to peering through the blinds. There's a light on in the apartment: the woman and Tito.

"Who is she?"

"Can't you see her?"

50

THE SECRET HOLY WAR OF SANTIAGO DE CHILE

"*Nein.*"

"Donkavian's agent. La Maga. Typical. They put us in charge of a job that's got no purpose. Without a budget, without clear objectives, without a deadline. Later they reprimand you and blame western decadence, the human holocaust, the end of time. The bureaucracy makes me sick."

"Boss, don't get all worked up."

"It's probably better if you give me the phone."

He dialed the number for God the Father, unknown to those present. It only took the making of the sign of the cross before dialing the ten numbers (10, the perfect number, the sum of the 4 elements, the 4 evangelists, plus those 3 who are one, plus the 2 eyes of our Lord God, plus the 1 eternally everlasting which is the Verb in the beginning of the beginning principles) and then there was the absolute absence of all humming or dial tone.

Right away they pick up at the other end and listen.

"The body of Christ."

"Amen."

"He's getting away from us. We need to speak to Him."

"You're crazy. He's sleeping."

"Wake Him up. If there's one thing He doesn't suffer from, it's insomnia."

Tropical orchestra music is heard in the background at the other end.

"He says to bring him in any way you can."

"Let me speak to Him."

The thin guy keeps on spying. Tito has turned out the light, or la Maga, who knows, and we can all imagine what happens next. Now there isn't any mystery in the mystery, now it's public knowledge, now no one can play innocent. Erotica has died under the weight of advertising. Pornography is commercialized, the body is becoming weak, it's disappearing. It's not a threat, it's not a Pandora's box, nor Dante's hell, nor Swedenborg's heaven. It's nothing, do you hear Tito? Only the darkness through which Tito descends, now intending to try to prove the contrary, and the thin man tries to see, whistling: *Nothing more than shadows, between your life and mine.*

A Subaru goes buzzing by on the avenue, and the tall guy listens to

51

the boss, who hangs up. He gets on his knees, gives thanks and looks at him.

"He says for us to bring him in."

"Now?"

"I don't see what's so important about following this guy. All because he's the great Triviño's son. As if he were a marked man. I think this one's a lost cause, but you know the boss." Both of them crossed themselves. "He really likes challenges."

Both of them were spying. The smallest one, whose name is Rafael, took out some infrared binoculars.

"Do you see anything?"

"Bodies. Moving, of course."

"This isn't voyeurism, is it boss?"

Rafael looked at Gabriel, who also called himself a thin version of Javier Solís. Or, at least, those were their aliases.

"We're working for a good cause, aren't we?"

"Yes, no doubt about it."

"Then, get to it."

"Okay, boss."

They were watching. The street, the moon mixed among the sparkle of the yellowing mercury streetlamps, the pavement. Another Japanese car went by at more than eighty miles an hour. There wasn't a soul out walking, maybe some wandering neighborhood drunk who would be finished off by some German shepherds before daybreak, or denounced as a terrorist resulting in his being implicated in the assassination of some visiting minister who was investigating a previous crime involving another minister, in the same neighborhood.

"Task completed."

A little light showed that someone, presumably Tito, was going into the bathroom. The Latin American custom of washing the genitals after having sex. La Maga, to follow the ritual, left in the bed, would ooze her aroma of sperm and her own juices, her dangerous proud flesh writhing. The light went out, again.

"They lit cigarettes for each other."

The thin guy was playing solitaire with tarot cards.

"Are you telling your fortune? You can't do that!"

"I'm killing time."

"We'd better get some sleep."

"I'll watch and you sleep, boss."

"I don't think they're getting up."

"Let's both of us sleep then."

But when they wake up (all of them: Tito and this pair of guards) la Maga has disappeared.

"Look, Tito's alone on the terrace in a bathrobe."

"And la . . .?"

"Getting dressed now! Getting dressed now!"

"Her?" he anxiously demands from the boss who is adjusting the focus.

"No! Him!"

Let's go. On your feet, on guard, to the attack. They leave, and they position themselves next to the exit of the underground parking garage.

The preceding situation would be told to Tito Livio in great detail sometime later and he would cheerfully utilize it in a commercial for chocolate-covered caramels, sublimating the obvious sexual content and persecutory nature of the scene. He would win a prize for the best spot of the year, ignoring the underlying dark story. That's art, that's advertising. Mistrust: they both deserve it.

Tito is whistling, he has found a note from la Maga in which she says goodbye:

My Tito, there are times when it's not good to prolong something because good times can be destroyed. Wood kept for a long time makes a better fire. Don't try to find me. I know how to see you again. I'm always with you, close. With love, Maga.

Tito rocked back and forth whistling. While he was reading he got off tune. He thinks about São Paulo, about MacPherson, about Fatty Aspillaga. His memories are always a photograph album which he leafs through rapidly. He's going downstairs while he's playing with the keys to the Toyota. His thoughts about last night don't have a single shred of originality: *awesome woman*, or, *she was really into it*, or, *it was real chemistry* and other reflections like that. When the elevator door opens, he looks at himself in the hall mirror and finds himself to be young, good looking and handsome. Strong, intelligent, everything. He thinks he deserves everything that's happening and thinks that what's happening to him is the best. He believes in good things to come, but most of all he believes in himself.

He's getting closer to his car when he sees the two men approaching him. He takes out the Walter PPK and aims.

"Oh, he's armed, boss."

"Put that down. For your own good."

Tito is surprised but he's macho, head held high, a real Chilean.

"What do you want now? Huh? The same song this time?"

The men look at each other silently, not speaking, staring at him, irritatingly calm.

"You're coming with us."

"Why?"

"In the name of the Father."

On behalf of his father, on behalf of our Father.

There's a long drawn out pause. The pistol is getting heavy for Tito, his dry testicles are weighing him down, how he's going to get to the Toyota is weighing heavily on his mind. Life is weighing him down. All of a sudden everything is confusing, it can't be this way. Why aren't things like in the commercials I write? Pack and leave. Without risks of any type that might scare the target audience.

Then a noise: a young couple with a little baby in a stroller gets out of the elevator. Tito hides the pistol, putting it to one side, but he commits an unforgivable mistake: he looks away.

For a few seconds they fake it.

The family passes. The casting that you need for Cerelac, Tito, blonds like the clients want, smiling, rosy cheeks. But it's too late. Just one blow, clean, well placed, on the neck. One of them disarms you. Other arms grab you. The pistol doesn't even hit the ground: professionals.

Poor Tito. He doesn't know what's happening. Between dreams he senses the car leaving and the sun that's coming through the two-cylinder Citroen's windows. The street.

"Boss, it really bothers me to have to resort to violence, you know?"

"Come on, don't act like such a pacifist."

Tito tries to say something but can't. He listens, with difficulty.

"I hadn't done that for such a long time."

"You love it, you love it."

But he can't. Once again there's total darkness. *Blackout.*

10

The word of God

Morning in La Vega is morning in La Vega. It's the sun which makes its appearance on this spring day and peeps through the luster of the stubborn clouds to abandon its shepherding of the sky. It's the music from the Salvation Army amidst the humidity of the fruiterers and the florists in la Pérgola, next to the covered swimming pool. It's also enormous trucks, with their workers clinging to the racks like monkeys on wooden banisters, climbing down carrying sacks over their heads which look like medieval capes, the merchandise which this Saturday will feed the Santiagoan week. And above all it's the smell of chloroform on the hand of the bolero singer, the whistler of America who has not stopped whistling the complete repertoire of the Trío Los Panchos, and who is getting out of the Citroen holding up a wavering Tito Triviño. Dark glasses, his face reflecting the tower of the church of Recoleta while they keep on walking as if they were carrying a drunk, the short man and the thin guy, towards a bar and restaurant which, without pretentiousness, has a lighted sign on the front with the simple name of El Cielo, next to the beer logo for Pílsener Cristal.

"Heaven?"

"That's where we're going, Titito. It'd be better if you was quiet."

A rain of plastic strips let the three cutout shadows pass through, contrasted with a hymn from the Salvation Army in the sunny plaza of the humid Mapochian spring. Penumbra: a waiter with a tablecloth for an apron, his sleeves rolled up, puts the chairs which had been placed upside down on the table in proper order.

"What can I get you?"

Tito stares at the thin fellow who is asking him that seriously, although it sounds like a joke. He's thinking he should run away. The short guy has lost himself behind the counter, in the back room. They are whispering. Tito feels really down, definitely lost in the frailty of all perspective, studying the development of the events. He doesn't recognize this place, but he feels he's been here before. The mural with clouds and angels which has been crapped on by every fly in the world intimidates him, the blinding flashing neon light, the cutouts of soccer games played before his time: Raúl Toro in the faded color cover from *Estadio*. This is heaven?

"What can I get you, I said."

Tito makes an attempt to get up and leave but finds himself tied up, or it's as if he were tied up. The fact is, he can't move his hands.

"A pilsner? A Bilz? Some papaya?"

There's a rancid smell, stale urine, cheap beer, soaked into the wood in the tables, counter, and walls. The bar is eagerly wiped by the waiter who doesn't seem to take notice of the presence of the mistreated Tito and his guard. There are some shiny spitoons, dented in by some drunk after the last goal by Chato Subiabre, Manuel Muñoz, Atilio Cremaschi. This is heaven?

"I'd drink a mineral water."

"A Cachantún?"

Tito says yes.

"A sandwich? A pork roll, a roast, cold cuts, a sub sandwich?"

Tito asks himself if la Maga and the whole ordeal of pleasure existed, or if it was only a remote fantasy in a high school summer, an adolescent masturbation. If by chance it's the truth, the only one, that's all it is: the religious refrain calling for the salvation of souls, there outside, and the silent flies that pierce the heavy dark air in this place.

The trucks passing by three feet from the door are so far away, the carriers are so far away, the farmhands yelling out their produce. The smell of fresh vegetables.

"No, thanks," mumbles Tito, and his throat goes dry on him: the chloroform, he thinks.

The Cachantún stands up on the table and looks at Tito. Vintage '52, the bubbles were lost, perhaps, in shipping. A thick glass bottle, chipped at the edges. He drinks. It's lukewarm but it tastes wonderful. He can open his eyes well now, he can take off the dark glasses. He feels like they've given him a beating. This is heaven? Or, is it a secret barracks for the political police?

"How do you feel?"

"Better."

"Should I get one for myself?"

"It's a little flat, to tell the truth."

The thin guy thinks about it.

"My name is Gabriel," he says as he offers his long bony hand, with a ring made of precious stones that looks like the coat of arms in a bar logo. "But you can call me Gabby."

"Oh, yeah."

"Do you like it?"

"Your name?"

"No, the place."

"It's not bad."

"I think they could modernize it, you know?" says Gabby confidentially. "Bring it more up to date. Those cherubs, for example."

Tito looks at the third-rate Rubens painting, or, where the flies leave their appreciative deposits.

"That's about to be the latest rage. In a few years, you can sell it for a million dollars, you'll see."

"Really?"

The curtains move in the background.

"Uh . . . Here comes God the Father."

Tito watches without paying much attention. The short man appears, whose name is Rafael and whom they call Rafi, and someone else is behind him.

"Watch yourself, Don Titito."

"Oh."

A man of medium height, heavyset, bald and rosy cheeked, with a beard, like on a Christmas card. All the men bow, Gabby gives him his chair. In his thick, rosy hands, like those of a large and hairy angel, he has a greasy deck of cards.

"A game of *brisca?*"

Tito remembers some type of game in the back of his mind. He was a little lucky, he knew how to lie. He was great at *truco*, but when it came to betting he had no backbone. Count to forty. He was forgetting. Count, count, friend. He was forgetting. Tito Triviño was given to distraction: a lot of women on the horizon where he could let fall eyes-fingers-mouth which squeeze her nipples, the back of her leg, between her ass cheeks through her woven jeans, about to . . .

"There, I'll shuffle them, let's say."

He begins to cut the cards.

"You're going to have to learn."

"At least for appearance's sake," whispered Gabriel, and he gestured towards the street. The music and the singing of hymns had stopped, and the singsong voice of a preacher filled the area.

God the Father, because it was Him, looked at Tito Triviño, but the one being stared at chose to lower his eyes. Something was bothering him, he was letting himself stare at the floor, counting the cracks in the planks, he was nauseous, he tried to raise his eyes but he couldn't.

"Pick up your cards. We're going to be friends." *Vox dei*, as they're telling him.

Gabby and Rafi were arranging his hand. He looked at his king, his jack, the sevens. The spade was the winner. Forty: I've got forty! The king and the horse looked at him indifferently, like they were used to winning, as if they had God for a companion every day and they could say they had forty.

"Fake it," continued the Old One. "While I'm speaking to you, hold in your feelings and emotions. Act like any other novice *brisca* player. Bring another Cachantún, Maruja!"

Her voice came from way down and rebounded in a soft, tired *okay*, and Tito Livio imagined it came from an old woman. But the young woman that left had porcelain skin, snow white hands. The cards shook in his hand. He thought he had seen her before. He attributed it to the long night, the excitement of the rounds with la Maga, to the kick in the head, the chloroform.

"Hold on to your cards."

He continued the game, mechanically. The Old One was speaking slowly, like someone who slowly counts to one hundred, without any intonation.

"I need you, young Triviño. Things are tough and you're going to have to work for us. Nobody but you can do what Heaven orders. As the others also know."

"Who?"

"Keep your mouth shut. I'm telling you that they're looking for you. That child, la Maga, she wants you for them."

The spades were on the table. The trick was his with the king. Forty, forty. All of a sudden he revived: knock, knock.

"Good, good. Don't lose track. I like it like that. Be careful. You're probably asking yourself why we want you. But this is the word of God" — the other two crossed themselves — "and God knows what he's doing. Only you can help us. A lot depends on what you do. For us . . . or for them."

"It's the secret balance in the world," whispered Gabby, who had changed his musical sweep and was now whistling Peruvian waltzes: *Soul, Heart, and Life.*

They gathered the stack of cards.

Tito felt like ice was going down his back, from the very middle of his neck to his waist, that a scream was building in his lungs. Who wanted him for what? Who was following him, and for what purpose? All this was a bunch of nonsense. His father's crazy friends: his mother's voice in his ear. Crazy, no doubt. He quickly got to his feet.

"I'm going."

God didn't even move.

"Mister Triviño thinks we're deranged," he said while he gathered the cards.

"I'm going," repeated the timid Tito Triviño without conviction. The preacher's voice was cracking the morning air. The yells from the workers, the florists, the fruiterers. Aren't they ever going to shut up?

He took a step back, but the Old One had gotten to his feet, enraged.

59

"You'll be held responsible for what might happen!"

"I don't understand one damned thing! I don't get one little bit of what's going on, and I don't give a damn about staying here listening to an old crazy guy when I don't know what the hell he's getting at, and I'm leaving, I'm going, do you hear?"

"You big baby," muttered the Old One, but Tito didn't pay any attention to him. He was going to leave when Rafael jumped up, alarmed.

"They're coming."

"The shutter," screamed Gabby and they jumped towards the door. Tito was left turning around like a monkey on a string. He was understanding less every second. All of a sudden, before they finished lowering the metal shutter, he saw, in the distance, two blocks away, Donkavian's silver car.

God the Father had gotten up.

"The Lord is with you," he said, and the shutter closed.

"Everybody hit the floor," Tito heard someone scream out while a thin but firm arm pulled him face down. He didn't even have time to feel the blow to his ribs before a volley of bullets ripped through the shutter. Glasses were flying, he saw a line of bullets rake the counter, and they sped away outside. After a silence the Salvation Army band played, like nothing had happened. Everything was as if nothing had happened.

Tito's eyes were close to the dusty floor, his face besmeared. The whites of his eyes were floating like phantom boats in the darkness of the room.

"They . . . they . . . they tried to kill us."

"Mmmmmmmmm," said God. He had a bullet imbedded in the palm of one hand, which he took out with his teeth and spit into the other. God the Father remained looking at the others with his right hand opened, with a wound in the center. He put the bullet next to his heart.

"From a .38. Professionals. They know that these things can't do anything to us." He licked the wound and opened and closed his hand a few times. A cheap trick, confirmed the resentful Tito: the wound disappeared.

"You're the one they're looking for."

Get scared, Tito, it'll be better.

60

"No."

"Yes, you're the only one they can kill with these bullets."

"They're afraid that if you get to talk to us you might come over to our side. And there, losing you is the same to them. They would prefer you dead."

Triviño felt small, out of place, a lost child in a haunted house. He had the illusion that outside of this place everything would stop, it was only a fable, a lie, some nasty trick of the imagination, a plot for a bad TV movie. He wanted to leave, get out of there.

"Don't scare him any more," pronounced God the Father. "Look at me, Tito."

He tried to focus on anywhere else.

"Look at me," insisted the Oldest of the Old in the world.

He hid his face in his hands, his body trembled, he felt like some type of battlefield remains, in between the beams of light which were entering through the holes in the metal shutter: rays populated with dust particles.

"Look at me."

And Tito looked at him. And he saw the end and the beginning of the world, and he saw the oceans being born from an intense blue and he saw the power of the sun condensed into his index finger and he saw lions fighting over the body of a giant and he saw volcanoes and lakes overflowing and he saw the clouds opening up for him as if he were the last light in the universe until he fell to earth and he saw the silent peoples of the earth sleeping forever and he saw the destruction of Babel and the parting of the Red Sea and he felt all the water from the Great Flood flow over him and the annihilation of Sodom and Gomorrah and he was buried by the walls of Jericho and he heard a voice which was speaking to him in a strange but perfectly understandable language saying that the decision to agree or run away was in his hands and nobody would stop him except himself or the evil of hell or the depths of the earth or nothingness, and he saw nothingness and he closed his eyes, hurting, and he let himself fall into his chair and he felt everything was shaking, that his bones were turning to dust, that he could scarcely breathe, that his heart was going to jump out of his throat like a crazed bullfrog, and his body would be left useless and lifeless forever, for centuries upon centuries.

He opened his eyes again and the room was lighted, and they had opened the shutter and God the Father was next to the woman with the old voice, next to the door, behind the counter, inviting him to enter.

"Shall we talk now?"

11

The Lord is with you

If the room was dark before, this was night itself. He felt the floor, half covered with broken tiles, part hard earth and grasses. A half-open curtain permitted the passage of a ray of light, which spread itself over the back wall made up of shiny glassy objects: bottles. They were in a wine-cellar. Behind him, the short one and the thin fellow were closing door after door.

"What are you doing?" inquired Tito Livio.

"Sit down, we'll explain it to you now."

At the same time as they were moving the sliding doors, Triviño Junior was realizing that the darkness was approaching zero visibility, if zero was imaginable. He heard the doors lock like the fallen pieces in a deadly game of dominoes. Clack. Clack. Clack. The last one. Clack.

"Everything set?" asked the voice of God the Father through the darkness.

There was no answer. The shuffling of soles over the rough floor suggested to him that God was moving around. A lightning flash made him blink, blinded. A lightbulb was hanging from the roof, below a cone-shaped metal screen. It had been turned on and left swinging back and forth like a pendulum, alternately illuminating and leaving in the dark both God and Triviño Junior.

"Here we can have a good talk. This is all silver plated and nobody can penetrate these secrets."

"Don't you think you're exaggerating?" said Tito, as his old ironic humor came to his aid. He always resorted to it in moments of greatest helplessness. A lifesaving joke, it surrounded him with a cloud of disdain, it took him out of danger and alienation for a moment. In that way he had eluded old fossils at the university, monstrous clients at the agency, raging women with knives in hand. Joke for joke, verse for verse.

"When you finally understand what you're involved in, nothing will seem exaggerated. Let's just say you'll understand the way things really are. The right proportion, let's say. You're now becoming involved in balances that you never suspected, bases and structures that not even the most outstanding of mortals is capable of understanding. Accessible only to the crazy and sick. Perhaps some dying person in the middle of his delirium might manage to realize that the Holy War is continuing, but his look will become deranged and will continue fixed to his deceptive daily lucidity. The truth is not seen in any mirror, my son."

"Like for vampires," continued Tito, ironically.

"The serious thing, cheerful fellow member, is that you are caught right in the line of fire, and it's none other than you whom we must place in charge of the mission to reestablish the balance."

"Are you putting me on? You're saying, excuse me if I'm not being respectful, but do you think I'm going to swallow this line of bull that this hellhole of a business is made out of silver?"

"Well it's a thin plate, but . . ."

"And you think that because you talk a little weird, or because you put I don't know what in the Cachantún I'm going to believe any old story?"

God the Father raised a finger and Tito could not continue talking. He was moving his mouth, but there was no sound coming out. Silence.

"It's painful to have to do this to you, but you don't listen, you overdo your sarcasm and mouthing off with all your cutting little jokes.

You'll have to shut up and listen up for once."

That's how a father Father speaks.

Tito stopped struggling. His defense was failing him. He felt that they were kicking a goal between his legs, that if he didn't wake up they'd deceive him, that the ball was slipping through his hands. Calm down, he said to himself.

"Before they discover that you were here, you'll have to carry out the mission you're charged with. If they find out you're on our side you're a dead man, in body and soul."

"Why?"

"You spoke again? For centuries we've managed the situation, more or less alternating between them and us. We've prevented complete chaos, an essential asymmetry, that they intend to break with the regime of death and silence. The flickering flame as a sign of eternal life has been hard to keep. Well then, we're losing."

"But what do I have to do with all this?" screamed Tito. He shut up, abruptly. He was afraid someone would come in, beat him up, leave him tied to a chair. Or maybe put a spell on him that would transform him into a rat, a shrew, a cockroach. Tito felt like Gregor Samsa.

"Get those ideas out of your mind," transmitted Pater Noster by telepathy. "No one can listen in or perceive what's going on here. We don't have much time. You're Triviño's son, that's your problem, your responsibility and, if you do it well, your virtue. You have to carry out what he left undone."

"What's that? What's this mission you're talking about?"

"I don't know. What do you think I am, omnipotent and all-knowing?"

"But . . ."

"I'm not a manipulator of mankind, I love them very much and I help them. But the joke is in what you people do. Otherwise, any mistake would be my fault. Look at the impudence."

"So, you're putting me in charge of something that you don't know about, which I don't know how to find anything out about, and it's got to be done right away."

"They've put you in charge of worse things in advertising."

"Well, look at this brief. It's like a bad takeoff on *Star Wars*."

"On what?" asked God, who didn't go to movies very much.

"On nothing. It's just a stupid comment."

"If I knew everything about this, I'd put Rafael, or Gabriel, or Miguel in charge, or anyone. But your father knows what he doesn't know he knows."

"Oh?"

"That is, maybe he'll discover what he has and point it out to you."

"What does my father have to do with all this?"

"He worked for us."

"He worked?"

"And for them, too. Before. We won him over some years ago and he was the best double agent we've had. Until . . ."

"What?"

"La Maga grabbed him."

A bell sounded in Tito's brain.

"And put a bullet right here." God the Father pointed to the space between his eyes.

"But I saw him."

God's smile shone on him. There was a brief glow in the room.

"Seriously? Then everything can move along faster."

"What?"

"He's not going to allow them to grab you, or get you on their side, either," he broke into a divine smile, "and he'll get in contact with you there."

"What? You guys can't find him?"

"Do you think I can be everywhere at once?"

"But that's what they say."

"Come on, you know advertising. That means something else."

"Oh, sure."

"Get to work now. In the course of the day you'll find your father. Don't tell anything to anyone. Get down."

"What?"

"On your knees, I'm telling you."

Without knowing what he was doing, Tito let himself fall to the floor. It seemed to him as if a ray of light were spreading over him, soft and luminous, enveloping him.

"In my name, my son's, and the Holy Spirit's."

66

And then Tito recognizes the rough flapping of a falcon's wings, descending from the ceiling, and he recognizes the warbling of doves with their neighborly gossip, talking from the top of the wine-cellar, and a raven is resting on his shoulders, delicately, like a shawl, and Tito is going to take it off, but it vanishes.

"The body of Christ."

There is a small transparent host between his fingers.

"This is my body which will be saved by you."

He shakes his head. He's in pain. But then he accepts, the host breaks apart, bittersweet, in his mouth. There's a slight taste of alcohol, blood, burnt sugar.

"Gabriel! Rafael!"

Clack. Clack. The Lord's henchmen come in.

"To the lower door, he's going to the agency."

"Did he agree?"

"He's going to agree."

Tito stays on his knees. The light is making him uncomfortable and he prefers to remain quiet, with his eyes closed, but a fetidness surrounds him. They've opened a pit in the floor and Gabriel is dusting off a lantern.

"Now, down, Tito, let's go."

"The Lord is with you, son," says God the Father as he waves the fingers on his right hand like a child. Then he points out the hole, energetically.

"Go to it. You're one of us until you judge to the contrary."

Tito stands up and begins to go into the hole. Gabriel goes in front of him, whistling *El Loco.* It's a steep rung ladder, very steep. Rafael begins to close up the hole.

Before a new total darkness and a new closing, he manages to listen to a conversation between the old woman and God.

"Will he work out?"

"When you expect the least, you always get more than you hoped for."

"Then he'll work out."

And, clunk, he hears the heavy cement slab being placed over the hole, and he holds fast to the iron rungs and descends. Meanwhile he recognizes the voice of the old sounding young girl which now does not sound old, which is now the sweetest sound in the world, the one he would like to keep listening to, the one from the beautiful apparition in Villa Alemana.

And he descends.

12

A body in the torrent

D arkness. Still the very same and underground darkness. The very same Tito Triviño feels his body float in the terrible odor, strong and thick with decay where they've let themselves down, and where the lamp which Gabby, the bolero whistler, is carrying becomes dim, weak, insufficient, dancing with each of his steps, illuminating the pavement next to the cramped flow of water in which lies the intestinal matter from the inhabitants of the capital, the dirty secrets from the lower guts of the city, the now forgotten password, the innermost and darkest motive, very dark, in reality, perhaps too much.

"Did he put you in charge of the mission? Really?" as the whistling suddenly ceased, and the whistler kept staring at him. Once again the light was stopped, swinging back and forth and yellowing their faces: the slender Gabriel, and the stammering, perplexed, Tito Livio.

"Triviño! I'm asking you if he put you in charge of the mission?" He looks him straight in the eye, and the thin gentleman understands. "Yeah, yeah, you got it all dumped on you." He shakes his head half-confused and half-displeased. "Don't take offense, I'm not one to

69

second-guess God the Father's plans, but you . . . after following you
for over a month . . . you don't seem to me . . ."

He pauses. The lantern seems to move in front of them. They start
walking again, but he turns towards Tito Livio and moves the light up
to his face. The flame does something to kill the bad smell for a
moment, or lessen it, at least.

"He told you that you had to look for him? Yes or no? He must have
made it clear to you, really clear. Or didn't he?"

A pause. The water splashing against the walls of the underground
sewer added to the whistler's agony which kept getting worse. Tito
shook his head, saying *no* almost with pleasure. I don't know
anything, I haven't got the faintest idea. He doesn't have the least idea.
He didn't tell me anything, not even a clue, not a hint, nothing.

"God didn't tell you anything! Shit! God doesn't know either!"

The scream reverberated, echoed.

"They're putting you in charge, and on top of that they don't even
know what they're looking for."

A splash in back of them.

"Holy Mother of God . . . Quiet . . .!" A shove from whistling Gabby
pushes him against the damp wall. He hides the light near his body:
pistol in hand. Tito doesn't know anything else about weapons other
than his own Walter PPK and the ones that show up in novels, films
and comics, but this one seems unusually big. What caliber? What
range? An automatic that all of a sudden makes its profile shine in the
darkness. You're going to learn a lot, Tito, a lot. Just in case, it's a
Parabellum.

There's a long silence, like a still photo with no one in it, the
seconds running into each other, they can't see anything.

"There . . ."

A body in the torrent. Tito shudders: it's a corpse. Gabriel's wet foot
stops it and the dead man turns over. He shines the light on his face.

"He's been in the water for a while, do you see? His face is gone,
look at his shriveled neck." There's a soft flash of light reflected from
the flame. "He's a Frog. He must have been done in by some Lizard,
or a Falcon, or a White Hand. Don't worry, Triviño, they're factions.
Secret societies that spend time fighting among themselves. Sometimes they contract God the Father for some work, but they're like

70

hot-headed soccer fans: you're either with them, or against them. If you go to one side, their natural enemies will attack you. They're experts but real belligerent. Didn't you know about them? You're going to meet them now. They're everywhere."

Tito pretends to be brave.

"Why did you get so scared?" Tito asks. He kicks away the rest of what's holding back the body, and it continues on its way towards the river.

"Me? Don't tell anyone, I shouldn't have gotten scared . . ." Gabriel makes a new attempt to continue walking but puts the lamp in front of himself, and is met with a stare.

"No, it's better for you to get scared too," he completes the sentence. "Because you don't know everything that's coming into play here. The whole balance of this microcosm that's in harmony with the earth which is the balance of the universe. All this has always depended on small movements, all linked one to another in structures whose complexity is unfathomable to the human eye. They'll never understand what maintains the cupola of heaven."

They will never understand? Why didn't he say *we* will never understand? Why doesn't he include himself with human beings? Who is the whistler, Tito? Calm down, don't say anything, keep on faking it, search that brain of yours, champion of limitations and deficits, dying of fright, disguised as a lost hero of the last world war, the third, the coming one, the expected one. Pretend that Gabby has started whistling again and starts on the way again and while he advances (careful not to slip, Tito Livio), while they are going further into the complex labyrinth, he explains himself and tells you. What does he tell you?

"These last few years this delicate balance has been at the breaking point, it happens every so often, in history, in all histories, the daily ones, the biographical ones, the century ones, those with and without fixed dates, it happens. And every structure changes face, demands solution, crisis, becomes disturbed, and the secret war . . . Do you know anything about the secret war?" He managed something that could have been a laugh. "The war speeds up, until it reaches a new point of equilibrium. They want . . ."

"Chaos and anarchy." Tito played being the clever one.

"Much worse than that! They want definite order, static and

insoluble. They love symmetry, exact results, Euclidian geometry, and hitting the bullseye. They reverse the meaning of life, and they stop it in its appearance. That which seems to be everything and in reality is nothing. The cosmos is chaos in balance. Order is the absence of chaos, the loss of tension, death. We defend positive entropy, the leap of perpetual motion, confusing at first glance, impeccable on an infinite scale but always distinct, like snowflakes, without end, without any possible repetition, a new incomprehensible form which no one will ever predict, always a further meaning, project, negation of negation. Do you understand any of it? Understand?"

"Somewhat."

"Well, that's good, that you understand the meaning of the thing you're looking for. Sometimes it's an object, a ring, a gem, a picture, a poem, something lost and hidden which will tell us the truth about the present and future, or if not, a deed, an act, a gesture . . . even a crime. They're junctures between two eras, bridges."

He brought the flame threateningly close to Tito's face, as if to examine the eyes of an alleged assassin.

"It's a type of gymkhana," stammered Tito, playing the funny guy. "To bring things which give more points for the Queen."

The whistler doesn't like the joke. It's bad and out of place, the joke of a frightened man. Gabby hums a bolero. He pretends he's not listening but he keeps going, advancing in the darkness, more rapidly. *I'm going through the tropical wall, the night filled with silence with its lemon scented perfume.* Tito is afraid of stumbling.

"Not so fast!"

"Don't take this lightly, then. Did you see the frog?"

The silver frog around the corpse's neck comes to his mind in a flash. He shivers, sure he saw it, sure he remembers.

"It probably seems like a joke to you, but when the balance is lost, you won't be feeling like laughing any more. You and all the other mortals. Do you hear? In every region someone operates the correct point, if it's lost in one city, it's lost in all of them. If we get it back here, it's recovered in the entire universe. The structure is that complex and delicate, just as it's that important for you to obtain what you have to get, or do, or undo, what do I know?"

"How am I going to find out about it?"

72

"Your father has to know how to find out about it. Or if he doesn't know, he'll stumble upon it without discovering what you in fact will find out."

"And how will I find him?"

His silhouette there, far away in the Plaza del Hoyo. Like a Delvaux painting.

"He's going to find you, Tito Livio."

"Why didn't you find him? Why didn't you call him and leave me in peace?"

He doesn't answer him. He whistles *Scandal*. More than ever he looks like Javier Solís, reflected in a mirror from a house of thrills which elongates images. He moves forward twice as fast. All of a sudden he stops.

"We're below Lyon and Pocuro. A little further up we'll come out."

"But how come you're not answering me?"

The thin guy stops whistling.

"If they didn't tell you that, I can't tell you. Although they all know about it."

"All who?"

"Those who are in the business. The Frogs, the Lizards, the White Hands, the Falcons."

All of a sudden a new flash rebounded in the Triviñesque mind: Mina's neck, where there hung a silver lizard. Could it be possible?

"Mina," he stammers.

"Yes, they've got women too," misunderstood the bad Javier Solís. A stroke of luck, thinks Tito.

A light appears in the distance. At last a light, on the wall. A door. It leads out to a basement, for a change, full of bottles.

"Here's where I leave you. A last word of warning: be careful with that woman."

"With who? Which one of them?" says Tito. It's not a joke.

"Don't act like you don't understand. You know who I'm talking about. The one last night. Pretty, isn't she?"

Tito remains quiet, speechless, obstinate. Yes, pretty, maybe the best lover he's ever had: a globe-trotter when it comes to beds. Gabby doesn't say anything. He doesn't even whistle. The door closes and the odor goes away. He thinks about his clothes having gone through all

73

the muck, but he checks them out and they're impeccable, as if nothing had happened. Cautiously he climbs the ladder: a store where the clerk seems not to pay attention to him. He's waiting on a woman who also remains impassive, as if people come up out of manholes every day to fulfill missions charged by High Heaven. He walks out and is on Lyon. How come he'd never noticed this place before? He begins to walk towards MacPherson and quickly sees the white facade of the agency with his car in the parking lot. How? He's had a dream. Everything seems to happen and not to happen. He could think that it was madness, only his imagination, some short-circuit in his worn-out nervous system. Neurotransmitters, stress, a midlife crisis. He's read about that. But no, now it's too late, now he'll get it all together. Now it's better to say hello, to Barbara, for example, who's coming in and he smiles at her.

Tito can't help staring at the pendant she has around her neck.

13

Tell me, my friend

And Tito calmed down when he saw the silver cross, insignificant, dangling from the small chain over Barbara's secret cleavage, between her two wonderful breasts which at this moment did not concern him. He calmed down but not that much, enough to put on a proper face, in order not to give away what had happened, to pass in front of the glass door and see his reflection and think: Today is a day like any other one, it's the same body and the same innocent face as always. Lean and funny this Tito: long steps, wide smile, always ready to shake a hand. He's even doubting his own mind. How many now, Tito? How many times have you run through your memory and run through it again, the image, the past, to see if all the pain has you looking ill, to see if you're preparing a jig-saw puzzle without a single missing piece, a single bullet wound, a single swear word, no danger at all? Like a child in its mother's arms. And you're thinking: Maybe it's nothing more than the bad effects from too many drugs at Donkavian's house, too much of a woman in my bed, I'm drinking a lot, staying up too late, sleeping less all the time. And it also seems strange to him that he doesn't feel tired at all, that he's raring to go, like new, rejuvenated, when he opens the polarized glass front door and receives a blast from the air conditioner and the waves of piped-in music and the receptionist (he never learned her name) says hello to him.

"Two calls for you, Tito."

His stomach tightened up again. "Who?"

"I don't know, I sent them upstairs. Deborah should have the message."

The message, who? All this activity surfacing in his brain: the perfect host, Donkavian, dressed as a Huaso, the magnificent magnetic Maga, don't even say that it's Mina, maybe his father — my father? — his mother.

"I don't know, talk to Deborah."

He doesn't know how he climbs the stairs and finds himself bending over Deborah's desk, the department secretary. A woman's body. Tito liked that office when he saw so many females, when Fatty Aspillaga took him away from Walter Thompson to show him the employees, and he saw Barbara, and he saw Sandy the brunette, and he saw Deborah. Each one more of a knockout, each more perfect. It was enough just to talk to Deborah to stir up all his bad intentions, Deborah to whom he couldn't say hello without getting irate when he listened to her. The body of a goddess, cackle of a crow.

"Who called me?"

She doesn't look at him. She never looks at him. She's doing three things at once, besides shrieking when she speaks.

"I don't know, I left the note in your office."

Your body is a blessing, Deborah. You should respect it, know you're wanted, desired, needed; or maybe you know it and that's the reason for showing your claws, that's why: *vade retro*.

And you *vade* to your office and Fatty Aspillaga is there staring at you through his thick tortoiseshell glasses.

"Fat Man!"

"New working hours, I see."

"Where's that message for me?"

"What's going on with you? Yesterday you ran out of there like nobody's business, and you didn't give a clue ..."

"There's an important message for me, Fatty, we'll talk later."

"Oh, we'll talk later. Do you know what country we're in? In a country that's approaching thirty percent unemployment. In a country where there aren't any spoiled brats who do what they want with their soft jobs. In a job where you've used up all the slack we ever cut for you. You're in deep shit, stupid!"

He recognized the paper with frigid Deborah's scrawl on it. His hand shot out for it but Aspillaga grabbed it between his thumb and index finger, thick and agile.

"You're going to have to listen to me."

Tito gave up. He let himself fall into the chair.

Aspillaga paused, triumphant: he had the stature of a gladiator who is catching his breath in the arena, looking down, in a counteroffensive. Tito saw his open shirt and once again got the chills: a chainlink necklace. I'm going crazy.

The Fat One sat down as if there hadn't been any struggle.

"Tell me, my friend," he said, pleased with himself.

"Do you promise not to treat me like an idiot? Do you promise not to keep looking at me like you think I've completely lost my mind?"

Aspillaga laughed, slowly: How could you possibly think that? Okay then, thought Tito, let's take a chance, this has got to come out once and for all. He thought about lying to him, he thought about telling him everything down to the last detail, he thought about giving him a watered-down version. He chose the fuzzy dream, I don't know how to explain to you, a dreamlike story which you can hardly remember when you wake up.

"My dear Fatty, your friend has gone through a series of some pretty strange things. Yesterday he went to Villa Alemana to see the Virgin, to write a book of first-hand accounts, according to him, to deal with a little bit less shit editing crap for margarine, middle- and upper-class women, words to jingles, etcetera, and there, two men in a Citroen begin to follow him and they turn out to be . . ."

Bah, Tito stops and doesn't continue.

"Yes?"

"Fatty, it's impossible."

"But go on."

"Well, they're guys who say they want to save me from other people who are sent by . . ."

77

"What's wrong with you?"

"It's just that everything is really crazy, totally bizarre, it doesn't make any sense."

"Tell me once and for all, okay?"

"Well, some guys sent by Donkavian."

"Donkavian!"

"Shut up and listen now that you've got yourself involved in this mess. I go tearing off to my mother's house and later I find myself in my apartment with Mina who beats the crap out of me."

"Mina?"

"Right, the one and only."

"I told you she looked like a spy."

"You told me that?"

He looked at Aspillaga who nodded, wise like a father. Every bit a father.

"Meanwhile," continued Tito, "my father, no less, shows up to tell me that Donkavian wants to hurt me. Do you know what Donkavian is offering me?"

"A trip to São Paulo to work with Riveiro."

Take that, Tito.

"How did you find that out?"

"Please continue."

"But how did you find out? It was a secret."

"It's still a secret. Go on."

Tito looks at him. Aspillaga is changing. He's afraid of what he might be hiding around his neck, hanging from that chain. Aspillaga seems to understand because he takes out a silver frog and shows it to him without saying anything.

There, take that, Tito Livio. You thought you knew about everything.

"Fatty . . ."

Aspillaga puts his index finger to his lips.

"Just go on."

"Well, you know everything. I spent the night with la Maga."

"La Maga? Holy Christ! Do you know who la Maga is? Do you know why she's here? It's better if you don't find out."

"What?"

"Be careful, you'll be better off."

It was as if they had stuck a hot pepper up his ass.

"Look, I'm tired of everyone telling me to be careful, I'm tired of everyone telling me what I have to do and nobody explaining anything to me about it. How did you find out about the Riveiro deal?"

"Donkavian's secretary called, I pretended to be you. She spoke about a trip, ticket reservations, about what time you have to be at the airport tomorrow. I know that Riveiro is here and I know that they wanted you. And I know full well who Donkavian is."

"Who in fucking hell is Donkavian?"

Aspillaga looked through the large glass door. The air conditioner will become indispensable in a short time. He closed the wooden blinds.

"Let's work, it'll be better."

Tito huffed angrily to himself.

"My messages, at least."

"Donkavian's secretary was one."

"And the other?"

"Your mother."

"Oh."

Tito remained silent. What luck it's Friday, he thought. He glanced at the list of pending scripts: a production meeting in ten minutes, a promotion commercial, the new non-calorie margarine, the food that doesn't nourish, pure flavor, pure chemicals, masturbatory eating, without commitment. Could he really work?

He looked at Fatty Aspillaga who was editing a pamphlet for television.

"How did you get yourself involved?"

"In what?"

"In the frog thing."

"What?"

He looked at him. He realized that there were things that were said, but one didn't say them. All of a sudden he got scared: he thought about who they were working for now. Them, the others. And him? Which side was he on? Who could he believe? Can you tell me who Donkavian is?

Deborah's shrill voice. Like a parrot.

"Tito! Telephone!"

Mina's voice on the line.

"Tito?"

"What do you want now?"

From a little further away, I know what your game is now.

"I wanted . . . I don't know . . . to tell you I'm sorry."

A cat, totally feline.

"Oh."

"Can we get together for lunch?"

"Are you serious? After your martial arts exhibition?"

"I'm serious. I care about you a lot, Tito."

"Where?"

"I don't know . . . Do you like the Bistro?"

Expensive, thought Tito, but the way things are it doesn't matter.

"Sure, okay."

"At one o'clock."

"Okay. Ciao."

"Don't get mad at me, Tito. Sometimes I'm a little rash."

He was going past Fatty who pushed him into the bathroom: locked up. Clack.

"Didn't it occur to you to talk to the gringo about the trip to São Paulo?"

"I don't think I'm going."

"Nevertheless, don't say that yet."

"Look, let's get out of here. We look like a couple of flaming faggots."

"Pay attention to me, and be quiet."

"Who are you working for, Fatty?"

"What do you mean?"

"Let's not go on like this. We're both involved in the same deal. Something that's going down real heavy. Real hard. Who do you work for?"

"I don't understand you."

Exasperated, Tito grabs Aspillaga's chain at the nape of his neck. He's almost strangling him: there's no frog.

Seriously: there is no frog. An innocent little cross, a medallion from the Virgin of Carmen that they must have given to him when he was a little child.

"I'm sorry, I'm sick."

"We've got a production meeting."

Not one more word.

"Right now."

Frustrated, Tito went straight to the hall. In the meeting room, he looked like a zombie: he said hello without shaking hands, he spoke without thinking. There was a dilemma about accentuating a certain erotic content as a benefit to the product. If the first camera shot was going to be on the waist, the breasts, or the stomach. The client, mild, pretending to be repressed, the moral conscience that these creative people have never had, was saying that the female buyers, the markets, the target group, would be upset, they would back off, no one buys margarine for that. Tito thought about *The Last Tango in Paris* and threw out a joke. They laughed. Everyone except the client, who began to laugh afterwards, but only when the meeting had finished: "What you said was funny, but you know about the prestige of an international business, a multinational like Lever." Yes, yes.

"Tito! Telephone!"

"Who is it?"

It was Triviño Senior.

"Thank God you called."

"Find me, and be real careful." And he hung up.

He didn't get to say anything, he didn't get to speak to that quivering voice, he couldn't tell him everything that came to him in a mad rush. Click, only a click. He was left with the receiver buzzing in his hand.

What was he calling you for? Why did he tell you to find him without saying where he was? What was the reason for leaving everything hanging?

Aspillaga was staring at him. What for? Why was he looking at him that way? Why was he standing guard over him?

He slipped out towards the video room. Nobody was there. He looked for some tacky tape: a promo copy from Europe advertising powdered milk with vitamins.

He put it on and threw himself into a chair, faking it. To whomever came in he would say: I'm working, we've got ten spots in the works, leave me alone.

Images were going by, logos, the most spectacular and repetitive trademarks, blond-haired little children, gymnasts, loving mothers who mixed and mixed and mixed tablespoons full of white vitamin-enriched powder on overly laden breakfast tables, incomparable to those in the Third World, sticking out their tongues at the slums. He was easily distracted, he was trained.

He took a quick look at his situation. Where could he hide today? He wasn't going to talk to the gringo MacPherson. He didn't want to see la Maga. He didn't want to find out about Donkavian. He had to find Tito Senior before the others found him. He shuddered when he thought they could be outside, and he checked the time: almost two.

He left the agency saying that he was going to see some graphics at the shop, two blocks away. He left, breathing heavily. Sandra made a friendly face at him from the second floor. He returned a smile, but coldly. He had fear written all over him.

He walked along Lyon with a fake easy-going attitude. Halfway between the shop and the agency he hailed a cab.

He climbed inside like someone putting on a mask, like kids who cover themselves up to get away from the ghosts in a dark room.

He gave his mother's address. Maybe she knew something, maybe he'd get it from her, maybe, yes, maybe he could cry in her arms, which seemed the most important thing.

14

Is it true you're going to Brazil?

Tranquility is not being followed when you take a taxi, it's craning your neck, looking behind you and seeing the truly innocent Santiago traffic, without that nightmarish humor of a haunted house, that atmosphere of panic with rearview mirrors filled with hats, little Citroens and silver cars. Tranquility is everyday life. Tito found that out, totally engrossed in the taxi driver's copy of *La Tercera*: the Virgin of Villa Alemana was threatening to turn itself into a fiasco. Would it have been a good idea? Maybe. There was something behind all that. Like a flash, the image came to his mind of that woman who pointed out his car on that road, who wasn't from Villa Alemana, who was from somewhere else, nowhere, maybe, or from everywhere. His thought bothered him: he was becoming difficult, paradoxical, ambiguous. Now he was speaking like the bolero whistler. The image of the guy in the sewer made him jump. He wasn't used to this and it seemed that he was going to have to get that way. He thought about the fact that he shouldn't have left the Walter at home. He should be armed, everything was too dangerous. He was thinking about this when he saw his mother's building. A series of childhood memories came to him. Had he counted on her in this danger? Would she be there? Would they have found her? Could she have something to do with it?

He got out of the car looking all around.

His mother opened the door. She had on her bathrobe, made up like she was going to a party given by the Duque de Alba, but she was in a bathrobe. His Christmas present of a José Luis Perales cassette was playing. The singer of songs of adultery, abandonment, and goodbyes. His wife hated them. His ex-wife, I mean. He still wasn't used to the situation.

"Titito!"

She let him in. The house plants and the collection of saints were barely illuminated, as if for the most expressionistic director. Monochromatic, contrasting, almost burned photos.

"Are you going to have lunch with me?"

José Luis Perales was asking how he was. He thought about the protagonist's latent homosexuality, worried about preparing his wife for her lover. Ismael, for example, his ex's steady visitor. What's he like?

"I wanted to ask you about my father."

A pause. His mother's way. Sulfuric acid, her chin dropped.

"Are you coming here to spoil my day? You know what he did to make us suffer with his friends. His female friends."

"I need to find him."

"What for? Surely he won't even recognize you. Did he ever worry about you? For what reason, now that you've grown up and things are going well for you, are you going to get mixed up with him? An old crazy drunk. Do you know why they threw him out of the National Institute?"

"Mom, I only want to know where he is."

Communicate, Tito. The word left your head spinning, don't deny it. Do you ask her, or not? What does she know?

"Son. Is it true you're going to Brazil?"

"Who told you that?"

"A little bird."

Tito thought about how curious it was that certain secrets stubbornly tended to make themselves public knowledge, making things more difficult. Whoever was controlling the information knew what they were doing. The real secret was something different. Something else that he did not recognize.

"Maybe I'll go on a trip. I don't know," answered Triviño Junior, who in this house was Triviño Recart. On his mother's side, of course.

"When?"

"It'll be a surprise."

"Can I put you in charge of something?"

Tito Livio saw that the conversation was leading to his mother's tears. She wasn't ready to give any inkling of his father's whereabouts. Nothing, never, no one, and least of all, to him. She wouldn't give in so easily to her son. They could torture her if necessary and it would be equally useless, equally desperate.

"Are you going to tell me something about my dad?"

"I've already told you everything. If you want to know more, go get into his world, in those nightclubs where he used to hang out, all night. Do you know why they threw him out of the Rectory at the Liceo de Aplicación?"

Her voice was bitter, corrosive.

"I've already listened to your comments about that."

"He used to go to bed with the practice teachers, he seduced them, he got them drunk. He made them lose their virginity."

"Which nightclub did he use to hang out in?" said Tito, becoming distracted. He was playing with an image of the Virgin of Pompeii which was placed in a type of manometer.

"Put that down. It's blessed." His mother said some prayer as she returned the image to its place.

"Mom, tell me the name of the nightclub."

I've told you hundreds of times, Tito. Didn't you ever memorize it? I used to pretend I couldn't hear, play stupid, foolish, deaf. It used to hurt to listen.

"*El Limbo*! El Limbo! Where that fat pig Lili Salomé moved her rolls for him and got him so hot to trot!"

His mother was furious. She was turning her back on him and crossing herself. Tito began to wander through the other rooms followed by her accusations and insults. He realized that he did this same nervous walk every time she got angry. Later this made him need to go to the bathroom, and he sat on the toilet while outside she prayed one two three Hail Mary's for her pent up anger. One day he should tell Gonzalo. Or maybe not? Or could what came to his mind one time be true? That Gonzalo could have something to do with that excessive make-up that his mother used to hide the lupus? He rejected the idea. It hurt.

El Limbo.

"Thanks, Mom."

Lili Salomé.

"Ciao."

"Don't leave me."

"Ciao, Mom."

Taxi.

He gave the address: the corner of José Antonio Soffia and Toba-lala. Le Bistro was annoying him. To tell the truth, he didn't even know what it was that he was going to do there with a woman who had just given herself the pleasure of demonstrating her complete reper-toire of attack techniques for him. And now, she had invited herself to a French restaurant with all the pretentiousness possible from the difficult years they had living together.

"Let me off here," he said, when he made out the famous Mina's Honda Accord. She was waiting for him.

The driver, who was a laid-off accountant-auditor working with what had been the family station wagon, one of the first Daihatsus from the economic boom, passively obeyed.

Mina said hello to him, kissing him on the cheek in a way that said something like I'm-sorry-I've-treated-you-so-badly. Tito was tense. You could see it in every one of the muscles of his face. He looked at the menu with the same disinterest with which he checked out some ad published in a women's magazine.

"What are you going to order, Mina?"

"Don't you think it'd be better if we talked first?"

A nuisance, a pisco sour. Wasn't there something malicious in the commonness of the pisco sour, the suicidal and negating aperitif of all that is life? Or was it this same thing that was making it irresistible? To live the easy life. The aperitif in the line of fire, toasting with your enemy.

He kept staring at her. He found an innocent face. Once again he began to run through all the slander, his bad faith came to view, images of all the recent events were passing by. His mother out of sorts, sobbing and screaming: *El Limbo!*
He felt like believing it was true. He liked Mina's face playing the weakling, the one asking for forgiveness. Tito Livio liked the fact that they beat the crap out of him and later cried about their own spilled blood. There was the irresistible temptation to deny his own wounds, sympathizing with the torturer. Anita María did it at the beginning, later she became civilized: a deadly idea. Now you see how that marriage ended. Tito needed punishment. But we don't know what's coming. Let's not venture opinions, let's continue with the action.

Tito orders some insipid browned mushrooms, considering that this isn't the best place to order them, and a medium-sized portion of whitefish with capers. Mina hasn't been able to monopolize the conversation. Her roquefort filet was getting cold. With a slight lump in her throat she puts on a face that Tito enjoys, he obviously enjoys it.

"Tito."

"Yes?"

"The reason I made a date with you was to talk to you."

"It's true."

Tito lifts his head up and keeps watching her. The whitefish is slowly getting cold. It's a little overdone, the capers are small and blackened.

"I want to say I'm sorry. Really. Besides, I know who you were with last night."

"How?"

Now it seems to you like your life is on television, Tito. There's nothing else left but paranoia and royalties.

"I was really hurt . . . When I found out I realized I still loved you . . . It was only anger and spite that made me beat you up. Do you forgive me?"

Tito had lost his appetite.

"Who told you?"

"I'm asking you if you forgive me!"

Mina's angry cheeks became red. She was rapidly running out of

humility, her conciliatory attitude was evaporating. Tito was losing his
charm at a bad time.

"What do you have to do with all this, Mina?"

"All what?"

"What were you doing at Donkavian's party?"

"I didn't go."

"You have to have been there. What are you trying to get me mixed
up in?"

"You're going crazy, Tito, I don't know what you're . . ."

"Who told you what happened last night?"

"La Maga."

The woman let the syllables fall out dryly as the restaurant staff
looked on. They were frightened of the man who raises his voice, the
couple who argues. She's calm now, he's hurt now. What's the matter
with them?

Tito is silent. That woman wasn't there to ask his forgiveness. He
didn't understand what was really happening, to tell the truth he
understood almost nothing. He ran through what had happened in his
mind, without being able to organize it. He had made the decision to
investigate the Supreme Father's request, finding his own father in-
trinsically involved in an as yet unclear mission, and all of a sudden he
was backing off again, and then once again they would get him involved
in a mess.

"I was with la Maga," she broke her silence. "And she assured me
that she was going with you to São Paulo. Are you going to live
together, Tito?"

Triviño meditates. Maga's movements were intimidating him but it
was a relief that they didn't know anything about his trip to La Vega, at
least it appeared that way. Did Mina want to verify that?

He took a deep breath and put on his best well-what-do-you-want-
me-to-say mask.

"Mina. Well, maybe I should clear this all up for you."

"Oh, now I see why you left me."

"Yes, really."

"All it takes is for another woman to show up and you leave. I really
believe that you deserved to be beaten to a pulp."

Triviño was frightened to watch the way she was moving her chin while she was speaking to him. She had started eating again. The meat was coming apart between her teeth. Tito was asking himself if she could be eating a piece of himself, and for a second he placed a protective hand over his crotch.

"You're a piece of shit, Tito," she said, wiping her mouth with her napkin before drinking some mineral water.

All of us think the same thing sometimes, Mina. But you, do you know what he's thinking? The problem is that Tito doesn't know either, but he's beginning to find out.

"I'm in love, Mina." Triviño Recart's face had pulled itself together with a great last minute effort, the strength that makes champions, the grasp, the sprint, the *Indian scores from behind* as his father, the Colocolino fan, was saying, celebrating the final offensive thrust and the winner's cup that they won from the Wanderers in an overtime game. It's before the World Cup in '62, you're listening to it on the radio and your father is crying, he hugs you and with a fountain pen he draws a new star for you on the small flag over your bed, and it absorbs the ink. It's a few years before separating from your virtuous mother.

"I imagine it has to be that way," she adds ironically. "I see you fall in love quickly, faster each time."

"That's the way I am, Mina, if love expects us to get together, we'll see each other again . . . I have to be with her to find out if she's really someone important in my life . . . It's been so strong, so unexpected, so intense . . ."

Who are you stealing that script from, Tito? Which radio soap opera? From *Secrets from a Mirror*, from Mireya LaTorre and Emilio Grau, from your mother's boleros?

Even Mina seemed to be moved. Tito took her by the hand. His hardened whitefish waits to be thrown on a fat cat's plate from the French restaurant, surprised at such a big leftover.

"I don't have any other explanation. I'm a detestable person, I suppose that's what you're thinking."

"And what a great job you're doing at being one, right? You must have learned it from your father. You're getting together with him again."

Suddenly our hero's view became unclear.

"What?"

89

"Your mother called me. Before I came here. Why do you want to see him?"

"I don't want to see him."

"You're going around asking where you can locate him. Do you want to take him to Brazil with you, too?"

Tito was within an inch of telling her he wasn't going, of telling her everything, he felt his worries churning up in his stomach. A damnable acidity was coming up to his mouth mixed with the worm-eaten capers and the badly done whitefish. One of the mushrooms, of course.

"I've got my reasons for seeing him . . . Before the trip."

Tito tried again. He thought he should control himself, he remembered the volley of shots, the body in the sewer, and it was enough and an impulse to keep on guard came over him. With a quick glance he searched for some chain on her neck but her blouse was in the way. There was something there and Mina wasn't exactly a Catholic. The silver lizard must be verified.

"Then we only have to talk."

There was a pause. The waiters were returning to their chores, calmed by what seemed only to be a bad connection, a small short circuit in the electric wiring of human relations. But, just as Tito was recently discovering, nothing less than a battle from the secret war was taking place, from the secret holy war of Santiago de Chile. This battle seemed to end and would not be memorable: Tito was paying, Mina was putting the cigarettes she had not smoked back in her purse.

They left almost without talking to each other. "At least I think it will go well for you in São Paulo," she muttered. Without wanting it to come out friendly.

"Oh, sure . . . Sure . . . That's real good . . . For my career . . ."

"Yes, not only for your career."

"Oh, the Maga deal. Sure, well, we'll have to see. Why talk about that, it's too painful . . ."

"Don't be so vain. You aren't hurting me that much, Tito."

Mina smiled. She knew about radio soaps, too. She also was playing the nothing's-the-matter-with-me role. Outside now, some footsteps were heard moving away.

"I can take it from here, Tito. It was real nice, you know?"

"For me too, Mina."

THE SECRET HOLY WAR OF SANTIAGO DE CHILE

It wasn't true, the beating flashed through his mind again. The important thing is that she left.

"Ciao," she said and threw him a kiss. She was six or eight feet away. Tito's sight isn't bad, so we shouldn't mistrust what Triviño Junior could see, what he saw and what made him shudder: when her blouse moved, it opened up a little bit and briefly but precisely displayed the figure of a silver lizard. One second, but the best, the fairest and most precise, to find out about the interweaving of certain apparent coincidences.

Tito watched her leave. She didn't notice his profound paleness. As soon as he saw her get into her car he went back into the restaurant.

"Can I use the phone?"

He dialed. He waited for Deborah's voice on the second floor. She should have returned from collating by now. But Aspillaga answered. Fatty?

"I know," answered the voice. "Take the afternoon off," and he hung up. Tito contained his surprise, said thanks, left, and once again got into a new taxi.

He knew where he had to go.

91

15

I'm looking for a cabaret

The Diez de Julio neighborhood was tasteless now. There were only glaring signs, clashing colors, yellow with red letters, white letters over green, red and orange backgrounds, logos for spark plugs, tires, insignias for all types of cars: the Renault rhombus, the Peugeot lion, the Citroen emblem, were repeated like old testimonials of a battle for hegemony in the Chilean automobile market, invaded in the past few years by that Nipponese jargon that made any after dinner chat seem like a samurai convention. Houses which at some other time were houses of worthy presence for the middle class, now painted like crazy canaries, like blind parrots, peeled off and painted over again, to molt again in a continuous rainbow hue, almost infinite.

Tito got out of the taxi between Portugal and Vicuña MacKenna. He was sure that this was the sector to investigate. He asked himself why he didn't wait for nighttime, he could go to the apartment, or to a movie, have a few drinks. The talk with Mina was going around in his head. To throw me off the trail? A trap? Were they watched? Time was a factor in this and Mina had wanted to distract him, there was no doubt about that. If she wasn't Donkavian's accomplice, she was at least his puppet.

You better get moving.

He looked all around fearing they were following him. Who? Whoever, any of those factions in which he saw the combat divided. Mina's lizard, now verified, had ended up convincing him. It had made him relive each blow from that woman. Professional, of course, irritated, phallic, all they want, but professional.

The only clue he had about that other world was that complaint reiterated by his mother in the old conjugal disputes during his childhood: *The bar girls at El Limbo, the queers you're involved with, that whore Lili Salomé who's got you panting, and has you so tied up you can't even come to see your sons, you're never at home, no one knows where to find you, always in El Limbo.*

"Listen, I'm looking for a cabaret . . ."

The car parts store employee was left dumbfounded. He was straightening up some sports steering wheels, small, compact, one could say muscular and bronzed if that were possible. Tito had thought about one of those for his new car that he would never have.

"A cabaret," he repeated.

The salesman thought he heard wrong. Maybe it was a new tool, there's nothing they don't come up with now, and they give such strange names to those things.

"It's called El Limbo . . . I don't know exactly where it is."

The guy rubbed his nose. He hung up the sport handle on a shelf full of small boxes of headlights, rear lights, signal lights, multicolored reflectors, silver and chrome distributed in a type of fancy metallic trimming.

"It's just that in the daytime . . . I haven't seen it as far as I know . . . Could it be La Sirena?" and he pointed towards the mountains.

No, that wasn't it, La Sirena was legendary but later on. He was familiar with it and it was closed now, leveled by that Santiago de Chile repressive night.

He mumbled a frustrated thank you and continued to inquire. The scene was becoming monotonous, repetitious, senseless: no one had the least idea. One guy recommended El Paraíso where there was a sensational comedian and a pregnant stripper who was seven months along. More than one guy kept looking at him with a puritanical and censoring attitude: here we've only got nuts and motors, no strange things. What could they know if this was the daylight world, they would leave when dusk fell, the street would be left to the mercy of others, those who are now sleeping, those who toss and turn in some rumpled bed with yellowed sheets, cursing the sun through the badly fitting lace curtains, putting up with a mild wholesome hangover with a couple of poached eggs.

Who to ask? He thought about the whores from San Camilo. It was just a matter of walking a little to see the legendary prostitutes of high school rumors. Never in his life had he showed up around here. Curiosity was enough for him, with well intentioned female friends who were running into each other in their rush on Friday and Saturday to make up for the suffering of an incomplete week, annoyed, forbidden. Now even sin isn't what it used to be.

He walked, totally into his role as an angelic investigator, towards San Camilo. He was surprised at the humbleness of the closed-up houses. There was almost no one on San Camilo. There was a person sweeping who was wearing highly ambiguous skin-tight jeans. A white shirt with satin glitter, floating in the air. When he turned towards Tito, he noticed that the guy had recently had his eyelids painted: make-up. He could see dark roots in his straw colored blond hair which was stained like a war flag.

"Listen, I'm looking for a cabaret."

"At this time of day?" His voice seemed strange, it didn't sound feminine at all. It was even firm, deep, and it confounded him even more than he already was.

"Well, the fact is I'm looking for a person . . ."

"Don't you think I might know her?" smiled the guy, or the girl, I don't know. Tito was looking at him: Queer, he thought, he thinks I'm hustling him.

"I don't think so."

"What's the name?"

"Mine?"

"The name of the person you're looking for."

Tito wondered if he would lose anything by giving it a try.

"Triviño. Tito Triviño."

"That's you?"

"No, the person I'm looking for," but it's also me, hell, although he only thought that. He didn't say it.

The other guy thought for a second. For an instant he got scared that it could be possible that this guy and his father knew each other, he even imagined that they could have been lovers, confidants, that his father was there inside, in that house, with his eyes smeared and his hair dyed. Enough now, Tito.

"No, I can't place him for anything. Is he tall, blond like me, with a mole here next to his mouth?"

"No, to tell the truth, no."

"Oh, that's too bad . . . What a pain not to have been of any help to you at all . . ."

There was something pathetic sounding in that sentence, said with a harsh voice, critical. He was asking for something and it wasn't seduction. Right away he read pain in those parted lips in that old face illuminated by the late afternoon sun, unstable, barely warm, from the newborn cretin spring.

"You can probably help me . . ."

"Tell me how . . ."

"Do you know where the cabaret called El Limbo is located?"

"Is it still in business?"

In a flash, Tito saw the demolition ball, the rubble from the old building falling over old posters, photos ripped to pieces, shredded lamé curtains.

"I don't have any idea but I need to find it."

"Oh. Look, it used to be over there, on the other side of Diez de Julio, one block down on Portugal. Do you see?" and he whistled imitating the trajectory of a fast bird. "To the south. In the middle of the block, more or less. I still remember. The place wasn't bad. Lili Salomé used to dance. Did you know her?"

The way he spoke gave away a turbid rural origin. Lili Salomé? Sure I know her, of course I don't know her. Is she still living?

"Thank you," Tito said to him and retraced his steps. He didn't look back. The painful gesture from that fellow had intimidated him. But if he had turned around for a moment, the truth is he would have

95

got a lot more frightened, because when Tito Livio Triviño Recart turned down Diez de Julio the guy with the broom hurriedly went into his home, and because, we're not sure but we can assert it, on his chest there vaguely shone a shape which we could well call a frog, a silver frog.

16

Just like your father

Tito's walk is wavering. He has circled the whole block and is beginning to show signs of disgust. If someone is watching him they will realize that his visit is that of an investigator, who stops and scans the doors, the moldings, the windows, to see if he finds the definitive sign, the one which for him confirms the existence of a legendary cabaret. Perhaps in the most remote past, where his father had probably gone to avenge the emptiness of an uncertain and wild marriage.

Tito's only question is where a fourth-class cabaret is located, a damned misplaced cabaret on the outskirts of downtown Santiago. At this moment he sees a narrow garage in which a pretty well beat-up Peugeot 404 waits its turn, edging out towards the street.

He goes over towards the door. There are few cars, one with its mouth completely wide open is swallowing a man in overalls. Another mechanic seems to be nursing from its underbody.

"Hey. Can I ask you a question?"

His face was not as black as he might have imagined, nor as dirty either. Only his blue overalls betray him: the grease paints a cloud-like map on his pockets.

"I'm looking for a cabaret. Don't get me wrong. I'm talking about a cabaret that used to be around here. Or that maybe is still here. They told me it was around here. I don't know if I'm lost. Maybe you can help me."

The guy brandishes his wrench. He's afraid it's a case of a crazy madman who's looking for dreamed-up places. A story from this so-and-so to fool him, something that arouses suspicion. Could El Limbo be a dreamed-up nightclub, a sham, an illusion? Maybe.

"What did you come in here for? This is a car repair shop. Didn't you read the sign?"

"It's called El Limbo . . . or that used to be the name."

"El Limbo?"

The estranged look from the mechanic produced a pregnant pause. From under the front of the car, the small guy who was hanging from the motor leaned out and let himself slide over the grating to look at the stranger.

"But that sucker closed down a long time ago."

"Did you go there, Monkey?"

Tito is thinking that the nickname is right on the money. If it weren't for not having a tail he'd be one: a little ape.

"Yeah, sure. It was right here. Before they put in the shop. Right here. There was a stage. There! Where we put the pit. I went in that place when I was a kid. There was a great *mina* that used to dance there."

"Lili Salomé," said Tito, now without being surprised.

"Yeah, that's the one. Did you know her? No you couldn't. You were real young. You must have been a little kid."

Tito Livio approached the pit. He had the impression that he would see his father's corpse, the famous stripper's, or his own. Will you end up there, Tito? Why not?

"And afterwards? Where'd they go?"

"Who knows. Now, besides the whores on San Camilo, we work here all day. Chained to our work. Do you see?"

"Now I see."

Tito was becoming disillusioned. Where to go? What clue to follow now? The end of the trail, a blind alley. He made a goodbye gesture and started to walk towards the street. They said something behind his back but now he didn't care. His resignation shielded him. The end of the line: there was no opening, no bridge. There was only going back and running into Donkavian again, Fatty Aspillaga, la Maga, even Mina. Bad timing. He even thought about leaving for São Paulo. That's what illusions are like.

He stood in front of the garage for a while and then began to walk in a southerly direction. Without any destination. Suddenly, out of the corner of his eye he noticed they were watching him. The short lace curtain was drawn and a face hid immediately when he turned his head. He stopped.

They could have located him, and they were following him again. It's been a long time since anything has happened by accident. He retraced his steps and peeked into the garage. The mechanics were continuing with their daily tasks. He crossed in front of the door of the shop, as if some remote hope existed of seeing the now definitely spectral cabaret. Nothing. He remained in front. Someone was coming from the opposite direction. He recognized him, he was the funny character from the whorehouse, the one who was sweeping the sidewalk. The guy stopped in front of him.

They looked at each other.

"To find what you're looking for it's better if you come at night," he said without any preamble or protocol. "Pay attention to me and don't ask." His tone had changed. In reality it had become firm and solid.

"I need a place to hide." Tito shook before saying this, but now it was too late for pretending. Let's cut the bullshit among friends.

The other guy raised his hand and his nails showed a bright shade of green sprinkled with glitter. He pointed towards the house where Tito had seen the lace curtain raised up.

"They're waiting for you in there."

"There?"

He was going to turn around and look at the guy's face, but the only thing he saw was his back: his mission was over, over and out. Tito Livio was alone again on a street which was beginning to be covered by clouds, next to what would have been his objective. El Limbo does not exist, there's no door to the other world. Or is this the one, which he's going to knock on now?

Knock knock: that's the way it sounds. The door opens up. An older woman, appearing older than she really is without a doubt, her painted eyebrows above her wrinkles create make-up lines which join only when she smiles. A shawl is draped over her shoulders. They could have used her for a commercial: the perfect grandmother, a little crazy, but marvelous. For advertising a short story magazine for children.

"You're Tito Triviño's son, right?"

"How do you know that?" Our hero seemed stupid repeating the same old question.

"You're just like your father," the little old lady smiled nostalgically.

"Did you know him?"

"Come in. Come in and we'll talk. I'll tell you."

The outside door closed behind him and the woman in question carefully drew the curtains. Tito remained standing in the middle of a tenuous penumbra which was illuminated by an opalescent lamp.

"Pardon me for lighting the lamp so early, but I prefer it that way," said the old lady. Tito thought about his mother's apartment. The smell was distinct, humidity, a closed-up room, like lavender.

She pointed to a chair upholstered with palm trees and tropical designs. There were Gobelins on the walls and a bookcase with old books to the rear of the room which had lost the glass in its doors. He recognized some editions, *Zig-zag, Ercilla,* softcover books, bent at the corners through use, coming unbound. He squinted, trying to read the titles on the spines. For a moment they seemed familiar to him.

The woman sat down at the other end of the room. A pleasant silence fell. She picked up her knitting. Tito thought about how absurdly normal the scene was. Only he didn't fit in.

"Who are you?" he asked, after a couple of minutes in which the only sound was the clacking of knitting needles at full speed, as if trying to defeat time. One of the Moiras, was a thought which occurred to Tito, and from there, the question.

"Do you really want to know?"

The old lady's voice sounded strange to him. It didn't match her age. It had become emphatic, firm, mature. It was from another body. A certain latent sensuality made him uneasy.

He took a deep breath before speaking.

"Well, I'm a little tired of meeting people who come up to me without even telling me who they are and what they want."

She smiled.

"It's clear they know full well who you are and what they want, isn't it?"

Her voice was definitely different. The provocative tone was increasing. He imagined the headlines: *The Old Lady Ravisher of the Diez de Julio Neighborhood*. Please, ma'am, behave yourself.

"You're your father's son. Does it seem unimportant to you?" she added setting her knitting to one side as if she had reached a goal.

She looked at the door.

"Well, it's getting dark now. You'll understand everything there."

"Getting dark? It's probably only around four o'clock in the afternoon."

The old lady didn't answer. She stood up (her agility was unusual too) and opened the curtains. The streetlamps shone into the room. It was true. Tito was startled.

Her eyes. It wasn't her anymore.

"Who are you?"

"I thought you would have recognized me."

"Should I have been able to recognize you?"

"Maybe. Maybe you saw my picture. Maybe they've spoken to you about me. They've talked to me a lot about you."

"Stop this once and for all!"

What's the matter, Tito? Are you dying of fright again?

"Don't get all worked up," she said to him. "It's not good or necessary. Calm down."

She put her hand on his forehead. Her skin was smooth, too smooth. Tito let himself fall into the armchair.

"You're safe here," said the old lady, or the ex-old lady or whatever she was.

"What do you know about my father?"

Tito understood everything. The books were his father's, those that he had sneaked a peek at as a child, the same shelf, the cold air smelling of lavender.

"They assume he's dead."

"Impossible. I saw him yesterday."

"That's good news."

He's putting his foot in his mouth. He had revealed what was the most secret fact. How could he be sure that this strange specimen of a woman was not one of Donkavian's agents, that she wasn't the Devil himself, a succubus trained in Transylvania, a witch? She was a bewitcher in every way, her magic web was controlling the course of time. Where had she gone to stop Friday afternoon? Squeezed between the points of the needles? Where?

The estranged Tito Livio swallowed what little saliva was left in his very dry mouth.

"Who are you?" he asked again.

A pause.

"I'm Lili Salomé, Tito Livio." Flashback: the name of the treacherous woman who would justify all the punishment at home, the name that was conjured up during every meal alone with his mother, he and his brother, every one of her fits of temper, every incomprehensible impulse. Lili Salomé, cheap whore, evil sinner, who corrupts the marriages of the lower middle class with the temptations of a bordello. You infect, *vade retro Satanás*.

"I'm not so bad, never was. Do you know what your father was to me? A gentleman. I loved him very much, very much. He used to come to talk to me about his troubles, his children, to hide himself in the heat of battles that you'll now understand. He protected me from pimps, thieves and drunks. He used to walk with me from El Limbo to my front door. While he was married he never went past the front door."

"And after?"

"Why do you have to know everything, Tito? It's enough for you to know that he was a unique man with no equal who knew how to love a woman."

"That sounds like a soap opera," deciphered Tito Livio. She blinked her eyes in slow motion. Yes, it was sensual.

"I don't believe a word of it," added our hero.

An ancestral worry was coming over him. That woman was a legend and now she was telling him that the myth was different, that it wasn't true the sun circles the earth, that the earth is round, that no one lives on the moon yet.

"I was very pretty. I still can be. But only at night," said the lady who was not at all old, raising her dress up slowly.

Tito Livio looked at her legs. Marlene Dietrich was an amateur compared to this woman. He started not to understand his father, or to understand him better: she was from another planet.

She shook her hair. The old lady disappeared. A mature woman, voluptuous, sweet, replaced her. Her breasts were floating towards him among some sequins. Her smile shone like a Cheshire cat. A white patch shot out like a lightning bolt the length of her thick dark hair.

She extended a hand to Tito. Fantastic bracelets danced on her wrist, twin slaves to those on her ankles. There was an air of an oriental veil dance in her rhythmic movements. Tito accepted. Warm, fascinating.

Where are they taking you now, Tito? Where? What happened to your fear?

Tito?

17

The select public of El Limbo

So they're leading you, Tito, by the hand. They're leading you
like they do blind people, like little children, like the chosen
ones. Like Virgil with Dante, like Dido with Aeneas, like Theseus led
by a sympathetic and tropical Ariadne, no thread, no messages or
Minotaurs, once again the labyrinth, the laborious unique labyrinth
that is all labyrinths.

You descend on a suspended spiral staircase and you're afraid of
missing a step, but she, the woman, always the woman in front who
leads you, calms you down and she says *calm down*, she says *quiet*, she
says *keep going*, and you allow yourself to obey. Maybe sometime you let
yourself be led like that, when you lost confidence, when you joined
the human race and you discovered the hesitation the trick the pushing
the treachery when you had to open your eyes every time that your
mother your aunt your girlfriend your wife your lover Mina Nicole
Nancy Nicole would take you by the hand enticing with laughter in
order to tell you come with me now like this here.

Do you hear the music, Tito? Do you hear the laughter? Do you hear the clinking of glasses, certain they're glasses, the bottles, certain that's that what it is? You remember: you as a child, as a little kid pretending you're asleep, auscultating the night to catch your parents' obscene secret, to invade the parental privacy with your hearing, but running into screams, threats and condemnations. Your mother's cascading voice, the worn-out scream of the supreme priestess cursing your father — who's drunk? who remains irritatingly quiet? — who all of a sudden roars, *augh?* The threat from hell. But the noise that comes out superimposes itself on your remembrance, and it can't prevent Tito Junior from stopping and being affected.

"Don't be afraid."

Did you hear, Tito? Did you hear? Keep calm, hide yourself in your bed, start up your windshield wipers to scare away those memories. Notice that it's beginning to get light. Notice the hand is holding you firmly and Lili Salomé stops and is coming closer to your ear.

"We're here."

A sliver of light cuts through the darkness. It looks like a curtain. On the other side, there's a salsa orchestra playing at full blast, and on the other side someone is laughing his head off, someone who turns out to be in reality a lot of people drinking, toasting, celebrating. The night has begun, Tito Triviño, the night in which your father lived and your mother cursed, persecuted and outlawed night, the secret and starlit night.

Lili Salomé opens the curtain and a spotlight falls inexorably upon her. Through the lighting, touching the rim of the circle of light, he sees a hand coming out of a shiny suit. An amplified voice, distorted by a microphone from the 50s, rounded, crowned with call letters, announces her: *The Queen of the Secret Holy Night of Santiago de Chile. The Lady of El Limbo! Lili Salomé! . . . And with her, Tito Triviño!*

The applause which was coming like a wave to surround her on her ample hips breaks up to allow itself to fall over Tito, to startle him beyond belief. The floodlights diminish and he can now see the room. It's the same garage, it's emerged from the same pit, between the towtrucks jacks batteries chassis there are now tables, bottles, glasses, there are waiters who file by with trays like far-off signs for Viña Santa Carolina. A melancholy Tito inspects the night bespattered with stars, a night of boleros above his head, and the orchestra elevated on a flatbed truck. The master of ceremony's hand, replete with sparks, grabs him by the arm. A toothless gypsy's smile applauds him and greets him.

"Tito Livio Junior is with us. What do you have for us?"

He places the microphone in front of his mouth and he doesn't know what to do or what to say, I know nothing, I see nothing.

"I don't know, really . . ."

A loud burst of laughter crushes him like an insect against the curtain behind him. The orchestra sounds the brass instruments: the great fart of the night.

"Have you ever thought about being a comedian? You're very funny, Tito Livio. Let's give him a hand!"

All of a sudden he feels he's on TV, on *Sábados Gigantes*, in a great contest winning a brand new car for himself, answering questions about the origin of dinosaurs, the last words of the founding fathers, the color of Olivia Newton-John's t-shirt. A gesture pushes him towards the orchestra pit. The applause continues while an old man, with the clear and definitive look of a crazy person, gets up from a table. He offers Tito a chair. He's rather short, with short white hair that covers his perfectly round head in which the black circles of his eyeglasses stand out, and a white beard surrounding an incomplete laugh.

"Come on up, Tito Livio, welcome."

He sits down afraid, with the same fear that's a habit now, the type which superimposes itself over the daily fear of living in Santiago, in Chile, one more kind. But the die is cast. What good would it be to resist now, where to flee? Besides, if you already understand that all this can't be, that it's not possible that this noise is not waking up the whole neighborhood, that this cold that's falling doesn't chase away the chorus girls that he's looking at out of the corner of his eye, that this pile of vagabonds from sleazy hotels which make up the audience (he can examine them now that he's seated) is not hauled out kicking by a group of military police. He looks at the waiter with his frayed jacket made of thick, white fabric. They all seem to have been dressed by an old wardrobe man from a run-down theater. He thinks about *The Threepenny Opera*, about the frozen bodies from the Arctic cold waves that fall on the capital in winter, over the beggars and the needy sleeping near the river, under bridges, in church doorways.

They serve him a glass of wine. I wonder what shit these lunatics are drinking?

"Just in case, it's wine for mass," the old crazy guy tells him.

On stage the Sonora Matadero (that's what the orchestra was named) launches into a cumbiamba: *I'm leaving, I'm leaving tomorrow.*

Tito has oriented himself, and now that he's done that he wants to escape.

"I don't want to drink anything. I think it's better if I leave."

"Leave? But you just got here!"

Our fleeing protagonist is getting up when the crazy guy with the white hair laughs at him, grabbing him by the lapels to look him straight in the eye.

"I suppose you've got a lot to do besides. Something very important. A se-cret miss-ion."

Tito lets himself fall into the chair. The publicity about supposedly secret things is overwhelming him.

"How do you know that?"

Someone explain this paradox to me, please.

"What? Didn't you realize we were waiting for you?"

The orchestra attacked: *Welcome, sir, welcome, welcome to our song, may you dance this way, may you dance that way, may the whole city dance along.*

They were looking at him from the other tables, they were smiling, whispering, almost to the point of pointing their fingers at him. It's true.

"We haven't had an authentic Triviño here for so many nights that this really deserves a toast," said the old guy as he raised his glass. "For you, for your faraway father."

"Have you seen him?"

"What? Don't you know that no one's been able to find out where he is for quite a few years?"

"But he spoke to me a little while ago."

He hesitated to say it, time was something so dubious, everything was so dubious.

The old beggar's enormous bugged eyes would have been big enough to fit Saint Peter's Cathedral and everything around it into them.

"What? Have you seen him?"

"Yes."

"With your own eyes? With your very own eyes? Have you seen him in the flesh, really?"

"Yes."

The old guy got up and screamed to all the tables with his glass held high. He spilled some wine.

"He's seen him! He's seen him!"

The uproar lashed out through the audience. Everyone toasted him, they shook hands, and they applauded separately. We have to have fireworks, clamored one, no, streamers, carnival games at least, we have to get drunk anyway. Long live God, long live life, long live the night, look, even the stars are shining brighter, and the moon, the moon came out to see you, Tito Triviño Junior, big Tito, little Tito, long live Tito Titito.

"Wait. Just a moment," announced the MC's voice. "Let's give a big hand to such a great guy, but let's remember the sobriety which characterizes the select public of El Limbo."

The select public was calming down. A last hand, brief and distinguished, like for a string quartet, returned Tito to his exchange with the old demented man.

"It's the best news tonight," as he chugged a drink. Tito thought that it was about the fifth since they had run into each other. The old guy was pouring another glass when it struck Tito that something seemed familiar about him.

"Excuse me. Haven't we met each other before?"

"It could be. It could be." The question seemed to leave the old guy very contented.

"You're . . .?"

"But . . . Doesn't a name come to mind?"

"Well, to tell the truth, no."

"Hee . . . They call me . . ." He drew close, confidentially: "Sigmund Freud."

18

The library where angels don't get lost

The idea of insanity fixed itself in Tito's mind. For a moment it seemed to be the only alternative answer. To think of everything as having come from a psychic blunder, from exhaustion, from an encephalocranial trauma, from his own anguish about survival in such an unstable social situation. He had heard something about strange and perverse hallucinations which affected those with multiple traumas. The kicks which Mina had given him, no need to go any further. Sure, that was all, the gentle and delirious conscience of an insane man. And he was the insane one. He, or everyone around him. Everything was a result of that cruel sun in Villa Alemana, of that stubborn staring at the sun until it burns up the retinas, until smoke pours out from the pupils. Yes, the binge with Arturo Estevez, Fatty Aspillaga's strange look, his own deformed mother, his father's impossible appearance. It all fits under psychosis, the disruption of that world of rules in which he always felt himself to be on shaky ground. Sure, now all he had to do was calm down and wait for it to go away. Maybe, he thought, he could even get something out of it. Writing

109

about his experience out of the bounds of reason. But once again a wave of doubt swept over him: if he was able to think like that, then he wasn't so crazy. Then, were they? That seemed terrible to him. His mother was crazy, Aspillaga was loony, the whole city of Santiago was insane. Or, there were remnants of sobriety, of mental health onto which he could cling. Mina was crazy, of course, just look at the way she beat him up. And la Maga? No, or yes, crazier than all of them put together. And Donkavian? It was frightening to run through it all again. At the very least, this old guy was indeed crazy. He thought he was Sigmund Freud. That crazy Freud, totally mad. An out of control toast, looking at him out of the corner of his eye. Tito Livio was pale, shaking from panic now. This all had to end quickly. He had to get up and leave. Or, was it an office joke? The old lady with a wig who turns out to be a kind of still too pretty Joan Collins, a type of time machine with knitting needles that was a joke, one of those terrible macabre jokes by MacPherson, who found out about where Riveiro was going on his trip and got jealous. No, that was exaggerated, no, it would be too much, the gringo wasn't capable of that. What's going on, then? Where did all this staging come from? All these deranged old men shouting along with a cumbianchera which is rocking the back of the stage, and the little guy with the mustache who is scrambling up to the stage, which is set on drums of gasoline, to sing a bolero.

"It's the gospel truth." Old Freud dried his mouth on his sleeve. Shiny little laboratory rat eyes behind his thick pop-bottle glasses. Tito is trapped in the depths of his reflection, confused with the glitter from a ballroom globe which turns in the spotlights and spreads out petals of light on the audience and stars on the heavenly cupola. Is this the origin of the galaxy? Maybe, at this point it can be anything, perhaps.

"I suppose you don't believe me, Tito my friend. Well, you should know that no one ever has. Everyone keeps looking at us like we're from another planet, like we're the strangest thing they've ever seen, when we introduce ourselves, when I tell them that right here are all those who managed to be the greatest figures in history, those who were able to change the world. We managed to get on book covers, in almanacs, in puzzles. They could have made posters with us on them, of course. They would have held serious seminars about me, they would have invented a prize with my name: Roberto Romero."

THE SECRET HOLY WAR OF SANTIAGO DE CHILE

"You told me your name was . . ."

"My man, that's what they call me. I'm not a demented person who thinks he's Napoleon. The fact of the matter is that my name was lost in the shuffle because of my nickname. That's the tragedy of Chile, being almost a country, an imitation, a pastiche, a parody, an eternal internal vision of the exterior world, a microclimate. When, inspired, I finished my best work, they negotiated with me and they told me to wait, because of this, because of that. When I managed to get the word out, forcing myself through the official channels, I found them praising a Viennese who was saying the same thing as I was. What I wrote was already written, what I thought he immediately thought, in unison, a European author, where things that are important to historians happen, where images are emitted of which we are only a reflection, the northern hemisphere which gives names to peoples, authors, and things. They read my work and as a great honor they nicknamed me the Chilean Freud, apocryphal Freud, Sigmund Freud Romero, and now simply Sigmund Freud, immortal of mediocrity like all these souls who have written the past and future of the West. Ignored forever, our souls are condemned to wander in this nightclub as a testimony to the other side of history, the night side, the one your father knew in all its glory, and that now is nothing but a shadow of its former heyday. It's a sign of the times. Do you want to come with me?"

Standing up, the Chilean Freud stared at him with his embittered elegance, the defeat of the impossible, the pride of a genius ignored, unearthed for certain eyes only. What would he gain by declining? Tito Livio looked at the bolero singer and followed Sigmund Roberto alias Freud alias Romero.

"There's Marcelito Aceituno, the Proust of Las Condes, who discovered that memory only serves to remember what's useless, the unimportant, the everyday, and he wrote infinite tomes which no one ever wanted to publish in this isolated country, buried by envy, captured by copying, plagiarism and innuendo. He wrote pages about a delicious capacity for evocation, pristine, well defined, moving, entering into a new psychology of novel characters. He indeed recovered lost time, look at him, shriveling with a chronic bronchial condition, a flaming faggot. He has white mice on top of the table so that he can wear out his eyes and be able to masturbate. Look there, at Marx Martínez

111

quarreling with Pedro Nietzsche, suspicious of appearances of reality like agreement, lost in their booze, with their livers shot and their days numbered. But we're immortal, therefore it can't be helped, nobody saves us from the pain of cirrhosis, from the nightmares from which we never awaken, the evils which don't give in. There's no death that's coming to save us, only an eternal and mediocre suffering. Look at Jaime Froilán Joyce, blind from birth, who narrated unfathomable peripeteia in the jargon of the gods, inventing words over again. But all his books were already written. Look at Ernestino Einstein de Conchalí, a genius but latent. His work wasn't worth the trouble, when he entered the competition it was already old hat. Do you see the fat lady by the piano? Isadora Duncan de Vivaceta, who used to dance like an enchanted princess, but they only took her at most to a high school festival. The woman over there, the one painted up like a clown, is Madame Curie de Quilpué, pretty, intelligent, she discovered things everyone already knew. She hid them when they were new, and when she finally dared it was already too late. Further over there is the Kant of Nuñoa, irritable and meditative, who keeps on editing useless texts. What's the use? The critics sent him to this half-lighted hole of failures and miscarriages. The names will blend together in the mire of oblivion, custom, seeing who you look like before knowing who you are."

Tito was looking at the wax museum surrounding him, the living corpses, so similar to their alter egos. Nietzsche in a frayed Superman suit chugging a bottle of cheap table wine, his face full of swelled cirrhotic marks like his round frog-shaped gut. They were humming *The Internationale* beside a very large dirty man with a pale face whose long scraggly beard gave him away: Fyodor Dostoyevsky who later found out his name was Eustaquio and that he had been a detective in Valparaíso at the turn of the century. Freud hid himself behind a beat-up station wagon, inside of which the supposed Lou Andreas Salomé Covarrubias was in a clutch with a certain Richard Wagner Brothers, as Sigmund his guide told him.

There was a small door hidden in the wall: another passageway? No, it was a small stairway heading down. Descending carefully, almost on tiptoe. An oil lamp was struggling to shed light on a librarian who looked like a young eagle, with blond eyebrows, who seemed to be writing passionately on his desk while he played with himself with his other hand. He looked at the visitors with a lascivious smile.

"Jorge Batalla, I'd like you to meet Señor Triviño."

"The son?"

He was getting really fed up with being his father's son. Why couldn't his father be the illustrious stranger again, like before, like when he used to ask him for money at the office? But he remembered himself as a kid. Tito Senior, and Tito Junior, floating along the streets of La Vega. Every fifteen feet there was someone who greeted them, who congratulated him, who gave him a tip for the Hippodrome. Now he understood it, they were contacts. Sure. He had been involved in this whole thing since he was a kid.

"I knew you when you were this tall," said Monsieur Batalla, putting his hand about knee high. He had a French accent and sounded like one of those television programs dubbed in Mexican Spanish. "I used to have a fruit stand in La Vega. As a front, of course."

"I want him to see our library," interrupted Freud Romero.

"Come on in," said the man in charge, with ill-disguised pride.

Tito looked below the flickering flame at the withered faces of both immortals. There was another door which opened. He saw rows of shelves overflowing with manuscripts, incunabula, ancient editions, loose yellow pages with frayed edges. Batalla balanced the lamp and led the way. Tito didn't understand how, but they were in some very high-ceilinged rooms, about two or three stories high, traversed by separate balconies which met at twin desks of the same type where Batalla was writing. Uselessly, he tried to calculate the size of the subterranean room, the basic structure, the fake building. He didn't know where he was. An odor of old books filled the air in that enormous library.

"Here are all the books of Western culture, the ones written in an untimely fashion. They were either written so much in advance that no one understands them, or so late that they were already of no importance. The treatises on physics that will turn into literature, contemporary history which will later be poetry in prose, fiction which will be read like the new metaphysics. The whole history of incomprehension or blunders. In some rooms there are even books which we don't know what they correspond to, new concepts of space and time, a whole new theory of man based on the tides and the movement of the moons of

Saturn, fundamental discoveries about the repetition of historical cycles and the denial of evolution, tomes and tomes that demonstrate the fallacy of apprenticeship and the presence of instincts in man. There's an interminable work on the secret of art which asserts that there is only one great work which is written in code among several connected brains who are ignorant of their mission and which will be read by a final reader who will understand the Tetragrammaton at last, the sacred word to give life to clay, the word which when discovered will end with man, God, and the Devil, creating just one race. Of the damned according to some, of gods according to others. When man makes himself it will be his epilogue. They say there are three letters already deciphered and that the fourth is circulating innocently."

He remained silent for a minute. Tito thought about the deterioration of so many pages of dubious utility.

"But it's impossible to read all this. Now it's even difficult to go through. Don't you get lost?"

"One only goes through it in dreams. I just recently dreamed of a great book, which every time it's opened has a different story in accordance with the wishes of the reader. It's a book which is self-sufficient and was banned for creating addicts, eternal satisfaction for its owner, the worst drug. Its author was burned and one volume is restricted to one place in those bookshelves. It's a book that never ends and which will fascinate even the most reluctant person. Dreadful. Don't you think?"

He scanned one of the shelves.

"This is our underdevelopment," he said and showed the dubious names, within reach, in printed letters, on the sides of cartons, with haphazard numbering which didn't correspond to any order. "Look at the names: Rubén Gomez, the Spengler of Talcahuano, Miguel Yañez, the Wittgenstein of Huasco, the Melanie Klein of Licanray, the Celine of Puerto Octay. We even have a small petty tyrant in Puyehue who writes us every week from a small prison in the foothills about the relation between power, the masses and the telegraph."

"But, this is all rotting . . ."

"And what does that matter? Of what importance is it to classify them? There is infinite mass production. All the lost keys to a civilization. Its holiness and its twilight. Destiny alone decides if someone finds what they're looking for. This country is destined to disappear. Just like this library, it's a cemetery. It doesn't try to betray the principal element of nature which is to fuse life with death and end up with only one principle, that of original chaos, sooner or later."

"Why don't they burn everything once and for all?" demanded Tito, bothered, faced with so much skeptic vanity.

"That's just what the Devil would want," shrieked the librarian, making the flame in the lamp flicker. "He wants to speed up the process and therefore lead us headlong to destruction. To deny that man did this when he could, inspired by a brilliancy that was leading to the unification of all countries, and which was pointed out in the one which history favored. Not ours, that is evident. To burn all this would be to deny the work of the Great One, manifested in consciousness. He was guiding our hands."

Tito could not help remembering the evident masturbation by Batalla under the table. Shut up, troublemaker, you never learn.

"An angel would not get lost in this library," said the old Romero. "The chosen ones don't need card catalogues, Tito, nor computers, nor clues, nor any kind of reference."

Freud and Batalla seemed to congratulate each other with a knowing look and then they focused their attention on Tito Junior, who sensed the scurrying of mice, the decomposition of so many pages, of so much effort, of so many ideas coming apart right before their eyes, the useless books in which was contained everything the world needed most.

"A great number of the authors are upstairs, getting drunk so the kingdom where they can resurrect their words will come."

"But that's defeatism!" clamored Tito, a fervent believer from the optimistic world of the neoliberal economy. "Yes, it's true we have to rescue it. All it needs is a little publicity. Give me a chance, just a chance."

He launched a fist towards the bookshelf but Freud's strong arm grabbed him by his forearm.

"No!"

They were frowning as they stared at him.

"It's better if we go upstairs," Sigmund mumbled. Tito caught the drift. There were things he didn't understand, but which he understood he shouldn't understand. Or, at least for now he couldn't.

"Yes, let's go," agreed Tito.

"Lili Salomé's going to perform now, right?" whistled Batalla, newly libidinous.

Freud laughed.

"That's also something you have to see. That's another library."

Tito let himself be guided towards the exit.

"Good," said Jorge Batalla. "One is not conceived without the other."

"Maybe you'll finally understand there, my son," pointed out Sigmund Romero, near, warm, almost putting his hand on his shoulder. Just like a father, thought Tito. Like when I was a kid. Just like that.

19

Señorita Lili Salomé

S ure the master of ceremonies had a strange appearance, like the
last office worker from the last layer of bureaucrats from the
glorious times for the Chilean public employee, when half the population punched a time clock, retired with cost of living raises, bought
themselves Raglan coats in Falabella, had respect for the banks, listened to soccer on the radio, had flings without commitment in sleazy
hotels on London and Paris streets. That's what he was like, dressed in
a three-piece suit with wide lapels, his long hair held down under a
thick cover of gel, reflecting the dim but sufficient light in his wavy
locks. *"The only true light is that from the secret conscience in the back of the
brain,"* Roberto Sigmund Romero would say to him, *"the only light that
really collects, traps and selects is the daily memory network, the unusual and
involuntary memory, the only one that matters. The show could be entirely in
darkness. In any case, for each one there will be a special and unique show,
the one anchored in his unconscious burning a false image, nonexistent, an
imaginary imago image, guardian of the watchtower which makes day from
night and constructs truth in the false reality of each hour."*

117

That's what Freud said, taking a seat, pausing, making himself comfortable, pinching one arm, then the other of the very much incredulous and anguished Tito Livio Triviño Recart who was about to become a spectator for the show. This was the much awaited moment, the most fantastic epiphany, hierophant, a sacred manifestation of the word made into flesh, made into woman, made into fire, the condemnation of all sin, the pardoning of all virtues, the dance made female. Today, here on this very stage in El Limbo, for our select and distinguished audience we present the most unique dancer in the world, who comes direct from the most elegant stages of the European capitals.

Who's coming? thought Tito. Who could it really be? Who can be appearing on this stage that makes me afraid they might show up, that makes me afraid my delicate condition might be changed, that scares me that they're coming to pierce me with deeply repressed desires from the inner chambers of the farthest depths of my mind where I never want to return again, not to my legs, nor my face nor my poor sleeping heart, numbed, truly in pain, mistreated.

She's coming! Sure she's coming! The master of ceremonies stretched out his neck like a chicken about to die and vibrated his larynx, his uvula, and he inflated his abdomen so his diaphragm would launch forth the full, penetrating, magnificent vowels: Lili Salomé!

Everyone at the tables applauded. Freud, Marx, Hegel Cabrera, Aristotle García, Rembrandt Valdés de Coinco, Martín Henriquez Heidegger de Saladillo. Tito followed the faces, moving and disappearing in the semi-darkness with anxious gestures of approval and desire. Bravo! Bravo! He thought that, more than a cabaret it seemed to be the canonizing ovation of a public megalomania for the genius of the interpreter, the composer, the deaf genius in his glorious Ninth on top of a platform which no one surpassed. He thought about the confusing aspect of the action, he thought about the night which seemed painted with stars by the still moon, hung from somewhere, perhaps at this point hung from the finger of the Maker. Why not? Why not, if Lili Salomé was the incarnation of the most distant image of Mother Earth. Sure! What else can those badly dressed, deteriorated, old and wilted men applaud? Those old withered glotti screaming *hurray*, *bravo*, and becoming silent all at once faced with the

THE SECRET HOLY WAR OF SANTIAGO DE CHILE

orchestra's introit, a long solo from the tenor saxophone and later, the bongos and congas which begin to create strains of a Caribbean air, but not really.

No. It's something different. The same music is different. Tito Livio is thinking about tropical spectacles, about the depressing bachelor parties in nightclubs at twilight in line with the curfew; disgusted, looking at the sterile intentions of the stripper in her eagerness to fake being ravenous or to disguise dubious appetites in the middle of that misery, that cold, the loneliness of some half-drunk poor souls screaming comments devoid of all intelligence, dark, insolent, and therefore stupid, which is the worst aspect of obscenity. Isn't it true, Tito?

No. This was different. The piano struck some notes in a tight, precise rhythm, it began to heat up the night until a light, nobody knows from where, fell from the zenith. Transparent, a sacred zone where the priestess will emit her incantation and will put us in direct contact with the deity. This was it, Tito Livio, it was a religious ceremony, this was the white light, clear and sharp, which was being concentrated there.

He didn't find out where or how Lili Salome appeared in the center. Transformed, even younger and smoother than when he believed he caught sight of her in the dark tunnel under the street. She was shaking her flowing hair slowly, as if each one of the strands had its own intention, harmonically placed in order to create the sensation of a multitude that is slowly becoming feverish.

The diva began to breathe to the same rhythm and her breasts felt themselves vibrating friendly, hard, turgid. Tito battled his saliva. A loud blast from the orchestra marked the first motion of her hips. Here and there members of the audience cleared their throats. Unhurried, the beautiful woman, the only one, the one from another world, who if she was not beautiful made you believe she was, was heating up. She raised a foot, a leg, her thigh. It's not that she was infinitely beautiful nor terribly sensual, nor perhaps diabolically exciting. Let's not get apocalyptic. No, nothing, more than that, previous to sex, to the vagina, the penis, before the minimal birth of minimal differences. There, was a kind of hidden source of life, from the same life which we believe we savor at times about sex, innocently, naively, about sex. Salomé was shaking. Beyond sex, beyond. The orchestra was following her, or was she following? Or was everyone following her? Or was she following everyone? Or, were she and the music all one? Or was it she, the same she, who launched the sounds from her bones, her skin, her fingernails? But could that body, that figure, that essence, that ectoplasm that was now so agile, enticing, irreproachable along the stage, have bones and intestines?

Tito Livio was absolutely mixed up in his consciousness. Knocked out, groggy. Seen from the outside he looked like a zombie. The dance continued nonstop and it could have been hours, minutes, seconds. Time is dying in the beautiful one, seduction is the enemy of history, thought Tito, if he did think about it. It was like being in a dream, and as in all dreams time was capricious and fortuitous. It was changeable, foreign to the world of fascination.

Tito Livio then looked at Lili Salomé's eyes and understood the knife, the blood, the wound, the harmony. Let's say we don't know why Tito, for an instant, had the image of justice, of hope, of the beginning of life, if in fact he has images outside of clichés. He probably had some kind of images, but he knew that they were what he felt they were. In the dance he learned about the function of truth in man's understanding, in each thrust of her arms he understood elemental values of respect, liberty, and forgiveness. In her body he learned about tranquility and prudence, in the rolls of her waistline, shaking, he understood the presence of death in every minute of life.

In the last vibration from the membrane of the saxophone the light went out. A fearful pause was left hanging, a second in which one could have heard the saliva in their throats, the obstructed sigh in their lungs, the incessant cracking of cartilage. Tito recognized a tear which she let slide down her cheek. Not a single hand clapping. Heads down, heads in hands. One guy over there broke into tears without modesty, he let out loud cries which contrasted with the sobriety of others, drying a perhaps bad-mannered wetness off his eyelids with the corner of his handkerchief, swallowing a lump in his throat. There was an attempt at some hurrahs, like a weak breeze which covered the moved assembly. Darkness hid the commotion: sparkles from the glasses drinking small pieces of nighttime, of wine, of sadness, of shared anguish.

"*Fiat Lux!*" screamed the MC and the light came up on the stage. Tito found himself constricted, having difficulty breathing.

"I don't understand what's happening to me," he said to Freud Romero.

Sigmund looked at him smiling.

"I believe, on the contrary, that you're just beginning to understand."

The old hand, full of veins, aged, patted the back of Triviño Junior's hand.

The MC announced the finale. The night of El Limbo has ended, you can stay and dance with the beautiful women, etcetera, etcetera.

But there weren't any such women.

"The fact is things aren't what they used to be," muttered Freud Romero. "Life has been wasting us away."

A waiter touched Tito's shoulder.

"Señor Triviño Junior?"

Tito looked at him with mistrust. He nodded, still confused.

"The señorita wants to see you."

"What señorita?"

The waiter smiled. He came closer to his ear to whisper to him.

"Señorita Lili Salomé. Who else?"

20

A dark and dangerous secret

He had to retrace his steps in the tunnel through which he had entered to see the show. Once again he managed to think amidst his vigilance: I'm being led through catacombs and passageways, once again there's a guide in front of me whom I don't recognize, who's taking me to speak with someone who frightens me. Who am I, what am I doing here, where am I going?

"We've arrived," the man said as he stopped in front of a fluorescent green colored door with a brilliant pink star placed at eye level. "The gentleman should behave himself, the lady rarely receives anyone after a performance," he advised, his mouth, surrounded by a thin mustache and an overgrown beard, coming closer. "Just between us . . . Who are you really?"

Tito managed to catch the shine in the waiter's eyes when a burst of light signaled to him that the door had opened. Against the background, weakly illuminated, Lili Salomé's silhouette was outlined. The man moved his face away, feigning his intention to confess Triviño Junior. Who am I really, and what am I doing here? That's a good question, a very good question.

"Come in." Her voice was soft and friendly. Tito heard the waiter's fleeting steps slipping away behind him. He tripped a few yards further on and the "*oh*" of his fall was clearly heard, followed by the clicking of his shoes on the floor in his submissive run. In the distance was the orchestra music: *Cheek to Cheek*. Tito remembered his parents dancing to Frank Sinatra. I must have been very young, he thought, they even used to laugh.

"Well, what are you thinking, sir?" Lili was being formal with him. She crossed the dressing room dressed in her Chinese silk robe. Tito briefly examined the room: a bedroom furnished with antiques, with an old bearskin over the bed which had a polished bronze headboard, a lot of black and white photos, some of them withered by time, displaying an evocative sepia tone. There was a pink painted chest of drawers crowned by an enormous mirror surrounded by lightbulbs, the majority of which were burnt out. It had the air of an old house from the southern part of the country, with wallpaper weathered by dampness, high ceilings, and spiderwebs in the corners. A Gobelin with lions testified that the Santiagoan consumerism had not entered this room. It sort of reminded him of visits when he was a child, with his father to a transient grandmother who, perhaps, caressed him slowly. What a beautiful child. Just like you, Tito Senior. In a certain sense, he felt that Lili Salomé was saying the same thing to him. They looked at each other.

"Did you like my number?"

Tito gulped. Certainly. Or worse than that.

"I understand that you can't say anything," continued the woman. "It's rare to see, I don't even know very well what I'm doing, and maybe that's the only reason for doing it. Not ever knowing what my body is going to do on stage and then creating a movement that might describe something that is more than words, more than a mere image, even more than a symbol. Your father used to like it a lot. He told me it used to go beyond perception, beyond consciousness. Besides, it has been so long since I danced, it has been so long since we've gotten together. We only do it in exceptional circumstances. Ours are not peace parties, but rather parties of war, of emergency, celebrations of alert. All this was done because of, and for you, do you understand?"

"What do you want me to understand?"

"That you're very important. That what you might do or not do in the days to come can be essential."

She had let her words fall with pauses, like seeds, like a string of pearls that were slowly rolled towards Tito Livio's feet in order to form an asphyxiating and perfect line around his body, a sign, or rather, a design.

"Important for what?" he stammered.

"It's uncomfortable to tell the truth, it's not at all amusing, and the worst thing is, it's not clear at all. The only thing I can tell you is that it's dangerous."

"They've already told me that," replied Tito behind a brief sigh.

Lili Salomé did not answer. She abruptly jumped towards the door and opened it all in one movement. She looked around carefully, searching for some spy. No one: she delicately closed it. She remained standing, looking at Tito Livio, leaning against the doorway. Her immense clear eyes opened and closed several times, subtly. Tito was afraid that she was going to hypnotize him.

"We don't have much time. The important thing happens at night and each night that ends is time they have gained. You must act now, before Sunday if possible. Before the sun comes up. You've been chosen to follow your father's trail, and I know full well you don't have any idea where it is. I'm going to tell you."

She came very close. Tito felt the dancer's breath, her close skin, her eyeshadow weighing down her eyelashes, a soft film of sweat. The heat from her body, the same as from the dance. She backed away.

"Your father was mixed up in something very important. He was the only one who knew things that many people wanted to find out. Don't ask me anything else, I'm being as clear as a woman who loved him very much can be, a woman who heard him talk in his sleep, who sheltered him in pain and loneliness, hiding him under that bed while putting up with his desires to get involved, even in his mind. Tito Livio, your father was in charge of a dark and dangerous secret entrusted to him from on high and from ancient times. He was our agent. He was their agent."

"Whose?"

"You understand me. Look for your father and get him to give you the clues to complete the work that he can't carry out now, as he finds himself being watched. Do it before they do it."

"I don't understand a word . . ."

"Maybe your destiny, or ours, isn't important to you?"

The dancer had gotten to her feet, raising her voice, but as soon as she perceived his fright she returned to the deep calm with which she was speaking to him. Very, very far away one could still hear the orchestra. Swing, but the melody could not be determined.

"Go now. The only thing I found out about your father was that he was staying in a boardinghouse on Cienfuegos Street. On the third block. You must find him now, before anyone, before everyone. Please, because of what's most important to you, don't mention me if they find you."

She kissed him on the cheek: he could see the woman's eyelids closed with emotion, out of the corner of his eye. It was an affectionate kiss, more sad than erotic, more full than stingy. Tito: a combatant kissed by his mother on the platform minutes before leaving for the trenches.

"Good luck, the best in the world," Lili Salomé said to him. Tito remained quiet while she went directly to an enormous three-door armoire which occupied one side of the room. She opened a flap in which an oval mirror cast Tito's image, deserted and numbed. It was like a camera panning, but with sufficient time to know that he was not a supposed chosen one of God. Yes, the image of an individual involved in a mess, in a dangerous mess, very dangerous.

She pointed to a hole inside the armoire.

"Leave through here . . . and quickly."

Total darkness.

"But there's nothing there."

"Leave, I'm telling you!"

And there you heard footsteps along the passageway and you had an uncontrollable desire to cry out loud. Without thinking about it, you threw yourself rolling into the dark hole until you found yourself seated askew on a kind of slide, a metal surface on which you rode gaining velocity, until all of a sudden you noticed that instead of going down you were going up. The momentum carried you until you began to brake. A wall (darkness was now a habit and your eyes were adjusting to it) appeared in front: end of the line.

125

He was in the street, a street which he couldn't recognize, but clearly outside the buildings of El Limbo. Where to go now, as soon as he managed to recognize the blocks, the north, the city where he'd spent his whole life? Would he go home or to visit his mother or to the unknown boardinghouse on Cienfuegos? He thought he needed a weapon. But, where could he get one? He had left the Walter PPK in his closet and now it wasn't possible to go near there without being discovered. By whom? He didn't have any idea, but indeed, whoever it was didn't have the best intentions. He advanced along the street. The mechanical strength of the sound of the traffic whispered a song into his head, hummed by an affectionate mother who waits for the aroma of apples from a *kuchen* in the oven. The traffic lights could be native trees in the countryside of the homeland, the contaminated air the breath of life which gives tranquility and hope. He checked over his body during the walk: it was all there. The flavor of the mass wine, still moistening his cheeks, reminded him of where he was coming from. The kiss from Lili Salomé was still floating on his cheek. He couldn't help wiping off the kiss, faced with the insistent uneasiness of that uncomfortable caress.

He leaned out into the street where the new tunnel he had traversed ended. He was on Diez de Julio, unmistakable in its glory and majesty. The night was plied with everyday persistency by taxis and micros and he was alive. He breathed deeply with an end-of-the-chapter look on his face.

What Tito didn't know, among many other things, was that Lili Salomé, after closing the armoire, had let a man into her dressing room. He had asked her about Tito and she, with a sigh that denoted severe discouragement, had told him: yes, but she hadn't confided in him at all.

"You'd better follow him," she said to him.

21

A handful of pocketknives

What were the motives Tito Livio had to choose to make his way towards Cienfuegos Street? He never found out. He made the decision without even flipping a coin. He just turned his head in space and leaned towards where his intuition pushed him, which is how great battles are won and the worst disasters are experienced. So the real history of events is illusory and dangerous.

Tito Livio vaguely remembered Cienfuegos along lower Alameda, past the Bulnes Plaza, in some erratic trip with his father to the headquarters of the glorious Colo Colo Sports Club, through privileged entrances for a memorable game with the Italian Audax. He remembered the Audax by the bad parody of an Italian accent that his father had attempted with some friends, members of the white club with the dark-skinned leader's profile over the insignia crowned with stars which he never got tired of counting. A mixture of an Argentinian accent with his own terms for tasting spaghetti. That was what the Italians were like for his father: passionate, gluttons for pasta and bolognese sauce, excessively effusive. Actually, he had used the same

127

image in a detestable and successful (sometimes in advertising it's almost the same thing) campaign for a brand of noodles: the Italian-looking guy was not really an Italian, it was his father becoming the Italian-Argentinian in a large converted mansion with colorful stained glass windows and gothic columns which housed an immensely populous and debt-ridden sports club, the parody of a parody, a shadow of an imitation, the desanctifying of the desanctified and at least, perhaps, the resanctifying of a cliché. He wondered if maybe Santiago could all be like that, a piling up of small sections of imitations taken from the capricious memory of a tourist, stubborn in wanting to remember the postcard photo of his own city, preventing him from having his own personality, preventing him from thinking, avoiding all possibility that the streets might meet each other, that the city might feel at home, destroying the familiar air in which its inhabitants could begin to relate to one another, in order to once again seem like Paris, London, New York, any part of Latin America except Chile, except Santiago.

The relaxed Tito Livio was continuing to meditate on this while he walked, exercising that incredible capacity for getting terrified and then pretending not to know, like someone who finishes a task and closes the folders in order to be able to go home, turn on the television, help himself to a drink, how did it go at work my love, nothing important honey, thanks. All the same, on automatic pilot, he had chosen the most traveled avenues certain of being protected. He had picked up the idea from some American television series. He imagined himself on crowded Fifth Avenue, lost in a dangerous and anonymous crowd. But in passing he had also forgotten that he was in Santiago, Chile, and that nighttime was an uncultivated space, a no-man's-land where other inhabitants appeared unexpectedly.

A few blocks further on there were some long-haired guys, a debasement of the last batch of possible Creole hippies, pasting up posters announcing the upcoming concert of a national urban rock group. In the distance there were some stupid-acting cops covering the corners around the big tower in the Diego Portales building. When he thought about the name of the building he briefly remembered having been inside, before they fenced it off, when it was called the Gabriel Mistral building. It was during his university years, although he couldn't remember clearly what career he was studying for at the time.

He had fallen head over heels for a great girl who was a communist. He couldn't help smiling when he thought about it. The brown-haired girl sheathed in a garnet colored blouse, seated in an underground café which led out to the plaza where there were some abstract erotic sculptures which no one looks at now, only the city guardians of law and order passing among them, distracted by the new slogans each morning. The communist girl, crossing her legs in her short black skirt and black stockings, and he crossing the holes in the subway, not even qualified to enter this excessively styled cafe. There was a bookstore in the back where he finds the first copy that he will see of *Tiro Libre* by Skármeta, recently published by Siglo XXI, which makes anyone who wants to be a writer in the future extremely envious, a member of that unexpected Olympus that was the Latin American "Boom."

But in those times he didn't know anything, he was only in love, which is the best way to live. With her he read poems by Cardenal, Neruda, Mayakovsky. In amazement, he used to watch the folksong groups practicing in the Student House on Villavicencio Street. Where could that girl be? Surely out of the country. It suddenly occurred to him that she might be dead and he felt a pain in his chest. Vague, transient, this breathlessness that was like a habit when he was re-membering. It was as if, suddenly, he had understood something else, beyond the tranquility of the city, cold, illuminated without pity in this whole stretch. He quickened his step looking away from the building, leaving behind in it the origin of so many bad times. The bars bothered him, they were telling him that a part of his past would not be there any more, now there would not be any way to come to look for it, no way to reconstruct it. It had been swept away and now there was nothing left. He was very much in love then. Perhaps it was the last time, before Anita, that he had read poems, that he had written them. He had gone out with her so many times walking along Lastarria, and he had sat down in a little theater of wicker chairs to see Oscar Castro and the Grupo Aleph. He was very much in love. Oscar Castro was now in Paris, he had read something about him a while ago in some credit card magazine. He had been stopped in Chacabuco and had left for Europe. Someone had told him that his mother had been executed. Could that be true? People say so many things, he thought, trying to make himself feel better. His internal calming mechanism used to work better, that's what he called it. Phrases like: good, things happen, something must be being done, better turn the page, that's life, the innocent must often pay for the guilty. They were more efficient when he was involved in the department, or flying in his car, or when he was cooling himself down with a glass of red wine with some woman in heat. Anita bothered him about that. He remembered her looking at the ceiling from their double bed while she was lamenting the latest news that had just been delivered between the music on the radio: What kind of country is this, what kind of country will we give to our children, what are we doing to change things? They didn't have the little girls yet and now he wasn't paying much attention to her. Could he be less in love? He didn't write poetry now, he didn't cross lower Alameda on foot as, mind you, he was doing now with this soft wind, skirting Santa Lucía hill. He thought that if it hadn't already been midnight he would have taken the subway. He thought that there he indeed would have felt like he was in a spy movie. When he came to the center of the hill he switched to the north path searching for utopian serenity. But the faces didn't calm anyone down.

A couple was embracing strangely in a corner next to a closed kiosk, doing something remotely similar to making love. A completely intoxicated fat woman was dancing a kind of dance *noir* in front of the barred and dark showroom windows of the Almacenes París store. A distant memory of buying school uniforms passed through Tito's head. Some vendors, stragglers who were left behind and were survivors of the police raids, were hawking nailclippers, plastic toys, pirated cassettes, umbrellas, gloves, blancmange candies. They were anxiously watching Tito, the only passer-by they could possibly sell anything to, the sole objective of such a quantity of irresistible offers. He was the last buyer who could save them the disgrace of that masked begging, giving them direction with his money. He was afraid of being so weak that he would buy everything. The vendors kept staring at him, hawking their merchandise in low voices, directly at him. A hunchback dwarf approached him waving a miniature pocketknife under his nose, an imitation of a Swiss Army knife. A hundred pesos, sir, a hundred pesos. Tito looked up: the others were coming closer. They were all quiet, only using gestures, and the objects were swinging back and forth in the shadows. The silence spread like a fire alarm among the last strollers. They were coming towards him. A hundred pesos, sir, one hundred, two hundred, fifty, a hundred fifty, for your kids, for the woman, for you. I don't have any money, I don't have any money. They grabbed him by the lapels, by the rest of his clothes, they had him half-immobilized. A blind man sang a bolero in his ear. For the love of God, a little alms please. Is this the cosmos whose equilibrium I have to save? Who's saving me? One hundred pesos, sir, fifty because it's you. The pocket-knife was swinging back and forth in space, their breathing was like the snorting of an anxious herd. Yes, fine, okay, whatever you want. He searched his wallet, he would write them a check, anything whatsoever. Suddenly something disturbed the tide. In the distance a couple of soldiers.

Terror spread among the street vendors. The cops, the cops! Like a swarm of locusts, they gave flight in a second in a desperate race. Tito got caught up in it and began to run. It was as if the crowd were a live body, one groaning body now becoming one with the buildings, it was disappearing between the lowered grilles of the stores, between the squalid trees in the gutter. He looked behind, seeing what looked like someone grabbing him. He had the feeling that they were beating him. No, soldiers don't do those things. His arm began to hurt. A pull carried him towards one side. He rolled between the pillars of the State Bank. It was the same imposing image which was on the savings books when he was a kid, the same savings bank into which every child of the Chilean middle class was received. Savings as a base of the state. Those were other times. Now there he was, grasping his legs. The snorting dwarf with the miniature pocketknives.

He took out one hundred pesos, no, a thousand pesos. He was left with a handful of pocketknives with acrylic covers in his hand. The dwarf was running, singing, hiding the bill. He was disappearing along Bandera Street towards the north. What was he going to do now? He was more alone than any of his pursuers. Everyone must have had some place to go, including jail. Not him, he was sheltered under the protection of a pillar where at any instant a drunk could come to anchor himself, or a beggar, or a couple of scoundrels. He looked at Alameda, the illuminated University of Chile, the statue of Andrés Bello who continued to look down, with shame. A slack look above the sparse traffic. He thought he saw a silver sports car. It had just recently

131

crossed in front of his eyes tracing a diaphanous line between the slow nocturnal minivans and the drifting taxis hungry for lost passengers. He had seen it a little while ago. But where? He gulped. He arranged the pile of pocketknives in his pockets before getting up. Afraid, he leaned out to the sidewalk. Could they be following him? Now he didn't understand what could happen to him, where the danger was coming from, in whom he could confide. He smiled when he thought that now, if worst came to worst, he could say to himself that he was armed, he could offer some attempt at resistance. But who was his enemy? Trying to deceive the slight and uncomfortable fear lodged in his epigastrium, he began to walk. He was trying to find the most inconspicuous walk. The one of a nocturnal stroller? That of a man in a hurry with his collar turned up returning from a clandestine love? The walk of a person who's going to his night shift? That of a drunk who's lost his sense of direction and is wandering, confusing the streetlights with the moons of Saturn? That of a prostitute's john who is disappointed with his extraordinary catch? The walk of a person terrified of the curfew who can't stand the sirens that make him remember his long days as a prisoner in the National Stadium? His own, his own walk is better, one that does not seem out of place in its look, in its appearance. The only walk possible was one of fear. Alameda was becoming darker and more dangerous with each step. It would have been better in a minivan, sure, and less risky. But he looked inside the yellowed windows of the collective taxi and at the immobile heads, staring like mannequins, like sitting ducks from the *Diana games*, they seemed the same or more threatening. Walking is better.

He crossed Norte-Sur Avenue with a dry mouth and he began to breath a little better. Next would be Cienfuegos and he would be safe. Safe? Did some place really exist in this city where he could feel safe? He didn't know how, but a kind of resigned smile came to place itself on his face. He was laughing at his idea. As if he could be safe. He was thinking about this when he came upon the sign in black and white indicating that he was at the corner of Cienfuegos and Alameda. He couldn't help looking all around before turning. There wasn't anybody, not a soul. Or, at least that's what Tito Livio thought. He sighed, for a minute he imagined his father greeting him. He saw himself as a child waiting for him to open the door, the gate to the house that they had one time on Maruri Street, to go running and track down some present: a top, a kite, a watering can, a miniature bakery truck. It was an almost forgotten image. He feared his was made up, a calming fantasy which he needed the most right now: someone who was more powerful than he, who came from outside this threatening world to cover him with his great filthy tweed coat, to put his enormous legs out front in order to hide him, to feel that he would never again be cold, or hungry, or bored, that he would never again walk along Cienfuegos with this paleness shining in the darkness in front of shadowy buildings housing the most diverse companies: the air force, an order of priests, the Colo Colo Sports Club, until he arrived at the third block.

Could they have demolished it? Could Lili Salomé's memories be so old? No, it was on this side. One of the houses closer to the next street. Sure. He took a deep breath, he needed it. His fear had been replaced by emotion, and now the emotion by fear, another kind, distinct, now it wasn't fear of someone being behind him, but rather that of what was coming up. I have to ask for my father, he thought, and he began to walk slowly, changing his gait, towards the house that he guessed was the one she meant.

22

Sara's boardinghouse

The outside gate was ajar and it was enough just to push it gently to conclude that it was meticulously oiled. Not a sound. Whoever managed this boardinghouse knew how to give the appearance and atmosphere of a well maintained house.

Should I fake having a recommendation? Should I say right up front that he was a relative? Should I ask for him without beating around the bush? Should I imply a possibly urgent message that must be delivered personally?

Now, standing in the small space between the outside door to the street and the gate he perceived that, in spite of the late hour, they were expecting a visitor. All without a key. That was extremely unusual in this neighborhood at this time of night. He closed the door with a soft click and opened the gate. The soft shine of a low-intensity yellow lightbulb lit up the corridor. Who should he speak with? He patted the pocketknives in his pocket without feeling any more self-assured.

"Samuel?"

The voice frightened him. An older woman shuffled her house

slippers towards the dark entrance hall. When they saw each other she fell silent.

"Good evening." Courtesy above all else, Tito Livio.

She was looking at him slowly, turning her head to one side, like birds do. She examined him with one eye, then the other. He thought she really was a bird, a retired ex-bird of prey: her pointy face gave vague testimony to this just the same as her long eagle-like nose. She was almost like a cartoon witch, if it weren't for the total lack of a chin. The curve of her face became lost in her neck which was hidden, in turn, in the floppy lapels of an old brownish-purple housecoat.

"Who are you looking for? You haven't ever come around here before."

"I'm looking for someone."

"That's what I asked you. Who are you looking for?"

Just dive in head first, Tito. Now you've gotten yourself involved. You have to face the consequences, this is a blind alley. Just like in the story, your father would say.

"Alberto Triviño."

He waited for some type of reaction in the old woman's face. All movement stopped. Her face froze, her wrinkles stopped twisting, the shine in her eyes diminished. She pursed her lips, that was all. Perhaps her ears moved smoothly along her hair which was put back in a bun.

"He's my father."

He let the sentence fall as if he were stepping on some ice of dubious strength. He felt that everything could give way with one step, and that someone might be listening in back of the door where he had spoken with the old woman when she asked for that mysterious Samuel. And who was this mysterious Samuel? Couldn't he be in back of him right now? No, he had astutely closed the door. If someone were to come in he would notice it. But why were they waiting for someone who didn't have a key? Or is it that someone had just left? Someone especially careless?

"They told me that he lives here."

It was a monologue now. Telegraphic but a monologue.

"He used to live here," said the woman and Tito shook. Used to? He stopped living here, or he simply stopped living?

"Are you really his son?" The woman's voice had become somewhat softer. Tito felt for an instant that she was asking sincerely, with a true desire to understand, that she wished he were. Tito showed her his identity card.

"Is it real? It's not a fake?"

The woman passed a hand with swollen joints back and forth over the photo, almost caressing him. A kind of smile came to her face, but it didn't last very long. Once again the woman put on her bird of prey look. She examined him up and down and made a gesture of reproach.

"You should have come before. How long has it been since you saw him?"

"We saw each other outside. He didn't ever want me to come here," lied Tito quickly, curving himself in the air to get the ball in the corner of the goal.

"Maybe he was ashamed of old Sara," said the woman to herself.

"I don't think so. It's a beautiful house. I think there must have been some other motive."

"What do you know if you have hardly seen past the door?"

"Maybe he didn't want me to come so that no one would find him," ventured Tito.

Something happened with that sentence since Sara, that was what the woman called herself, went on observing him with strange resignation. She shrugged her shoulders and looked at the floor. She probably stayed that way for a few seconds until Tito's uneasiness brought her out of her meditation.

"What's going on?"

"He's not here now."

"What? What do you mean?"

"I don't know, he left or they took him away, I don't know."

The answer didn't amuse Tito.

"He left . . . or someone came," added old Sara.

Tito felt a sudden and total dryness in his mouth.

"Who is Samuel?" he asked.

"Samuel?"

"You asked about Samuel when I came in. Who is he? Why do you leave the door half-open for him?"

"That's got nothing to do with anything. He's a nephew of mine. He's sick. He goes out at night."

136

All the hardness in the woman disappeared. He was cornering her. He looked down also.

"When did he go? Or when did they take him away?"

Both of them with their heads down.

"Recently. Less than an hour ago. A group of men came in and, I don't know, they did something in his room. One of them took me by my arms, firmly but delicately. Do you understand me? They knew what they were doing. They were friendly but impertinent. They didn't make a sound. They left me sitting in the little living room, in the dark, one of them sat me down and ordered me not to speak. I was very afraid." A sigh began to build up in the poor birdwoman's chest. "When they left I went running to your father's room and there wasn't anybody there. Everything was turned upside down, papers, all his things, and there wasn't a trace of him. Poor Don Tito. I don't know if he could have been there. But he's not there now."

"What? Was he there or wasn't he? Did you see him leave? Did you see him come in?" Tito Livio shook her by the shoulders. He was anxiously searching for her scornful eyes.

"Don't hurt me." Sara freed herself from his hands. "I don't know, I never know where he's going. He's very nice when he greets me but very quiet. He reads or writes in his room, he leaves sometimes and I don't know if he came in or not. I don't know if he was in his room when they came. Maybe he's still there, but I didn't dare to look very carefully."

"He's still there?" repeated Tito angrily.

"I mean dead . . . or wounded, he could be, couldn't he?"

Tito's chest was hurting him now, his back, he got really uptight. He turned pale all of a sudden. He took a deep breath before taking the initiative again.

"Where's the room that my father was living in?" he said, as with each phrase he felt that an arrow was twisting in his guts.

The woman searched in the pockets of her robe for a key ring. The unmistakable sound increased Tito Livio's uneasiness. What could he be going to find? Who? He felt like crying, he was afraid of dying from pain. The woman asked him to follow her as she checked the bolts on the gate and the door.

"And Samuel?"

Sara didn't answer, she shrugged her shoulders. What did it matter now, she seemed to say to him. Tito followed her down the corridor, both of them stealthily. The moon could be made out through a narrow gallery where flowerpots of ferns testified to the old age of the decorations. The woman stopped almost at the end of the corridor. Tito stood studying the outline of the windows on the floorboards. An old round rug interrupted the design. There were legs of old and dilapidated furniture. The sound of the door when it was opened brought him back to reality. A part of him didn't even want to know what was happening, he preferred to be far away, in the remotest state of experienced ignorance, but he put up with it.

The woman switched on the light.

"It's better if I leave you alone," she moaned, and went away like a retreating shadow towards the living room. Tito Livio didn't move. He listened to the mixture of sighs and the dragging of those slippers. The light coming from the room mixed with the moon diluting the shadow game. The round rug confessed some dirty reddish colors, grays and blues. The concentric circles were interrupted every now and then by a tight darning or an indelible stain: planets in orbit in a forgotten mandala. Tito looked towards the room. He thought about crossing himself but he didn't do it. The only thing he did was once again to pat the pocketknives like a multiple amulet. After that he went in.

23

Difficult moments

Tito Livio looked at the room, the hovel, the minimal lodging. It was in intolerable disorder with drawers overturned and scattered all over, articles of clothing, ripped up papers, the bed torn apart: pillows ripped up and their stuffing spread around the room. Everything had been torn to pieces in a rage. Rather than a search it was a complete demonstration of bad intentions. Someone had overturned everything that had been on top of a small three-drawer dresser. An orphaned bottle of after shave lotion was teetering on the brink of the abyss: Atkinsons. The old man's stubbornness, always out of style. Between his fingers Tito grabbed some shirts that had lost their buttons and were unraveling at the seams. Who could be capable of so much destruction? So much chaotic power? So much viciousness? He thought about the beaches when the tide goes out, about those crowded seaside resorts and the morning walkers avoiding bottles, refuse, bodies of birds soaked in oil, solitary shoes twisted by the ocean. He felt like he was invading the fallen body of his own father, passing through his entrails.

The slanting bed with all its emptied contents was an abdomen undone by slashes from a knife, its dried blood converted into t-shirts, socks, underwear, spread among jars of cosmetics and fragments of pages of his father's inimitable flowing handwriting. One lonely chair was showing off, still upright in the center of the room. Could Sara have used it for sobbing? Could they have left it for him? Could the exterminating agent have sat down there to look at his work? Or, could he have reflected on the site in order to capture something which seems to have escaped his furious search? Could that be the explanation for so much rage?

He looks at the old torn paper, the dresser damaged in the search for false bottoms. He grabbed the papers: copies of letters from his father. To whom? Unknown, unconnected notes that no one could understand now. Could it have to do precisely with that? Like Leonardo's codices written to be read in a mirror. Was his father trying to hide something? For whom? For what reason?

He sat down. The only light fell from a ceiling lamp, opaque glass where some Greek dancers were drawn under a circle of fretting, like caryatids in movement, freed from the weight of the arch of a temple in order to remain motionless, circling some 40 insufficient watts. The light fell directly on his head, hiding his face in shadow for any observer, as well as on his hands with the white papers and the characteristic handwriting which this time was incomprehensible. The window led to a small interior patio whose curtain had also been slashed and shapes could be sensed, badly arranged ferns in mildewed flower pots. All of a sudden he spotted something underneath the glass of the bedside table leaning out of its unique enclosure like an exhausted tongue: a photograph. Who? He couldn't manage to make it out but it wasn't important now. Maybe it would be better to leave, he thought, I'm confused, it'd be better if I got far away from here, why not to São Paulo, this is a lost cause, it's better to take off for there, any city would be less dangerous, better to get totally into some more superficial work than this absurd deal, this thing that makes no sense with mystic overtones that's got me fed up, sitting in a broken down chair, hardly breathing, surrounded by my father's mortal remains, in a place where it would seem impossible that life could take root again.

This is a city ravaged by the plague, he imagined, the bodies were the only thing missing. Insanity, crime, and other offenses running rampant and taking away all traces of structure, all laws, any semblance of order. It wasn't the first time he'd felt like that in Santiago. He used to wake up suddenly with that image, on certain mornings, drenched in a cold sweat and his heart trapped in his throat, which he attributed to the overload of stimulants misused for an advertising campaign that bombed, or to an insane combination of small lines of cocaine at a party for artists, entertaining like no other, sickening like most. He wanted to smother himself in the one and only Mina's tits, he would even forgive her for the kicking, everything. How frightening, he would like to lose himself even in Anita María herself, he was sure this was not happening to the parents of families, to those who respected the limit between the earth and sky, to those who didn't intend to construct the kingdom in this world and be gods this same afternoon, not recognizing sex, age, fatigue, death. How beautiful it would be to go far away, go far away, how beautiful it would be.

The photo.

Why hadn't they destroyed it like everything else? The papers strewn around, the torn clothing, the slashed up furniture. The photo was intact like a lure, like a trap. Messages from hell had the same appearance as signals from God. Be careful, Tito.

His curiosity was stronger. He stood up and advanced on tiptoe clearing a path. It was a photograph of his mother. In black and white. His mother and two small children in a sunny provincial plaza, or the Santiago of those times which was, is, and has been the province of the world. He was one of the children. He recognized himself with a forced smile, trying to be funny and stand out next to his brother. I'm the favorite, I'm the best, I'm without doubt the most amusing. If I'm not, may the photo be ruined. Both of them immodestly innocent. Gustavo with the same silence as usual, the silence of a good student, a good professor, a good husband, a good father, hiding everything behind his black, calm, impenetrable eyes. I'm even noisy in photos.

Am I four, maybe five years old? My father must have taken it. My mother looks happy. She's a pretty woman, before old age and menopause. Before they began to fight, or during a break. His mother had hidden all the photos of the two of them together. She used to look at them on the sly. One time I caught her, on the sly, what's she doing if not praying. She was looking for a long time at the photos of Alberto Triviño, Tito Senior, and her.

I said to her: "Mother, all photos are tragic. It's something that's no more, that's ceased to exist. The theme of photographs is always death. Haven't you read Barthes?"

The house in the background was absolutely unfamiliar to him, or worse, vaguely recognizable, perhaps in a dream more than in the waking hours. The composition surprised him: his mother took up the whole lower right, with Gustavo and Tito Livio in her arms, his face in the upper right. Tito Junior was under his face and Gustavo to the lower left. The house with a door in the center was occupying the whole rest of the picture. It was as if it were ready to be published in a magazine, the text could go over the uncluttered space. He thought: It's the gap my father would leave. This was enough and a strange affliction lodged in his insides. It was rage, he wasn't in the mood for sentimentalities now. He had an impulse to tear up this raggedy edged photo. No, he said to himself, it's the only one left, maybe his mother would thank him. That's it, his mother would never think that this photo was with his father all the time, there, on the nightstand. He looked for pieces of other possible memories. Nothing. The only thing was now in his pocket: the photograph. A clear remembrance of times that must have been secure and sweet. Before all the wars there was original peace, primitive tranquility. He felt protected, just as if he had received a sacred image, the bone of a saint, one of the nails from the cross, the authentic olive branch from Noah's ark, a consecrated host from the Last Supper. Now he didn't need all those ridiculous pocket-knives. He took out the handful and spread them over the mattress. He seemed like a sower letting fall his philosophies and Taiwanese seeds in the wounded furrows of wool. What could he grow there? Resentment, revenge? Or, could it be a trap for the possible return of those strangers. Tightly packed, threaded fakirs in the knives that would grow like bearded darnel shoots to take them by surprise. No one would go to sleep again in this bed. Only to die, only to be killed. He kept one of the small pocketknives and tested the blade. It was no larger than a little finger and thin in the same way, but it was enough to open the heart of an enemy. The little knife and the photo. His benediction, his weapons.

He looked for the light switch and went out to the gallery, leaving the room in darkness. While he was closing the door he felt the total, resigned peacefulness of having completed some mission, of having gathered the only important thing, that this was all he needed now. To know that his father had him, his family, still so close. He began to mull over the question again: Where had they taken that picture?

He found Sara in the small living room next to the front door. She still hadn't recovered from her crying, still hadn't regained her composure. A small deformed man was with her. Digging in his memory he recognized Down's syndrome, slightly blond, mongoloid eyes, his eyes almost at the same level as his thick neck. It was Samuel, without doubt. He didn't talk, he only stared at Tito in all his graceful stupidity.

"Did you see?" moaned the woman. She was controlled.

"Yes, I want to pay for the expense."

"No, please, he'll return and take care of the costs."

Tito kept staring at her. Would his father return? Would he dare show up around there? His soul was pained. And if they had done to his father what they had done to the room? Maybe they aren't even looking for him, they only wanted to spoil his possible trail, convert him into a fleeting accident, destroy him as a part of history. Make him disappear. No, he couldn't tolerate that. Who would want that? Who?

"I'll pay you, Sara," he insisted, opening his checkbook.

"That's more than generous, they're cheap things, we're poor," she said, after seeing the amount.

Tito smiled. How dearly his father had held that woman in esteem. He bent down to kiss her head softly. The idiot laughed, raucously, in a string of guffaws and retching.

"Samuel," she reprimanded him affectionately.

Then she looked at Tito.

"In spite of everything . . . did you find something?"

"Nothing," lied Tito instinctively, without knowing why.

"Yes, what were those scoundrels going to leave?"

Tito made a goodbye gesture.

"No, don't go, it's very late, you can stay if you want."

"I don't want to cause you any more problems," insisted Triviño Junior, moving away towards the gate; but he didn't manage to open it.

143

Where could he go? Where would he be safe? Maybe it was better to accept the invitation. There were still a few hours before daylight and then it would be easier.

"I'll stay," he said.

Samuel rattled his smile again and Sara got up, purposefully.

"We'll open a room and get a bed ready."

Tito imagined his father in a conversation with them, listening to Sara's troubles, commenting over a cup of maté, a brazier, next to the electric stove, the portable stove with a pot of water and orange peels. She knitting and he immersed in a rereading of a Simenon novel. He sensed that he also wanted them to take care of him.

"We're ready," pronounced Sara, suddenly coming in, followed by the idiot who was snorting happily.

The room was almost identical to his father's, but in another arm of the gallery. In the morning he should find out where the house ended, how far it went back.

The door closed and Tito could not resist the temptation of placing his father's photo under the glass of his bedside table. He lay down without taking off his clothes. He only put his jacket and his shoes on a chair. Before falling asleep he ran through the whole turbulent day to the wild night. He reflected on the possibility of once again visiting that strange library, that crazy guy who believed himself to be Freud who had sparked a sympathetic feeling in him. When he was at the point of losing consciousness he got up to take off his pants, folding them meticulously. Like my old man, he thought, and he closed his eyes, wearily leaning his head against the pillow and covering himself up to his ears. Like a child, sure. I'm going to sleep well, he thought. But he couldn't. Over and over again he dreamed that knives coming from deep inside the bed were penetrating him.

24

A very pretty lady

A seguidilla of soft knocking on the door woke him up: Sara's woodpecker hand that was saving him from a new nightmare. He opened his heavy eyelids, feeling his chapped head as if it were going to fall to pieces at any moment. He held it in both hands. A hangover from the mass wine? Maybe they've drugged me? He felt himself in the middle of recovering from the late night, as if he could never get up again. For a second he remembered the Agency. Relief refreshed his pounding head: it was Saturday. Washing, getting dressed: eternal paths that he would never manage to travel.

After a few minutes he managed to focus on the ceiling: Sara's boardinghouse. Could he find out what he was doing sleeping there, in the place that at one time his father had occupied? Almost in the same bed, the same house. There was some secret in this act which was escaping his grasp. With the effort of a port crane he sat up in the bed and checked the bruises on his body. When his hands got to his back he was afraid he would touch his broken ribs poking out, bloodied, with an infinite number of pocketknives buried to the hilt in his lungs.

145

He was happy to be able to breathe with minimal effort.

Ten o'clock in the morning. If his watch was not lying it was already ten o'clock in the morning. The boardinghouse should be emptied out now, there was probably some old guy in the corridor reading a newspaper successively pawed through as if a distorted story, still not written, were important. Was it sunny or cloudy? Who would get his copy of *El Mercurio*, from which he read only the business ads and the sports page?

He found the photo on the bedside table. He had almost forgotten it. He could have gone off leaving it behind. Did the same thing happen to those prowlers? He saved it in his jacket pocket. He didn't feel like seeing it. It reminded him of everything that had happened, it told him that everything was true, it overshadowed the strategy of the nightmare and the restful feeling after waking up. He wasn't in his house, he was in a room close to where his father's abstract body was lying.

Sara knocked again. She informed him that the bathroom was free and that in addition, if he preferred, she would run a hot bath for him.

Samuel was the one who led him to the bathroom. When they entered the birdwoman was testing the water temperature with a large thermometer. A paleolithic heater was panting like a Model T to heat up the promised tub. An enormous bathtub with lion's feet, like in old illustrations, like in a large old house where he could have stayed with his parents at some time, with his brother, where the cockroaches hid between the tiles. He remembered a faraway grandmother in the north who used to fill her tub from mythical washbasins for baths that wrinkled the soft flesh of your fingers because of so much immersing and submerging.

The water was ready. Samuel and the woman excused themselves replete with courtesies. They seemed to have wanted to make up to him for what had happened in his father's room. Tito requested a toothbrush, toothpaste, deodorant, a comb, and a disposable razor. During one of the many exchanges of instructions and thank yous he believed he saw a number tattooed on Sara's forearm. The idea of a concentration camp passed through his mind. An exiled Jew in this corner of the world. What is she doing here? Why here? How did she learn this damned language? He tried to review the conversation in search of some signal of a central European accent. Maybe. The guttural *r*'s. Maybe.

He was seated in the tub meditating on nothing, letting himself be cleansed by the hotness of this space where he fit completely and his muscles could return to their proper places, when the door cracked open and Sara's hand left something on a wooden shelf, very bashfully. It was the package from the pharmacy and the change, with the coins neatly stacked. The number became evident. Auschwitz, Treblinka, who knows? His father had an ability to surround himself with immigrants, survivors of impossible persecutions, the damned, lost causes, serving them as a guide, as a translator, as a Lazarillo de Tormes, as a Spanish teacher, or rather, a Chilean teacher. His father doing favors which no one could pay back. Or were they doing it now through his body? He calculated how much it would cost to pay the board and room in this boardinghouse, deducing that his old man did not use the money that he had given to him. He could have stayed in a hotel if he had wanted; but no, he had preferred this place. Maybe he supported the old lady and the idiot, maybe this guy was a bastard son of his, maybe his half-brother. Water. He dunked his head to see if he could stop thinking about his father's stories. He rested a bit with his head supported on the rim. Now this was a bathtub, for his size, to really let himself be in the warmth of the slow and desirable hot water. Silence: just someone far away who was listening to a morning radio program with a mix of oldies and new songs. He smiled when he recognized a jingle from his very own hand. A broom was carrying out its task near the door. He closed his eyes, attentive to this sea of sounds so different from those of his apartment where he listened to the latest model new cars blaze by, or parties with stereos blasting, or frenetic television sets repeating the same hectic threat: *stop or I'll shoot, anything you say may be used against you, if you leave me I'll kill you, I love you, I love you more than anyone, don't back up, careful.* Ring. Like that, ring, the bell rang. A rough, coarse electric doorbell came to interrupt the peace of that so distinctly imbued silence. It could be some customer, the mailman, the kitchen worker bringing vegetables for an ever-present stew, a chicken salmagundi, a cabbage roll, a stuffed potato. Then he could hear the noises from the kitchen and the smell of the stew would happily invade the midday. Only the sound of machine keyboards dwelt in the office,

147

Fatty Aspillaga's comedy routines, the impertinence of the account executives, the excessive uproar from so many ceremonial greetings in the hall, irritating histrionics, slaps on the back, canned phrases. Without smelling like anything. The São Paulo offer emerged in his mind again when he imagined Donkavian on the wall to wall carpet in an exclusively designed Danish chair. A lost cause, he said to himself, and he dunked his head again to submerge his aching neck. He was drying off when Sara's voice snapped him out of it.

"Señor Triviño?"

"Come in."

The bird head leaned in like a papier maché puppet.

"They're looking for you. It seems that it's your wife."

"My wife?"

"A very pretty lady," she smiled with a certain roguishness.

Tito Livio rapidly reviewed the unfortunate archive of his understanding. Anita María, here? No, that couldn't be. It was impossible. Mina? Would she have gotten it in her head to blow over here after taking their restaurant meeting as a reconciliation? On the contrary, she had left mad. Then it was Lili Salomé, sure. But she wouldn't seem at all like his wife. It had to be a young woman. Anita María was getting involved in his life again, or that stupid Mina. Nobody else could be that clumsy, lacking in judgment, absolutely imbecilic.

"I'm coming. Tell her to wait."

He was boiling mad. He had never brushed his teeth with such anger, almost filing them down. The bad thing was not knowing who he was going to insult. One detail just didn't fit in at all: how had they found him? How had they found out, whoever it was, about his stay? He thought seriously about the idea of a new escape. He got dressed quickly and began to sing in a Neapolitan style, trying to hide his uneasiness behind the scenes. He began to run the noisy faucet in the tub. What to do? They had trapped him. Salomé was the traitor, or someone who had followed him, whichever. The thing is that there in the living room, there was a woman talking with the old lady, Sara, making herself pass for his wife. No, she would have to have noticed that she wasn't wearing a necklace. Or, she wanted to warn him about something? Maybe the woman herself was the one who had given him away. Sure, sleeping until ten o'clock in the morning. She could have called, or she could have known where to find him. Surely because of his father and then . . . But who? Where? Only to his mother. And how did she find out? No, I shouldn't have told her that I was looking for Triviño Senior, not ever. That was it for sure.

Entangled in questions and without putting two and two together, he felt like screaming out loud and long, becoming deformed like a Munch painting. The noise of the water was beginning to shake him up. He decided to turn off the faucet and face whatever there was. He combed his hair in funereal silence. As if preparing his own body for the coffin, he adjusted his tie, his dirty shirt, his pants. And he went out.

25

Did they tell you that the world was at stake?

He recognized her before going through the doorway to the living room: la Maga. Her immense green eyes also saw him, returning an enchanting smile, as if they were old friends. Tito couldn't help shivering. She was there again, with her hair, which before was wildly flowing, now well-placed into a bun. She wore a two-piece suit which concealed the geography which he knew to be exciting, almost torturing. He had the feeling it wasn't good to look at her so much, that she could turn him into a pig, a rock, a shadow. Hey, come on, she was doing it, she was going to put a spell on him.

"Hello, Tito."

A pointed affection in her voice.

They kissed each other on the cheek, painfully affirming a cordial look. All his anger had faded away. Fear was the problem now.

The three of them were seated as if for a whole weekend get-together. Sara was looking at him like a doddering grandmother with these beautiful recently married grandchildren, on the verge of asking them to pose for a Polaroid, telling them about the Christmas presents,

150

making them look at postcards and birthday cards. He thought quickly about the photo in his pocket and then erased it from his mind. What was la Maga doing here?

That thought was enough to have her look at him sweetly. He shivered again: she was beautiful, pretty and well mannered. She was talking with Sara as if she really were a charitable spirit, a fairy, someone who was coming to save him. Tito was frightened by the strange relaxed feeling which was creeping through his chest. She was reading his mind or something like that: that look had told him, *I'll answer you now*, he had heard it with total clarity, with the same voice that was saying she admired the antique furniture, the porcelain on the mantel, the large old house, the uncertain future of the western barrio in old Santiago, in a tone of voice in which Tito, at times, heard that there was a similarity in accent to that of old Sara. La Maga transformed herself into what you wanted to hear, she had all the gifts, all the powers. How to resist, how to deny himself faced with such a woman, so, but oh so beautiful. Above all he, Tito Livio Triviño Recart, who never had managed to put a limit on the influence of a beautiful woman who popped up right in front of him. He, accused by his ex-wife of being a genuine fraud, incapable of prioritizing his feelings, a type of chaotic cavalcade of promises and deceptions. Yes, he was condemned to be an advertising agent.

"Well, we have to be going," said Tito, suddenly.

La Maga smiled. She stood up in all her exasperating elegance and said goodbye to Sara. The birdwoman was thankful. When they were leaving she took Tito by the hand again and whispered to him: How pretty she is.

Tito accepted her opinion.

They were going out the door and the gate towards a still vacillating sun. La Maga's silver BMW was parked there in front of the door, like a guard chosen for a princess. He looked at her so expeditiously when she opened the door. Tito thought again about fleeing, leaving in a dead run, getting into a minivan, disappearing in the nascent hustle and bustle of the capital.

"Be careful," whispered the old woman. The tone broke the previous cordiality. It was more of a complicit tone than anything else, said so that only he could hear. When Tito drew up the balance sheet of all the things that occurred he would remember that signal very well: the gesture from old Sara when covering her mouth and drawing closer to his ear while making him bend down with a soft pull on his jacket sleeve. *Be careful.* Of whom? Who are you talking about now?

He got into the car with la Maga. An automatic transmission in drive: they left. Not a sound.

"You probably want to change clothes," she said.

Tito looked at her legs, what legs, under the steering wheel.

"Before that, I'd like to know how you got here."

"What's a girl like me doing in a place like this?" implied ironically the green-eyed woman.

In her humor, Tito perceived he was trapped. No jokes were coming from him. His tongue felt gummy, the funny guy felt boring, she was the one giving the orders. He remained quiet: I'll pass.

"I'm here because I worry about people who are of concern to me. And you're of great concern to me, Tito."

She spoke without looking at him, she was driving effortlessly. At the first stoplight she let down her hair. She owned the world, a perfect model, her precise movements, without a mistake, it bothered him. He was trying to cling desperately to the fear which had moved him the whole night. He rejected the blasphemy of the seduction. It would be so easy to become fascinated, so easy to let himself be charmed. Something was telling him that it wasn't good, that he should avoid it at all costs, at any price. But it was very hard for him to do. He felt so much like being happy, he had such desire to stop suffering. I'm so weak, he said to himself, so weak.

"I tried to find you yesterday, I spoke to your friend, Aspillaga, a treasure. He was a love to give me all sorts of clues to get to you, after talking with your mother, such a charming lady. You have the same eyes, you know?"

Her, drinking tea with his mother. Sure, Mom could be charming with her, just like with everyone at the beginning. She must have seen the car, she must have acted like a real lady, she must have fascinated her, just like Aspillaga. She would say to him in a week: I think she's an airhead.

"Just as you're thinking, we left the best of friends."

Tito was startled, he shouldn't open up his thoughts for one second, enjoy yourself, enjoy yourself.

"You shouldn't be afraid of me," she continued, set in her mind. "I've never done anything bad to anyone I really like and I'm telling you truthfully, you've really gotten to me. I've found out the whole story, and I think you're good, you're almost a genius, you could go far. I read your book."

"My book? Where did you get it?"

"Come on, there are three thousand copies."

"Yes, in a good many old bookstores, for a hundred pesos, they're sick of them around here."

"No, Donkavian lent it to me."

Vade retro Satanás, thought Tito and la Maga bust out laughing. Then she looked at him sententiously, puckering her mouth with coquettish seriousness.

"You're a love. You shouldn't be so naive, my Tito."

Now she wasn't talking with an Argentinian accent, nor with the Hungarian one from the boardinghouse, now she was talking like him. The debate inside your head: give in, no, please, no, give in. What did this woman want with you, Tito?

"You shouldn't think like that, you're very confused, well, that's just why I came looking for you. Your mother told me you were looking for your father, and then I really got moving and I found out where you could be. Looking for him I found you, isn't that funny? I was intending to talk with him and you show up."

"And for what?" answered Tito rudely, relinquishing all secret thoughts.

"In order to show you the true order of things, and in that way save you from a deadly trap that they want to catch you in."

"To save me, to save me, everyone wants to save me, everyone wants me to save the world. When's it going to end?"

"They told you that?"

"Who?" Tito wanted to have bitten his tongue.

"Whoever. Did they tell you that the world was at stake?"

They were now driving along Costanera and la Maga was weaving through the spaces between the cars without giving it a second thought, in a slalom at ninety-five miles an hour. It was useless to continue. He felt like opening the door and throwing himself out: his body crushed, tossed around between the tires of the cars that hit it, broken into pieces, scattered all along the avenue, getting bumpers dirty, mud flaps, fog lights, nauseating drivers and passers-by. Identified only by his dental work, encrusted on the bottom of a willow tree.

"The things that occur to you, Tito! How can you think I want to hurt you? You're totally lost. Poor dear, they've poisoned your brain. Well, if they told you that . . . Things are much worse than what I imagined. Much worse."

"What do you mean?"

"We'll talk about that in your apartment. You don't know what you've gotten yourself mixed up in, Tito."

The BMW was entering Vitacura. He had never seen anyone drive that fast. They didn't say a word until Tito closed the door to the building. He had anesthetized his thoughts with words from songs, ice cream ads, mnemonic devices about the Chilean provinces, and erotic fantasies about all the inhabitants. But fear was beginning to reappear. While that was happening she was softly caressing his forearm, the back of his hand, his thigh. Like a little kid: It's over, it's all gone, never again, here's your Maga, it's all gone.

"Put in the key," she said to him. Tito followed her instructions: a submissive dog, a frightened slave. I listen and I obey.

Surprisingly she took his head in her hands. She was tall, almost the same height. Her mouth was just about chin level. She kissed him softly on the lips.

"Poor Tito," she said to him.

The infallible strategy of compassion. He watched her check the rooms. Tito felt alien in his own house.

"Sit down," she said. "We have to talk, or do you feel like changing your clothes first?"

Tito accepted the last offer, trying to win some time. He was going into the bedroom when la Maga put her hand on his arm.

"Please, don't be afraid of me, I came to help you, you know very well about the danger you're in and I know many things that you don't know. Things that neither your father, nor Donkavian, nor Lili Salomé know either. Things that even God the Father himself doesn't know."

As soon as she mentioned them Tito felt that he was turning into glass again, a frozen and fragile glass that would break with only one more blow. Before he began to cry like a little kid, he entered the bedroom, falling doubled up onto the bed. The moans were welling up in his throat. La Maga approached him softly and began to caress his hair. He couldn't take it any more and the torrent of tears came out like a volcano of crying, a cry of death, of not being able to stand it for one second more, of not wanting to live, of not wanting to have been born. He felt that his blind and feverish heart was going to be yanked from his chest, that there weren't lungs that could stand it, that he was becoming black and blue like a newborn. La Maga remained patient while Tito was crying. Little by little he was calming himself down. His head hurt but he was still alive. He looked at the green eyes of that beautiful woman, assuredly beautiful.

"What can I do?"

"Change your clothes and we'll talk," she commented serenely, as if nothing had happened.

Tito even felt a little ashamed, he was beaten. He got up to get ready and a last cry grabbed him in the sternum. Short, the last one. At least he had let off some steam. He went into the bathroom with his clothes and he changed slowly, like leaving a sanatorium, as if not wanting to risk this fragile recuperation with each movement. He returned to the bedroom where la Maga was looking at herself in the glass, fixing her hair. She seemed painfully vain to him. She perceived him, and through the mirror she fired out a smile only she knew how to give. Tito was too tired to have continued resisting. He found her marvelous, resplendent, he let himself be bewitched and he returned her smile. Let whatever happen, happen, let others write his destiny, now he wasn't offering any resistance.

"Sit down," la Maga said again. They were in the living room and a cassette by Thelonius Monk was playing which had accompanied him on some seduction of Mina, or with Francisca, or when he invited Barbara out of frustration. She had served a couple of glasses from a newly opened bottle of Chivas Regal and his was in front of him like the most enticing commercial, like for the most strived after position: the golden glass of expensive whisky and the admirable car. Starting the day with a drink: It was almost a joke.

155

"No, it's not a joke," answered the painfully telepathic Maga. "I want to speak to you seriously. You should know at last what you're really involved in and what the truth really is. They've deceived you, Tito, they want you to collaborate with your worst enemies."

"What?"

"Calm down, have a drink and I'll explain it to you. I really appreciate you and it will be good for you if you listen to me while you're very relaxed. Do you know who your father really is? Do you know who he really wants you to work for?"

I don't know anything about anything, thought Tito. La Maga confirmed that this was true. In a light scanning inside his head, she perceived Tito Livio's absolute innocence, incapable of noticing if he was committing a crime or begetting a son, incapable of distinguishing the moon from the sun, night from day. La Maga smiled.

"I'm going to tell you, Tito. Listen carefully."

26

Listen to me carefully, my Tito

"*So, you need to know, Tito that there was an ancient time in which they had the power and kept us enthralled with the idea of a superior order and they convinced us that we were all one, but we weren't.*

"*They hid science, knowledge, and hope from us. They were the masters of time and of space and of space-time, and there were some who found out that something was being taken away from them, that such a union was illusory, that there was nothing more than a dream in our heads and that death was sleeping in the breasts of women, in the growth of fingernails, in the falling out of hair, that innocence was the disguise of tragedy.*

"*Therefore, anxious, the ancestors of genius and light stole the fire from the secret and revealed the masquerade, one life, one body. All the rest were stories, deceptions and tricks for children.*

"*That unleashed the struggle, caused the expulsion. They will tell you that they did it with tears in their eyes, that they didn't want to do it, that death was a necessity unleashed by the desire of others. It's not true. It was the scream of a child discovering the nakedness of the regime. If we rose up, it was to free them, in order to bring life to life, in order to go beyond death.*

157

MARCO ANTONIO DE LA PARRA

"We tried everything: reincarnation, gene alteration, cloning, spiritualism. We enriched life, we prohibited the words death, passing away, destruction, pessimism. We fought for many years but they are still in effect. They're strong, they're certainly strong, my Tito. They plot traps with words: faith, hope, the good news of the resurrection. They promise us a celestial body beyond this body, a kingdom which won't be of this world. They assure us of the necessity of dying and dying in peace. Can you die in peace? Can there ever be any death in peace? No, it's always a scandal, it's always the greatest infamy on earth.

"They make life absurd, they make hope intolerable. We want to save ourselves, bring the kingdom here, abolish what is invalid, give everyone the structure of angels, the pure life, the true benefit of what it is to be omnipotent. We invite you to the day when all need will be abolished, where liberty will not even be needed because being will be everything and having obligation will disappear from the face of the earth, beyond body and soul, beyond good and evil, bodies with spiritual attributes. We will imitate God, we will be like Him. Having all information will be our power, knowing everything, controlling everything.

"God cannot prevent us from achieving universal memory some day, the grand memory that He believes to surpass forever. No. We are accumulating and accumulating until there are no secrets nor chosen ones who possess them. We will have everything in our minds and therefore in our hands. There will be insatiable appetites, infinite pleasures, we will go beyond time. There will be no limit to our dreams. Information is our strength, intelligence our weapon, the body our room where life will become life.

"Tito, there are many things with which I could enlighten you, many words, the visions that would introduce you to the world of secret knowledge, but you're still not one of ours, you've still got one foot on earth and one in this myth of heaven.

"Look at yourself, look at your ingenuity, your presence of mind. Couldn't you agree to all these powers? Don't you deserve to accede to invisibility, immortality, magic? Wouldn't you perhaps deserve to dissolve the limits of matter and morals without losing all the potent sensuality of your body?

"You're involved in a struggle for information and power, you're involved in the very center of the war and any movement involves you more and more. You'll have to decide whether to come over to the superiors or let yourself be carried away by the despicable ones who sooner or later will be exterminated.

THE SECRET HOLY WAR OF SANTIAGO DE CHILE

"I really appreciate you. I've known many men and many have believed they possessed me. I would give my all to you, Tito, I would love you like no one has ever loved if I knew that you are going to be one of ours. Next to me you would know all the recesses of my skin, the sound of my breath, the fire of my embrace, the peace of shared silence. I would do everything for you, my dear Tito, if you would just come over to our side and collaborate with man, with the free world, with the earth which unaware and innocently believes that it controls destiny and history in its ideologies. Don't the leaders, the politicians, and the anarchists with their infamous humanities and their infantile proposals talking about good and evil make you laugh? Evil doesn't exist! Good is a convention! Everything is knowledge or ignorance. That's all the power, all the magic and He, that god who makes your head rust, holds on to it.

"Your father was ours, and among the best. He joined up with us and here he drank the most pure and transparent honey, but something made him go mad in his damned slave brain, in his wretched so-called body. Your father was of no use as a magician, I'm asking you to forgive me if I offend you. He was weak, enchanting but disloyal. He promised us faithfulness, perseverance, permanence, even chastity and service. He swore to abstain from any other guidance, to be one of ours. He ate with me, from these hands. I ate from his. He was like you, a man full of stars in his mouth, the words that came from him were scanty but luminous. He used to listen to the point of even forming music from silence. He learned from everything, he retained whatever perception he received in his prodigious memory.

"He seduced us and we gave him the confidence to accede to the most guarded nuclei. He came down to our clubs, he sat at the tables, he became intoxicated with poetry, knowledge and looks. It's bitter, it's painful to remember him. The nostalgia and rage make my heart beat fast in my chest. When he knew the most about us, when he was aware of our most profound intentions, when he was put in charge of the definitive mission, he abandoned us.

"He went over to the enemy, he left everything and sank into his dirty back alleys, his fourth class establishments, his buddies with pompous phrases and foul-smelling outbursts of laughter. He became a religious zealot and sanctimonious, he was repentant, the imbecile, traitor, the man I curse a thousand times. There are not enough hate words sufficient to describe what he was.

"Just like with you, he abandoned us. We're all his widows, his castoffs,

we've all lost him. Tito Senior was the most immoral and unscrupulous enemy of all those we've ever had. He was someone who was in our ranks and then went over to theirs.

"We wanted to forgive him and he rejected us. He even killed, yes, yes, although you don't believe it, several of ours, of his own brothers-in-arms of other times. He became a scoundrel.

"In time we found out that he was the one who came to guard the final secret, the letter that we needed. Letter, yes, letter, the fourth letter of the Tetragrammaton: the missing letter in order to be able to pronounce the sacred word which makes life from clay, which allows man to make other men, which overcomes death, which makes us equal to the gods.

"He carried it, excuse me, he carries it. He must be walking around with it. Do you understand why they wanted you? Do you understand now? Tito Senior is perhaps giving this knowledge to Tito Junior and therefore they want to dupe you and possibly eliminate you, or make you crazy or leave you an idiot for the rest of your life. Because your father, and here comes the worst part, also hid from them. We don't know why. Maybe because of an order from the top in order to be safe even from our infiltrators, our double agents, or even more brilliant traitors. Perhaps it was to prevent someone from under-standing the truth and leaving the false spell of heretical liberation, and returning to us might locate him. I don't know, nobody knows anything about him, and no one even knows where and how he's keeping the secret text. In what formula? In what key?

"You can help us search, you more than anyone, Tito. While I've been speaking to you I'm discovering in your eyes, your beautiful child-like eyes, beautiful child, that you understand, that you're gaining knowledge of the hidden truth.

"You can be one of us. We wanted to avoid it by sending you to São Paulo, but you entered the battlefield and it's better that you're on our side. You will help man to free himself from the yoke of sterile hopes. You can be immortal.

"Come here, kiss me. I know that we'll be together forever. We will kiss for centuries, we will make love for eternities, our orgasms will intertwine each other for weeks. You, who have known the leftovers of love, will have in my arms the certainty of a superior existence.

"Come, my Tito, be mine, be ours, help us to find your father, and more than your father, to find the fourth letter of the Tetragrammaton. Say yes, tell me yes, kiss me, forget that loyalty to a father who never loved you, who went *out of his mind in order to forget everyone and betray everyone. He's ambitious, vile, perverse, a father who didn't ever think about his children and who left them at the mercy of death, discouragement, anguish.*

"Come, kiss me, I know you're dying to make love to me, kiss me, let me be yours which is the only thing I want and I can't stand the desire any more. Open your shirt, your mouth, your legs, your ears, close your eyes, give me your tongue, I want to drink it, give me your juices, I love you. Screw me, stick it to me, penetrate me until there's no part of you outside of me. Fill all my holes. Now, now, come here, now. Mine, Tito, mine, mine, mine."

27

A longtime desire of yours has been fulfilled, Tito

After love, made at full volume, scattered among Maga's blazing words, Tito opened his eyes and kept staring at the ceiling. He inspected the white paint, there was a hole in the smooth ceiling, the result of a lamp from a previous renter. Something was leaving the same kind of hole inside of him. He didn't understand it. Each time he would finish making love, in the ebb, after the ejaculation, in the silence after the whistle from the orgasmic referee, a sensation would come to him of celestial distance, of light years, of where am I that I don't see you? Financial doubts were assailing him, esoteric problems, his body was leaving him, it was becoming detached from him. He would end up looking at himself from the ceiling, from this same ceiling perhaps, the following night. But now it was different: equally strange, however, was that it wasn't unpleasant for him. A kind of prayer for the dead, a morphine high, a sensory mattress upon which to repose a confused mind, a spirit which would be afraid if it found out about itself, a stupor, the old songs of anguish.

La Maga was walking all around, stretching. She was humming

something from Julio Iglesias, turning the stomach of the sprawled out Tito Livio Triviño. But no, he answered himself, I'm relaxed now, better than ever, she explained everything to me, I shouldn't feel like that, I'm fine, I'm very much okay. Once again he looked at the badly disguised hole in the smooth ceiling. He sighed: No, I'm not fine. He sat up in the bed. La Maga was searching for some music. She asked him from the living room if he had something more modern, something in vogue, something romantic, something tropical, something she was familiar with. She finally found one by Caetano Veloso which she put on while she commented on the discotheques in São Paulo. Tito was familiar with them. He had brought back a kilo of cassettes with him when he filmed a diaper ad in a studio there, with animation. His kids had really liked it. That was before he was separated. So long ago? The years go by and other nostalgic images flooded his digression. Can we know what's happening to you, Tito? Haven't you gone to bed with a tremendous woman? Didn't she allow you to do positions and maneuvers that no one had ever put up with? Didn't she guess fantasies of yours which turned you red when you admitted them? Didn't she move around on top of you the way you like it, put herself under you the way you like it, move the whole time in the rhythm you like best, act passive the way you like, be wild the way you like, suck you the way you like, let herself be licked the way you like? Didn't she ask you for more, and here, and there, and like that please, don't stop now I'm dying, as if she were reciting Henry Miller sucking on your ear? Didn't it end up five times in a row leaving your skin burning and satisfied like I told you? Wasn't it one of those lays suitable for framing, for a pedestal, a diploma? Wasn't it unbelievable, one to tell your friends about, to make them eat their hearts out at school, in the office, the stadium, to stay hot your whole life by just remembering it?

Tito frowned. La Maga was in the bedroom dancing the samba and speaking Portuguese, smiling about life. He thought about a model for *Kem Piña.*

"Let's be happy like never before," said the woman, planting a closed-lipped kiss on him which was like a jab to the jaw. Tito fell down towards the bed and had to laugh. She took his head in his hands.

"This very afternoon we're going to São Paulo."

163

"This afternoon?"

"Uh huh."

"But the tickets, permission from MacPherson, I should go see the girls, I agreed to go to the movies with them, it's impossible."

"Tito! You're crazy! They're following you to kill you! It's your professional future! You have to do it! Call your daughters, explain to them that it's an emergency, promise them Brazilian dolls, whatever. Bring some jewelry back for your wife, the latest in clothes. Don't let her argue: we'll take care of MacPherson. And who do you think will worry about the tickets, the lodging, the money? Your beloved Maga. Do you know you upset me, Tito Livio?"

She kissed him again and began her speech again but Tito was disconnected, spaced, something was protecting him from her spell, something was keeping him safe, superficially distracted, it was permitting him once again to put the images in his brain in order. He was gratefully surprised at this new cell of distrust where one could take refuge. A few hours ago, when la Maga had finished her frightful explanation, anguish had exploded in his soul, he had thrown himself into her arms like a shipwrecked man jumping from a burning boat, and only there, in her arms, her caresses, with her mouth thrown forward like a perspiring skier descending in kisses as far as the tree of knowledge itself, the very same phallus fellatio in which he accepted everything, where in the waves of her lips he just managed to gain back a vague sense of infantile believability, of now-whatever-you-want, anything-you-say. But that sensation had evaporated. Now once again frowning inside, smiling outside. He agreed with la Maga who would once again clarify the situation, his danger of death, the treachery of his father, the need for the trip, his future, the secret balance of things, the urgent need to get out of the capital, the noble and just cause of intelligence, reason, and man's progress. Yes, he would be ours. Isn't that right, Tito?

All of a sudden he stood staring at her.

"What's the matter?"

"With me, nothing."

"You're spaced out, Tito."

"What?"

"You're full of doubts. You don't even believe me. Poor you, you

164

feel I'm butting into your life, that I'm giving you too many instructions. Although in a certain sense it's true."

Tito shook. This woman was walking inside his brain, she was reading his mind.

"Sometimes I've treated you like a child and maybe that wounds your male pride. And the fact is I like you. All the pain you're suffering really affects me. When you love a man you can't avoid perceiving his weaknesses and wanting to alleviate his pain. Now it's something personal for me. Do you understand?"

He felt that he was beginning to believe her again. Her hands on your waist, in her embrace. But why is her smoothness bothering you, Tito? Why does it upset you to let yourself go, give in. Come on, Tito! Now we all know how inconsequential you are. Or maybe you feel she's bad, dangerous, a poisoner offering you the forbidden fruit?

"Or do you feel I'm bad, Tito?"

Tito hugged her.

"I don't know what's wrong with me. You've told me the truth . . . You've saved me."

La Maga caressed him at slow speed, a motherly cadence, like a soft breeze at the beginning of summer, warm.

"Let's get dressed and let's go to lunch, what do you say? And afterwards we'll get ready for the trip, okay?"

"Okay," smiled Tito when he listened to her. He was stuck on that *okay*, an old saying of his father's who was accustomed to put yankee-isms in his speech. He remembered him screaming in the Santa Laura stadium: *don't overdo it!*, to the left wing of the Chilean team, tempted with the haggling in the corner of the grounds.

But where had la Maga gotten this *okay*? Was she also chameleon-like?

"Okay," said Tito, separating himself, "but I have to take a shower."

"You first. I'm going to pack your suitcase."

Caetano Veloso was making his guitar dance from the speakers in the living room.

If anyone had seen them they would have seemed like a pair of lovers in a mutual and indelible agreement, a lifetime project, in that full instant in which one prepares a honeymoon and the fire is postponed for better and more prolonged causes than a happy coupling.

Tito was looking as bright as can be, if not radiant. We could even go as far as to say he was relaxed, comfortable for the first time in a long time in his skin, in his bones, nodding his head slowly. But some happy child was betraying him, some subdued child who finally accepts this mother who's so good, so understanding, who swears to you that they'll never hit you again, they're never going to beat the hell out of you again, they're going to leave you alone, that nobody but nobody is ever going to separate them again. A mother who clearly shows the child the risky areas, a child who respects and understands that if he behaves well he'll know paradise and that hell is all those things which mother doesn't like. Underneath his peaceful face, behind his resplendent smile and his look, trapped in la Maga's green eyes, fear was still there. The same fear that in the last few days had been rising to the surface with everything, ceasing to be this deaf noise over the city, crisscrossed by helicopters, a rattling of weapons far away, fleeting, a surge of electricity, a stampede that I would say, can be, perhaps is, something like a bomb.

And so our hero crossed the bedroom toward the bathroom. In that way he contemplated la Maga's body which seemed magnificent, splendid again. There was a marvelous absence of tan lines from a bathing suit in a continuously and totally bronzed body. That thing which made him sick about Mina, about Anita María herself. Pretty, as if visibly dressed, as if they had painted the nipples, the pubic area, the navel. He preferred them pale all around, without breaks. La Maga, no. She was entirely bronzed, with the splendid skin of a liberated Brazilian, from a French beach with naked bodies stretched out on the sand in a perpetual chain. He imagined her skiing in a spa, naked, without finding it strange that she was capable of doing it.

He closed the door to the bathroom while the smile remained on his face. He was looking down on his slight erection. He looked at himself in the mirror and insisted on smiling, but it didn't last very long. To his left, standing in the bathtub, he made out an unmistakable shape: a man.

With one swipe of his hand he pulled back the shower curtain. Anger that gives way to fear.

Freud Romero in person. He recognized him immediately, the face of an old gray-haired drunk, his scraggly hair, the short beard over his half-toothless chin. His mischievous blue eyes dancing at him behind his glasses. The old guy had his finger to his lips, and with his free hand he saluted him in Indian style: *How!*

Tito was going to speak but Freud Romero put his hand over his mouth, staring at the bolt on the door.

"What are you doing here?" whispered Tito without knowing why he was lowering his voice.

"I came looking for you. I want you to come with me."

"Son of a whore, I'm getting to be real popular. Listen to me, you're going to leave right now, the same way you came in. Do you mind telling me how you got in here? Maybe you're an old pervert who gets off going around listening to couples? Maybe you were spying on us?"

"Let's not argue about that now. It might be, and it might not be. The important thing is for you to come with us."

"What for?"

"Do you want me to tell you now, here?"

"Tell me whatever you want because I know the truth very well. I don't know what faction you're from, but I'm getting out of the country and afterwards I now know for sure what I'm going to do."

Freud ran a hand over his face and then rubbed off his fingers on his old raincoat.

"I'm going to São Paulo, today."

"I think it's better if you come with us but you're not going to believe me. Or, one part of you might believe me and the other, no."

"Why would I believe you?"

"Because we found your father."

"You found him? Where?"

"I, and Marx Martínez who's down there below waiting for us in a green Renoleta. We found him."

"I've had it up to here with my Old Man. Besides, now I know who he really was: a traitor. As far as I'm concerned it's better if you don't even mention him."

Tito stretched out his hand, groping for the doorhandle.

"Well, a longtime desire of yours has been fulfilled, Tito," interrupted the old man.

"What do you mean?"

There was a theatrical pause by Freud. Tito stopped.

167

"That he's dead."

"Dead?"

Cold is the word they use to describe what happens to people when they receive news of this depth. Cold, a sensation of emptiness in the stomach, a trembling in the legs like when they're going to faint. All this came down on Tito, that and more.

"You'd better come with us."

"How could it happen? Was he sick?"

Freud Romero's eyes grew large, like in a zoom lens.

"They killed him, Tito."

The cold again.

"I understand how you feel. A deep guilt must be coming over you and it's natural. While you were making love with such a woman, your father was dying, murdered. Too much satisfaction for old repressed desires."

"Do the cops know? Investigations?"

"You know they're not going to get involved in this."

"What do you mean?"

"If everything is as clear to you as you say, then you should under-stand it."

Tito held back the knot in his throat.

"I suppose that I'll have to go with you."

Knocks on the door: tap tap. What are you doing in there, my love? A cliché just like that, but then it's nothing more than that. Tito: I'm talking to myself, hee hee. Like that, too. Freud with his finger to his lips: then the whisper.

"We'll wait for you below."

"Where?"

A new signal to be quiet.

"Don't use your car, walk, we're two blocks further up. Take all the time you need."

He watched him go out through the window. He couldn't under-stand how he could have opened it, nor how that old man with the look of a beggar was able to climb with such agility. He latched the window and got into the shower. Under the water he tried to think up some strategy but his thoughts were in disarray because of the pain that was squeezing his chest, making his mouth dry, compressing his calves. He was half soaped up when a crying fit started to invade him. But when he thought he should still deceive la Maga he shivered. The pain was replaced by apprehension: la Maga was going to find him out. Who had killed his father? But he had things so figured out. Why not simply ask la Maga herself? And if Freud Romero were the real fraud?

The idea that this was only a lie designed to ambush him calmed him down enough so he could finish taking a shower, and he even thought about telling everyone and everything to go to hell. Now it was Gal Costa who was singing in the living room. Yes, he said to himself, it's a trap, and he left the bathroom.

But a very distinct idea, as if the shaken and ailing son Tito had thought it through before, escaped from his mouth.

"You know, Maga? I'm going to go see the kids. I'd like to speak to them in person, okay?"

La Maga smiled. They agreed to meet each other later on in a French restaurant: the *Arlequin, par example. N'est pas mal, non?* La Maga, immaculate, planted a finger on his forehead. Tito was fresh as a daisy. In front of her, in plain view and calmly, he put away the Walter PPK in his underarm holster.

"With the story you've told me I prefer to walk around calmly."

"You're not going to have problems with me, but if you feel better."

"Ciao."

There was a new exchange of kisses. A revived Tito went out to the corridor and descended the stairs towards the parking lot. When he was standing up next to his car he noticed a mental block. The mental block had impeded the telepathic penetration of la Maga. She had not seen the news of his father's presumed death nor the appearance of Freud Romero in the bathtub. He got frightened again: and if it were true? He didn't even dare put the key in the lock. Stories about bombs, crimes, terrorists. Autos that exploded when contact was made. He shook his head. The scission was confusing him. What did he want to do exactly? Go to where Freud was, go to where the girls were? Why not walk? Tito began to be happy about his double consciousness. Without knowing where he was going he knew where he was going. He walked towards the south. Moreover, it should be said that the girls' house was in the opposite direction.

In the Renoleta, Freud Romero was waiting for him with another guy with a curly beard and a round nose like a ball: Marx Martínez. Nice to see you, nice to see you.

What am I doing here? What am I doing here?

He looked towards the street in fear.

"I knew you were going to come," said Freud Romero.

28

In an old building

Marx stopped the car on a signal from Freud Romero. Tito recognized the Estación area, the movement of the buses towards the coast, the loaded trucks, the minivan taxis looking in desperation for some patient clients who would put up with suggestions to go see the wonders of the International Fair in Cerrillos Park, to look over the prodigious advances in technology that they will never be able to reach even with fourth class imitations, returning to their condition of irritated, greedy, voracious, envious beings. He himself had written brochures with splendid and glittering sentences in order to justify the familiar walk among tractors, the stands of Dutch cheeses, the retractable colored pencils brought directly from Germany, the Austrian beer, food and bottles and then broken in a run-down hovel, watching *Sábados Gigantes*, leafing through the book of sports predictions to see if this week the miracle is fulfilled and it listens to our cry and we get what I told you.

Marx and Freud remained quiet; Tito didn't feel like doing anything. Waves of panic were coming over him which were almost

171

enough to make him get out and start running, or begin to scream, or think about anything else but remembering about his father. Winking at the thought during the whole trip, avoiding the memory, the well-known skill of amnesia which opens up and leads to its result of old searing pain, as if new, sharp, burning.

"They're not coming," said Marx Martínez suddenly.

"No?"

"No."

"They must be around here."

"I don't think they come out at night," disagreed the driver.

"Shall we go?"

"Let's go."

Freud Romero let go of Tito. Marx opened the door for him. They lined up, one on each side. The pair of old decrepit men were surprising him with their studied behavior. Their fingers felt like pincers on his forearms, protecting but firm. These guys know what they're doing, my friend, you're in good hands. Expert, at least. But are the experts to be trusted?

"Don't look at anyone, as if you lived here," whispered Martínez.

There was a blind alley which he swore he had never seen before. There were some wooden buildings, survivors of any number of earthquakes and fires, of the type that house deadly boarders, unusual suicides, pairs of lovers in the agony of love and misery. Marx stayed next to the small stairway, took out some dark glasses from his pocket and a small metal cup where he dropped a jingling coin.

"You go up with him, Sigmund."

A Siego sign was at the level of his chest. Tito saw him crouch down and bend his back. He knew what he was doing, sure. The push from the other old guy submerged him in the darkness of the corridor.

"Be careful."

They began to climb the stairs. With each creak Romero made them stop and listen.

"If you've got a weapon, use it, Tito," he said in his ear.

Tito obeyed. His armed image, rather than calming him, over-whelmed his adrenaline reserves of panic. They arrived at a small resting spot on the stairway and Freud had to push him softly against the wall. He was petrified. The old guy stationed himself in front of him and looked at him harshly. With a gesture he indicated that he should imitate him. They went sliding little by little against the wall. If Tito had known anything about pistols he would have worried more. The other guy was carrying a real Magnum, one of those that can blow a guy's head apart with one shot. He found it to be large but he shrugged his shoulders. He was saturated with fear, now everything was making him feel the same. A new gesture by Romero paralyzed him. The old guy approached a door stealthily and pushed on it. Then he gave an indication that he should stay where he was. A stronger push opened the panel wide open. The fading light from some window crossed the room and illuminated the worn floor in the corridor. He saw dust particles in the air and breathed the acid smell of a badly kept bathroom. It gave him a scare: the smell of a decomposing body? He gripped the butt of his Walter PPK, the one he had never used, his fetish in order to feel impressive, to frighten thieves, to go around telling stories to the *minas*, to the *mina* named Mina, to whomever. His preoccupation with showing it off used to annoy Anita María. What for? Maybe you're getting mixed up with that type of people? Or is it your macho Latino insecurity? That was what she used to say to him in the last months before the separation.

Freud returned from the room and motioned with his hand.

He was next to him in two steps.

"Come on, there's no one here."

The old guy let out a whistle aimed down below. After a minute or so he heard a little bolero that the sentry Marx Martínez was singing slowly and like a drunk. Everything was set.

"Come in," Freud said very seriously.

Tito, as you can all well imagine, would have preferred to go back, he would have gone down the steps three at a time, he would have rolled down, he would have broken his teeth if that were necessary, anything at all. But it was too late. Let it be whatever God wants, or the Devil, you know how these things are, Tito my friend.

Come in, open the door, Don Tito Livio Triviño, and look. Look at the half-open window in the station building in front, so much like the Eiffel Tower, such an historic monument, the gargoyle at the end with the open mouth illuminated by that spring sun that's just coming out. Look at the yellowed wallpaper mixed with patches of old newspapers

173

where you can find photographs of Vicentini, Tani Loayza, crazy Rendic, the old glories of the national sport, the face of General Ibañez, Gloria Leguisos, Natacha Méndez, look at the bed all torn apart, once again the mattress slashed with knives, look and feel how your chest is beginning to hurt, your joints, your insides, look and feel how you want to stop looking, look at the hand, the human hand, the hand you know, beloved, badly forgotten, leaning over pale next to the old dresser with open drawers turned upside down, look at the same scene as the other boardinghouse repeating itself, but now infinitely your father's presence, the body of your father, the possible face which approaches.

"Get closer, look at him," Freud says to him.

And Tito moves slightly, just a centimeter so his father's head comes into focus, the same as yesterday, from the other day, the same one he dreamed, remembered, smelled from far away. As a child he looked at him on his pillow in his conjugal bed sleeping off the late night in the morning through the opening which the neglected door leaves, badly closed, his mother's stupidity which permitted this child to stare at his father's head, with more hair but equally disheveled, with wrinkled pajamas, maybe the same color, the same pink and white striped flannel, flannel frayed through use. My God, why have you abandoned me, why, Father? Why is your face against the floor, your nose smashed, your hand extended forward, the other one next to your body with the palm upwards, and a coagulated blood stain on your back, a brownish red definitely staining the pajamas, that shell, that carcass of your dead father face down in a hovel in the Estación Central area where you never thought he would be, where no one could have found him except them, them, whoever it was that shot him, one shot, one blast right in his back. Could he have been going to sneeze, getting out of bed to blow his nose when he received the blast? What was his last unfinished movement? Who knows, only God, or the Devil, what do I know at this stage? It's fine like that, Tito, that you're letting your feelings surface, it's good that you're slowly getting on your knees, it's okay that you're stretching out your hand to touch him, and when you touch his pajamas, his fingers, those white fingernails, it's breaking your heart and your face is getting long, you're grimacing and sighing,

174

yes it's okay, Tito, cry, it will do you good, it's the only thing you can do now. And for a long time.

Sigmund stared at him bent over in his struggle. Every so often he would look out towards the corridor or listen outside waiting for a danger signal. When Tito got up he instructed him to wait and took out a pocketknife from his pocket. A switchblade: the blade shone slightly before plunging into the cadaver's back.

"What are you doing?" exclaimed Tito Livio furiously.

"You stay quiet," Freud's pistol stopped him threateningly. "This has to be done. We haven't got much time and I imagine that you'll want to know who killed him."

Tito's pain coagulated in his throat. He nodded, turning his head the other way. A glimmer was coming up from the wound.

"It must have been in the early morning, they must have taken him by surprise."

"But there's a curfew!"

"Don't be naive, Tito, you still believe in Santa Claus. Look . . ."

He was holding a silver bullet between his fingers. Tito remembered the Lone Ranger for an instant. The idea was so ridiculous that it took away from the sadness of his loss.

"I think it was a Falcon," pronounced Freud.

"A what?"

"A Falcon. They must be working for them: they're traitors and impulsive. In other words, they don't define the limits of good and evil very well, their morals float as well as a paper boat on a lake."

He remembered the scene in the sewer.

"And who are you?"

"They call me Freud Romero. I don't belong to any faction, I'm me and I like it that way."

Tito took advantage of the fact that Sigmund was looking at the bullet to aim at him with the Walter.

"What in hell are you doing with that move?"

"Don't be ridiculous, Tito. Your bullets aren't going to be able to do anything. You'd have to have one of these."

"What are you saying?"

"Your father was like me, one of ours, those who aren't allied with anyone, of unknown affiliation. Like those you met in the nocturnal library, those who are separate, the ones on the fringe. Sometimes we work with some of them, or others, but not because of moral problems, nor for money. We have much stricter and unrewarding ethics: those of truth."

"I'd rather you didn't go on, I'm tired of speeches, the only thing I want to know is who killed my father."

"Me too, Tito, and it will be better if we get out of here, unless you want to find it out in an unpleasant manner."

Tito lowered the barrel of his weapon.

"Running into them . . ." concluded Freud. "And getting a dozen of these . . ." He shook the silver projectile. "In *your* bones."

They went down the stairs on tiptoe, rapidly but carefully, and arrived at the first floor. Before going down, Tito looked at his father's body out of the corner of his eye. How do you say goodbye to a dead person?

"Don't go back up," said Marx, who noticed him hesitating in the doorway. He had disguised himself in the meantime as a vendor selling paper pinwheels.

"There's nothing to look for, they already carried away everything, they didn't find anything in the other boardinghouse either."

"Looking for what?" Our protagonist was getting irritated.

"To the car, we'll talk somewhere else."

Tito let himself be taken. At times he was sobbing, at times he was furious. More and more shaken, more crushed.

"Where are we going?" he asked upon closing Marx Martínez's door, always moving fast, flying.

"First of all to a phone so you can call your little friend and your daughters, afterwards to someplace where we can talk and eat."

"But I've got to go to São Paulo."

"But nothing, Tito, you're already very involved in this matter. The next one could be you. The ones who are looking for you and didn't find you, they know you might have it. Do you understand?"

"I don't have anything."

"They don't know that, Tito. Until they leave you like your father they're not going to find out."

Tito sank his head in his hands. "Dad," he stammered.

Freud patted him on the back.

"Cry, Tito, it's okay to cry. Just cry."

29

Things become complicated

They're waiting for him outside the store where he found a phone. It was a pharmacy and, in the image of an analgesic reflected in a mirror, he saw them walking along the sidewalk, pretending to be street vendors or drunks discussing politics or preachers announcing the end of the world. They kept changing roles in a studied sequence.

He spoke with Anita María and it was difficult to hide his sorrow. When he heard her voice on the phone he thought about telling her, she knew his father, she even loved him and he loved her also. Tito Senior had been the only one to take the trouble when he found out about the separation. With her he could cry and be consoled. But it was impossible, he was looking at Marx and Freud outside the pharmacy, understanding that he had to be cautious. Don't delay, Tito, you don't have time. You put up with your ex-wife's anger, you tolerate the guilt because of the kids, you put up with it, nothing more than tolerate. You listened to the recriminations from your ex-wife: What's the matter with you, Tito? You're stranger every day, the kids need you, you can't just think about yourself, nobody can count on you for the tiniest thing. He felt the lump in his throat so he hung up. Later on, sometime, he could explain it to them. But would they understand it? When his throat cleared enough to swallow he called his apartment number. La Maga was impeccable, pristine in the air, beautiful but icy, it came out like the dubbing on television, well positioned, almost plastic. It even left an aftertaste of anger in his mouth. So you were the ones who did away with my father, sons of whores, you'll see, you'll see who you're dealing with. He felt that his rage was keeping his mind safe from the scrutinizing telepathy of la Maga, of the Witch, as Tito said when he looked at the silent, hanging telephone. All his words were reduced to absurdities faced with the body of his dead father. Witch, your whole legend is going down the fucking tubes. For whatever reason my father has been killed, there are no excuses that compare to the crime.

"There's nobody around," pronounced Marx Martínez when he returned from where they were. "Let's go to Torres."

They left the Renoleta parked on Dieciocho. Tito looked at the young people in civilian clothes with excessively short hair who were getting off a bus, all of them with dark glasses.

"Don't worry," whispered Romero. "They're from another war which doesn't concern us."

They seated themselves. The window advertised crab, sirloin steaks and turkey stew. They drank their beers slowly, without speaking. Freud was studying Tito Livio with a stare.

"My father used to come here a lot," babbled Tito Livio, feeling his breathing becoming difficult again, and the image of his dead father weighing on his soul. "We used to come when I was a kid. It's changed, it was different, I don't know. I got my first taste of Barros Jarpa and Barros Luco here. We used to sit down next to the window, far away from the door, he used to say it was dangerous for kids, that there was a lot of traffic on Alameda. I didn't think it would hurt so much."

"The task of mourning is just beginning," smiled Freud Romero sweetly, raising his full glass to make a toast.

Tito made his glass clink sadly against the other.

Rather than crying, he felt like staying quiet, slowly drinking an infinite Pilsener, which would never end, nor ever make him drunk, nor ever satisfy him, for all eternity. He wanted to make that moment perpetual, contemplate the foam until its disappearance, not have anything in front of him except the smoothness of the beer passing through his throat.

"Those guys knew what they were doing." Marx Martínez's voice broke the pause, but it had an unpleasant aftertaste. "They're professionals. Trashing out the room so much is unusual."

"That depends," answered old Freud. "Maybe they don't know what they're looking for."

"Yes, they certainly didn't find it, everything was smashed up too much."

"And if it's a fake clue?"

"Romero, they don't need it. They know we're behind them and they know that having the . . . the . . ." He looked at Tito. "Wherever it may be that they find it . . . Our following them is not important to them now. We lost and that's that. They wouldn't have to leave false clues if they had it."

"Do they have the other three?"

"Shhhh."

"Come on, Martínez, he has to know about it. You understand, Tito? Don't you?"

"What?" said Tito, distracted.

Freud moved closer to him. He had lost his gentleness of a little while ago. Our protagonist caught something unusual in his eyes.

"I'm asking you if you understand. If maybe you know what they're looking for."

Tito put his depleted mental archive in order.

"I've heard something. Some stories about a word with four letters . . ."

"The Tetragrammaton."

"That they only need one more . . ."

"Exactly."

"If they have it, they'll have everything," added Marx Martínez.

"But to people like you that shouldn't be of concern. It's the death of God!"

Marx put his large hairy hand over his mouth.

179

"None of us wants His death. We need Him. Although it may be like an illusory image, idea, representation. It's part of human equilibrium. It's the last prevailing instinct."

"An illusion of an undeniable future," toasted Freud anew.

"Listen, I don't understand anything. I don't know anything about philosophy, nor metaphysics, nor psychoanalysis, nor political economy. My father has died and I want to be able to think this over in a quiet and isolated place."

His next act was to make a movement to get up but Marx's rough hands grabbed him by the lapels.

"Don't be an imbecile!" He sat him down again. "If you don't cooperate there will never be a peaceful place in this world where anyone can think about anything! It's a matter of life or death! That's enough emotionalism, Romero," he said to the other guy. "You have to understand that your father is barely a cog. That we're nothing. We're only accidents of history. A product of coincidences."

"Martínez, you know it's not so much that way."

"Listen, Romero, the real reason is that historical forces are in motion when the cycles are fulfilled."

"Just a moment: death is confronting this man with his own realizations and his own finiteness. The death of a father is a challenge to the most elemental identifications."

They wrestled each other in a brutal struggle of theoretical arguments. Tito didn't understand anything. Suddenly, losing patience, he hit the table with the palm of his hand.

"What do you want from me?" he screamed.

Marx and Freud looked at him.

"You must know what they're looking for," Freud Romero said to him.

"Maybe you have what they want," added Marx.

"What's that?"

"I don't know, something that might be useful to understand where, or with whom, or how one can obtain the fourth letter of the Tetragrammaton."

They stared at him.

Freud continued to talk, whispering, hypnotically.

"There's something that you might have taken or received or caught on to in the past few days. It's very probable that your father has handed something over to you or left something in your care, or pointed something out to you that might be useful to us. Something apparently innocent which is put in safekeeping in your hands. And, something which makes you safe, Tito, and so you wouldn't be the next cadaver."

Tito Livio felt his spine tremble, Freud Romero's beady eyes were burning him. He looked down. The photograph came to mind, he had it in his jacket, sure. He started to look for it.

"I think I've got something that could be it."

Marx moved forward in visible haste.

"Seriously?"

Tito continued to look. Suddenly he had it between his fingers.

"Here it is," he said. "Take it."

But neither Freud nor Marx managed to grab it.

A whizzing sound flew through the air like a silent and invisible report, and the body of Freud Romero fell face down on the table with a singular death rattle. A stream of blood came out of his mouth. Marx managed to take out his Magnum, but another whizzing sound opened up his hand with blood gushing out. A third shot burst out his right eye and he collapsed next to the table.

A man of medium height, with a penetrating look and a carefully trimmed beard was carrying a pistol with a smoking silencer.

"Close it up," he heard him order the waiters. Tito thought he had gone crazy, it was the unmistakable voice of Freud.

"You, Tito Livio, come with me through another exit," he was telling him.

"Who are you?"

"They killed your father, Tito, follow me before they come for you."

He stared absolutely amazed. The whirr of the metal curtain descending was accompanied by the gradual dimming of the lights. A couple of customers he had taken for lost drunks got up, armed, from a neighboring table and placed themselves on guard at the door that led to the street. The waiters were opening a secret exit behind a gigantic mirror, placing a Viennese chair there as a step.

"I just don't understand."

"Things are very complicated. I'll tell you outside."

"I'm not moving from here," said Tito in a stubborn rage. He grabbed his Walter PPK.

"Get your hands up and tell your bodyguards to throw down their weapons."

"Don't do this, Tito, you're holding us up."

Tito picked up the Magnum. Wielding two pistols he stood up. The place had the Persian blinds down and the neon light was making their faces appear blue.

"Drop your weapons."

Freud, or whoever he was, shrugged his shoulders. He clicked his tongue before speaking.

"Pay attention to him," he ordered his men.

The three of them threw down their pistols.

"Tito, you're making a mistake."

"Everyone tells me the same thing. Let's see if you convince me now. Because if you don't, I think I'm going to kill you. With silver bullets, lead, antimony, with whatever."

He heard a noise behind him. It was a waiter.

"You guys too," he pointed to the waiters. "Get over there in a line, with your hands on your heads, with your backs to the bar."

For a minute Tito watched how they obeyed him. He was beginning to waver, but he caught his breath making sure all their hands were on their heads.

"Can I explain to you?"

"Do it well if you want to live," said Tito. The line was from an old film, but whoever has had a Magnum in their hands, let them try not to imitate Clint Eastwood.

"You're not going to believe a word of what I say, but if you think a little bit, if you have any reasoning power left in you, you'll take my statements as the truth. My name is Freud Romero."

"Don't make me laugh. You just died. They've saved me from la Maga."

"They're her allies. Imposters. They found your father and they killed him. La Maga herself let them into his apartment. They were trying to confuse you at any cost. They know your weak points very well, and they knew it was better to fill you full of contradictions rather than convince you to go in one direction. They've never thought about sending you to São Paulo, aside from being a way to rid themselves of you in another city where your death would go by unnoticed. La Maga got you out of the boardinghouse because she knew that Sara had arranged to meet there with your father. They went there, eliminated Sara, took him to the hovel at Estación Central and arranged this whole plot."

"They killed Sara? How did you find that out about Sara?"

"Through Samuel."

Tito had to grip the Magnum tight again.

"He survived, they ignored him. He was a witness to the whole thing."

"You're lying to me. You're not Freud."

"Can I go up to one of the bodies?"

Tito had his doubts.

"Okay, but don't forget that I've got you covered."

Freud knelt down and grabbed the skin around the neck of the dead guy.

"Do you have a pocketknife?"

"How do you know that?"

"I don't know, I'm asking you. If you don't, hand me a knife from the bar."

"Wait," said Tito. He let go of the Walter and, without lowering the barrel of the Magnum, he threw him the remaining pocketknife. Freud opened it, and with the small blade he lifted up the skin without spilling a single drop of blood. Then, he pulled up a mask which was finely attached to the skin on the body. He dangled it next to his face: they were the same.

Tito felt that the pistols weighed an incredible amount. Freud came closer but Tito raised the weapons again as he swallowed the rebellious lump which was forming in his throat.

"I'm going to kill you! All of you! I can't stand any more! You kill my father and you do what you want with me! It doesn't matter now who wins and who loses!"

"It does matter, Tito," Freud spoke calmly. "It does matter. For your children . . . for your father's memory . . . even for Anita María."

There was a break in his soul. He let himself slide down into a chair. After a few seconds of hesitation he let the pistols fall. Freud didn't rush him, but sat down next to him. Nobody moved.

"It's not a good thing for us to be here for such a long time. We should leave. Here nobody's going to have any doubts about killing anyone, not us, not them. It's not the time for reflection or diplomacy. If we don't make the evidence about the fourth letter disappear we'll continue to be in danger."

"Make it disappear?"

"What do you think your father was doing? He was carrying the key, and one should eliminate the bearer if necessary."

"But I thought it was a letter?"

"Usually, yes. But not only a letter, but a person or a place or someone in connection with that letter. If they get the three letters, we must kill the fourth man and then everything will start over again. They'll choose four more people or places, another four letters and the situation will return to the beginning . . . to peace, to the millennium."

"The millennium?"

"They've waited a thousand years, dear Tito Livio. The word has remained secret and the place must be changed. The century will be filled with wars until it's decided if they obtain the power, or if justice is initiated again. It's eternal, it's the equilibrium of the times. Whether we like it or not. You and I can do nothing more than collaborate."

"It's absurd. But why have they left the letters within everyone's reach?"

"It wouldn't be fair, do you think?" He pointed to heaven. "He could have kept all the information, but that would not be very loyal, but realistic, and besides not very motivating. What man is searching for is the sacred word, the Tetragrammaton. To be like God."

"I thought it was to kill the father and go to bed with the mother."

"Well, that's the sacred word. To be God the Father oneself."

Tito became quiet. Freud's peaceful face made him remember the man from the night in the nightclub on Diez de Julio.

"I've followed you at Lili Salomé's suggestion, and I think we'll continue together. Come with me and we'll talk about that photograph."

"Which one?"

"The one that you were going to give to those imposters."

It was on the table, surrounded by bodies. The blood of who knows who, alias Romero, had not managed to stain it. He got up, grabbed it, and put it in the front pocket of his jacket.

"Did you kill them with silver bullets?"

"Yes, it sounds like it comes from a vampire novel but that's the way it is. Can we pick up our weapons?"

"Yes, sure."

Freud gave a signal.

"I'm afraid," said Tito.

"You'd be crazy if you weren't and you wouldn't deserve our confidence. We're all afraid here. If we weren't, we wouldn't be fighting for this cause."

"Where are we going?"

"Follow me. Have faith, Tito."

They walked towards the mirror.

30

On the other side of the mirror

W hen they were on the other side of the mirror Freud positioned himself a few steps in front of Tito Livio. The closing
of the secret door behind him made him tremble in fear. How many
doors are still left? How many would he need to cross so the fear in his
soul would disappear and he could feel the need for this risk? How
much was each threshold which was passed through changing him?
Something in him was changing, his beliefs were becoming shaky, his
faith was going up in flames, or was wavering like the flame of a candle
in a breeze.

What la Maga seemed to clarify was becoming much more confused. The shooting at the Torres sweetshop had relieved him somewhat of the memory of his father's death. The war was not leaving time
for pain. His panic was changing into courage and once again his
instinct for survival was riding high. He wouldn't give up his weapon
for anything from this point on.

"Wait a minute," whispered Freud to him as they were coming up to
a door which was poorly lit by weak bulbs placed along this winding

passageway. The old man's hand was bent back to gracefully open the panel which made the hinges squeak. A ray of light filtered through: outside there was daylight, the city and its stupid innocence in its naive march faced with assassinations which no one would find out about, face to face with a secret battle which would be ignored, about which maybe someone, someday, could write or tell in some drunken state, when nobody would be affected, when it wouldn't be of use, protected in the disapproval of alcohol or literature.

"No one," judged Freud and he opened the door completely. A patio filled with crates of mineral water and beer was waiting for them. Tito remembered the episode in Villa Alemana. Would there be a beautiful young woman with winged feet coming to save him? From far away one could hear the noise of what he calculated to be the kitchen in the Círculo Español restaurant.

"We'll go out here."

"You can eat well here," thought Triviño, and then he became gratefully surprised at the courageous attitude he was beginning to develop. A magnificent paella came to mind, some scallops *à la madrileña*, just look, an authentic Miguel Torres wine, from the ones brought in from the peninsula, from before they installed themselves in Curicó, in place of half-baked danger. Would that be the only alternative in the days to come? Scarcely a banquet over the remains?

They crossed through the rooms of the Círculo Español like two somewhat absentminded passers-by, like habitual customers, without paying the least bit of attention to their surroundings. No one could have perceived their condition as survivors from a pitched battle.

They stopped in front of Alameda. The midday traffic was efficiently polluting the air, making the view gray, irritating, making one's throat hoarse with each mouthful inhaled.

"Fake it," mumbled Freud Romero. "Make like you aren't looking for anyone. If they're around here, they've already found you. If not, it doesn't matter, what you do is absolutely immaterial."

"But . . ."

"Fake it, I'm telling you."

They remained silent, rocking on the sides of their shoes. Tito imitated the role of his guide.

"If they're following us, they must have located us by now, although

187

I don't think it's possible. They must have confided in your people, they didn't have any reason to believe that someone would protect you, Tito."

Freud Romero walked towards Dieciocho Street, with the same moderation, the same peacefulness, the caution which grants calmness. To go unnoticed feigning calm, the clear objective, the talked about walk. Only the nervous movements of Tito's eyes could have attracted any attention.

"They staged this whole thing, Tito, they know you. They've probably been studying you for some time. Someone at work, in your family, in your neighborhood. Some lover you had who could have been their agent. They've certainly got a file of data on you that's thicker than the telephone book. They knew you couldn't resist la Maga's good looks, but they also assumed that she would intimidate you and some kind of mistrust would flutter around inside you. Because of that, the second part in order to confuse you, to shake you up. They must have seen us talking in El Limbo."

"How did they find out?"

"Someone in the same cabaret, or in the library, who knows, there are so many nihilists, so many mercenaries running around, everyone works for everyone these days. Nothing is safe, nothing is certain. Because of this, things are like they are. They arranged the fake Freud and fake Marx and ambushed you. It's an old trick. They had found your father a couple of days ago, don't ask me how, but they must have interrogated him first, in order to get the facts about the fourth letter, that same photo perhaps. In some way your father arranged things and left the photo for you, maybe it's part of a chain of clues. He was a very smart guy, that's why they had to kill him."

"Did you know him?"

Freud didn't answer. He kept looking at a shop window of religious books. He went in and walked around among the cases. He leafed through a history of religions by Mircea Eliade. Tito imitated him submissively and gently.

"What are we doing here?" he asked him.

"Have you ever read the Bible, Triviño?"

His mother livening up lunches on the weekend with reading parables. Tito used to make jokes about that. Isaac and Jacob selling the primogeniture for a hamburger. Noah, drunk on the deck of the Ark. Joseph who joined the Communist Party. He became an expert in blasphemies, something fundamental in all advertising: a degraded religious feeling.

"No," he lied.

"Read it, it's good literature. Aren't you familiar with the Book of Job?"

Very vague rapid readings in sudden youthful repentance, closer to superstition than the most elemental simple faith.

"God and the Devil betting on the faith of a poor believer. His anger, his internal struggle and his reconversion after painful renunciation. It's really exciting. The prophets also. Have you read Jeremiah?"

"No," stammered Tito. His mother used to recite them in such a way that the boys preferred to turn a deaf ear, Gustavo would become upset, inundating the noodles with tears.

"I don't know how you're mixed up in this. Let's go," announced Freud.

"But why are we going in?"

They left with the stubborn silence of Romero. A few steps further on the old man continued his speech.

"The other Freud, the one from Vienna, wrote *The Future of an Illusion*, and when I read it I realized that I had written it badly, thirty years after. At this point I doubted all faith, I already thought that everything was a psychological necessity to find some sense to my famous precariousness. I was going to shoot myself when they contacted me from the Service."

"Which one?"

"What does it matter which one? I, like your father, got to know many flags."

"You met him there?"

"Let's say that we weren't only mercenaries for the Falcons, the Lizards, or the Dogs, have you heard about them? But rather, we were searchers for the truth. Go ahead and laugh, these days it seems romantic and out of date. I got out of it, he preferred to continue. I abandoned everything, I started an office at the end of Toesca, almost at Ejército Street, and I write a little there, I read less and I hope that something happens, anything. Something that's worth the trouble of making it happen. Let's say that I proved how useless human efforts are, that the truth has other criteria of reality and the category of illusion itself was illusory."

At this very moment they were arriving at Ejército. They turned towards the south. In the show window of an auto parts store Triviño could see himself reflected next to the old man. Teacher and disciple. Going where? Learning what? Becoming initiated in what secret knowledge? Left behind were the bodies of his father, Sara, and the laments of the unfortunate Samuel. He understood his suffering. Both relatives, orphans.

"Let's go to my office," said Freud.

"Excuse me, but . . . what type of office?"

"What?"

"What kind of office is it that you started?"

"Everything and nothing. Let's say trauma therapist, private detective, spiritual guide. Something like that. Invent a name for it if you want. You're an advertising agent, right? What I offer is privacy . . . and action. Eyes and ears and at times answers when there aren't better questions. The ones I don't have, I look for with the consultant. I don't charge much, enough to clothe myself and eat something. I don't eat much."

And you dress badly, thought Tito Livio. He couldn't imagine that supposed office.

"On my card I put 'Private' which is the only thing I have clear. The rest, I don't have a clue."

They saw a military bus pass by, filled to the brim with armed recruits.

"Did you see them?" continued Freud Romero. "Those are the protagonists of the public war, the one that lives below the apparent peace. Below the public war is the dirty war, the clandestine one, and below that hidden war is the secret holy war of Santiago de Chile, the one that you're witnessing, Triviño. Sometimes they get mixed up, you know? Some of ours have to join up with the others. They habitually confuse them. Power, lust and fame make them crazy. I like it too, in its time. I could have been a very important guy, you know?"

He turned his back and went into a rather ancient building, square, with four floors. Small iron grates boarded the windows in classic restraint. He began to climb the stairs.

"What was your job?" inquired Tito, sincerely interested.

"Me?" asked Romero. "I was . . . ha . . . I was almost a doctor."

"Almost?"

"Almost. I also became disillusioned. In those days I wanted to be omnipotent. Do you understand why I fell in with them at the beginning?"

Tito nodded. They were on the third floor landing. Freud stopped in front of one of the doors which displayed a plaque: *Sigmund Romero: Private.* The door opened after a difficult movement of the key in the lock.

"It isn't exactly a private place, is it?"

"What for? To believe that I can hide myself from my enemies? No, you never manage to flee from a dangerous creature. It's possible to flee from friendship, affection, from a loving wife and hide yourself, but not from death. I'm waiting for it here, peacefully, it will arrive when it's my turn."

"Maybe you aren't immortal?" smiled Tito characteristically.

"So-so. Partially, let's say. The fourth letter would be the only one which would give us immortality."

"Then it doesn't matter to you that they get it?"

"What for? In order to fall into the absurdity of an eternal life with a miserable body, limited, with a primitive and fragile mind? So that everything loses its meaning? The most similar thing to nothingness is everything, dear Señor Triviño. Our condition is destined for mortality, without it we would need another body, another style, other desires. Eternal life is precisely the death of all impulse, of all satisfaction, of all caprice, total satiation. It doesn't know movement, desire, uneasiness. In another state, perhaps beyond death, but nobody knows."

"No one?"

"In the sense that we understand knowledge, no one. In another plane of categories, yes: all those who have passed the threshold of death . . ."

"My father?"

"He knows it now."

191

Tito retreated.

"Don't be sad. Sit down, you'll feel better and let's take a look at that famous photograph."

He pointed to an antique sofa in the small room: an old leather armchair, a chess table where an unfinished game was waiting for the moves to follow.

"Do you play with Capablanca?" asked Tito.

"How did you find out?"

"I read it somewhere."

"You're not as foolish as one might believe. At times you seem like your father."

"Thanks."

"I'm going to look for something to drink," said Freud leaving the room.

"Before showing you the photo I want to ask you some questions, Señor Freud. I hope you won't mind."

At this, Freud returned with two glasses of Coca-Cola.

"I hope you don't drink alcohol."

"You disappoint me, you seemed just like a detective in a film noir."

"I do what I can. I'm pretty old to be going around looking for someone to imitate, do you understand me?"

The Coca-Cola seemed heaven-sent. It was what he needed, to be seated, apparently safe, with that old friend of his father's before him. It was like being with him, maybe that's why he was so calm.

"What were you going to ask me?"

"Oh, yeah. How did you find out about the trap, the ambush, as you called it?"

The old guy smirked.

"I've followed you, Tito, and I've followed your pursuers. I've been following you around ever since the library."

"Why? Love at first sight?"

You're the best, Tito. There's no stopping you.

"Don't joke around. Do you think this is really a detective novel?"

They caught you, Triviño.

"But why did you follow me? You haven't answered me."

"In a certain sense they had, let's say, assigned it to me. Suggested, if you prefer, and I decided to find out about it personally. I stared at

THE SECRET HOLY WAR OF SANTIAGO DE CHILE

you while Lili Salomé was dancing. You reminded me of your father. I loved him very much, you know? I was sure they were going to kill him, he knew it too. He spoke about you a lot."

"About me?"

Once again the pain rushed to his throat. Calm down, Tito.

"Yes, about you, and about your brother. Even about your ex-wife and your mother. But about you above all. You worried him."

"Worried?"

Your pride is writhing in pain. You feel that it's gone pretty well for you, what worry can you have? Maybe he hasn't seen your salary?

"He felt he was on the wrong track. He wanted to leave you something as an inheritance, something really important in which you could recognize yourself, so you would do what he could have done."

"I don't understand."

"That you could obtain peace by saving the fourth letter. I don't know, something like that occurs to me. He never left it very clear."

"You're telling me!" Tito said suspiciously.

"He only pointed out to me: that he does what he deems convenient, that he decides, that the world belonged to him for a few minutes. I told him this present didn't make much sense and he answered me: You never see the meaning of anything, you only believe in death and in sex and the world as a stage of this incessant struggle. It's a somewhat literary phrase, but we were fairly smashed when he said it to me. There's no one more literary than a drunk philosopher. Your father was a thinker, did you know?"

"A philosopher?"

"There are books of his in the library."

"Books?"

"Yes, some crazy theories on language and geometry, on words and identity, names and destiny, on the biology of incantations, an exhaustive argumentation on supposed neurophysiological functions of the sentence, of mantras, of the power of the verb up to . . ."

"To the Tetragrammaton . . ."

"Do you see that it's not at all stupid? Your father even wrote novels. Maybe you have one of those talents. Well, let's see the photo."

At this moment Tito began to hesitate. Did your shirt get heavy? Did you feel the weight of the mission handed over by your father? Did you have doubts about handing over, just like that, the only proof, the only foundation of your existence?

"And if you aren't who you say you are?" he asked.

"If you don't believe me, don't show it to me."

"It's just that . . . you could be from any faction."

"That's true, as a matter of fact I was. In a certain way I still am."

"What?"

"I'm doing this to complete a cycle, in order to help you, so that in the end you can decide what you're doing with the proof that we might discover. I'm outside all this. I'm doing it as . . . let's say . . . as a sentimental commitment."

"To my father?"

"And to Lili Salomé."

A questioning look. Tito, you seem like a child. Once again the confusion is softening you up.

"I would recommend to you that we hold on to the photo. If I belonged to their faction, I'd eliminate you and I'd have it. I don't need anything else. When they find out you have it, you're a dead man. At the least, they would want to torture you to look for some information that could shed some light on the possible meaning of the picture. But outside of that, they couldn't care less about you."

Freud drank the last swallow from his glass. Tito was pale.

"It looks like you're going to need something stronger. Should I get you a glass of pisco?"

"No, thanks. I'd rather we took a look at the photo."

He took it out and put it on a table in the center of the room, covered by an old Sunday supplement which Freud threw to one side. He opened the blinds. The light made stripes on the wall.

"What do you think?" asked Tito after a few minutes of studying the photo.

Freud lifted his head up to speak but at that very moment the doorbell rang. The old man brought his hand up to his lips indicating silence, and then he nervously pointed out a door.

"Hide," he said to him in a whisper.

Tito obeyed and closed himself into an old empty armoire. A strong smell of humidity trapped him. He listened as Freud arranged things without leaving any clues. In the quickness of his flight he had not forgotten the photo. He hid it again in his jacket, while in his other hand he tightly gripped the Magnum of the supposed Marx alias Martínez. He had learned the lesson: at times you have to use silver bullets. He was growing to resemble his father.

The doorbell rang again.

31

Señorita Wonderly

Hidden in the armoire, Tito was not only submerged in the darkness of the closet, but also in that of the events. The pistol was burning his hand. This is a war, he said to himself, trying to diminish the pain for his fallen father. He managed to remember, among many other memory flashes, the day in Villa Alemana trying to get some benefit from the Miracle of Peñablanca. He was surprised to see himself in the past so proud, such a master of the world, so contemptuous. And now, in the dark, he was at the mercy of whomever came in.

"Come in." He heard Freud's voice. Someone was sitting down, they were moving some chairs, the sound of their steps was muffled in the rugs, in spite of them being worn out. He thought they could be a woman's high heels.

"Thank you," said a feminine voice. It was a young woman, mature but young. A beautiful voice, but why are you getting upset, Tito?

The noise of Freud's body sitting back in his chair.

"Well. How can I help you, Señorita?"

"Wonderly," she said with a perfect accent.

The name left Tito gagging. Where had he heard it before? Think back, quick. Or, maybe you read it? Come on, think and calm yourself down. The silence was worrying you more, her breathing, the squeaking from Freud's chair.

"Could you? I thought . . . That is to say . . ."

Her voice was revealing a certain anxiety, she was gulping rather hurriedly.

Tito continued to think that there was something strange going on there. He imagined Freud smiling and nodding his head as if he understood everything she was telling him precisely, as if it weren't a serious matter at all. His confinement was making him feel his own physiology like a torrent, a textile machine at full speed, a motor with the exhaust pipe loose.

"Why don't you tell me everything from the beginning, and then we'll know what needs to be done? Recall the past as much as you can," said old Romero with all the calm in the world.

"Well . . . it was in New York."

New York? Did you hear, Tito? What does New York have to do with all this?

The story the woman told was very complicated. Tito tried to follow it, keeping his breathing in check so as not to miss a single detail. She was saying she wanted to locate a lost sister, but after that she was talking about a guy, a foreigner. At times she was unintelligible. Señorita Wonderly, or whatever her name was, was wrapping everything with moans, sighs, and sobs, fidgeting with her purse and grabbing at her skirt.

Something about all this seemed profoundly artificial to Tito, but he didn't dare to move.

"I understand," interrupted Freud suddenly. "You want us to find your sister, take her away from him and bring her back home, right?"

There was a pause, short but opportune. Tito gripped the Magnum, wet because of his sweat. The confinement was asphyxiating, the weak wood of the door was becoming thinner.

"No," said Señorita Wonderly unexpectedly. Her voice had changed, not only the tone. Tito's heart accelerated to full speed.

"But . . . !" Freud's voice let a shadow of fear and surprise escape.

197

"Don't move," said the woman. "And tell me where he is."

"Who? Where who is?"

"I don't care who. What I do care about is you-know-what. Did you kill him? Did he manage to hand over the clue to you?"

Now that's sweating, Tito, you're soaked from head to toe, the only thing missing is for you to piss your pants from fear. Did you recognize the voice, Tito? She's aiming at him with something. Do you realize?

He heard how the old man was getting up and the woman was following him. Now her heels were tapping on the parquet. They had probably gone next to the wall, in front of the armoire. If I open it up they'll be at point blank range, I'll have a split second to shoot. He raised the gun, he lowered it, he cursed his cowardice. Weak, made to be vain, spoiled, a paper doll, a cardboard cut-out, a stuffed animal.

"This pistol is loaded with you-know-what, Romerito, so you'd better tell me where he is."

"If you shoot it will be a relief, Señorita . . ."

"My name doesn't matter. You played dirty with us. Who are you working for?"

"For nobody."

"We all work for somebody. Don't play independent. Nobody's independent. You've got the clue, right? Maybe you want to get a good price for it? Fine, let's talk business. How much do you want?"

"Now I know who you are."

You too, Tito. You don't dare think about it, you didn't know this side of her. She looked so pretty in bed, didn't she?

"Give me an answer to the question, you old bastard."

Her voice sounded caustic, terrible. That woman was a dangerous beast. Tito heard her lifelong voice coming through, in his very own ear, as if barely this very same morning he had said goodbye to her.

"You're the famous Maga, as they call you now," said Freud.

Steady, Tito. Your legs are still there. Don't let go of the pistol. La Maga! He hadn't managed to recover when he heard a woman scream, and a gunshot with a silencer. He didn't recognized it for a second until he remembered the shooting in Torres. He became terrified, imagining another carnage of the same type right there outside, but the screeching continued. Freud and la Maga were beside themselves. What are you waiting for, Tito?

With just one kick to the door he was facing them. Freud was in back of his desk and she, at this moment, was holding on to her gun in the center of the rug. She was beautiful, her patchwork skirt from what must have been her original disguise was climbing up her leg showing her fancy garter belt, and her blouse had been ripped up to the neckline. He knew what that woman was protecting there: the treasure of youth.

There was less than a second to think, but Tito had it filled with images. He, aiming at her, and she, looking at him first with her saucer-like eyes, and then closing her mouth at the same time as she pulled the trigger. Tito saw her making love to him, he saw her telling him that long story about the true state of things, he saw her affectionate, flirtatious, close, seductive. And all of a sudden he saw her there, her staring eyes which already were leaving surprise behind for an infuriated aim at his chest, at his head, between the eyes, eyes that were steel, powder, a shot, a wound, death, the very same hand that was frantically closing around the grip of his weapon and was sending him to another world.

"Be careful!" He heard the scream from old Freud who threw himself at la Maga's feet like a running back. In Tito's head the bang sounded like the twelve o'clock cannon shot from Santa Lucía hill, like a whistle outside. The bullet broke through the molding of the armoire and ricocheted into the ceiling. A chink in the plaster was evidence of what could have happened to Tito Livio Triviño. La Maga got on her knees, enraged, and aimed with more determination. But a real gunshot, without revulsion, without shame, with the honesty that clean guns have, inundated the room with the smell of gunpowder, and made her lunge forward with her neck curved in an arc, and her mouth open as if she were making love, in an insane smile, without meaning, a brief and smothered moaning, a silent scream, to make her flop down like a rag doll on the rug.

A revolver was gently smoking in Freud Romero's hand.

The shaken Tito Livio looked at him trembling.

"I couldn't do it," he whispered.

"Women always have a one-second advantage, Triviño, you have to kill them at point blank range or they'll blow you away. There's no such thing as inferiority, they can even be more ferocious if you let

199

them. Never lose sight of where their hands are."

He put his revolver away.

"I did a real stupid thing by taking the silencer off and leaving it in the case. I'm catching your naiveté, Tito."

Tito could not stop staring at the body.

"Is she . . . dead?"

"It was a silver bullet, one of the best. One wastes a fortune on ammunition in this business."

Tito had an impulse to touch her but he held back. His father was enough of that for today.

"Did she want to kill me?"

"I don't know if it was her original plan, but it seems that she thought it was best when she saw you come out of the armoire."

"But this morning . . ."

"You made passionate love? You slipped through her hands, Triviño, and she wasn't going to let that happen. If she was famous for anything it was her pride. It was you or her, do you understand?"

"Why did she ask if maybe you had killed me?" asked Tito after putting his heart back into his chest.

"Because it seems that your life doesn't matter to anyone, Tito Triviño Junior."

He finished saying this and remained contemplating his interlocutor's lividness.

"They only want the clue. Calm down, Triviño, if I had wanted to eliminate you I would have done it in Torres. God has other plans for you."

"I can't imagine what else can happen to me."

"It'd be better if we get out of here. La Maga never travels alone."

"They can kill me as soon as I go out on the street."

"I don't think so. At least not while they have doubts about who has the photo."

"The clue?"

Freud Romero smiled.

"You're a sharp listener. Come on, leave the pistols here and go out through the window."

"Through the window? And unarmed?"

"You said it yourself. They're outside. There's nobody around here, but they could have heard the shot. In a few minutes we're going to have them here. And if you didn't use your gun in here, you'll use it even less outside."

"Are you going to leave the body . . . there?"

"Do you want to take it with you as a souvenir? It won't be the first time I've moved. If the soldiers find it they'll know from the silver bullet that they have to get rid of it."

"Like my father," said Tito with a heavy heart.

"Exactly."

"She's not going to have a grave? Or a funeral?"

"She won't be the first or the last. Come on, this room stinks. Go on out, I'm telling you."

The window was wide open. With one pull the grimy venetian blinds stopped letting in the indecisive spring sun.

"Now, you have to disappear. Tonight I'll want you to decipher the photo. Get out of here, I'll throw them off the trail."

"But where will I go? Where can I hide?"

"Where nobody will look for you," said Freud putting away Tito's arsenal. "What do you think about your ex-wife's house?"

"I almost never go there."

"Then it's the perfect place," pronounced old Freud and gave him a shove outside.

Tito had to support himself on the thick cornice of the building. Behind him he heard the blinds closing. He thought he caught a glimpse of the crazy old guy smiling. In a little bit he was immersed in darkness, now totally outside. In the air, better said. He looked below but the only thing he managed to see was a bunch of roofs. He calculated that with a small jump he would land on the flat roof of a neighboring building. He took a deep breath to jump. A shot startled him. Far away, down there, it was difficult to locate.

Yes, he had to get away from there.

32

This isn't my house

A
nd that was how Tito Livio Triviño found himself in a minivan
on the way to his wife's house. Seated in the back seat, slack
sailing towards the east in time to the music on the car radio: a tune
from The Police which was suddenly interrupted by a dubbed over
promise for the latest news, extra well-informed from Cooperative
Radio.

Where are you going? Where are you going, Tito my friend? What
are you doing on the way to your ex-wife's house? Let's not call her ex,
since you're not even annulled much less divorced, since here we don't
have a law for that. Is it true you thought about going over to your
mother's house? Is it true you almost cried while you were crossing
Alameda with a stride that was moving you along from pure nervous
energy?

It's useless to try to uncover the hidden part of a worried mind like
that of Tito Triviño: he's lost his father and he's been an accomplice to
the death of a mild-mannered landlady. She looked beautiful until her
death, he's thinking, while he's listening to some news about mobiliza-

tion by the opposition, possible understandings which seemed like such weak ideas, childish fights which didn't protect anyone, which left them as defenseless as Tito was feeling, half lost in the ascending collective taxi which left him a short way away from his ex-wife's house, his own house in the Fleming-Tomás Moro neighborhood, a few yards from the maternity home where Caroline and Janine were born. The good times, he could have mumbled ironically at some time, when they used to seem happy. While Anita María used to go to the obstetrician and he would wink at the clinic's receptionist, or just after arriving at MacPherson he would start on Ruby, the sketcher for the business, petite in her tight jeans. You're so bad, Triviño, your wife about to give birth and you here with me, she would laugh wickedly, remember it used to bother you. And if she had also been part of the plot, the Devil's siege, evil, constant temptation?

He looked all around and calmly crossed the sidewalk, recognizing the colors of the minivans, the school, the newsstand, that everyday smell which creates nostalgia and shows loss with impunity. You were there, Tito, you would reluctantly walk with your daughters, the little car, the cookouts with the in-laws whom you hated, your father getting out of the very same minivan taxi with his weary walk which at times you feared was caused by his damaged hip, like a cripple, a veteran from a war which you didn't even imagine existed. My father, he thought, what would my father say?

When he was within a stone's throw of the house, he tried fruitlessly to stop the flow of memories, to put some alibi in his memory, some trick that might avoid that scarcely perceptible delineation between remembrance and guilt about to stab him in the back. He stopped in front of the gate and contemplated the care given to the garden, meticulous and middle-class, Anita María's hands, she squatted down with gardening gloves scraping under the privet, the speedwells, the jonquils, the snowballs, the hibiscus brought from the near north. So different from the designer gardens in the rich neighborhood where you'd sometimes take a walk on those days you felt like a writer and you'd say to yourself: I'm going to go out and think and avoid the barking dobermans, the German shepherds, the long-haired English sheepdogs which had become so much the rage with their inability to see, which he remembered from his readings of jokes by Pompomio in the Sunday paper. Or the chaotic garden of his youth, not even the rustic and honest garden of Anita María, much less those of Vitacura, the ones with high walls, large leafed begonias, the English ryegrass of the Polo Club, the aroma of the stately robust Holm oak trees. How awful not to know how your own neighborhood smells, not even to give it a name. He indeed was acquainted with that garden, the smell of wet earth, the quackgrass, the colored flowers of the lantanas. He walked over the flowers with the stealthiness of an elf. By the absence of her car, a Charade, he deduced that Anita was not home. He was going to ring the doorbell when the door opened. It was Nena, their lifetime employee. At some time, in a leftist delirium, he had tried to convince her to rebel against her employers. She told him to go to hell. She now said hello to him with quite a bit of hesitancy.

"Don Tito . . ."

"Don," thought Tito. "Why are they using that title, Don?"

"Señora Anita is not here . . ."

Señora, as if that feudal relationship still existed, as if the marriage between us remained in force. That word alone warded him off, her way of saying hello. No, Nena, four years have gone by. How is it possible, we broke up with the boom, we fell with the country, before. The house was full of appliances from the years when the dollar was low, full of the unchecked waste which was alleviating their sins, their raids before, after and during working hours. The fact is I can't stop, he used to say to Gonzalo, and his therapist would quietly look at him, silently censuring Tito, who like all the others felt he had all the rights in the world. Completely, it was a question of throwing away a few dollars to make life easier, and that was that. Instead of confession, it was absolution from the credit card.

"Can I wait for her?"

Nena smiled again, pleased.

"It's not for anything special," Tito tried to calm her. "Don't make a fuss."

He was trying to be trivial, as if that were possible. To see if he could play dumb, to see if it could pass as a simple visit: Look, I was in the neighborhood, I saw the light, and I said to myself, why not?

She let him come in. Melancholy opened its wings inside Tito. The furniture, the same furniture. He didn't recognize some accessories, some souvenirs from a trip to the south that she made with the famous Ismael, her stable and constant suitor.

"Have a seat. Can I get you anything?"

"No, thank you, Nena, thank you."

He dropped into a chair. The afternoon was becoming unbearable for him, too many memories, too many times that were too difficult. However, he could breathe calmly. The warm protection of the middle-class house which the ideologies of the seventies had scorned so much, along with him, too, in his daily irony, with jokes which denigrated the familiar ads from Lever, the testimonials from happy mothers in which he read the bitterness that he knew so well. The arguments which you devoted yourself to when you left this house also, Tito: Marriage is a decrepit and obsolete institution, we made a mistake, my Anita.

Surprised by his own relaxation, he closed his eyes and by pure chance ran across his prayers as a child: *Now I lay me down to sleep, I pray the Lord my soul to keep.* How long will your relief last, your peacefulness, that possibility of breathing effortlessly? And if they fooled you? If they're waiting to enter without taking any risks and haul you off, one on each side, pulling you, screaming, to which everyone will turn a deaf ear? And where will they take you? To heaven? To hell?

While he was waiting he had the tempting idea of going into the bedrooms, to find out if Ismael had come to get into the sack with Anita María, her sweet thin arms and legs, her fawn-like fragility opening herself for another perhaps with more enthusiasm than for him, always a little lazy at sex time, first timid, then accusing, afterwards jealousy, resentment, mistrust, the exit. When she managed to be his wife it was already too late. She used to cry when she got excited, everything hurt after an orgasm. No, I can't go on, she used to say to him. Tito Livio would smoke looking at the emptiness of the bedroom thinking about someone else, in a refuge where problems didn't exist, the stupid problems of marital love, the most threatening, the most essential. What a hassle, he said to himself during those years, the happy years for Lever. He got up and ventured a look towards the corridor. The kids' bedroom, a poster of Luis Miguel which made him smile, imagining them making up a love story, idolizing him, a feeling between their small legs, combing their hair in front of a mirror with their looks of love. That hell of puberty where Tito feared at times he had become perpetually marooned.

Anita's bedside table, so respectful, it didn't even have a picture of Ismael. Only the kids and the Virgin over the headboard, the same as her house when she was single. He wondered if inside the drawer there might be some contraceptives, prophylactics, something like that, what underwear could she be wearing, how did she probably like to make love, where? What does it matter to me, what am I doing butting in where I shouldn't? he said to himself, and went back towards the living room. He was going to sit down when he heard some car brakes outside and it made him jump. Let's get back in the game, he needed a weapon. Because of the time, he calculated that it could be Anita María returning from dance classes with the kids.

And if it were not?

33

Hello, Anita

First Janine came in, smiling, her short brown hair floating in the luminous air, dressed in tights, with her purse dilapidated from too much traveling to school, acting class and ballet class, singing a Victor Manuel song. Face to face with her father she acted silly, void, her unexpected father coming out like an image from the Sacred Heart of Jesus in the middle of the living-dining room of house DFL 2 in which she lived. Next there was Caroline who ran into her sister and let her braid fall down over her shoulder.

"Hi, Dad," she stammered, they stammered.

Tito hoisted, as much as he could, the pulleys of the smile he had before, in order to receive Anita María who was wrestling with a box from the supermarket and calling to Nena. The employee left asking for an unnecessary authorization from Tito Livio Triviño, ex-head of this terrain, ex-inhabitant, ex-husband, almost ex-father. In some way Ismael and his narcotic moderation, the cordiality of a successful lawyer without the least prepotency, already had that house, the aroma of his pipe impregnated the curtains, he spoke in slow motion, he gave the kids presents of Swiss chocolates with suggestions for dental health. The father of the year, as in the advertising for an Isapre, from Parque del Recuerdo, just like the psychiatrist recommended to Anita.

Tito caressed the kids and they hugged him, above all Janine. How old were you when I left you? Did I even think about you when you were born? The fuzz on your neck, the same smoothness in your hair as your mother's. They asked him something in a mad rush, if they were going to go to the movies, if they were going to get an ice cream, if sometime he'd take them to see those planes which used to make him disappear into a dot on the horizon in order to have amorous adventures of the type where he'd return with dolls, blouses, and fantastic jewels in order to calm the deceived aborigines from this side of the world. The daughters from an ex-marriage are the third world of the family, Fatty Aspillaga used to say to him, the kids are the proletariat, Marxist trash. Tito remembered the aforementioned trip to São Paulo, la Maga's insinuating voice, his father's body. How are you going to explain about the call? May it be what God wants.

Anita was pretty, with that weathering of time which subtly furrowed her so well with wrinkles, finally granting her her point of maturity, the strength which Tito fiercely mistrusted before. She was strong, less weak, less nervous. Ismael had been good for her. On the other hand, how was he? Could he feel equally as confident and mature? Or was he the remains of a shipwreck which was bringing him to his house of origin which was already given up for lost?

"Hello, Anita."

She stopped and took a deep breath, as deep as the ones separated women breathe upon running into their ex-husbands, mistrusted from the beginning, ready for combat, making sure the tracks of the true crisis were avoided at any cost. All appearance of weakness and all nostalgia will be banished. Don't even bring up thinking about this stupid guy that I miss, that I was sorry to lose. Like separated men also, sure. Anita felt the whirlwind of her eyebrows going up, the nose of a bloodhound. What are you getting into, Tito Livio? This house is not your house now.

"I want to talk to you."

The kids left, fearing the old quarrels which they had recorded in the walls of their souls. But Tito Livio's attitude was different and

THE SECRET HOLY WAR OF SANTIAGO DE CHILE

Anita watched him. She wasn't an elementary school teacher for nothing and she smelled her ex-husband's pain from a block away. With a friendly gesture she pointed to the bedroom.

"I don't know what Ismael would say!" threw out Tito in jest, but he took it back. "I'm sorry, don't pay any attention to me, I'm being silly."

The kids cheered up, life goes on. Janine threatened to show some drawings, Caroline sat out of the way on the lower bed of their bunk beds decorated with drawings of Barbie and Strawberry Shortcake. From her hair a Walkman flowered. What are you listening to, honey? What type of electronic musical confinement are you getting into to protect yourself from me?

When Anita closed the door Tito looked at her calmly. She was just as thin as before but with a better shape. She was getting better with age.

"What's the matter?"

She ran her hand over her face.

"I don't know how to tell you. It's hard. You wouldn't believe it."

"Look, Tito, if you're going to try to lie to me with another of your stories, leave it for some other time or for one of those women you like to go out with."

Tito looked at the floor. How he hoped that she would at least give him an opportunity, put herself in his place, believe him sometime. Zero for trust. But then he felt a kick in his chest: his father's body on the floor of the room facing the Estación Central.

"It's my father," he said.

"What happened to him?" Anita's face went through a change, she loved him, they loved each other. His father shook his head, bothered, like a horse, when he heard about the separation. He didn't lift his head up from his bowl of soup, he became quiet and refused to eat. Tito understood his anger, he really liked Anita, they used to laugh together. She used to prepare special dishes for him, she missed him.

"What happened to him?" Anita repeated the question.

He's dead, Tito heard himself say in his mind's ear and it sounded terrible to him: *He's dead, he's dead.* He thought about other ways of saying it but all of them were useless: euphemisms, sentences doctors used, all cold. He couldn't say it any other way.

"He's dead," he said to her.

209

She threw her head back, like a dove drinking the water of bad news. The poor dear, she mumbled.

"When was it? Where?"

Hold your feelings back, Tito, look how your mouth is getting dry, look how your neck is tightening up, look how your eyes are filling with tears.

"They found him today. In a cheap hotel . . . down there."

"Where?"

"In the Estación Central. In a sleazy boardinghouse."

"The poor guy," broke in Anita gently. "When is the funeral?"

"I don't have any idea."

Anita looked at him, somewhere between a reprimand and a strange look.

"He's not going to have a funeral. He won't have anything. It won't even come out in the paper. I'm never going to see him again."

Anita's hand movingly crossed the space between them and rested on his shoulder.

"You don't know who the old man really was," continued Tito, uncontrollably. "They took me to see him. They murdered him, Anita, they murdered him."

The crying came to him like a waterfall, a fire hydrant opened in a spasmodic stuttering. A man's cry, without practice, artless, without style. Anita did not move, she remained in her chair, one of the ones they had bought together when he was breaking in his Diner's Club card, the very same one where he put his clothes, where perhaps Ismael would put his. Maybe, perhaps.

When he caught his breath he looked at her as she was bringing back her hand to dry her own eyes. Her sharp, white nose was turning red.

"Who killed him?" she asked. Her calmness attracted his attention, the kind he couldn't have.

"You wouldn't understand it, it wasn't a criminal, nor the secret police, nor the communists. It's much more complicated than that."

A pause.

"You didn't know anything?" she said to him. "Your father never told you anything?"

He shrugged his shoulders. Caught again. No, nothing, never, nothing.

"Maybe he didn't trust you," she continued. "He told me. He came to see me after you left. He warned me that sometime you would have to confront this secret, which was a curse, that I should take care of you, that I shouldn't worry about the kids, but I should about you . . . that it was written that you would return."

"You knew everything? The thing about God? About the Devil?"

She neither nodded nor shook her head, she only raised her hand to her mouth with her finger across her lips in order to point to the door. Walls listen, windows spy. Quiet, Tito, or you're a dead man.

"How long are you going to stay?"

"I don't know. Do you think something might happen? That they might look for me here? What did the old man tell you?"

Anita shrugged her shoulders and put her hands on her face.

"I'm afraid too, Tito."

They hugged. The kids were spying on them from behind the curtains. Father and mother, consoling each other. We're in danger, Anita. Don't go away, I should hide someplace else, no, stay, stay.

"Really?" He looked at her, so close, so close. It reminded him of millions of movies, commercials, popular songs, radios and televisions turned on at old-time series time. He tried not to believe her, but Anita María's mouth made it impossible. There she was, the same as before, even riper fruit. On top of that an inopportune erection started. Still more, more. What was this damned lustfulness doing coming to him in the middle of struggling with his father's death?

Calm down, thought Tito, and separated himself carefully. You're very sweet, Anita. He didn't say that to her. He sighed and limited himself to letting himself fall on the bed.

"Thanks," was the only thing he muttered.

And Anita opened the door.

34

I don't know what Ismael would say

Not even in the most outstanding of his creative excursions could Tito Livio have imagined what came next. Caroline's smile at his side, such a serious little girl and now with this shine like a Christmas star, Janine's drawing which she was handing to him, a picture of herself holding an enormous balloon which was going towards the sun. That's the way you feel, daughter, like that, in the air, that's how your father feels too, a small basket from a Montgolfier which at any moment could sink without a moment's hesitation. So Tito also let himself be rocked, and he sat down at the table and ate lunch between the childrens' stories, face to face with Anita María and the girls talking about school, ballet classes, Ismael's idea of course, who else could truly think about them.

Now he couldn't even look at everything from a distance. Neither his sly skepticism, nor his mainsail vanity from a boat in which he was moving away from the world in order to triumphantly contemplate everything, were saving him. He ate the spaghetti and meatballs calmly, just like those he had insulted in the past. Now he was having fun, he was even in his glory, he let himself be caught up in an immense outburst of laughter faced with a very funny anecdote from his oldest daughter. It didn't seem like a Lever ad, it *was* a Lever ad. Worse yet, this is what the Lever ad was trying to capture, this essential feeling of the family of which the ad campaign was only a perverse idealization.

The girls asked him what he was doing, if he had started to write again (in their infantile minds his leaving was always in order to write a neverending novel, to become famous, you, Daddy, you're going to be famous, they used to say to him amid the freezing cold of the divorce, around the clash of the separated parents, among the labyrinths of the stores in the Apumanque where the bookstores turned into places where they could find their father's name, the one which they had proudly cut out of newspapers when they confiscated his book because of blasphemy, disrespect, irreverence, and rejection of the establishment).

Tito was embarrassed. He hadn't even written one decent line, barely any of those commercial phrases that they thought were divine. Their father did all the advertising in the world. I'm as much of a liar as advertising, he wanted to tell them, I pervert the use of words without wanting to warn that in that way I'm corrupting myself, I'm losing my ideas, I transform the magic of language into witchcraft.

But the girls were not interested in his *mea culpa*, but rather in his presence. Two or three times Anita María had to tone down the kids' excitement. When they got up from the table he looked at her with a smile that Tito never thought he'd ever have again.

"Are they always like that?"

"No, they're that way with you."

She offered him a cognac. Where did you get it from, Anita?

"I don't know what Ismael would say."

"I hope that's not a provocation," she smiled.

Tito shrugged his shoulders.

"I've instigated so much. Not only with you. I'm past that."

Anita looked at him with a don't-come-to-me-with-crocodile-tears look and handed him the glass. How does Ismael toast with her? Jealousy is infinite, my friend, perennial, extemporaneous. It's better not to say anything.

"This isn't a secret concoction, is it Anita?"

Aren't all women witches, all of them fairies? In your mind, Tito, at least.

"It's incredible," he said after inhaling big mouthfuls of the atmosphere, which was becoming tense from too much not knowing what to say to each other. "This is the place where I least thought I could be received, however, it's the only place where I don't feel I'm in danger of dying. I envy Ismael, Anita. He knows how valuable you are. I'm sure he doesn't hurry you, nor yell at you, nor cheat on you like I've done."

Anita swirled the cognac in her glass, with a moderation which Tito didn't recognize from her.

"Everything isn't so ideal, Tito. He's a mature man and he has his bad habits. On the other hand, I'm the one who doesn't rush him and he's the one who doesn't commit himself."

Anita had just finished the separation game. For a second, Tito felt the temptation of taking advantage of it as a point in his favor but then accepted that it was derisive, almost immoral: to bite the hand that feeds. He quickly took a drink of cognac, and changed the subject.

"You don't listen to music now?"

She shrugged her shoulders. The dust on the sound system, the former glory of the economic boom, betrayed her.

"It's just that . . ."

"Ismael doesn't like it," finished Tito. She nodded with that chameleon-like quality which explained why she was shy. With him she listened to blues, Cannonball Adderly's jazz, that song from Jimmy Heath which obsessed him with memories: *Gemini*. He said that to her. She told him that sometimes she thought about going to this or that concert: "Tito's probably there," and etcetera.

"When there were dollars to bring them here," he laughed.

"There will be again. You'll see . . ." she corrected him.

At this moment the temptation of memory and nostalgia began, that train which passes by slowly in front of our eyes without stopping, telling us everything we've lost. From commenting on the survival of the Japanese auto, the Korean television, the blender, right up to speaking dangerously about the first time they met. Anita balanced herself on the edge of the worst in lack of enthusiasm, the abyss of collision, illusion, and the ghost of a dead love. Tito noticed the rise in temperature in his pelvic region and flattered her: You're more beautiful than ever. Her critical capacity was in pieces. They were talking about the wedding party when the image of Tito Triviño Senior came to mind, Triviño Junior sighed. Anita asked for details.

"Some people who I thought were loyal took me to see him. He was dead, wounded by a bullet, but later on they themselves turned out to be the murderers. Do you realize? In order to get me to . . ."

He was going to continue but Anita's interest aroused suspicions in him: And what if she were one of them? What if Ismael himself were one of Donkavian's agents? And what if she, because of resentment (how could she not feel it) had joined up against him and was waiting for his surrender? What if Freud Romero were another link in the sequence, another turn of the screw to push him to this apparently wonderful picture of love which would be the spiderweb where she would get the truth out of him? He was silent. Anita leaned her head forward.

"What happened to you?"

"I'd rather not talk any more," he said coldly.

She drank the last swig.

"Your father interests me, not state secrets."

Did she perceive his mistrust? Was it because of that that her look became metallic, cold, like steel? Or did she feel she'd been found out? Careful, Tito, you've already lost the last of your soul's virginity.

Tito Livio's hands got cold. Yes, this was nothing more than another Lever ad, as deceiving as his. Even the kids were puppets of the wretched Donkavian.

"It's a plot, isn't it? I deserve to die like this, for being such an imbecile."

"Tito . . ."

"Shut up," he said to her, trying not to raise his voice. He thought about the girls who were playing in their room. "Don't keep on trying to make eyes at me."

Anita got up.

"Tito, listen to me. You're very smart. I think you get it from your father . . ."

"Don't talk to me like a psychologist," he muttered. He kept on thinking at high speed. And if he were right? And if the effect of waking up that damned friendliness in her terrorized him more than all the silver bullets in the secret Santiagoan holy war? It was certainly a lot more work to be tender than to shoot guns right and left. His book was pure bad temper splashed in everyone's face. Love was making him frail, it was annihilating him with language games, with witticisms, everything that was affection felt corny to him, like a Hallmark card, one more piece of foolishness with which to go more insane in a schizophrenic world. A nauseous feeling surged in him from deep inside. The idea of a secret potion flashed through his brain. That was his private insanity, his personal war against all that might arise from that thing they called love, so well-known, and damned. He had to destroy it all and just like that he had done it. He also had been an agent of Donkavian. He wasn't conscious of it before, that's all.

He looked at Anita as if for the first time. He was pale and disconnected. He had never spoken the truth with her, if he stopped to talk it was to put her down, to demonstrate his superiority to her, his control. If he seduced her it was because of envy, to steal away the tenderness that he lacked, in order to destroy her and hurt her as he felt he had when he left the house, wrenching all those qualities from her that she reproduced again, always more wholesome than he.

A dry tree, he felt penetrated by a seed of destruction, a sickness more venereal than the worst case of syphilis, which would prevent all contact without leaving a wounded and purulent mark, through which the last vestige of affection was escaping which he could have felt sometime, and where he was planting the standard of pride for his own gleaming contemplation. That was being famous for him, and because of this his meager creative flow was drying up, stopping at the arches of MacPherson which adorned him with praise and toasts and trips. All of them were Donkavian's agents. The Devil didn't even need to be present on earth, everyone was carrying him in their private mirror, in their inflated image of themselves. The only thing that was missing was the Tetragrammaton, the sacred word with which to give life to matter and forget about God, forever.

"If I don't believe you I don't believe anyone," pronounced Tito, anguished. Anita came up to him and he had the impulse to let himself seek refuge in her. Don't touch me, I'm hurting all over.

"Tito." She hugged him.

The protagonist didn't cry this time. He remained confused, softly rocking with his eyes open, no part of his discovered consciousness looking at her. He had never been truly with Anita in his life, nor with his father, nor with anyone. Now he was dead and it was already irreparable.

"Anita." He returned her hug. Her thin body seemed precious and precise to him, the smooth opening up of her hips without theatricality nor exaggeration, the slope of her shoulders, the enticing outline over the column of her light and elastic muscles. He didn't feel the erection which wasn't needed, nor the urgency to captivate her. No, nothing like that, only the passivity of the afternoon and the smoothness of Anita's hands in his hair.

"I have to go to drop off the kids at a birthday party," he heard her say.

They separated without anything else and she got ready in her room while Tito watched her through the doorway. Her beauty hurt him. Now not even Ismael mattered to him, his own loss was making him anxious, it was as if only at that moment he understood the separation, the succession of useless conquests, the deceitful affairs.

"Take a siesta, it will do you good. I'm coming right back." She said goodbye among a to-do of hugs from her kids and arrangements of hair, dresses and jokes. Don't go, Daddy, Janine said to him and the idea shook him. The time that had gone by bothered him, the battle given without knowledge, the cruelty of his naive egocentricity. He ran his hand over her head and kissed her with all the tenderness possible for him. Caroline, more serious, was going to wave goodbye but he kissed her, wanting to take her in his arms. He gave her a big hug.

"Your dad might not be here when you get back so give him a big goodbye now."

Anita's words only made the storm worse. More kisses, more hugs, Caroline's tears streaming out against her will next to the naive reproach of Janine. I'll return, I'll come back, stammered Tito, trying to calm them down. They had to have their hair combed again for the party, the stitching straightened, ties for the dresses, the wrapping paper on the presents straightened out that had been wrinkled from so much affection. Tito finished by waving from the window, fearful of being seen if he went out onto the sidewalk. Before leaving, Anita threw him a kiss with her hand and Tito felt a shiver run down his spine. He thought about Ismael with extreme envy. He imagined him to be a skillful and difficult bachelor, who deep down inside hated kids and compensated for this with all that good management of upbringing, he being such an adult. That settled him for a little while but then his sorrow returned to the attack. He lay out on the ex-conjugal bed, you could almost say with fear, and he thought that he wasn't going to be able to go to sleep with so many emotional jolts. But he did it. As soon as he closed his eyes the most beatific dream overtook him completely. He was completely drained.

35

The warrior's rest

Together with the sensation of slowly waking up, Tito realized he was sad. The pain when he breathed communicated this to him. He opened his eyelids little by little and he noticed it was getting dark, that he had slept as if he were hibernating, without dreams, without moving in the bed. He was curled up in a fetal position, on his side, turned towards the window, and he could make out the diminishing light of the sunset through the curtains. He tried to ward off the pain but couldn't, it was like a bird perched on his body, an animal which he felt was dangerous to wake up. He remembered the siestas of his childhood, the room made dark by his mother (who had closed the curtains this time? when?) and his eyes half opened trying to poke around in the sound of his parents' room, pretending to be asleep, adventuring on some fantasy with Captain Nemo or Jim of the Jungle or the Phantom or Tarzan, read in an ancient edition stolen from an agonizing godfather. Those were warm and alleviating siestas. Tito, without any other worry than the heat or an unexpected excitability which the solitary job of masturbating would alleviate. Not now, now it

219

was the pain, the grating of bones in his soul which barely let him think. My dead father: how many more times will I have to put up with the image? That hellish close-up, the dried blood, the stained pajamas, the bullets, the holes in the ceiling.

That emptiness invaded him, which he would resolve as a child by leaving to take a walk around the block with no particular destination, or immersing himself in a lethargic game of pool or in front of the electronic rhythm of a pinball machine. The same depression which condemned him later on to change careers, girlfriends, offices, on which he blamed everything that came along: that long period without writing a word and which he couldn't accept as a test of his diminished talent, but rather blamed on his household routine, Anita María's bad character, the kids' demands, and later on each one of his bosses, his girlfriends, the girls he was trying to get close to. He would blame the moon if that were necessary, with a blind faith in change, a new year and a new life, the faith with which he would begin everything while fleeing from that shadow, from that restlessness which would not go away and would catch up to him again one afternoon, one morning, waking up, until the next insane flight towards another job, another boss, another string of successes which slipped between his fingers without being able to satisfy that intolerable thirst for he didn't know what, that bitterness which right now was coming into his mouth, not feeling like waking up, something very similar to dying, sleeping for an eternity. Why not? There I would be warm, guarded, I would not realize it if death trapped me from behind, perhaps like my father whom they caught sleeping and he didn't realize, and now he's probably peaceful, now he won't bite his nails, he won't pull his hand over his face, he won't be worried about the track, the horses that won't ask about you, old man, where you went, where you were going when I wanted, eternal darkness. Or isn't that right? Or were you there looking out of the corner of your eye, playing the cat in the back of the house, watching your sons whom we believed you were renouncing? Maybe my brother was right when he claimed you were a good man? And me, accusing him of being oedipal with words stolen from the mouth of Gonzalo, who pointed out your present absence to me several times, the niche in my mind where he insisted you were like an image of the Virgin of Lourdes on the patio of an agnostic, like you are now, omnipresent, on your feet over my shoulder, which is how the people killed by violence are, the beloved beings.

That was what Tito Livio Triviño was thinking when he heard the door creak and he excitedly recognized Anita's hand turning the doorknob, observing him through the crack.

"I'm already awake," he said to her turning over in bed.

She entered like the wind. He saw her against the backlighting and couldn't avoid following the line of her body. Years doing this, he thought, occupational hazards.

"How do you feel?"

"So-so."

Anita sat down on the bed.

"You shouldn't have let me sleep in a bed that isn't mine now."

He thought he saw her smile in the dim light, she was quiet.

"And the kids?" he asked.

"They're at my mom's."

"It's better. You're afraid for them. Isn't that right?"

Anita nodded.

"I don't know why you let me in, Anita. I just bring problems."

"It won't be the first time," she said with a certain irony.

Tito smiled. He saw himself like a whirlwind in the harmony of the house. The slamming doors, the early morning tennis, the renowned changes.

"And Nena?"

"She left too."

The idea of being alone slightly excited him. Had they ever really made love? Had he thought about her when he was penetrating her? Where have I been all this infamous time?

"I'm sad, Anita," he said from inside, from way down inside.

She remained motionless for a few seconds. All of a sudden he could see her hand ploughing through the air and resting itself on his shoulder. Tito felt an impulse to grab her, the call to arms down there in his groin, but he discarded it as absurd.

He looked at her guessing what her eyes were saying. He felt they were soft, serene, although maybe they were as terrified as his.

"Anita, they can kill me."

He felt her other hand. Don't come closer, Anita, don't come closer.

He couldn't avoid it, he grabbed her by the shoulders and brought her a couple of inches from his mouth, she smelled like roses and he liked that. He was going to kiss her when he felt a pulling from her. He also realized it. This wasn't either love, nor lust, nor anything, it was the behavior of corralled animals.

"Better not," said Anita straightening up.

There were a couple of minutes of silence and she lay down by his side.

They didn't say anything. They let time pass until Tito checked her breathing, its rhythm in the darkness, her skin so close, his heart beat faster and blood rushed to his head. With true gentleness he let his head fall on her shoulder, thin bones, delicate, crystalline, he felt as if her hair were shining, as if he would burn it with movement and he reached out his hand to explore her waist. She didn't move, neither in favor, nor against. She wrinkled her nose and then let it be done. The tenuous curve of her abdomen, her navel, time which does not pass in vain but is even beautiful and captivating. Then her hand came back gliding in the minimal space which the bodies were leaving, and it grabbed the bottom of his neck, the wishbone under his chin. The gentleness of her desires surprised Tito, that caressing full of fear, the blind awkwardness of fear, the stupidity which only heavenliness has, the splendid wisdom of the fever possessing her. He listened to how her breathing was speeding up and he became excited, she was caring for him, not only admiring him or letting herself be seduced, or it was a product of some irresistible exhalation, a magic elixir like the lotions of his commercials, Van Heusen shirts or the long shining car, it wasn't the devoted hand which at times he received like a trophy but rather a hand which opened his skin depositing the seeds of desire, those of true desire, which dazzles, which one repents from feeling, which only her mouth could satisfy, perhaps, only her womb, only her legs.

He turned towards her, searching for the lips which he found waiting for him, tongue at the ready submerging itself in a kiss which he had already forgotten, he didn't recall it as so full, so wet, so free, a mocking voice leaned into his brain reminding him of Ismael, what he had probably taught her, but he chased the voice away, discarded it, and gave himself over to her warm embrace, an embrace which would have no end, ever, don't go further away, and then he hugged her and she wrapped him with her muscles and he managed to feel her most private temperature coming toward him, towards the banner of his so beaten virility reined in for this ritual combat. The forgotten tender moments, so much making love without making love, the routine of sex, rather so much destroying of it, one could say. Rubbing against each other with intensity, with the courage of a schoolboy his fingers searched for her freed upright nipples, yes he remembered them, loved, yes, he loved them, yes, he loved everything about them, a ray of brilliance came to him when he maneuvered that active body between his arms and they kissed each other as if they were condemned to death, which perhaps they were, until all of a sudden she jumped back. Tito's hand was galloping between her muscles opening up a wet path, but she pulled it away.

"No, I can't," she said holding down her breathing.

"What's the matter?"

"It's not the right time, Tito."

He let himself be conquered and he fell to one side. It was true. What did a screw have to do with that? What the hell was he coming here for if it wasn't to try to cover up the terror, the nausea, the duel?

"Forgive me," he muttered.

He sensed that she was smiling in the semi-darkness.

"It's strange to hear you ask to be forgiven."

Both of them smiled, a nervous smile shook them and then there was silence. Once again, in spite of everything, he felt like kissing her, asking her who she was. For a fleeting second he feared an incarnation of la Maga, another accomplice, but he shook off the idea. The pause expanded when there was some knocking on the window.

"Who is it?"

Anita got up with professional caution. She stealthily opened the curtains.

It was Freud Romero.

223

36

A trip to the north

He left with Freud Romero almost without saying goodbye. Barely a quick kiss on the cheek, a *be careful* from her which she let fall while they were separating and Freud waiting outside among the trees in the garden, below the storied abutilon tree which he never learned to appreciate and in which the girls assured him lived the entire population of hummingbirds from the whole block.

"Be careful."

"Take care," answered Tito Livio or he thought he answered. He lowered his head, stepped between the flagstones spread among the Bermuda grass and put himself at the service of Sigmund Romero. He heard Anita's voice in his ear like a diminutive guardian angel while he was waiting for Freud to finish climbing the garden wall at the end of the patio. That's how some goodbyes are, out of sheer importance they seem hollow.

"Where are we going?"

"Don't ask and get a move on. We haven't got all the time in the world."

They dropped to another patio where they heard the noise from a teenagers' party. They waited among the cans and bags of garbage for a group of girls who seemed really happy to enter, all dressed in blue, their hair artificially kinky, screaming out the names of their boyfriends while they greeted the one who was acting as hostess. When they went in the music got louder.

"Let's go," said the old guy, and they jumped out towards the street, crossed through another gate and another garden entrance in order to then slide along next to a hedge of thick hydrangeas. The bark from an excited German shepherd made Tito Livio jump and slide down into a sitting position.

"Get on your feet!" Freud scolded him. He seemed like a Marine sergeant. Tito thought about answering him with a foolish statement. He didn't have the soul of a recruit, he didn't understand the reason for having been like this, in this trance, with his wife and then having to leave running like a thief. He was going to protest but the image of his father's body stopped him. I'll never be able to stop remembering you, he thought.

"I'm coming," he begged. "Wait for me."

Freud was now a half block ahead of him.

They made out the buildings at the corner of Tomás Moore and Fleming where it was said that during the protests they shot tear gas against the windows shattered by banging cooking pans and trumpets making an uproar and protesting against a regime with mythical deafness. The Alamo, thought Tito. Freud was calling him from behind a closed newsstand which was now waiting for morning. He wondered what time it was. He made an attempt to answer, but he was interrupted by the appearance of a pair of elevated headlights like on a tank.

"Triviño."

He pressed up against the wall in a reflex action. Who were they? He trembled from head to toe. He couldn't see Sigmund Freud Romero from there and he only heard the noise of a machine coming through the night in a prehistoric fury. They caught me, I'll fall like my father, like la Maga, I'll end up with my guts ripped out all over the ground, my blood like my father's will filter through the grates in the street to feed the insects and be lapped up by dogs. He let himself fall face down on the pavement, the cold cement scraped his knees like those of a child spreading out on his knees for the ritual of marbles or to play with tops. He managed to hear himself pray when he made out the roaring truck full of recruits. It was an enormous Toyota stuffed with recruits with their faces disfigured with black war paint which made the weapons in each one's hands seem more frightening, the ones the Devil carries, who else could it be? They didn't even look at him. They spread out through the streets of Santiago occupying their nighttime guard posts for the curfew which was approaching. Terror was establishing its manifest reign. Nighttime was a restricted area.

Freud picked him up in the air, treating him like an imbecile. What was he trying to do, was this any way to act? With a tug he got into an enormous Chevrolet Biscayne painted like a taxi which began its rapid march.

"You don't even know how to keep still for even one minute. You're not going to last very long if you keep on like that. The only thing left to do is put yourself in front of the truck so they can shoot you. Don't you have a better way of being invisible? Or do you want them to kill you?"

Sigmund was indignant. He was scanning the four points of the compass looking for marauders, furtive hunters, a sniper in a tree. He was foaming at the mouth. When the car took Balboa towards the east he seemed to calm down.

"Where are we going?" blurted out the startled protagonist.

"Where do you think?" responded the other sarcastically. The taxi driver smiled in the rearview mirror.

And him, Tito? Which faction does he belong to?

Freud is imperturbable.

"Do you think we'd be so stupid as to not have anything prepared and dive into the first taxi that appeared without even considering the consequences? You'd do that with your childish impulsiveness, you never look before you leap. Obviously this guy is one of ours." The taxi driver laughed again. "You're very changed, Tito, I should have guessed that your father's death would leave you out of action. That's why those bastards did it, to knock you out. The hardest blow that a man can get in life is when his father dies. They read it in my books and look how smart they are: they have you scared."

"But where are we going now?" inquired Tito. He didn't like them to scold him.

"There are things that you don't know and our people don't know either. We've got to gain some distance and time. We have to find the ones who can think for us to see if they tell us what it is they're looking for and suppose you have, that your father had and probably gave to you . . . That photo, for example."

Tito felt the picture was like having a target painted in the center of his chest. What had seemed to him to be an innocent souvenir of family life now destroyed, was now a death threat, a condemnation to be pursued with a price on his head. It was better with Anita María. Damn the time when I separated from her. Who put the crazy idea in my head about being such a wildly successful famous writer? Was that the sentence from advertising? To be seduced by the dream of oneself being the product to be promoted? Receiving the adoration of the target group, fetishist contemplation of the consumer society aimed now at his name, the name of the thing being more important than the thing itself, the advertising which is written more attractively than the thing it's advertising? At one time he had thought: What I do is better than what I sell. Why don't I sell myself? The second step, the inevitable one, the one which will produce the fall, Lucifer's temptation: Why can't I be God, aren't I the most beautiful child of His? Why get married like the rest, live like the rest, if I am *so* special?

Well, you made your own bed, now lie in it, Tito. Surrounded by gods and demons, bearer of the secret letter, the destiny of the cosmos in your hands. What else could you want? However, you don't seem very happy.

"What really transpires happens in the dark," spoke Freud, who was translating his thoughts from the gestures of his face, the wrinkles on his forehead, the sighs in Morse code. "Only the illegitimate is visible and open to discussion. Fame is one of their inventions which pretends to deny the necessity of the truth being revealed, and they want to invert the order of the relation between lies and falsehoods. They want to deny all differences, all oppositions. They have canceled out sex and don't be surprised if you find out around here that la Maga was sometimes a man and Donkavian acts as a woman and tries to deceive you. Death is their next goal and that's why they want the Word. The attraction of fame is attraction for the transient, the mortal as if it were divine. It's to offer God's attributes to any mortal for fifteen minutes.

To be everywhere, to be above everyone. Illusion, delirium, suicidal fantasy. It's the way to possess us that they've chosen."

Tito damned the minute in which he remembered traveling full speed toward Villa Alemana, just like now as they were ploughing through the Santiagoan night, believing himself to be the future of the Chilean novel with the enviable plot of the holy child. Get out of the way García Márquez, Vargas Llosa, Donoso, please, here comes Tito Livio Triviño at full speed. Was coming, I mean, I put a curse on my daydreams, my daily hallucinations, my walks around the room imagining chapters which never reach the light of day on the typewriter, and had already seen themselves translated into twenty languages, with lecture tours throughout the whole United States, pointed out by the young people crowded into Charles de Gaulle Airport. My God, save me if you can.

He closed his eyes tightly. Freud observed him with a certain tenderness.

Santiago was just getting dark, the businesses were pulling down their metal shutters with the noise of guillotines decapitating the day and leaving the street mute until the morning, until the sun rescues life drop by drop, which seems to support itself halfway in a taciturn city, until the following opaque night, inhibited, from hard times, curfewed, from this Santiago without a life of its own. A provincial city, settled by priests from those who came before, a military camp from which all that was missing was the bugle call. The nostalgia of lodging for the entire large city.

Tito recognized the road to the airport, now with another name like all the rest. He remembered crimes in those sectors, strikes, the rotten smell from the garbage dumps while the inhabitants must have been making themselves comfortable in front of their color televisions, crowded with ads which he would write, masturbator of the proletariat's soul. Yes, I'm a very famous author, kids sing my jingles, adults take my sentences and convert them into jokes made to liven up mealtime. It's disgusting.

Suddenly the speed diminished. It wasn't hard for him to recognize the San Pablo neighborhood. In the distance they were closing the shutter on the last visible business: a bakery. From the light from the street lamps he could read the name: *San Pablo Scholastic Academy. Everyday and Special Bread.*

Freud lifted up his hand, stopping the flow of his thoughts.

"We still have to wait," he said to him.

"What's going on?"

"They have to close everything," said the taxi driver, opening his mouth for the first time in the whole trip.

Old Freud asked him what time they would be able to go in.

"No more than half an hour and everything will be ready," uttered the driver, a polite man, a strong constitution, friendly. "I have to go. You know what you have to do later?"

Tito became nervous. On foot, at night, with the curfew?

"We'll know how to take care of things," pronounced Sigmund Romero just at the same moment they were closing the last shutter in the bakery.

"Where are we going?" asked Tito again, who didn't have much hero left in him, less sardonic, and why comment if there wasn't any courage left?

"To the bakery," Freud said to him and opened the car door.

37

The password to the bakery

They stopped next to a wall. At night all men seem like cockroaches and they weren't out of place. The neon light contrasted its cold illumination with the lower facades on the street, a clash of two eras. Tito scanned the windows, now grated over with thick, half-rusted steel, now covered by thick wooden shutters. There were old metal plaques with white numbers over the doorways, the kind which were divided by an unused flag pole: the country was different in the days when those places were built. An apartment building a half block further up the street testified to an inharmonious attempt to modernize the neighborhood. The doorways dispersed fragments of private lives: a head which was watching television, a couple who entered and left the room all worked up, a family late in finishing its Saturday dinner. Freud, very calmly, was looking in his pockets for a cigarette which he slowly lit.

"We have to wait," he whispered and took a second drag on the cigarette.

"Have you got another one for me?"

Freud shook his head.

"Nein, in the first place I don't share my poisons."

It was probably healthier to remain like that, calm, as if nothing were happening, thought Tito. He sat down on the ledge of a window closed by the metallic shutter of a grocery store. The street seemed completely unfamiliar to him. He knew very well where the neighborhood was, but he didn't have any idea which part of it they were in. What bothered him the most was to have time to think, to take into account and calculate the frenzy of those days: the party with Donkavian dressed to the hilt as a Huaso, the night at poor dear old Sara's boardinghouse, his dead father, Anita's closeness. His role as a protagonist was weighing heavy on him like a suit of armor. He scribbled against the hardness of the surface which prevented him from falling asleep, ignoring, at least in this way, that dead time which never seemed to go by. He looked at the ground, the old tiles like those one never found anywhere anymore, replaced by the municipal officials through the famous decrees, pieces of dubious quality, less tasteful and frankly dangerous for the passers-by. They were making downtown Santiago uniform, eliminating all vestiges from a previous history. Wasn't this a demonic desire? Beginning everything with oneself and exiling the past like a bad dream, someone else's dream on top of that. Just as he would have wanted to be able to eliminate all the dead people from his mind. Why had he survived? Why wasn't his brother, who was much more together and worthy, in his place? Why not him, in Spain, happily married, a happy middle-class professional with no major aspirations in his whole existence?

"It's almost midnight," judged Freud taking the last drag on his cigarette butt so he could crush it on the ground. "From here on the hardest part of the mission begins. We're going to see and hear things which nobody will believe if you tell them. All of Santiago sleeps or gets ready to sleep without ever finding out about their own night. Everyone dreams dreams which the majority of the time are nothing more than futile attempts at combining their miserable daily lives with the truth, which you're now going to see revealed. What you're going to learn, Triviño, you mustn't tell, if you don't want to succeed in having them laugh at you, or classify you as insane, or if you're lucky, as a dreamer. Nothing that you'll see is forbidden but for some reason you'll notice they fight against it. The soldiers know full well the power of the night. They protect everything new, everything subversive, everything which comes to disrupt the pagan order of the day. In sunlight grow the biological and material, and by the light of the moon the spirits, ideas, passions, things which those who wish to maintain the order of death will want to crush. But it's useless. Life, truth, night, continue. It's the meeting place between the dead and the living. Nobody leaves here innocent."

Tito felt they were trying to scare him, that Freud had come straight out of a Gothic novel with a black cape and fangs dripping with blood. Half imitating, he let loose a small laugh.

"Tell me about the werewolf now," he said in a sarcastic imitation. Freud gave a half smile.

"Don't be childish," he said to him. "The night is much more than that. Maybe you believe that werewolves don't exist? Maybe not in that version dedicated to frightening bored old ladies or young ladies who are weak of character. The night is the source of life, the place where the sun rests and recharges." Tito felt he was losing patience. What is he trying to tell me?

"First of all an agreement that you'll take seriously the fact that what is coming is not easy, and secondly, I'll try to allay your fears because you're very nervous and I have to give you your weapon."

Tito remembered his Walter PPK abandoned in the flight through the attics bordering Freud's office. Marx's Magnum and his own pistol, still virgin, left on orders from the old guy.

"My Walter?"

"Not by any means. An uncommon war doesn't use common weapons. It's thought out for you and for the enemies who will come."

Tito expected a double-bladed ax, a necklace with garlic, a wooden stake. He felt like he was in the middle of Transylvania, but it was only the old armor of his irony. Romero took something out of his pocket. He opened it, and it twinkled in the light from the streetlamps: wrapped in a woman's handkerchief was a pistol. Tito recognized it. It was a Beretta, small, easy to carry, easy to handle. He had seen it in James Bond movies, and one time he wanted to make a commercial with that theme for a man's lotion. But now it was real.

"Do I really need a weapon?"

232

"The fact is it's not just any weapon. It belonged to your father. Compliments of Lili Salomé."

What are you going to do now, Tito? You need real guts, a mask of courage won't be enough. It's the gun your father didn't use to defend himself, the one he preferred you defend yourself with. You can't go back. That's it, take it. It's cold like a reptile. It was waiting for your hand.

"It has silver bullets," continued Freud. "Be careful with them. There aren't very many of them and they're difficult to get."

"I don't know what I'll do if I have to use it."

"Maybe your Walter was a toy?"

Tito thought that for him, yes. He had handled a lot of adult things as if they were toys. Even people, even his own life. Once more he felt like throwing everything far away and running out of there.

"You don't seem like your father's son," finished Freud, rubbing it in.

"No, not at all. I suppose he was real brave, isn't that right?"

Freud moved his head from one side to the other, not convinced.

"If we consider someone who betrayed us to them courageous . . ."

"But that's not good, I suppose."

"A traitor is someone never totally to be trusted."

"Although he comes over to your faction?"

"Not so fast. It's not exactly my faction. Nor am I very brave, let's say. I do my work, they pay me the allotted amount and that's it."

"What are they going to pay you for this?"

"That's not important. Besides, it's indeed very important to me to avenge your father."

"Have you worked for them?"

"In my profession there are no ideologies . . ."

"You're an immoral person."

"And you aren't?"

"How do I know you didn't kill my father?"

"You already asked me that question and I already answered it. You either believe me or you don't. You don't have any other alternative. Leave if you want, shoot me with the Beretta, give it back to me and start with a clean slate. But if you had ever worried about truly knowing Alberto Triviño, your father, you would understand that I can love him and be here with you, although I might feel you're an overgrown kid,

233

an unbearable immature cowardly show-off."

Tito gulped, what little he had left. He tried the weight of the pistol in his hand.

"I believe you."

"You won't be sorry. Don't waste the bullets, like I told you. Don't shoot them at just anybody, they only do their work on one of them. They're true death, the one way to hell with no return."

Tito recalled the instructions for shooting one time on a country estate, an office party, fooling around, shooting at some Nescafé jars on a fence. On that day he almost thought he was Dirty Harry.

"I wish this were only a movie," and he clicked his tongue.

A loud noise distracted them. Tito Livio's heart jumped to the center of the sidewalk. A half block further down, from where Tito had thought he heard music from a television, they were clearing out what seemed to be a nightclub, a discotheque, something like that.

"It's starting," said Romero.

"What's that?"

"Get further back in the alley and shut up."

Some soldiers with loud voices made the myrtle trees buzz. There were moans from the drunks bashing into the pavement like wooden sticks. Tito made out women's voices, also liquored up. The beatings lasted a few minutes. Someone thanked the police. The moaning lessened, the noise of the bodies against the ground signaled that they were being dragged away. A pair of shadows was coming straight towards them. Tito gripped the Beretta. Freud's hand calmed him down through the darkness. They were coming towards the alley.

"What are we going to do?" whispered Tito, anxiously.

Freud didn't answer him. Meanwhile, the drunks were swaying and humming an old Mexican song: *The bed has to be hard as rock, and the pillow a stone.*

"They're ours," said the old man. Tito swore he saw his smile through the darkness in the alley. What could he mean? Our what? He didn't ease up on the gun: If they move I'll shoot them, he said to himself. He tried to think about what his father would have done on this occasion, the valiant traitor whom he didn't know. *The woman that I love,* hummed Freud. Was he crazy?

No, on the contrary, it was like a magic word. The drunks' mistreated and sinister air faded away altogether and they appreciated it like dwarfs ready to revel on the hidden forest past.

"We were waiting for you," said one. The drunk had a voice like a woman, a young girl, rather.

"We didn't know how much longer we were going to be going around in circles," said the other, a young man. Tito, in spite of the sparse light, noticed that they were disguised. They didn't smell bad, nor were they dirty. He sensed a wave of gratitude upon verifying that allies existed, some ally, somewhere.

"Who's the visitor?" said the woman curiously scanning the darkness where Tito was hiding.

"My, don't we like to butt in," retorted his companion. They seemed to be laughing together.

"That's not part of the deal," Freud stopped them, pushing Tito Livio backwards with his elbow. "You just give us the password to the bakery . . . and goodbye."

"Did you bring yours?"

"Everything's okay," said Freud.

"Get to work, little angel," said the guy to the woman who seemed bothered by not being able to discover the identity of the one hiding behind the puny figure of old Romero. Making a grimace he rummaged in his pockets. Half amused, she showed her empty hands and shrugged her shoulders.

"I've lost it."

"No more jokes please, nighttime doesn't last forever even if we want it to."

The fake drunks chuckled. They seemed to have a spirit of fun rather than conspiracy.

The young woman stifled her laugh with her hand, craned her neck to spy again in Tito's direction, and then came close to Freud's ear and whispered something.

"It can't be," said Freud Romero.

"All passwords are absurd," answered the woman shrugging her shoulders in turn. "Now the pay."

"How do I know if it's the right one?"

"You either believe us, or you don't," said both of them almost in unison.

Triviño Junior could not help but smile. He wasn't the only one trapped in this net of weak power positions which came undone at the first confrontation with someone else.

"Who's going to assure us that you won't shoot us in the back as soon as we take a couple more steps over there?" added the woman in a surly tone.

Would that be possible?

"At night all cats are gray." The young guy stretched out his hand, continuing the negotiations.

This time Freud was the one who searched the pockets of his coat, putting a packet in the other guy's hand. Drugs, thought Tito. A drop of cold sweat ran down his spine.

"It's less than we were expecting."

"Everything's very expensive, do good work and I'll get you some more."

The two of them looked at each other. A movement from the man pointed out the other side of the alley.

"Bring it with you next time," said the woman by way of saying goodbye. Tito couldn't help trying to look at her ass as she was walking away.

Freud ran his hand over his bald white head.

"What's going on?" asked Tito.

"I'm wondering how they found out that I had orders to kill them."

"What?"

"Don't be surprised. Today they're ours, tomorrow they're with them. In less than an hour it'll come out in the newspapers that we were at the Academy."

"They weren't ours?"

"They were," said Freud, and he pointed at the shadows moving away. Tito looked in horror at the gun barrel in front of his nose and he gave it a slap.

"Don't shoot. I've had my fill of crimes."

"We're at war! Don't you get it? Or do you want us all to turn a deaf ear like you, with your life which is so clean and orderly?"

He was going to aim again but the two of them had disappeared down the streets. He looked at Tito Livio with hate.

"If we fail it will be your fault."

"It's immoral."

"In the zone we're in, morals do not exist. I make the decisions."

"It's worse than them."

"Ha . . . It's easy to see you don't know them."

There was a noise of footsteps on the paving stones which continued for another block.

"Here they come," spit Freud and they ducked down again.

Shadows of men were arriving at a side door to the building where the bakery was, and they were slippping inside with such stealth that at times Tito was afraid that he was seeing only figments of his imagination. Then nighttime once again, silent.

"Now let's go. Good luck to both of us, Tito, and remember: now all of them are rivals. Don't say anything that can give them the clue. The bakers are our allies while we're with them, but they're so neutral and such lovers of the truth, that they don't recognize the difference between friends or enemies. So close your mouth and leave it to me. We're running from everyone, understand me?"

They were going to cross when Tito assailed him with a question.

"Listen, Romero."

"What do you want now?"

"What did those people say to you?"

"Who?"

"Those people, the drunks."

"The password."

"And why didn't you believe them?"

"Would you believe in a password that went 'Long live the Mother Superior'?"

38

The San Pablo Scholastic Academy

"It's time," said Freud suddenly, without any warning, as if a switch had been thrown inside of him.

"Time for what?" Tito Livio broke out of his trance. He didn't have the least idea how much time had gone by. His muscles were asleep, and his toes freezing cold.

The old guy raised a finger in a signal perfectly resembling one from a German expressionist movie. The world was now black and white and the shadows oblique and startling.

Tito looked. There was the hermetically sealed bakery door and suddenly, for a change of pace, faraway footsteps. The kind that nighttime distorts and multiplies. Sigmund Romero forcefully brushed him back against the wall.

"It's them."

There's no comment more disquieting. Them who? Them them? Or them, us? The ones we're waiting for or the ones we don't want to see? The good guys or the bad guys? How he wished he were a spectator for this movie, seated in the Valencia de la Plaza Chacabuco movie theater with a paper bag full of cookies on his knees, watching a horror film which would be interrupted by the breaks in the film, the projectionist's mistakes at which the whole theater would whistle; all right now, I've got it.

And this movie, damn it, doesn't break. More steps. Playful ones like a Gene Kelly movie, repeated once again on TV in another movie anthology, splashing through the puddles which don't exist here, but it's as if there were. More steps.

"Everything right on time. That's good."

"Why don't you explain yourself a little more, for Pete's sake?"

"Just hold on and you'll understand."

Like a little kid, they're treating me like a little kid. As if I didn't have any patience, as if I didn't know how to wait until it was my turn, as if I didn't want to receive the famous promised lesson. Well then, I can't wait. I'm impatient and revved up. My muscles hurt, my feet are falling asleep, Freud, for Christ's sake, what are we waiting for?

"Almost everyone's here."

Freud was smiling. The silhouettes were getting close to the door. Everyday men, ordinary, cutting through the curfew like blind people in a dark house which they knew by their fingertips. They were entering the bakery as if they didn't need a gateway. In a moment, the effect of the lights and shadows seemed to merge with the wall and they disappeared like ghosts from a thick turn of the century novel. He couldn't even manage to see their faces, make out their ages, what they were wearing. Freud waited a few minutes more after the last one showed up.

"They were a little late but they're all here."

"The bakers?"

You stepped over the line, Tito, you're beginning to understand. Didn't they tell you that it was a matter of waiting?

Freud nodded three minutes later.

"Long live the Mother Superior," he repeated for himself and shook his head. On your feet, both of you, it's time for action.

Tito caressed the Beretta.

"You're not going to need it yet."

Without looking in any particular direction they crossed the street. Their heels sounded soft and perfect like drops of indestructible steel.

They stopped in front of the entrance. Over the door Tito recognized the holes from a recently disconnected Heart of Jesus. The round outline with no paint was still there against green paint cracked by the humidity. Freud pressed what appeared to be a doorbell. Inside a kind of cicada chirp was heard.

He looked at Tito Livio.

"Nervous?"

"More or less."

Footsteps inside. By the sound of the soles, there was a wooden floor over an empty space and then tiles. All of a sudden there was silence again.

Freud was surprised. He rang the doorbell again. He knocked softly with his knuckles. Three times. The knock repeated itself identically. He frowned.

"Long live the Mother Superior," said Tito, speaking very quietly, to the slot in the door.

A noise of chains, a lock, a heavy wooden bar which must have been blocking all possible entrance of strangers. Freud congratulated him.

"Now you resemble your father."

What did Tito mean with that head movement? Thank you? Yes, I knew that? I'm happy? It's better not to talk to me about him? The one sure thing is that the door is opening. A white dust emerged, letting an eye lean out.

"Long live the Mother Superior," repeated Freud Romero, losing his appetite for so many steps.

"Inside, quickly."

They obeyed.

What was Tito Livio Triviño Recart, our hero and protagonist, feeling?

Gripped by fear he entered the doorway, leaving the refreshing Santiagoan night, typical of the Central Zone of Chile, cool afternoons and pleasant nights in which hot summers or impassioned springs take refuge, insisting upon accelerating the course of change of a season, to a space of another texture, in the same way as the Dutch darkness in Rembrandt's paintings or those attributed to the master, to another space in which to visualize through dusty hues, glazes over whites, creams, wood hues, colors also from the Low Countries but more à la

Vermeer, and the murmuring conversation from the men who strike the dough on the table tops to the sound of a deep canticle of which he can't distinguish the words, a mixture of a military air, paganism and a religious party which makes one think inevitably of Orff's *Carmina Burana.*

Where did they take them?

With a gesture from the one who opened the door, who was a baker's assistant, they entered the corridor which, on the other hand, was the only possible path through which Tito and Freud, in this same order, reached the Great Room of Primordial Bread, so called by the members of the San Pablo Scholastic Academy, in which they were gathered without ceremony nor any comment, merely a resounding silence which is not a contradiction with desires for a literary paradox, but rather the only possible description of the mechanical rhythm of the work of the bakers, guided like galley slaves through this rustically flavored song which seven members were intoning, dressed in matching white, a color whose mystic content is described only too well, with their arms dusted with flour up to their elbows and large balls of dough on the ancient wooden table which Tito, idiot in the world of vegetation, recognized immediately as oak by the grain and the color, making a gross mistake because it was a southern laurel, which was out of place in the ritual atmosphere, if we're frank and we avoid the idealizations which our protagonist would encounter.

How were they received?

Said with honesty, nothing special. At first cool indifference, and secondly the stare from the one who was the boss, the Great Baker, Master of the Spatula and Oven, and thirdly his voice which deserves special mention since it had a unique tone like a bronze bell with bass tones ringing out in a medieval esplanade, in the era in which bells were the only signal of civilization, which if you don't believe me, ask Huizinga.

What did he say to them?

What you're going to hear now.

"You're Triviño's son?"

Tito to himself: The son of, now my name isn't important but rather my lineage, I'm my father's son, the one I should have been, I don't get anything out of denying my ancestry as I've done up to now. He felt the

241

temptation to get on his knees. On the other hand, he raised his head and agreed with a nod.

"And you?"

"My companion," said Tito who now had assumed his role as bearer of the mission with increasing interest.

The boss, the Great Baker, studied them for a while. Then he grabbed dough from the trough to his side and hit it on the table three times in order to slowly mold a type of fuselage with his nimble fingers. His hands were moving amiably and forcefully at the same time. Experts, I already said, to the point of irritation. Suddenly Tito caught himself with his mouth hanging open like a child at a puppet performance, dazzled by the rhythmic movements and the harmony of a work which was becoming a body. He understood: they were thinking over what to do with him over the dough mixture. As Tito would discover little by little, the head is not the center of thinking nor of consciousness.

"I came for your advice," said our hero. His voice merged with the flour and there was no answer. Like a cormorant which submerges itself in the sea and doesn't come to the surface again.

Tito tried to demand an answer or at least hint at the questions which brought him to the Academy, but an unequivocal change in rhythm of the movements of the bakery signaled to him this man's discomfort upon feeling bothered, which in addition was the necessity of total concentration and answering without asking, which is the height of wisdom. The six remaining ones and the mixer continued a melodic intonation with their lips closed: a humming of gigantic bees was coming from their larynxes.

"I don't know if you know . . ." insisted Tito, who was having a difficult time distinguishing whether it was fitting or not.

"I'm the one who doesn't know if you really know why you're here," said the head of the bakers all of a sudden, the Great Kneader, Master of the Spatula and Oven.

Tito had to accept that his ignorance was much more plausible than theirs.

"Well . . ." he stammered like a panting football player asking about the penalty which cost the game.

"Do you know what bread is?"

Tito got quiet. Questions which seem stupid tear mental plans to shreds. He searched for a hurried definition in some branch of his basic schooling. Our daily bread. The only thing that came to his mind. To the bread, bread, and to the wine, wine. Bread for today, hunger for tomorrow. His head was a world championship of lack of imagination.

"Do you know why Christ made his body change into bread? And not rice, wheat, cereal, a sausage, water, milk, mashed potatoes? Maybe you know all about the rites in which enemy soldiers are left in water until their bodies are softened taking on the color of the most purified flour and then they are devoured by the tribe? Did you know that bread is the flour of the earth? Do you know anything about what goes on every night in this room?"

"I didn't have time to explain it to you," Freud humbly intervened.

The Great Master seemed brutally annoyed.

"And whose idea was it to bring novices here?"

The dough slapped against the table with the noise of thunder and then picked up the rhythm again which the other bakers followed immediately. A second phase of the rite was clearly beginning. A sharp and dissonant canticle came from the mouths of the kneaders, their rhythm ruled by the blows from the long mixing spatula on the floor. It was like a sailor's song passed through a synthesizer. Tito scanned the large slaves' quarters through which emerged the oven smokestacks which seemed in disuse beside some obviously new equipment. However, the largest of the ovens was fired up and was progressively heating the room and drying the air which the mixer spattered every once in a while with sprinkles of water taken by hand from a bucket. It's the Sacrifice Oven, Tito said to himself, and he feared seeing himself made into bread like Hansel thrown into the fire by the witch and changed into a gingerbread cookie.

"We'll eat and afterwards we'll know what to say. First was bread, then the verb."

"Okay." Freud heeded the boss's words and moved towards some benches to sit down. He didn't manage to stay one second in that position before someone opened the door for them, also described as the mixer or assistant, and showed them a hanger where white clothing was hanging next to a pot full of dough.

"It looks like we've got to work," said Freud.

They got dressed. The rhythm of the songs was changing its beat in short intervals, following a sequence which was impossible for him to imitate. Each time he thought he caught on, the tone changed and a new seguidilla of chords was begun.

Five minutes into kneading along with the members of the bakery, the boss of the San Pablo Scholastic Academy stopped his ball of dough.

What a way to order a pause! The kind which come wrapped in Latin.

"You two do the feet," he said, however, in Spanish to the visitors.

They obeyed. Kneading in the early morning. What am I doing here with my father dead? What am I doing here with a bunch of insane bakers playing let's make a human figure with dough like my kids usually do?

Next to him Freud was working seriously as in everything he did, thorough, meticulous. He was slowly sculpting a foot as others were a hand, a muscle, a man's torso, a face.

The great lifesized figure was spread over the table.

"Doesn't this all seem strange to you." He looked for Freud's complicity, our flour-covered hero speaking *sotto voce*.

Sigmund Romero was tight-lipped, not saying a word. He took a little bit of dough and formed a big toe on the right foot. Hallux I, our hero and his companion, Tito Livio, remembered from his medical school studies. We still have a memory, citizens.

The work was soon finished. Tito recognized the speed of the rest when everyone had finished and he was still involved with the toes and the ankle. He looked up and could make out a complete human body, the stomach, the genitals, the sloping shoulders. It was a large older man, around fifty years old. He was far away from his face and he couldn't make out who it was. The boss caught him craning his neck so he authoritatively covered his face with a white cloth. One of those present grabbed what seemed to be the handle of a great spatula in order to lift the doughman and put him in the oven. Above the figure the Great Master whispered something which Tito was incapable of understanding, while he was sifting flour through a fine sieve. Another guy opened the oven door and a burst of heat licked the skin of our protagonist. The flames did their number with ill-humored dragon breath. He had to close his eyes. The dough body entered the fire. At the last minute the head appeared clearer and Tito thought he saw his father's features. No, he said to himself, it can't be, I'm joking: but he understood immediately that what he was agreeing to was a burial, a ceremony of change, of death and resurrection, a different one, in another state. He broke into a cold sweat. What are they doing to me? The oven door closed and he didn't find out anything else.

Definitely not. He stayed sprawled out on the floor, his skin white, his clothes too, totally conked out.

39

The turbulent revelation from freshly baked bread

How many minutes went by until the aroma of freshly baked bread woke him up? He never knew. He opened his eyes and saw the enormous fans in the roof with blades the size of propellers on a B-28 from the Second World War. The hardness of a sack of flour in his head, his back. Freud was on his feet and one of the bakers (all of them looked the same under their flour masks which gave them the look of Kabuki actors) leaned down towards him. His white cap suggested a nurse's outfit and he thought he was at the Public Health Hospital, perhaps pierced by thousands of tiny pocketknives. My father, he then said to himself, and he remembered them putting the dough into the crematorium. The smell of bread reverberated in his soul.

"Do you feel better?"

What does it mean to feel better? Wasn't it better to be sleeping, maybe feeling less? Wasn't amnesia better than anything? Or feeling better was to make perfect sense of everything that happened until he didn't hurt and he could grasp reality like someone putting out an ember by crushing it with their hand until it went out leaving an unbearable wound?

A uniform murmur like a mantra was coming from the oven room. The baker who was helping them spoke with a lisp.

"Nothing special. Baking, the usual thing."

It's my father who's in the oven, and that's not anything special. Where'd you get such an outrageous idea. But he didn't say it. And if they think I'm crazy?

"What did the face look like on the . . . the . . .?"

"The body?"

"Yes."

The baker smiled.

"No one, they never have a face. Everyone will see one of their ancestors' faces, the one from whom they will receive the message."

Tito has a questioning look on his face, like a black hole.

"When we eat their body we'll know something about ourselves. It's a special recipe which they say comes from far away. Sometimes some bread made from this mixture escapes. Careless bakers or other jokers. Those are the days when people go around telepathically on the street, or have intuitions or foretell the future. Avalanches of prizes in the lottery are won, fortuitous winnings, fights over discovered adulteries, meetings by simple desire, poetic inspirations, scientific findings which they didn't suspect were even possible. It's the origin of all powers. You will receive it now."

"Don't exaggerate," said Freud. "It's pure suggestion."

"One can see you're not familiar with this profession," answered the baker without even turning around.

"One can see you aren't familiar with mine. I'm tired of listening to legends and dreams that don't lead anywhere."

Freud sat down on a pile of sacks. His pants were white from the flour.

"What good have your ceremonies been if we're heading towards the end of everything just the same?"

"The end of everything?"

The baker looked at him. Terrified.

"Everything," he pointed at Tito. "Not even he knows what he's looking for."

"You're coming here to ask that?"

Freud nodded.

"And does the boss know?"

"I don't think so. He never lets anyone speak."

There was a sharp clang of a bell which announced the end of the baking process. The baker made a couple of genuflexes and returned to his position. Freud helped Tito get up.

"Fear will help them concentrate."

But Tito was the only one really frightened. What did all that mean about his not knowing what he was looking for? Why Freud's scorn for the Academy? Why had they come here then? He was going to open his mouth, that mouth which wasn't at all adequate in its questions, when Freud warned him and made him be quiet. The ceremony was beginning. The oven was open and the fans were accelerating. It seemed like the cover of a whaler in the middle of a storm.

Had you ever seen such golden bread, Tito Livio? Had you ever felt such an intense intoxicating aroma as that of the primary food? Is there anything more inviting, always inviting, than warm fresh bread? Wasn't this his father's face, his closed eyes, his complexion obscured by the fire, the calm in each of his features? Did you know that calm? At any time have you been able to obtain it in your task? Or are you confusing peace with euphoria, parties with routine, fireworks with omnipresent stars in the night which you haven't even looked at for such a long time?

Enough questions, I should bow my head to my chest while I really feel that I'm praying. A strange language is possessing my larynx and making my ribs, my forehead and my jawbone vibrate with changes in tone which I didn't think I was capable of making. How horrible, at times I'm embarrassed, at times it's ridiculous, at times sublime. Or is the transcendent absurdity seen from the outside?

Enough questions, Tito, Freud is the only one who's still mute and you're following like you always followed the interminable prayers from your mother at mass, trying to feel that nothing touched your heart, without perceiving that you're possibly praying your father's prayers, the ones which you denied all your life. Get on your knees at least mentally, bow, faced with the inevitability and perfection of the bread. The sentence is not ours, Tito, the Supreme Baker says it, the

Great Master of the Spatula and Oven, the tall large and rosy man who washes his enormous palms in clear water, free of all stains, from the select flours with which he has made the mixture, to indicate that the bread is now ready to be eaten, which is when the fans stop and the rising heat reinstates itself like a combat suit on the Sahara front.

"We should wait a few hours and taste it when the sun is going down, but our guests are in a hurry."

It's the first time he's been friendly with us, Tito is thinking, and he stretches out his hand towards the Body.

"Not so fast." The administrator of the ceremony took on his dominant air. "Repeat ye the Question to yourselves and in the bread ye will receive the light."

Tito looked at the others: they were closing their eyes and mumbling some strange noise, like the squeaking of a newly born rat, a puppy, of a little bird lost in its nest. After this they were furiously grabbing pieces from the body, in an act of mutilation which hurt Tito in his own body. He moved back.

Freud gave him a push. What did we come here for if it wasn't to eat bread?

Tito choked: Eat my father's body?

"Cannibalism is a natural instinct," said Sigmund Romero. "It's not going to hurt you."

"I can't."

The rest of them, meanwhile, were gobbling it up with pleasure. The bread still seemed steaming hot. A column of steam was coming from the pieces in their hands which were so heated up it made them juggle the bread back and forth between their hands to cool it off. They were blowing on it, eating it with their mouths open. In a little while they began to laugh as if they had smoked marijuana, from the eastern plains of Colombia, from the heart of Mexico. Sometimes he had used it to go to the agency, day and night stoned on weed. That was another era.

"Come on, Freud."

The push this time sent him reeling back to the table. Either he was eating bread or he was forgetting everything. The loud laughs from the bakers were increasing in volume. They seemed drunk, stoned. Their eyes were shining, alcoholic voices, they were beginning to strike the table, euphoric. One of them stood on a stool and began to tell an old joke about an Englishman, a German, a Chilean, and a monkey. He got all mixed up and threw in a parrot, and then got it confused with another one, a variation on the fall of the cross of Jesus Christ, and finished off with a gross joke about condoms. All of them seemed to follow him with disproportionate outbursts of laughter. He hadn't managed to finish when another baker got up on the same stool, pulling the first fellow down, to recite *Nada* by Carlos Pezoa Véliz which halfway through was replaced with a tongue-tied version of *La Casada Infiel* by García Lorca.

"Please, let's go, Freud."

Romero lost his patience. He grabbed a piece of bread and began to chew it spewing mouthfuls of steam because of the temperature of the dough. Tito hesitated and reached out. He took a section of the foot and brought it up to his mouth.

"Forgive me, father," he said to himself.

He took a bite, thinking about the photo, about his progenitor, about his question. The bread was hot just as he had foreseen, but tolerable. He ate a piece, and then another and another. Terrified, he waited for the effects, but nothing happened. Nothing. The bakers were amusing themselves for all they were worth. A third one was intoning *Granada* by Augustín Larra and was now mixing the words with: *I'm selling some black eyes, who wants to buy them,* and fragments of *Poema 20* by Neruda. Applause, sobs, and laughter capped off his presentation. Another fellow danced a hybrid of a *jota* from Aragón with a *chilote* and a northern *cueca*. Everyone was slowly gathering together in the middle of an insane canon. He made out a political discourse which never finished: *Ladies and gentlemen, mayors, professors, members of neighborhood groups, Mister President, generals, director of the firefighters from Talagante, from Fresia, from Maullin, secretaries, nurses, etcetera.* The last one was shouting sharply in the tone of a nightclub singer, in the face of another guy who was announcing evangelically the coming of the Lord in all His glory and majesty. Tito couldn't stand it any more.

"But this bread is a fraud!"

The yell silenced the ritual. Freud's eyes opened wide. The bakers turned towards our out of tune protagonist who was breaking protocol at the very climax. How the eyes opened up, the mouths. The Great

Boss, Supreme Priest, Elder Baker, squinted, his eyes sharpening the most persecuting stare.

Tito was beside himself.

"This is a bunch of trash!" he screamed. "Blasphemies! Absurdities!"

With a blow from his fist he smashed what was left of the bread on the table. He began to destroy it in front of the astonished stares of the celebrants. Then he grabbed the head between his hands, he raised it above his own and took a violent and terrible bite out of it. He pulled off the nose, the cheeks, the eyes and the mouth. He spit out the crumbs and continued his destructive task until he left a pile of warm wet mush spread all over the floor. With his mouth still full he headed towards the exit.

"Calm down," Freud grabbed him.

Useless. People were grabbing and pulling. A stumbling Tito Livio Triviño found the path.

"This is a lack of respect! Heresy! Imbeciles eating bread as if it were the host! A fraud for ignorant people!"

Insults followed until he fought with the multiple locks on the door without being able to open it. He became more infuriated at his powerlessness. The chains took off one of his fingernails, his hands were covered with wounds. From inside, the bakers and Freud, who was watching him leaning up against a pillar, were listening. A huge laugh exploded from the mouths of the group. The Great Baker, old Sigmund.

"It seems we overdid it with the mixture," he said to him.

"It's unbearable."

"He needs it. Now he'll know what he wants to find out."

"Listen, sometimes I also doubt if all this is nothing but nonsense. Third rate Latin sayings, a pastiche of orientalism with sacred songs and then an occasional dash of a Zen Koan."

"It's not a bad recipe," laughed the Supreme Baker.

Where did he get that sense of humor? When did he become such a joker? Tito was going on like a kid in the middle of a tantrum, fighting with the door and clawing at the bakery.

"Get him out of here. In a little while the second phase is going to begin and it's not a good idea for him to be here."

One of the bakers, having difficulty controlling a fit of laughter, accompanied Freud Romero. The door was freed in an instant. Tito left, slamming the door to go along with his overexcited state of mind, as if there had never been a curfew, as if there were no danger. Freud was behind him. They threw their ritual clothes far away.

"Don't you think that's the limit? Aren't they the same as my father?" screamed Tito Livio, blind with rage. "It's just a trick, a facade, a bunch of cowards, queers, incompetents. They're not anything, mediocre people who spend their time kneading bread and think that they're doing something sacred. They tell each other a supernatural myth so they won't feel like the scum of the earth from a night which nobody gives a damn about. All of them are full of shit, with a terrible salary, in a miserable sham, and they think they're the wise men, the ones who can do everything, the enlightened ones. Trash! That's what they are! Pieces of crap! Garbage!"

Tito's screams were resounding all through the street.

"It seems as though you're looking to get yourself killed."

"Me? Who's going to kill me?" laughed Triviño Junior proudly, and he began to dance like Nijinsky in his delirium.

Freud stopped and looked towards the west.

"Oh, no," he said.

It was then that Tito noticed the headlights. He clearly heard the roar of the motor coming towards them. The great snout of a large and elongated military vehicle which was bending at its frame under the headlights, stopping the flow of the metallic polish from the bodywork, without respecting the dead signal lights, menacing with the most determined and cruel crew. Panic in a liquid state covered his skin. Soaked, he ran towards Freud.

"In the corner," he ordered him.

He searched for his Beretta.

"They're going to kill us, they're going to kill us."

"Damned bakers," said Freud.

"All this is just a bunch of crap."

Tito wasn't listening. Fear was making the words clink in his ears. His mind went blank, empty. Stuck to old Romero, trying to blend into the wall. On the street again.

"Quit trembling," Freud scolded him. He immediately let out a moan.

Damn, was what he said.

"Damn what?"

"Get on your feet. We're going right now."

"But . . . What's going on?"

Sigmund Romero's eyes opened like heavy artillery cannons, they remained powerless faced with the inherent stupidity of his companion.

"They're going to the bakery," he pushed him.

The blast shattered his brain. They ran, ran, ran. In the distance the slamming of the car doors rang out like explosions. There were several, asynchronous.

"Hit the dirt."

A few blocks further away they found peace and quiet. Garbage cans, the hollow of one of the old doorways. They caught their breath little by little. In the distance a volley from a machine gun made their stomachs knot up. Freud covered his face with his hands. Shooting again.

"Son of a bitch," he moaned.

Tito remembered pieces of the nights of insomnia from so many years with those noises in the distance. Above all when he lived with Anita. Falling asleep to bullets, falling asleep with a helicopter overhead. Like now, once again.

The winged bug crossed the night with a potent searchlight which raked the darkness of the street. Tito and Freud squeezed against the wall, standing up. Shapes, invisible. Again and again the mechanical dragonfly. Then it disappeared looking for other quarry for its luminous claw. The x-shaped arms gradually became silent.

"What happened?"

"It's better if you don't even think about it." The old guy was drained. "Was it useful at least?"

"Was what useful?"

"The bread, I mean, the bread with drugs."

Tito hesitated, he was still confused. Incomplete images were going through his mind, sentences, leftovers from a consciousness which didn't belong to him.

"Think hard," insisted Sigmund. "Haven't you had some vision? A sentence? An answer?"

Tito shrugged his shoulders. Freud swore again.

"Everyone dead for nothing."

That was when Tito saw the photo in his mind, like a bodily presence, like a large three-dimensional blackboard. Above it were triangles, squares, geometric figures, the Pythagorean table drawn by Jimmy Scott in a book of math for the Humanities, a photograph of his father which had gotten lost without being missed. Then once again the photo found in the boardinghouse, and a bolero: *I'm involved in a triangle, without a solution or reason.* That's how he heard Los Hermanos Arriagada, as if it came from a small transistor radio which had become lodged in his brain. Foolishness, he said to himself, and it all went up in smoke, the photo, the song, everything. He came to again.

"Did you find out anything?"

"Nothing, pure foolishness. What did they put in the bread?"

"Nothing is foolish. Maybe at first glance it seemed trivial to you, but don't put it out of your mind. Retain it as well as you can. The thing which you feel to be the most idiotic might be the one which will give us the clue. Tell me what you thought."

"Seriously?"

The old man nodded. In the middle of the night Tito Livio hummed the bolero. Freud kept staring at him.

"It can't be," he said.

"Well, that's what it was. Nothing more."

"I don't understand it, I don't understand it. Does it remind you of something?"

"Shall we go ask them?" suggested Tito, innocently. His recent lucidity was impeding his memory of the cars, the shootout a few streets away, the helicopter.

A squealing of tires answered Tito and he had a burst of memory.

"It's useless. There can't be anyone left alive," said Sigmund Romero, hurt. But it wasn't necessary. Tito had understood and was sobbing again. The image in his brain, that's it, it was his father's.

"I killed him, I killed him," he suddenly screamed and he took off running in the direction of the bakery.

Out of his mind, of course.

40

Right in the middle of hell

Tito arrived panting at the door to the San Pablo Scholastic Academy. Fear stopped him: the door was torn off its hinges, violently. The effect of a blow from a dragon's paw, the relentless claw of that dinosaur with helicopter eyes and automobile feet whose slobber of light had spelled misfortune.

"Don't go in," Freud requested of him, behind, pistol in hand.

He didn't pay attention to the warning.

Would you like to have another helping, Tito? You knew what you were going to find. Because of that you hugged old Romero, because of that you left running. How many bodies do you need to see so it won't affect you? Is it enough for you with blood all over the flour, bodies spread all over the floor, torn apart as if they were stuffed toys? When will the day come when you pay attention to someone, when you consider the authority of someone who knows more, whose advice doesn't irritate you? Look at them. It's my fault. No, it's not your fault, Tito. Yes, it is. I've got them all involved in the thick of things. No, no one got anyone involved. It's the law. Life, as they say. Don't think you're so omnipotent.

The most disfigured body was the Great Baker's. He recognized it by its majestic look, even retained in death. They had smashed him in rage against the wall. His face was smashed and blood was spurting along the wall to the floor. An enormous piece of bread was stuffed in his mouth like an apple in a roast pig. Tito stopped cold. He knew he had gone too far but he needed to see it. I need to hurt, to not have them let up on me, to hurt and not heal, get used to the horror without any possibility of denying it, so it won't be just a newscast which can be turned off by pushing a remote control button, nor a newspaper where all you have to do is throw it in the trash can, nor a joke that's easy to discredit. Dead people exist. They're not television series or propagandistic maneuvers. They kill, they die.

"They really gave it to them. Styer automatic pistols with twenty bullet clips. All silver bullets."

Tito, with his last defenses, calculated the cost of the killing. They looked at the bodies for a few minutes. All of a sudden Freud yelled out an exclamation: *No!!*

"What's going on?"

Freud Romero didn't answer. He threw out his hand towards Tito Livio, but he couldn't manage to grab him by the arm when the squeal of brakes was heard again in front of the building. The city was deaf like a dead person. The light from the headlights came through the cracks. It was too late to run away.

Later on Tito would be surprised by his reaction: not a tremble nor a doubt nor a sob. Finally used to it, almost. Blood on the soles of his shoes, bodies in his sight, the smell of death and bread throughout the whole building.

"We'll wait for them here," he said to Freud, gripping his Beretta.

"You're crazy. Let's go out the back."

"Where?"

Freud was already moving through a labyrinth of sacks. He followed him. Someone came through the doorway of the wrenched-off door. Perfect silhouettes: armed with high caliber weapons.

Tito squeezed the Beretta, he had it ready like the muscles of a sprinter leaned over the starting line. The smell of the blood was slightly intoxicating, now not only from the bread, but from rage. He stayed where he was. The temptation was to try out the pistol on those guys. He understood the cruelty and the blindness, the taste of raw meat, the wolves.

The men came on stage. Tall, burly, well dressed. Very stylish. They looked like magazine models wearing the spring-summer collection from Ermenegildo Zenga. He didn't recognize them. They did recognize him.

"Tito!" Freud's scream.

No way. Tito raised the Beretta and aimed. For my father, for the bakers, for me. He squeezed the trigger. Click. The safety, damn, he hadn't taken off the safety. Your heart is pounding, Tito, your hands are getting cold. They're watching how you're bumbling with your gun. You don't manage to bring it up again when they get off a volley. You jump. The bullets were aimed at the floor. You jump back.

"Tito!"

Stubborn, you aim again. Again, in the floor, two volleys which leave perforations like the cave of a river rat. You jump, a shaking fit. They're having fun with you, Tito. Do you see how their teeth are shining in the semi-darkness?

An explosion rings out behind you. Sigmund Romero's weapon doesn't have the silencer on. One of the guy's shoulders is shattered, he's rocking like a carnival duck, he bursts like a ripe tomato. The strapping young man turns and aims furiously again: a wounded animal. You hit the dirt while above there floats a storm of bullets. You turn like a commando and you return the fire. For the first time Tito Livio Triviño Recart is shooting at a human being, or at least one of human appearance. *Bang*, is what the onomatopoeia of a comic would say. *Bang*, the body which jumps clutching the middle of his chest. The silver fist which shreds the silk tie, the explosion of blood which stains everything, his weapon shooting towards the sky, trigger-happy while its carrier falls to his knees, then bends over, then falls flat on his face, burying himself against the body of one of the bakers.

You're sweating, Tito, your clothes are stuck to your skin, the blow from the recoil of the Beretta, painful in the thin arm of an amateur tennis player who barely does exercises with a typewriter, jogging every

257

once in a while, stretching an exerciser which you've never managed to turn into a method.

The one with the wounded arm shoots again.

"Tito, let's get out of here once and for all." Freud is furious.

Another round from a machine gun. He remembered *El Cielo*, when he learned about the bullets. The wall opened up like one of those movie tricks, magic. Who looks like who? The movie like life, or life like the movie? You did this trick in an ad one time. The bullets wrote the name of an American cowboy blue jean. Now it's for real. You roll once more until you fall on your face. A sack has fallen on your feet. There's the wounded guy and a third guy you can't see very well, they squeeze their triggers again. A swarm of lethal silver insects whistles all around. The door opens up and you shoot again.

A hit, Tito. The Beretta shakes while the man flowers like a liquid geranium right in front of you. The third guy has hidden. Well, Tito. You really shot. But you don't feel good. You're confused, abused, you're having trouble breathing.

You feel the weight of the silence from the pause. You listen to your own panting, whistling. Death winks at you perched on your shoulder. Where's old Freud?

"Tito."

No, it's not the old guy. Who can it be? Who? Who else but Rolando Donkavian?

"You lost yourself a beautiful trip to São Paulo. You lost a lot of things that you would have liked. You shouldn't have gone so far."

You don't answer.

"You're a better shot than I thought."

A coincidence, Tito, that's really clear. Beginner's luck. Or, inherited from your father? He must have shot like that. Because of that you survived, because of that you took care of the letter, because of that. And if his spirit is who is guiding your hand?

"You're better than that idiot Old Man of yours. Why are you continuing to be loyal to a ghost?"

Shut up, Donkavian, I'm going to send you to hell.

He heard him laugh. Did he read his mind?

"We're right in the middle of hell, Tito. Yes, I read it. Soon everything will be like that. We're only somewhat discredited. Adding it all up, we're not so bad off. Why don't you come over to the winning side?"

He couldn't take any more. Impulsively he grabbed the Beretta. *Bang.* Nothing, only the whistle and the projectile smacking sharply into a cornice.

"There's no way out, Tito. You're surrounded. There are more of us and we're better, dear Tito. Come over to our side." He was quiet before speaking again. "I'll wait for you outside, Tito."

He heard his footsteps leaving. Slowly, calmly, sincerely, convinced of his strength. That's how he sold his ideas to his clients. No one could say no to him.

He looked for Freud. Where was he? Where?

41

Freud's last cigarette

"Over here."

His voice was weak. A whisper, a last gasp. Almost nothing. Darkness again. It wasn't easy to get his bearings. Tito Livio was feeling sick, his body was wet: sweat. Where are you, Freud? Here you are.

He saw him leaning with great difficulty against a sack which was leaking flour through the bullet holes. His gun was being held up by a lifeless wrist, his arm was bleeding. When he went to grab him by his sleeve he discovered it was soaked with a warm fluid. The unmistakable shine of blood, like oil, wine, its odor.

"You're wounded, my friend."

It was the first time he had considered him a friend.

"Nothing to worry about. They're lead bullets. I'll get over it."

"But you've lost a lot of blood."

Sigmund Freud's weak voice, like an out of body experience, confused. He's breathing in short gasps with irregular pauses. Does he have a bullet in his lungs? Like a sack of flour, like a wineskin with holes, bleeding to death.

"No, don't move me. I'll get over it. It's part of hell to suffer total agony without relief from death. This is immortality: martyrdom. I hope they never give it to you."

"They're outside."

"Someone must have told them about the photo."

He thought about Donkavian's smile through which he heard his words of steel. Knives in his brain. This was São Paulo, death all around him, Freud's blood which was getting his feet wet now, soaking through the leather of his shoes, in an enormous puddle which would grow little by little until it reached the street, until it flooded Santiago with this death in slow motion, blood which nobody would notice, only during the chores of the housewives asking themselves why the stains aren't coming off the sidewalks, the tires in collective motion staining the center of Santiago with the blood of the master until it blends into the asphalt, made from everyone's blood, that which no one dried more than the sun, erosion, despair, habit.

"You have to get out of here."

"We're surrounded."

Fear was beginning to flap its wings around Tito Livio again. He was free for so little time from this cruel bird, its claws in his back, the pecking which penetrates my heart.

"There's an exit that I'm sure Donkavian doesn't know about."

Tito questioned with his look. Freud didn't notice it. There was a little bit of light on his short, white beard, his mouth with teeth missing, his round face outlined by the light and shadow. Tito remained with his back turned, his face in the darkness, his profile which old Freud could still see.

With his good hand he pointed at the roof. "Behind those sacks," he stammered. "At the end of the warehouse." Tito couldn't make out anything. Then Freud asked him to light his last cigarette. He poked through the old guy's clothes and he could feel that he had caught a chill. He found it. He was going to tell him he didn't have any matches when he remembered a silver Ronson which he had seen him use when they left Torres. It was there. The spark caught immediately, loyal. By the light of the flame he noticed Sigmund Freud Romero's yellow paleness.

The old guy breathed with pleasure. One, two times. The third time he got a coughing fit which Tito thought was going to do him in. He didn't insist again. He handed the cigarette to Tito who kept staring at him.

"Go on, take it. It'll do you good."

Tito took it, suspiciously. He took a drag that burned his throat. What kind of shit was the old guy smoking?

He saw him smile, if that's what you could call the grimace which his weakness permitted. He changed his pistol to his other hand and aimed at the door.

"I'll cover you," he said. "They'll come in over there, and I'll give it to them good."

He said something like that. He could make out something like that between his effort to speak and the barely mumbled words.

"There's a hidden stairway between the fuses and a skylight that opens up," he said, in his last breath.

The protagonist had his doubts. It can't be, he was dying. He couldn't leave him there. He tried to tell him, but Freud put his hand over his mouth. Tito felt his rough, strikingly cold skin. Why did he seem happy, the old bastard, if he was dying?

"You don't understand anything, Tito. In a little while I'm going to be safe and sound. Take care of yourself."

"But . . . Where am I going?" It hurt him to have to demand a guidebook.

"Look in the library for something written by your father. Hurry up. They know you have to do it."

Tito imagined what that could mean. Bodies, the terrible sign of death in the Diez de Julio neighborhood. There, mixed with the usual, everyday tasks, everything looking the same.

"Hurry," reiterated Freud, clenching his teeth. Tito remembered his mission. He managed to take a step towards the narrow opening which he could make out between the sacks after a more attentive look. He returned to caress Freud's head. Freud made a gesture of displeasure.

"Enough sentimentality. Get going."

Okay, towards the exit. He found the stairway without any difficulty. A moonbeam fell, in a cropped off manner, like a spotlight. It was there that he hurt so much. On the floor, by chance, he recognized shell casings from the volley which had crushed the adobe and passed through walls. They shined as if they were silver. They were.

A new shot rang out behind him. He wanted to go down and look for Freud but his own voice, broken, almost extinct, pushed him again. Another shot, and another, and another. Sigmund Romero emptying his gun into the door. A machine gun burst answered him. Wide open, without a silencer. The people sleeping can screw themselves, let them get used to the noise of power. When he leaned his head over the roof the night was clear like a northern night, the air was like a marsh in the high plain, as if everything had been purified by the sacrifice which he was leaving behind, his own. He walked without stumbling over the changing surfaces, multiplied. Arriving at the edge he threw himself to the ground and looked over the gutters: Donkavian's cars. Rolando himself walking around smiling while two henchmen were aiming at the bakery. He thought about shooting him but a gesture from his target stopped him. Go in, he was saying to his bodyguards. He had to hurry. Get out of here. He ran like a cat bearing the weighty burden of his grief. He didn't even know where he really was. The weight of the Beretta was his compass, still full of silver bullets, in his right hand. It was the spirit of his father running at his side, directing the wind, choosing adequate trajectories for him, he had transformed himself into good luck, intuition, common sense. He was inside him, taking care of him.

During a pause he took the last drag on Freud's cigarette. He had kept licking his fingers as if it were a fetish. As if upon putting it out it would be the signal of his last breath. He let it go out and accepted the sorrow. He must be dead now, he thought. Then he heard the cars. Not one more shot, only the cars which closed their doors with that empty slamming, intolerable, sure of themselves, and then later on the motors sawing through a gap in the night. Were they going to the library?

He went down to the sidewalk. Never so feline, never so acrobatic. His father calmed him down inwardly. He was excited and confused. The walls were dancing and the floor was performing a strange ballet.

"Oh, shit, that old guy was smoking dope."

Dear Freud, he happily thought, you never ceased to surprise me. He said goodbye to him, beginning his long-lasting walk. No one, nothing. His footsteps, his footsteps again, all alone. The Beretta swinging up and down, like the baton of a relay runner.

At this point he saw lights and heard a motor. It can't be, Donkavian again.

But death makes one gain experience and Tito was a graduate now. Hidden behind a kiosk he waited with his weapon with the safety off, cocked. He was right in the middle of a war and he was beginning to like it. Marijuana, he laughed again, recognizing the uninhibiting effect.

The car was coming slowly. Another sound, another rhythm. He recognized it when he leaned out. It was clear that it was looking for him. But it wasn't Donkavian.

It was the taxi.

He and the driver looked at each other.

"And Freud Romero?"

Tito understood what he was asking him.

"Sons of whores," exclaimed the driver who didn't need the answer. "Let's go, get in. We have to get there first."

42

A door

Santiago at night, dead Santiago. Like an occupied city, like a closed museum, like an insignificant village to which the plague could have come, wiping out everything left of life in the streets and plazas. The doors closed tight. Some piles of garbage which the poor people would come to rummage in, looking for a possible treasure.

Nobody knew about the photo except him and old Freud. Who could have squealed on them? The waiters from Torres with that silent suspicion of servants, omnipresent witnesses to the masters' games, possessors of all secrets? An infiltrator in the ranks of the people in the library? The old guy himself? He wouldn't have taken a risk like that. And if all this were a trick, Freud's fake death, the fake death of the bakers, everything an interweaving to put him on a false trail and take him where they would want when they find out the truth and learn about the requisite letter? Hadn't old Freud said that maybe the person who had it should be eliminated?

He looked at the photo again under the changing light in the street, which with the movement of the car was rotating its angle back and forth, confusingly. What was there in it? Triangles, squares, a bolero listened to on the radio in his now very distant youth. His mother, him, his brother. Something clicked in his mind. Eureka! A change of temperature, the expansion of his chest to give more free territory to a heart muscle contracted for so long. He was familiar with the neighborhood in the photo. The house in the background was not his house but maybe the one in front was, the one which he could see from the living room window when he got bored in the patient weekend afternoons listening to soccer. Badminton with Magallanes, clear in his head. Yes, that was it. He let his memory moorings loose and little Matchbox cars entered the net, the first, a luxury of the era. Now they were selling them in drugstores. A child in front, a friend of his brother, perhaps very dark to please his mother who used to complain about the neighborhood which wasn't at her level of upbringing. I wasn't born to have poor, mediocre, everyday children. The little neighbor was dark-skinned and humble. They used to play guns on the dusty passageway near the Chacabuco Plaza. The houses had a letter over their portals. Later on they changed them. Something like that.

Like a movie machine with a timer, the image went out. Looking without thinking, he said to himself, let yourself go, like when he used to plan a campaign and he would think about the product until the image became deformed and words would come into his mind. He looked at the photo: I'm the one in the picture, me, Triviño Senior taking the picture and letting my son find me in order to tell him something that I couldn't tell him in any other way. Why didn't he speak to me in the apartment? I wouldn't have believed him. Like an idiot I would have given away everything to la Maga. His death was the message. His absence in the photo. Now that he was murdered his message should be deciphered. When my father took the picture he knew about his death, about my blindness as an adult, his destiny was as clear as day to him. His mission was to take care of it and hand it over to me like this, through his own sacrifice. Was I then designated as his relief? Why not Gustavo who got along better with him, they ate the same way, they moved the same way, they even look alike, looked alike, physically? He was in Spain, sure, and besides that the rush. I have to locate this letter and make it disappear. Although it may mean my death, although I also must be eliminated.

266

He looked at Santiago passing by the window. He would give his life for that sleeping world, dazed, rather, below the chloroform of the curfew.

"Do you want me to let you out here?"

The taxi driver's voice shook him out of his resignation. He halfway recognized the Diez de Julio neighborhood: the light was not helping very much. At night all landscapes look the same.

Help me, my Father, we've got to get out here, rather, we have to proceed cautiously. Behind, there is a door which goes directly into the library. Only those of us who have books in the library are familiar with it. Thank you, Father. You're welcome, we're one. My memory is yours, your voice is mine, I act through your body, you think and you reflect through my memory. Thank you, Father.

"I'll get out here," he said to the taxi driver who clicked his tongue again.

"Sons of whores," he swore before leaving. He disappeared into the night just as he had emerged, like an elf, a secret inhabitant of the curfew.

We have to act, thought Tito. Yes, he heard inside himself. We have to work, like an echo. He looked for the door.

It was small. It was situated in back of a pillar painted with lime. It was green or lilac (the scarcity of light prevented him from making it out clearly), it wasn't any taller than a ten-year-old child and, given its width, you had to turn to the side to pass though. Besides, it was closed. It didn't have a keyhole visible anywhere, much less a door-knob, a knocker, or a handle. Simply a door, without visible hinges. It could simply be built into the wall, like a kind of sculpted *trompe l'oeil*.

It wasn't very hard for him to find it. Its presence in a long white wall whose only flaws were the pillars every ten feet, seemed to be made on purpose to call attention to it, and then to frustrate. The house was buried in the sidewalk. Tito calculated that the library would be below street level, perhaps one or two floors underground.

He pushed a couple of times, no go. He leaned into it forcefully a third time but it persisted in its immobility. He felt enraged, impotent and alone, all at once, but most of all lonely. No one who would help him, no one who would advise him. He had lost the internal dialogue with his father like a fleeting radio signal which by chance finds an antenna.

He let himself fall in the minimal opening of the threshold, doubled up like a fetus, with the Beretta floating between his hands. Once more he felt like crying.

How do you open an impregnable door? The excitable effect of the bread was making his brain nervous. How do I open you, damned door?

He looked at it, stupid like all doors, like chickens, like armoires. Couldn't there be another one? He looked all around, he ventured to the corner recognizing what now in the morning would be the typical bustle of the neighborhood, full of cars and men in grease-stained overalls with monkey wrenches, and screams which announced the parts on sale Monday through Friday. Now there wasn't a single sound. He returned to the entrance, his own niche in which to take refuge, from what he didn't know. To wait for the arrival of Donkavian's cars and his flame throwers? That was letting himself be crucified. He wasn't cut out to be a martyr or hero or anything like that. He looked up at the sky.

"You made a mistake with me," he said. And he felt the pain of accepting it.

His mouth formed a perfect parabola. He beat on the door bitterly: knock knock. Like making a joke.

"Hello?" he said, imitating the voice of the old lady done by Sergio Silva on *Radiotanda*, a program he never missed when he was a kid, accompanied by his mother who found him irresistibly funny. She used to laugh, she was different before the lupus.

He continued joking with the door. *Rapunzel, Rapunzel, let down your hair*. He thought it was old Romero's marijuana which had gotten him like this, or the bread. What a crazy guy. He was getting back a subdued sanity and once more the labial grin of bitterness was spreading across his chin. Another joke.

"Open the door or I'll huff and I'll puff and I'll blow your house down."

The Wolf and the Three Little Piggies. He thought he was the wolf, foaming at the mouth, trying to break down the barrier of the hardest working piggy. A moralistic homage to strength and foresight. His father used to tell it to him, imitating the wolf so well who was made furious by the surviving pig. He felt like a stupid, contemptible petit bourgeois beside the impassioned register of the wolf, his omnipotence, his frankness. When I'm big I want to be a wolf, he told him one time. It's just that I'll worry about not being a stupid wolf who goes around believing that you can break down bricks with your breath. His father laughed. He told it to his mother. Lupus means wolf in Latin. I really put my foot in my mouth.

And the oblique moral of Ali Baba who deceived the thieves? His work was something like that. Tito Livio Triviño and the forty clients from MacPherson. A Puss in Boots, yes, he certainly was a savvy ad man. What a guy. Who was making fun of whom in his work? The stories of The Thousand and One Nights were beautiful. Read in their entirety, without cutting, with his father. With Gustavo they read Salgari in the darkness, and with flashlights, Ponson du Terrail. The old woman, totally inconsistent, would give us Poe in the complete version. I could swear I saw Justine on her night stand, I could swear.

He stared at the door, now all intentions of opening it were forgotten. The mere pleasure of waiting and rambling in his mind. Ali Baba.

"Open, sesame," he kidded.

And the door (which is how the cliché goes) opened.

43

Funiculí, Funiculá

Another stairway, darkness. Isn't there any place to go that isn't
dark and gloomy? Which doesn't have this smell of dampness,
of old wilted paper, with boards that creak diabolically, may God
excuse the adverb, when I descend on them?

I go down and I fall into a passageway illuminated by small little
windows which filter the pale moonlight. Through patches of darkness
I distinguish the walkways between piles of books, all in disarray. No
coded signal appears to help me find anything. They are placed in a
totally unpredictable manner, as if an illiterate maid had done the
cleaning meticulously but hurriedly, and interrupted in her task she
had left some volumes not only upside down, but with the bindings
towards the inside and the pages on the outside, or perpendicular to
the rest or simply thrown on the floor.

Piles of books are accumulating under the bookshelves and I don't
even dare ask how to get to one supposedly written about, on, or for my
father, which could give me clues with respect to this photograph that
I'm carrying in my pocket next to my heart. I'm in the midst of all this,

270

wandering and rambling among the interminable shelves when I perceive a ray of light coming from underneath a door. Another door. A dim yellow outline which borders what could be the passageway to another area of the library. I think and remember: Jorge Batalla, the attendant and librarian. I think and remember: a tenuous papyrus colored atmosphere like the one which emanates from thousands of lighted candles but which he could not see. I think: there was no identifiable light source. I squeeze the Beretta holster, cold and hard like a widow. I put my ear up to the door panel. I listen.

A Neapolitan song: *Funiculí, Funiculá.* Between his teeth.

"Open, sesame," said Tito.

But things aren't that simple: it didn't happen. There was a tacky doorknob and an everyday Odis panel which opened ungracefully. With the Beretta held in front of him, he went in. Whoever the Neapolitan singer was he didn't notice Tito Livio coming into the room. Surrounded by tall stacks of books, he was occupying Batalla's desk. Without batting an eyelid he continued funiculating until the mouth of the gun barrel installed itself between the cervical insertions of his trapezium muscles. He shut up. Ciao, Caruso. Tito could not avoid the Bogart attack which came over him. Raymond Chandler completely took over his vocabulary.

"Don't move or turn around unless you want me to blow your brains out."

He said this without a trace of modesty, like in an old movie on television late at night. Are there any other movies? The rest is pastiche or bad cinematography. Howard Hawks or nothing, black and white or nothing. Blow his brains out. Did you really say it to him seriously, Tito?

"It's no joke. So it's better if you tell me who you are and what you're doing here."

He watched him carefully. The poor guy, he was trembling. He had a thin, fine beard and a pair of thick glasses with black plastic frames. He was rather young, he looked younger than the age he could be. Younger than you, Tito.

"My name is Umberto."

"Humberto?"

"No, Umberto, without the 'h'."

271

"How do you know I said it with an 'h'?"

"Well, it's noticeable."

The know-it-all tone from the guy infuriated Tito. He squeezed the Beretta.

"How can you tell if I'm not pronouncing it?"

"It's just that . . ." The poor guy was trembling; which produced great pleasure for Tito, it's always more pleasant when the other guy is trembling. "Everything is pronounced. Not pronouncing the 'h' is only a convention which comes out in the cultivated ear and in the transformation of Spanish under Arabic influence which ennobles the 'j' and ignores the 'h' like a breathing pause. You said Jumberto and not Umberto, but with a soft 'j', almost silent. You came to the 'U' with suspicion, with fear. The 'h' acted like the minimal pause which I'm telling you about. It's purely a matter of training."

It's obvious that he didn't manage to say this entire paragraph. Tito felt like killing him and pushed him again with the Beretta.

"What are you doing here?" he insisted.

"I study, I read . . ." he trembled again.

"Who let you in?"

"And you?"

The man was quick. Tito searched anxiously in his bag of ready-made scripts. What would Sam Spade say in my place? Or Nick Charles? Or Marlowe? Nero Wolfe, whoever?

"I'm the one who's asking the questions."

"The old power play," said the other man.

"Who do you think you are? I'm aiming at you with a real Beretta and you're shaking like a leaf, but all the same you're speaking to me as if you were giving a lecture in Milan."

"You pegged my accent, isn't that right?"

It wasn't true but he said it was.

"Where is Jorge Batalla?"

"He let me in and then he left. You're a friend of his?"

Tito thought about what sentence would be the best answer. The scene had changed into a battle of wits. He felt the guy's talent in the air. He was one of those who went around with it stamped on his forehead. Where had he come from? He wasn't very tall, rather mesomorphic. He spoke strangely.

THE SECRET HOLY WAR OF SANTIAGO DE CHILE

"You must be looking for something here. No one comes in without a purpose. Maybe a nocturnal intuition, a Babylonian codex, a treatise in Sanskrit, a study on medieval culture written in Mapuche."

"There isn't any of that here," muttered Tito. Totally dominated by Umberto. He had the pistol but it was pure show. The other one was giving the orders. He had him trapped in a net of words and words and words.

"There's everything here. The whole universe is here. Disordered and chaotic, but all here. Apocryphal Middle Ages, false histories of the world, theories about the origin of the cosmos which can never be proven, but neither can they be discarded under any counterargument. Drawings of the Absolute, maps of the Infinite. It's the library of the illusory and useless, from the other worlds, from nocturnal wisdom just as Batalla calls it. Do you like the way he speaks?"

Tito was fed up. Enough, I can't go on.

"Don't get scared, I'm not going to do anything to you," said Umberto.

"How do I know that?"

"I'm not with Donkavian."

Tito tensed up.

"How do you know about that?" The question was old hat, but necessary.

"Everyone knows it. They don't talk about anything else."

Tito lowered his cannon. He didn't believe it. It was the hobby of the subterranean world of Santiago de Chile. Very little was lacking before the secret holy war would come out on midday television programs, those made for housewives, nurses, the aged, and the mentally weak. Meet Tito Livio, the man of the week. Would they transmit his murder by satellite? They were capable of it.

"Don't be distressed. It's inevitable these days."

What did he mean? He looked at him hatefully. The Beretta was aimed at the floor and Umberto had turned around in his chair. He definitely looked like a young man. He had the look of a person pleased as punch, an innocent smile spread across his face.

Triviño Junior shrugged his shoulders.

"Maybe you can help me."

It didn't matter if he was Donkavian's agent, or not. Freud's lesson

273

was repeated over and over in his mind: either you trusted or you didn't. You don't get anything out of racking your brains trying to unravel an intricate and irrelevant problem. A superior impulse was controlling everything. Or at least that's what he was hoping. Your faith is fragile, Tito, what are we going to do with you? He took a deep breath and contemplated the irritating smile of the Neapolitan with the accent from Milan. *Funiculí, Funiculá.*

"I'm looking for a book or something about a book. But I'm afraid it might be impossible to find it in all this confusion."

The other guy laughed behind his glasses.

"It's not like that, you are categorically mistaken. It has a secret order which is not common. Its disorder is apparent, a product of the greater complexity of its system. One frequently chooses the most remote decision which can still be the most obvious, occasionally at the same time. The obvious is rare and what should be rare is obvious. Words are numbers and numbers are words. God's order sometimes is man's disorder. Nature is not symmetrical but rather only by chance."

Tito's trigger finger tensed up. He really wanted to blow his head off with one shot, to see his brain full of coordinates and variables go flying in pieces.

"Something in particular?"

It was then that he recognized the shining chain on his neck. For an instant, a tenuous and fleeting brilliance. He closed his eyes, and opened them again.

"I'm looking for a book about my father. A book that tells the story I'm living. Do you think it's easy to find?"

"I'll tell you that everything has a method. We generally discover it later on, but it exists. All philosophy is like that, looking for God's methods. Until chance grasps it, only in those cases it's a matter of more lax and distant association, inaccessible to the human race. Let's say that it's a method in movement which has, at the same time, another method of change whose sequence is not intelligible, then the movement would need to be stopped in order to capture one of the concentric methods and with this the remaining ones disappear. Therefore one can never have access to the Great Method. The one of the Absolute."

"The Great Method?"

"The one which is put into motion with the Tetragrammaton."

Tito became pale. Since the lighting was dim and yellow he was confident that Umberto could not have noticed it.

"What does the Tetragrammaton have to do with all this?"

Funiculí smiled.

"Look at the coincidences. The Method is working. I said the Method, not the method. I don't know if you heard the capital letter as it sounds. Me-thod. Did you hear? I'm studying about this right now."

Tito leaned over the desk. There was a tall stack of unbound books. One of them open, with pages written in the most delicate disorder. Not a single one in its place.

"It's easy. This book has the cosmos and its hidden order as its subject. If you open a page it becomes lost forever."

"Quit talking like Borges! Okay?"

"You know Borges Mandiola? He comes from Curicó. They say he's going to replace Batalla as library attendant, that he's very sensitive to the other orders and will give a final touch to the perfect cosmos which this chaos encompasses. He's in charge of all the secrets of the Absolute. In spite of being deaf."

"Wasn't he blind?"

"Borges Mandiola? Deaf as a post."

The Beretta lowered its bad humored nose. A bullet in each nasal passage until they perforate the sphenoids.

"Look, Shorty, either you shut up or you're going to taste some hot lead, do you hear me?"

"Yes, I saw that movie."

"Don't tell me which one, I've had enough of your snobby attitude. Do you hear me, Shorty? I'm tired of it."

He pushed him against the books. He fell to the floor dragging with him a pile of volumes which remained next to the table. He sat down in his seat while he heard him complain as he rubbed his sacral area.

The Great Method. Wasn't this the quoted book? The one about the supposed chance, obedient to a supreme design? He read.

Somewhere, what seems complex becomes as simple as a kid's top, and transparent like a geometric figure. The most complex of the formulas refers indefinitely to the most simple arithmetic and the most elemental reflection waits to be discovered below the foundations of the most complex constructions

275

of metaphysics. All knowledge is in the words of a child. Culture extinguishes the whole universe summed up at first glance, segmenting it into particulates of wisdom which, because they are more broken down and extensive in number, require a much greater space, and many more words. All the books of the world can be one, all its pages just one, all words the only one, the Tetragrammaton. In it is the original principle of life whose function is to expand to the infinite through Man's mind, a corrected and augmented version of the divine principle which is greater and justly embraced because it's small and infinitesimal. The magnificent thing about Man is his vain effort to be God which one obtains in smallness and foolishness, in foolish acts and insanity, in the act of faith and irrationality. To look at the most pedestrian, starting from the missing point which is always the looked-for presence. Where what one is looking for is not located, there is what you're looking for. Understanding more is losing time, understanding less is regaining it. Between these points there is no transition greater than the light which already died out.

The page ended. He jumped a paragraph (a lifelong bad habit) and read without being able to believe it:

Alberto Triviño wrote a useless and impossible adventure about this whose name remains forgotten because its power did not have eyes which read it nor ears which managed to listen to it. His voice has faded away in the silence of this library, but in it remains knowledge in its raw state. Whoever looks for this book must trust or not trust and then he will know what no one can know and forget it. Superior knowledge is not cryptic as wise men believe, it is diaphanous and perfect and, because of this, it passes unnoticed for the vain. A simple child's song sums up the birth of the world, a cheap joke Man's creation, the moan of an old person all philosophy for becoming oneself. Read ye an adventure book and ye will understand the reason for so many deaths.

Tito was sweating. He turned the page and it turned to sawdust, right between his fingers. Umberto smiled, unconcerned.

"I told you that."

His only impulse was to pull out his gold chain and make out a frog, like the one on the dead guy in the sewer. Identical.

"Did you see my body floating in the stream in the sewer?"

It was the dead guy. The same dead guy from the descent to the Santiagoan underworld. What was he doing here? How was it possible? If he smelled bad, if he was rotting, if he had marks from rat bites, if he himself had seen him with all the gory details? He recognized him.

"I'll die this very day. That book will remake itself again and I will be reading it here again, and you will come in again and put your pistol up to my neck."

Tito Livio Triviño shook his head. Don't give me a line of bull, okay. I wasn't born yesterday, cut it out, please, I beg you.

But Umberto continued.

"You yourself will kill me, or maybe they will. A bullet will go through my forehead and my body will be thrown into the drainage ditch after the library burns down."

"It burns down?"

"Yes, I manage to realize this before dying. With so much repetition one develops a certain memory. Before, I always used to think it was the first one every time that it happened. Now I know what's coming."

"But what's the purpose of burning it down?"

"So there won't be any clues left. That's the reason for the disorder, it's a way of protecting the secret equilibrium. The chaos contains the cosmos. It's not its destruction but its disguise. And vice versa. Didn't Freud Romero tell you that?"

He looked at the bookshelves. He understood the disorderly appearance completely. Jorge Batalla knew full well about everything, they knew he would come. How could they not? How many times had he perhaps done this believing it was the first? How many sons and daughters were perhaps reuniting in front of the bodies of their parents. And in this book turned into sand they changed the name of the author who, he would swear, had been his father.

"Are they going to come?"

Umberto nodded. He was all twisted up and his trembling was not from the Beretta now.

"Am I going to survive?" asked Tito after a few seconds of anxiety. He was also trembling.

"I don't know, I'm going to die first. Up to that point I'm aware that you're alive."

Tito brought his hand up to his forehead: damp. A noise rang out behind him. An increasing racket.

"Are they coming?"

"Yes," said Umberto, terrified.

"What can I do? What have I done before, other times?"

"Well, you always run away, you always run away and grab a book by chance."

"And is it the right one?"

"I don't know. That would only be described in the Great Method and I already told you: one can't grasp the only explanation, but rather it's due to successive approximations which end up contradicting each other."

The wood of a door jumped out in a shower of splinters behind him. Tito didn't manage to see it. He jumped instinctively to one side, looking for the exit through which he had arrived in this place. It was a unique movement, in unison with a solitary and well-aimed shot which passed through the space which his head had occupied a fraction of a second before, in order to bury itself majestically between Umberto's eyes.

"See you next time," he said, mixing his words with a stream of blood bubbling out while he was falling on his knees and then falling face down on the earthen floor. Tito didn't see him again. He read it then, afterwards, in the book. He fell into the darkness and between gesticulations he grabbed the last volume from a bookshelf, absolutely flying, and he ended up at the small door, the secret portal which the taxi driver had pointed out to him.

Tough voices, electric, like robots, were coming through the walls. The sound of an explosion shook him. Then the crackling flames.

"Open, sesame," he said, but the door didn't budge.

Shit, you can't be like that. Open, sesame, again, horror, the silent door. He thought, thought, thought. He opened the book but he couldn't see even by bending over close. Suddenly another explosion left a hole between the shelves. The flames quickly devoured the paper. He recited prayers for himself from his prehistory: *Now I lay me down to sleep.*

Tall yellow flames illuminated the book. Badly, but they lit it up. Clear as a bell he found the diagram for the door and above it an inscription: *May whoever enters leave.*

"Idiots," shrieked Tito. The flames were coming closer. The shadows of the robot voices began to shoot to the left and right. The smoke was making him dizzy in the heat which in a few minutes more would be intolerable. A volley went right by his head. *May whoever enters leave.* Idiots.

Anger against Freud, against his father, against Lili Salomé, against all those crazy wild people who had transported him to hell, this hell in which the flames were in charge of consuming him like a sausage fallen among the embers. Neither more, nor less. The explosions increased, the bullets were ricocheting over his head. An unexpected hand grabbed him. Tito tried to free himself, desperately. He raised the Beretta. Not without a fight.

"Don't drop the book." The voice of an old lady.

Cleanly, through the door which had opened. The wind made the flames dance. A queen.

Lili Salomé.

"Come on."

In a second he was outside. A final and terrible explosion made a pile of bookshelves fall over the door, closing it forever, or rather, for that always null and relative time which encompasses another temporality, another scene, the reserve of clock time with which he was familiar.

"Run," said the woman's voice which now was not that of an old lady.

It was nighttime. In the middle, dark and closed. Still nighttime.

"Run," she said, and she kissed him on the cheek and disappeared.

44

The Perfect Biology

Y ou ran, Tito. Once again you ran for blocks and blocks. You ran
hoping that behind your fleeing silhouette, your rhythmic clacking of soles like a feverish metronome, the library would explode and
the fire would rise up in glory and majesty like a great tower of flames,
an infernal Babel above the houses of the Diez de Julio neighborhood
until it burned the moon itself as if it were a paper balloon which would
fill tomorrow's headlines, television screens, the vibrant morning news
on the radio which would denounce a terrorist attack on the sky, the
stars, the whole neighborhood completely leveled by a colossal catastrophe, that's what they would say.

You ran craning your neck to look back, breathing half breaths,
without stopping, checking that nothing was happening and nothing
was happening and nothing was happening. Only your feet clicking on
the pavement, the earth, the grass of some unkempt small squares.
Blocks later — how many? — maybe crossing Seminario, going along
towards Pocuro through the innocent sleep of a capital which believes
that another option other than insomnia still exists, you stop. You

panted, Tito. You panted again and the cold air burned your nasal passages, it made your lungs hurt, it irritated your nose like an abusive stimulant, the oxygen burned your throat, it made you sick. You summed up the military patrols near the Telecommunications Regiment. You skirted it by quite a distance but it didn't tire you out. You thought: It's the cold air that is stirring up my brain, it's the bread from the Academy, my father's body turned to energy inside, it's his mind transmuted in my blood. The most disturbing of the effects from that bread had dissipated, the mental and motor excitement still persisted.

Stopped in a doorway, you observed the morning very closely, the sun which was coming out from somewhere and the absence of those flames which surely exploded in the most terrible way, but secretly, far from the vision of that proud world which knows nothing about itself, about its own smallness, about the unknown limits of the universe. You sat down until the panting subsided and you grabbed the book snatched from the library which at this point would not exist, only ashes, waiting to revive. When? For another mission, another pursuit, another party in El Limbo, which you will not attend. Half lit by the neon light you contemplated its hard cover, bound in aged brownish-red leather, worn edges, whose fire-scarred gold letters which were peeling off announced: *The Perfect Biology.* It had to be your father's. The old crazy guy, reading in his bed Sunday mornings while mother was getting us ready to leave, I'm taking them to mass where you don't go, you old atheist, she said to him jokingly, that was how it went, it wasn't the battlefield which would come later on. Was it the lupus? Or did the old woman find out about all this?

Tito leafed through plates of the human body, the cell, the family. By the titles of the sections he could guess the content. *The philosophical knowledge of the Absolute can be deduced from human and animal biology. The body as a mirror to the cosmos, movement as a manifestation of love, the primal force of the universe: the essential energy of the word. Animal and vegetable life, hierophant par excellence. Biology as Applied Theology.*

The organic symbolism of a family. The title stopped him. He put up the lapels of his jacket to adjust to the minimal temperature. Spring was still offering rather cool nights, forty to forty-five degrees. It had even been a little cloudy the afternoon before. He curled up next to the text dedicated to his family and read: *Family Geometry*, he scanned the subtitle, *Essential plans and volumes which explain spatial harmony in movement, repeated in the atomic figure where we will be able to recognize the particles Father, Mother, and Children.*

It clicked immediately in his mind. What's the matter with you, Tito? You're stunned, a fixed stare, you blink your eyes. *Essential Geometry.* He looked at the laminas: *parents, children, triangles, lines, quadrangles, the son determines the primary plane, the father the spacial time. The Mother-Son line, the Father-Mother line, the intersection of the one which gives birth to primary bidimensionality.*

He smiled, almost against his will. Surprising lucidity from the Academy bread. He took the photo from his pocket. Where was it taken? He studied it in the poor street light. Click: the triangle from the bolero by Los Hermanos Arriagada was not the triangle with his brother, it was a different one. It was missing a vertex which he had supposed was whoever was taking the photo, but that wasn't it. It was his father who was the figure being ignored in the background. Sure, that's it, leaning against the doorway like I am now, in the opening of the door like he used to place himself when he was young, when he was my age, sure he was my age, there he is, blurred but present. Who took the picture of us?

That, instantaneously, was a message, a premonition of his departure, a warning. A secret agreement between his parents to protect him from this pursuit. Someone came to make them pose in a searching attitude in which the secret of the Tetragrammaton would remain included: the letter above the door, over his father's head.

He squeezed his crowded memory: a dry lemon.

Unconcerned in his pleasure, he approached the streetlamp. The light fell flat on the photo. He couldn't make out the letter. Its texture prevented all enlarging. He had to go to see it immediately, to destroy it before they arrived at the destination. Right away. He broke into a cold sweat when he thought that perhaps if he found out what it was, it might be necessary to give his life for the secret. But he had to do it. For everyone, for everything.

It was then that he heard the military patrol in the distance. Screams, don't move or I'll shoot, a password. He jumped as far as he could and disappeared along Miguel Claro towards the south. He ran again, fed by the tireless strength from that miraculous bread. When would its effect wear off? He had to get to Chacabuco Plaza, now. He heard a shot in the air among the houses. A car motor. He was now part of the scenery.

After an endless series of curves he decided to hide on the front lawn of a house with tall steel gates. While he was climbing he was afraid of a bullet in the back. With all his weight he fell on some scotch broom, untangled himself from the flowers and plastered himself to the wall. The noise of the jeeps looking for him, the footsteps of the thick regulation shoes. He embraced the book, the photo, the Beretta. He was enjoying being hidden. They didn't find him, they were going away. The jeep was vibrating towards the east. Why not spend the rest of the night there? And only then leave. Let's sleep, he said to himself in a dream state.

He closed his eyelids but the whole text of the book and the photo were coming at him. He searched for an opening with light between the branches of an almond tree. Half climbing up he opened those dearly beloved pages.

But now the book was a different one. The cover was the same but the inside had transformed itself into a novel. He read line after line without recognizing anything until all of a sudden it fell into place that what was in his hands was the story of his father's adventures, Alberto Triviño, running through the Santiago of the fifties, with a .38 caliber in his hand and a book underneath his arm which upon opening had changed in appearance. That book was his father's book, it was written for him. If he closed it, it would disappear. He read it shivering. Tito Livio Senior hidden among the shrubs in a garden where he was giving thanks that there weren't any dogs. Outside a band of marauders came out of the Black and White. He was hiding to read his book, checking that it was his own father's book, reading another book with the story of his father reading about his father reading about his father.

Getting dizzy by the game of mirrors he turned the page. Will I survive? Can I keep going? Will I have to die like him? His stomach tensed up. He anxiously glanced over the words. The father of his father had not died, he was the bearer of another secret, of another way, under another appearance. A song, a strange map of a country estate near Pichidegua. Drawn by pen, it illustrated the novel. Another page finished it. Quick, find out, quick, read more. He turned the page but the beam of a flashlight lit up the pages.

The shadow of his head contrasted with the paper, leaving it entirely blank.

He turned his head. Illuminated.

"You're going to ruin your eyes with so little light, Tito."

45

The cruelest theater

Donkavian *lui-même*. In person, live and direct, in the expanded and updated version, looked after by his lord and master. The unmistakable voice, like that of his favorite announcer on the morning program: *Let's get up, Ma'am, let's get up, Sir, the day is beginning.* Smiling under the streetlights with a flashlight in his hand, calm as if there were no curfew nor any firefights, nor helicopters sweeping the city every half-hour with their x-shaped teeth which pierce the Chilean sky.

Rolando Donkavian, the real thing, no imitation. Dressed in white, impeccable. With those attributes which only the Devil gives: not a wrinkle, not a sign of fatigue nor hunger nor thirst. Like the bread from the Academy has given to you, Tito.

"I'd advise you not to try to shoot," he says to you as you make a move to look for the Beretta. "My people have you covered from the roof."

Tito looked over his shoulder. On top of one of the rain spouts, a man's shadow was outlined against the violet dawn. The sun was coming up.

285

Another one leaned over behind Donkavian. Impeccable. Without a trace of so much death in back of them, nor the fire, nor the cyclical destruction to which they would commit themselves.

He wanted to be able to pass through them shooting like the henchmen from the bakery assault. He squeezed the book. Now he knew where the clue was, the fourth letter. They also knew that he knew. They didn't need to wait any more. Take care of him and that's the end of that. Don't bother with any more illusions.

"Will you come with us, please?"

I hate that little phrase, thought Tito, ever since he heard it in Villa Alemana, ever since that pair of clowns emerged from among the cases of refreshments and beer, those two inept guys in the little Citroen who didn't know how to watch me very well, who nobody knows where they are, who are incapable of watching anyone, tacky guardian angels, it's no wonder the Devil does what he wants.

"You're the Devil," he said to Donkavian, furiously.

"You honor me, Tito Livio. I'm scarcely his representative, one more agent in this war. A colleague of yours at this point, Tito."

"I'm not anyone's agent."

"If you want to go on feeling independent, let go of your ideas. Do you see it wasn't a bad idea to get you out of the country? We would have arranged everything directly with your Old Man alone, without conflicts. You wouldn't have discovered anything."

"Arranging is what you call what they did to him?"

"He knew the risks in his profession."

Just one shot from the Beretta, just one. But the mission? Don't tempt fate, Tito, there'll be an opportunity to settle things. Now, smart, cautious strategy, more tactical, esteemed protagonist.

"Come on down," said Donkavian to the one on the roof. "The gentleman is coming with us."

Tito watched him emerge on the front lawn. The daylight had progressed. The outlines of the shrubs were still effervescent, the strong smell of the wisteria had turned into a visible figure.

The one who aimed at him opened the gate and Tito passed through it.

The curfew must have ended. They aimed at him insolently, in plain sight of the whole street. An enormous van, totally white, with letters indicating a supposed laundry, Opera Dry Cleaning, was waiting on the other side of the street.

They opened the doors to the huge vehicle, those in the back. Tito remembered the police minivans dragging in demonstrators in the middle of Alameda. Some birds were chirping and the sun was fighting with a mostly cloudy morning.

Diaphanous Santiago at dawn. A rosy gray light was lighting it up without heating up his weary shoes yet. Only Santiago in the rain is more beautiful than in the first daylight hours, after a rain there is no lovelier city. You breathe fresh air, you rejuvenate.

Tito went into the van bowing his head. In its dark interior he made out some shapes.

"Anita María . . ."

"Do you know each other?" asked Donkavian.

She was there, hugging the children, Janine, Caroline, all embraced like cubs next to their mother, moaning, Daddy, Daddy, and Tito Livio's anger, they can't do this to you, you don't have anything to do with this and his hand searches for the Beretta and at this same instant one of the hired assassins grabs his wrist with a steel hook. One-handed, with a tenacity that almost cuts off his circulation.

"If you don't make a fuss, nothing will happen to you."

Tito handed over his gun.

"The book."

He handed it over towards Donkavian.

"Thanks, Tito. Now the famous photograph."

"How did you find out about the photo?"

"What business do you think I'm in? I let you escape from the bakery for a reason. We've known about it for a while."

They closed the door without any more explanations. He and his family were enclosed in the cargo section of the van, without windows. There was a miniature skylight through which the yawning morning sun was coming in, and a small grating which separated them from the driver's cab. The two armed henchmen were maintaining distance between him, his ex-wife and his daughters.

"How are you, Anita?"

The most absurd question on earth. There aren't prepared sentences for fear. However, she made a gesture of contact. She nodded, and was good for an imitation smile. My God, why are you letting them get involved in this, not them please, for what's most important in this world. As if it were possible to split a country in two, one for peace, another for war, as if the bullets could have prohibited destinations. Tito's daydream. A knife of pain was cutting into his liver. He checked out his daughters' eyes, little squirrel eyes in the darkness. The guns: a barrel in his neck, another pointed at them, changing heads according to a cycle, a rhythm, a studied cadence to terrorize him, break him down, make him repent everything.

He looked at Donkavian. The vehicle was advancing through the city waking up: Baquedano Plaza. He recognized the monument to the General, the military men who have saved the country. The pride of the statue irritated him, the dirty Turri buildings, the small river, resting from its summer flows.

"Where are we going?" His voice was wild, dry, with weighted resignation, tired of asking the same question, tired of not hearing an answer.

They were crossing the Mapocho river. Thin and barely distinguishable in its bed, whose channel appeared disproportionate to this thread of dirty water. No one is familiar with you, how you behave all of a sudden. When you went to get the kids from school in the midst of floods and the storm. The time when you got it into your head to have a Suzuki jeep. How am I going to save them from this downpour now? Help me, God, if you still have some power. The little frightened girls over there, and Anita María's voice whispering to them, singing slowly to them under the eyes of the guns. I can't stand it, I can't stand it.

The Bellavista neighborhood appeared in the windshield. He made it out through the thin grating which separated them from the driver. The back of Donkavian's neck: I'd kill you, Devil.

"What happened to Freud?"

"Who?"

They were turning along Antonia Lope de Bello towards the mountains. He remembers his trips to San Cristóbal Hill with his father. The perfect biology of his voice.

"Freud Romero."

"That old crazy guy? He's okay, better off than us. At least now he doesn't have anything to worry about."

Donkavian, don't get me any angrier, because anger makes me afraid, and with the fear paralysis comes back, submission, cowardice. Your power is based on instilling death wishes in me, irritating my patience, trampling on everything I love the most. Transforming me into you, what was you, what I want to stop being. That's enough.

The van stopped.

"Get out."

He could make out the previous climb, pine-filled. They were on the side of the hill itself. He didn't know exactly where. He tried to look but a gun barrel was sticking in his ribs. He heard the kids and Anita María descending like little rats towards an old house which must have belonged to an abandoned factory. Refrigerator factories. A neighborhood of Creole artists, evil was hidden among them too. With the guards' carelessness he made out the large house in Dr. Gandulfo Plaza, in front of Camilo Mori's house. Its exotic roofing, unexpected, like a witch's house, like a Gothic plot. Worse than that, impossible. They went in.

The light, once again, was poor. An order from Donkavian was enough to leave everything in absolute darkness. Nighttime once again, confinement, the kidnapping of the sun.

They seated him down in front of the little girls. The same room, crowded together, weak, like newborn children. Still in sleeping shirts, their feet naked, frozen stiff by the morning cold. Sons of whores, motherfuckers, what right do you have to come into someone's house, grab them out of their beds, their sleep, their calm. He had read about this, but it was something that happened to others, those outside the law, the communists, the damned. Now they too could disappear in a minute with no trace, without a tombstone, without any explanation nor prayers for the dead.

They tied him up.

"It's for your own good. It's like when they take you to the dentist or on airplanes. Consider it a type of seat belt."

He was tied hand and foot in such a way that he couldn't take his eyes off his family. The poor dears, the girls in front, not tied. One infamous lightbulb illuminated the room. There was a dirty smell, stagnant air, dusty. The sun was squeezing through the doorways making the dirt on the floor and the old tables evident.

The cruelest theater would come now. And Tito would be the captive audience.

"Now you're going to tell us everything."

"Everything about what?"

"Everything you know."

"I don't know any more than you."

You're being brave, Tito, but then you see him approaching the little girls, he's moving around them, a certain solemnity makes it even more fearful.

What are they going to do to them, Tito?

46

I wouldn't be surprised if we even forgive you.

"I'm not interested in last-minute sentimentality, Tito Livio," said Donkavian after a theatrical pause. "I'm advising you for the last time, think about yourself and decide the most rational thing possible. You can even still leave for São Paulo, your family will go away peacefully, alive and kicking to their house with everything taken care of."

Tito looked at Anita. I don't want them to do anything to you, I swear, I've always wanted to protect you.

"I don't know why you rejected la Maga. She's much better than your ex-wife, and more powerful. You could have had everything, even immortality, to be eternally young, to be a man or a woman at times if you wanted, never to suffer from hunger nor fatigue nor lack of sleep nor thirst. Why did you get it into your head to pay attention to your perverted old man? Besides you let them kill her. One of our best agents. But war is war. Everything is permitted when there are passions or ideals involved. I'm in favor of the final abolition of this whole stupid celestial hierarchy about knowledge, this foolish idea about the

291

superiority of God. It's all over. You tell us how to get the fourth letter and there will finally be peace and equality for everyone, never any more differences, not up or down, not women or men, not old or young, not life or death. Power for those who deserve power, and the rest will die without any pity, those without will be an extinct species. Like the unfaithful ones they are, unfaithful to faith in reason, in total knowledge, which will found the kingdom of this world."

"A beautiful sermon. Do you want us to sing a hymn now?" Tito put out his claws.

"Don't try to get me mad, I already have experience with that trick. You're a novice and you think you're superior, just like that old guy from God. Think it out well, that it's better for you to use your head for something more than dreaming that you're the most famous person in the world, inventing phrases of the type that will not leave any mark on this earth. Where's the letter?"

"Why don't you figure it out with a computer?" you said. The last slap from a drowning man.

"Don't pretend you're an imbecile," mocked Rolando. "The important thing is not the letter but the road to get to it. Each letter is an act, a singular strength of the material, it's not a mere sign. You don't know the difference between your ass and your elbow. Where's the letter?"

"What letter?"

The slap was masterful. A perfect drive that came out like a whip across your face. How do you like the taste of blood?

"The next one will be for them."

He looked up: Rolando Donkavian next to the girls. Janine hanging in the air by the one armed man's pincers.

"Janine."

"Where's the letter? What's the clue in the picture?"

"I can't . . . I can't . . ."

Janine's moaning with her arm twisted between Captain Hook's metal pincers. Anita made an attempt to save her but just one slap from Donkavian threw her against the broken down sofa they had seated them on, right in front of you. Can't you do anything, Tito?

"Daddy, please, Daddy, tell him to let me go."

Your eyes are filling with tears: baby, my daughter. Donkavian didn't even bat an eye. He's lighting a cigarette, it looks like a Tiparillo. The ember in the semi-darkness enters the area with the dying light. Your pupils have adjusted and they see what they never would have wanted to see. Anita screaming that they let her go: a blow from the butt of the gun right in her face. Blood on the corner of her mouth, on her nose. Anita, Anita.

"Answer, Tito. I don't know why you don't realize that everything depends on you alone."

Shit, he's putting the Tiparillo close to Janine's skin, to her arm. A sizzling sound, a subtle smell of burned meat. She recoils like a worm.

"Enough!"

Your scream reverberated through the whole Bellavista neighborhood, in all the innocence of the housewives who get up early on Sunday mornings to sweep the sidewalks in their bathrobes, the regulars at eight o'clock mass who lean out to check the morning temperature, students preparing for exams, joggers who are returning home satisfied about feeling eternal and perfect, convinced that angels have their shape, the supplements which they throw in front of each home in the thick Sunday paper with red-hot interviews about the tense situation between the government and the opposition. One more scream, what does it matter? It won't be the first nor the last. Torture? That doesn't happen in our neighborhood. The sun continues fighting with the clouds. It's too cloudy, if you're going to go out put on a vest. Mothers and children, shamelessly naive. Fathers who sip coffee as if they were stepping for the first time on the rediscovered Indies. All easily deceived.

Donkavian stopped the maneuver. Janine was crying.

"Do you want us to keep going with the other one? This little girl isn't bad at all. We could teach her some things about life. Do you think this might hurt her between her legs?" he showed the barrel of his Magnum. "That's how she gets used to it from the time she's a little girl. She can go far in this world if she knows what she has to know. Or shall we continue with your wife? Or ex-wife? How would she look with these big guys between her legs? Or with a slice across her face? Or on her breasts? What do you think if we cut her in four like a flower?" He took out a switchblade which seemed to have a shine of its own. "It's up to you, Tito."

You broke down crying. Another cry, one that you weren't familiar with, a new pain in your repertoire, total impotence and face to face with absolute cruelty. How weak we are, Tito, it's enough for someone to totally lose his scruples, and he can do what he wants with us. Evil is so strong, so strong, so strong. Are you going to confess, Tito?

He looked at Donkavian, defeated. He couldn't take any more, he didn't have room for any more threats, nor capacity for more grieving. Pain weakens also, it drains, it leaves you exhausted. He didn't have what it takes to be a hero, nor courage nor true convictions. He was discredited, a skeptic, a hero without true passions. All those things which hide weakness of character. They can't get to me any other way but through them. Anita María, you don't know how much I love you. I didn't know it either.

Donkavian's hand grabbed him by his hair.

"Are you talking or not, you fucking fag? Or do you want us to stick the barrel up your ass and blow your guts out to blow the shit out of you, you queer?"

Tito squirmed free, resigned. Donkavian perceived his triumph and smiled. Janine's body made a dull noise when it fell lifeless to the floor. Don't worry, honey, nothing more is going to happen to you.

"You're a good guy. I wouldn't be surprised if we even forgive you."

He heard something like the scraping of a chair.

"We'll know everything before noon," he said to the other guys who were congratulating each other.

Ladies and gentlemen, Tito Livio Triviño Recart's confession immediately. We're asking you to empathize with him. He really tried to defend the indefensible, a task we know is not easy and which each one of us renounces daily. Let's not accuse him of being a coward just like that. Let's not deny that in his place we would have done the same. We're with you, Tito. No one's free from your sins.

"The photo shows a place, a street near Chacabuco Plaza . . ."

"Which street?"

"Justiniano Sotomayor. It has a side outlet going towards the Chilean Hippodrome. They took that picture of us there. It's an ugly place, without charm, with a house, or an adobe wall in the background. There's an arcade where the letter is. You can't make it out in the photo. It's too grainy. You have to go to see it. It's over the head of the man who you can barely make out and who's my father. The letter is there. He put it there. He changed the order of the letters and . . . I don't even remember what it used to be . . . I'd have to see it."

A strange relief. No tension. He said it all at once, retching, like he was vomiting. He remained wretched but relaxed. The sensation of establishing himself as a coward. But is this really anything new, Tito?

"Nothing else?"

"Nothing else."

Like a body made of wool, hanging by a thread.

"Okay. Time to go, guys."

The one with the steel spoke. He had a pleasant voice, like an anchorman from a television newscast.

"Should we waste them, Rolando?"

The elegant publicist hesitated. He puffed slowly on his Tiparillo and then clicked his tongue.

"What does it matter now? Let him go. It'll be my good deed for the day."

They laughed. Captain Hook untied the ropes with his hook. Donkavian himself opened the doors, helped by his chauffeur. The almost fully dawned morning streamed in to make fun of Tito. Against the light, the sofa with his family was a single shadow. He waited to see Rolando and his people leave, feeling his defeat, freeing himself from the complicated knots and straps of the same type with which they had tied him down to the rungs of the chair. Affliction overcame his soul, weeping.

"Girls, Anita," he sobbed.

He got up, in pain from his forced position. It was like coming out of a several month long invalidism, stumbling, he reached the old sofa. With a last effort he let himself fall on his knees, extending his arms to caress them.

"Anita . . . Kids . . ."

But the embrace came apart in the emptiness. Horrified he groped, lashed out wildly. Nothing, nothing, not a trace.

"Anita! Janine! Caroline!"

He ran through the big room. His steps resounded on the boards mixed with the echo: Anita, Janine, Caroline.

"It's impossible. It can't be."

His pain turned to rage. They had deceived him, they had made him hallucinate the worst torture, the worst threat, they had driven him mad. They limited themselves to showing their power, discovering his weakness. Yours, Tito. I should have known it! I didn't have enough strength! Coward!

Calm down, Tito. All of us can make a mistake. Our epoch is an era of God-fearing souls. Don't blame yourself, don't be a martyr. They're professionals. No, I have to go, I have to go stop them. But what do you get out of it now? Everything is lost. Do you think that anybody is going to take notice of the defeat of God? We've accepted everything, isn't that right? Life is so short. What does a change in power mean to you if you've never had any?

You don't pay attention. You take off running just the same. The morning hits you in the face with light and pure air. Head down, you ran along Chucre Manzur Street to land smack in Dr. Gandulfo Plaza. There's no time for anything. Really worked up, you calm down because of a taxi. It found you: the old Biscayne in front of the Venezia Restaurant which, still closed, was waiting for the Sunday hoards going up and coming down San Cristóbal Hill, from the Virgin, from the zoo, from the parks full of picnics and lovers getting their underwear dirty under the trees.

"What are you doing here?"

Aren't you ever going to stop panting, Tito?

"I've followed you all night."

"And you stayed in the car? They were killing me a block away."

"I have orders. Besides I've never carried a gun."

Tito was going to swear at the sky but he chose to shrug his shoulders.

"Take me to Chacabuco Plaza right now."

"Okey dokey," said the driver, starting up the motor.

47

Like in a gangster film

The riskiest day for automobile accidents in the city of Santiago is Sunday, in the morning. The streets are an irresistible temptation for an accelerator pedal to be put to the floor, and the tree-lined avenues of the residential neighborhoods are the most perfect scenery for the sharp sound of tires squealing on a curve.

Luminescent and empty, the Biscayne cruised through the morning like a space ship, almost level with the ground, one could say flying, something which although Tito could not verify, the truth is he would have wanted that. They cut through, grazing the outskirts west of San Cristóbal Hill. Through the window Tito could follow the image of the Virgin, white and enormous, who is nearer to heaven and because of this she can do more, as his mother used to assure, expertly.

They're going very fast but Tito Livio isn't afraid of death now. He was confiding in the steel wrists of the driver who has the radio tuned to a big band song with full brass playing a tune imbued with swing. It must be just seven o'clock. Tito's digital watch was blinking with its same invariable insolence. Stupid, don't you realize what's happening?

297

Like all machines you ignore what's happening, you're the ideal of this society: doing without thinking, feeling without changing into history. You count the time but you don't have any idea of what you're counting.

The Biscayne was humming.

"Independence," the driver pointed out the street at the bottom.

Tito calculated the rendezvous point to be three minutes away. Donkavian removing the letter with pleasure. Studying it and then hiding it. Looking for the place pointed out in the photo. If he had any luck he would find it before him, and the situation would be salvageable. If not, fine, return home, think about it all again, let yourself fall into the arms of despair. It wasn't a new feeling, nothing like that. But now, let's get going, please. Let's fly if possible.

Chacabuco Plaza began to come into focus at the bottom. The turn was screeching and spectacular like in a gangster film. The stone horses of the Chilean Hippodrome, the grand sculptured heads presiding over the plaza, ordaining the immutability of certain places. Not so for the buildings which covered the horizon, the place where Independence Stadium used to be, where his father made every type of exaggerated gesture against the Catholic University, his mother's team, sure. The pleasure of hearing the roar when they scored a goal from the patio of her house. There's no sound which equals that. The sea, as much as they talked about it, could not hold a candle to it.

There, like a volley from his memory, came the aromatic flow of jasmine which inundated the patio of his infancy. A soccer goal painted green, covered with jasmine, surrounded by arum. The plastic ball and Gustavo at the goal who always cut across like the wind, always better than he was in sports. The passion of his father, who boasted of having been the great hope of the Chilean midfield.

Now, none of that. The stores replaced by miniature supermarkets, nothing of the bags full of vegetables on the road home from the open air market, nothing of the nightclub to which he had to go to get his father, dragging him away from his game of dominoes which for him was a theory on the relationship between mathematics and power, numbers and politics. Everything is in dominoes, my sons, that's why it's called that, dominoes, from "to dominate." The most important thing in dominoes in pairs is knowing how to give up your own triumph in favor of the alliance. That's the secret of dominoes. I don't trust the politicians who don't know how to play. They won't know anything about negotiating nor about transactions. They'll confuse power with war, they will be unaware that arithmetic is peace. Enough, Dad, let's go home.

The Biscayne stopped. Tito shook off the nostalgia as well as he could, the blows from that involuntary memory, insolent, forcefully placing itself in his motivation. He anxiously searched for the van, he ran towards the inside, the passageway, the passageway.

He didn't recognize the paved street, formerly grounds for hand to hand fighting and improvised soccer games with a rubber ball, dressed in the uniform of the Colo Colo Sports Club, illustrious bastion of everything Chilean. The short length of the tract seemed strange to him. He looked at what had been his house, estranged from its diminished magnitude, his loyalty. As if he had chosen to place himself in the waters of time.

He stopped immediately.

The pastureland wasn't there. The wide uncultivated terrain where soccer became something more organized, where the cowboys and Indians installed themselves, where once he was a commando and played out his adventures, now true to life, had disappeared. Not a wall nor a hole to slip into the great patio of that terrain. The dusty land where he was going to ruin his school uniform playing goalkeeper for a team of adolescents, the playing field amid thistles and dry pastures. There was nothing left of that. The street widened, it continued. New houses, diminutive imitations of a decent home in a more powerful neighborhood. It made him laugh. Like everything contemporary, the Chilean middle class collecting scaled-down representations of riches. Just as Vitacura was a smaller version of Beverly Hills, this was a plagiarism in miniature of Vitacura. Vestiges of English style, very small front lawns where they could get hold of something green, labor of a landowner who wants to have breakfast in the shade of the begonias.

He was not mistaken. This was the place, this had been it. The houses were different. The stable where he hid to read stories, Salgari, Verne, abridged versions by the Russians. A *Quixote* edited by Billiken, the *Odyssey* illustrated. Nothing. The urbanization, progress, everything had been taken away by a wave of bulldozers and Caterpillars. And the house in the photograph? It was a different one. It was situated at the passageway exit. He ran looking for an exit. The paperboys and bread delivery men looked at him strangely.

A narrow passageway led him towards the parallel street.

The van.

There it was, parked in front of a wooden wall. While he was jogging, drained now, he realized that the house didn't exist either. Not walls nor goals, not even ruins. The rest of this certainty was handed over by Donkavian's tense walk, his face showed frustration and rage. They had demolished it, they were digging up the foundations of a building.

He stopped his walk, smiling. A happy face, of glory, of relief. Panting, he got within firing range of Rolando Donkavian and his group. There they were.

They stared at each other.

48

The dogs from hell

I f Tito Livio lost anything it was his triumphal look, mocking,
scornful. Courtesy doesn't take away from courage, Tito.

Donkavian raised his hand as soon as he recognized him. Tito, too
satisfied, did not notice the Magnum. The shot made him shake just
enough so the bullet passed whizzing by his side. He felt its heat on his
right earlobe.

"Don't be so happy, Tito," Rolando shouted to him, feverish with
rage.

Tito didn't wait for the second shot. A moving target, he threw
himself into a flowerbed. The poor things, their thoughts trampled.
Why weren't the soldiers from the Fifth Precinct coming? Weren't they
just a few blocks away? Didn't they hear the shots?

"Get him!" screamed Donkavian. The two bodyguards and the
driver began to run, frightening Tito. In a jiffy they changed their
appearance. A lightning bolt, a crack, and the elegant suits gave way to
a lustrous dog's coat and their faces were changed like diabolical clay
into the ferocious heads of three doberman pinschers, blind and

slobbering with their fangs anxious to grab him. Running towards you, Tito Livio.

Our protagonist understood that he was going to die, that now there was no way to avoid the Devil's rage coming down on him. Nothing worse than a wounded giant. Its very progress, its same adored omnipotence had broken the symbols of the past into pieces, the last testimony of the sign of power. Its ire was the barking of those dogs, their crazy race which Tito was eluding.

Along the side of Chacabuco Plaza he was jumping over garbage cans, a spigot, a mailbox. Dogs from hell, real devil dogs. The curve in the street with Santa Laura Stadium made the pack spread apart giving him a second to breathe. The few inhabitants of the morning lined up to one side. They were going to kill him, the rabid canines from Hades would destroy his body with their teeth. Their red eyes would shine in the shadows of the street's low buildings.

He ran into the Santa Laura Stadium, now turned into a sky with multi-hued clouds, as if he were running to his father's arms. He thought he saw him in the very same door of the grandstand for members of the club, where they were seated facing the mountain range, watching the match between Unión and Colo in a packed stadium: Dad! He saw him with open arms and he also understood that this rendezvous would be his death. Seeing dead people playing, those who were playing on the parallel planet of those who aren't here, what formations they made on the field, stars of all time, a Chilean All-Star team which no one could stop: Dad! The neighbors got out of the way of the dead man and his pursuers. Meanwhile they were heating up bread and talking as they were taking margarine out of the refrigerator, that man is going to die over there, they're going to kill him there.

Don't you realize that these are the three henchmen from hell who are chasing me? Can't you throw some garlic at them, crosses, mirrors which will testify to their hellish nature? No one did anything. With his last breath he deciphered his father's appearance: the stadium was his salvation. The closed door to the stands opposed him. The blow that he gave it was not his, but rather that of someone who was helping him. He hesitated before making the effort, but when he heard the gross jaws with ferocious fangs at his heels he threw a foot into the air and

302

was taken by surprise: a stirrup of invisible hands lifted him up by his shoulders over the wooden door and other hands received him on the other side with a smoothness which none of the tennis shoes that he advertised could ever give. What polyurethane could match that! This was definitely the bounce of angels!

The dobermans were left barking impotently. Tito turned around looking for something to fight them off with when there was a sudden burst of a blue-green flame and a strong odor of rotten eggs which invaded the air. The dogs disappeared and three mountain lions began to climb on the wood. When the first one emerged, Tito, finally, did not hesitate to grab the iron which was serving as a door bar and give a blow like a baseball player to the animal's chest. Where did the strength come from, Tito Livio? The puma, which is what it was although Tito was unaware of it, gave a complete turn in the air before falling amid lightning bolts and sulfuric explosions. Witnesses accused of being delirious asserted that it changed into a bird, a fish, a bear, and a ram before becoming a burned body on the pavement, a kind of smashed mummy which the garbage men on Monday failed to see since the afternoon wind scattered it like paper ashes.

The two remaining demons retreated. There was a new series of sparks and emanations before a beautiful hawking falcon emerged with its sharp talons ready for the attack, and behind, Tito couldn't believe it, a shiny black panther with clear eyes like the most beautiful of females, climbing with difficulty. Tito started to run under the stands.

The falcon shot like a bullet to trap him before he hid himself among the crossbeams which held the tiers together. The turn in the air opened his pathway and they saw each other face to face. Tito surprised the bird of prey with a jump towards the first pillars of the stands, under the stairway. The falcon dove and made an enormous error: Tito whopped it one good one on the head with such force that the iron bar was bent when it bounced off the floor. Someone guided his weapon while Tito felt the pain in his right hand: he was also bleeding, wounded by the fragments from the metal bar, rusted. An iridescent image through which all the predators of the animal kingdom crossed, preceding the disappearance of the felled henchmen of Lucifer.

The panther was staring at him from the foot of the stairs. Its roar

303

was short and clear: You're going to die, Tito Livio.

The dark and ferocious feline advanced slowly. Tito barely had the strength to run. He brandished the iron without managing to intimidate his strong enemy. The roar from the panther, frankly, was mocking: You're going to die, Tito. No one makes fun of Mephistopheles, nobody conquers the one to whom you sold your soul.

What claws! What fangs! You imagined them in your jugular. You'd be beheaded by that animal. Resigned, he searched for a handkerchief to cover his wound while the complete Ave María came into his mind, indelibly. A hard object interrupted his movement: in the bottom of his pocket lay the small pocketknife from the nocturnal dwarf. He grabbed it and had to endure another surprise. Nothing remained of the small pocketknife for manicuring, made in Taiwan, an imitation of a Swiss Army knife. Now, opened, it was a large knife with a red handle. Its gleam made the feline blink.

From the Lone Ranger I've changed into Tarzan, he thought, with the last vestige of humor left in him.

They stared at each other, Tito and the panther. There was no doubt that rage clouded his judgment. Tito did not have any fear in him now. He had already seen himself dead, he didn't have any alternative now, he had nothing but strength inside now. Anything in order to survive: the courage of limited situations. The furious panther threw itself on Triviño Junior's body. An error of pride, of overconfidence, scorn for an unarmed enemy, who knows. The fact of the matter is that he didn't have to do anything except raise the blade of his knife with all his strength and the weight of the animal itself did the rest. Who guided your hand away from all harm, Tito Livio? Who put the beast's heart there, on the point of the blade? Who gave you the vigor to bury it up to the hilt and become part of the impulse of the panther who felt death coming in a flow of blood emerging like a waterfall through its snout, rolling on its side, with you embracing it, the proof being the claw marks on your suit, the acidic smell of an enraged cat which stayed with you for weeks?

The cat rolled away mortally wounded. You shook, waiting for the iridescent shine which didn't come, replaced by a new trembling of sulfates and sulfites and the return of the wounded and elegant hired assassin of Donkavian, gun in hand. He turned towards you, disfigured and bloody, the barrel vibrating, too weak to empty the chamber at you.

It was there that Davy Crockett's delirium came over you. Without any celestial help whatever, without any force from another life coming to help you, contaminated with courage by your own unexpected survival, you grabbed the dagger by the blade and balanced it perfectly, its weight impeccable, made for combat, and you threw it right on target at his throat where it submerged itself submissively and obediently.

The guy dropped the automatic pistol and brought a hand up to his throat: it never arrived at its destination. In its swing his fingers came apart in bones, dust, a gelatinous mass. His face disappeared, carbonized among lightning bolts and a malodorous smoke where Tito heard the noise of the jungle in heat, lions fighting, scavenging hyenas, the flapping of buzzards, coyote howls at midnight, snakes, alligators, a court of spiders which were fleeing from that volatile body to then disappear like a hallucination from *delirium tremens*.

The loaded pistol shone on the ground. Thanks, Dad, he said and picked it up. He still had one enemy left: Rolando Donkavian.

49

The Gorilla's Bite

While he was trotting back with the unfamiliar gun, a Styer pistol with a full clip, he realized what they had done to him. Through his entire existence he had been a paper entity, without muscles in his soul, without strength, a big chicken by profession, conviction and doctrine. He had merely been a contemplative cynic, a commentator on the process of the decay of the West. This was its final product. A sanguinolent gorilla, dirty at night, from the sweat of rage and fear, from other people's deaths, running with an automatic pistol through his native city. The secret desire of all the petit bourgeois.

An impulse to laugh came over him, but it was another type of laugh. I'm going to kill you, Donkavian, he said while he was running.

There he was.

Both of them with their weapons.

Music from Ennio Morricone was missing, Raoul Walsh's camera, John Wayne's face.

I saw these movies with you, Mom. We crossed over to the Valencia

306

theater, without thinking. These are my epics, this is my Troy, my Olympic gods were wearing pistols around their waists, my herculean works included a pirate boat, a duel in the afternoon, a last train to Yuma.

Donkavian couldn't believe it.

"Isn't it funny? You're an amateur and you're making it hard for us."

"You killed my father, Rolando. You don't have a pardon from God."

Do you hear, Tito? You're every inch a Western hero.

Donkavian threw down his Magnum.

"Throw down my Beretta too, okay?"

The Beretta came flying out.

"And your book," added Donkavian, throwing it.

Tito followed it in its aerial trajectory. It just fell to earth and turned to dust, one little hill of sawdust spread over the pavement. Tito raised his gun.

"I'm unarmed, Tito. Don't take advantage." Ironical and to the point, the dirty bastard.

He looked at him leaning over in total calmness, he opened a manhole. A key, a turn and a putrid odor which leaped to the surface.

"Don't you want to look? There's your famous father."

Tito approached with caution, very prudently. He craned his neck. The depth seemed unfathomable.

"What's down there?"

Steady yourself, Tito Livio.

"Hell."

You're a novice, Tito. You stood looking, dazzled by the stench of corruption and rot without being aware of anything else for a few seconds. Horror dazzling like beauty, darkness like the sun. You let your guard down.

Donkavian's blow was right on target, in full view of the people who had stopped on the sidewalks. What's going on? Are they fighting? The gentleman looks so elegant. Is he robbing him? What do I know? Who are you for? Let's bet.

He hit you in the back of the neck, literally, just one crushing blow and your knees doubled. The Styer fell from your wounded hand and Donkavian, with a dancer's movement, an expert in martial arts, like

Mina, sure, how did you not notice it before, delivered a kick to the gun which put it out of your reach.

You can't say anything and your wounded hand is on your back, your arm twisted, he's over you. It hurts like Drakkar Noir this time, the mixture with the smell of rot which burns your nose is unbearable.

"This is the difference between a master and an apprentice," he says to you with that breath which reeks of menthol and anti-tartar flouride. "You're a slow learner. You'll have all eternity to be sorry."

He pushed him against the mouth of the hole. They struggled. Tito stretched out his good hand, desperate, grabbing the edges. A stomp of Donkavian's foot smashed his fingers. Another kick forced him to turn, left with one leg in the void inside the septic well, he grabbed with his hands any way he could, looking for something to grab on to. Donkavian was agile, expert, squash sessions were installed in each muscular fiber, smelly gymnasiums, saccharine in all its forms, diet cola. He was strong besides, enormous strength in his trained arms. We've only come this far, Tito.

And he opened his eyes, frightened, and then our protagonist saw the Great Beast himself shaking among the flames with silhouettes of men with lions' heads, rams' feet, scorpion tails, he saw his chariots with wheels of fire preparing for the assault, he saw the infernal oceans where boats filled with condemned people at their oars were crossing among sea monsters which devoured them, pulling them apart in their jaws, only to be born again as slaves tied up in the bottoms of these galleys of death, he saw war bands ready for combat on the crests of reefs next to a wild and red ocean of blood and body parts where he could make out heads, eyes, tongues, and human intestines which sea vultures gathered at random, scavenging birds of prey, deformed pelicans, under the command of the aforementioned Beast whose enormous torso emerged from the fire with scaly arms and both hands gripping red-hot steel swords with which he flailed in the air, smoke which filled the space, the closed vault where the echo of infernally executed hymns reverberated from a brass orchestra under a shelter of bones which stood out on top of an escarpment. He saw how the boats and chariots and armies were advancing and he understood the coming threat, he understood the evil and its strength, he understood the idolatries of war, the strategies of Hades. He saw how they were making bonfires from books, how they were warehousing prisoners to exhibit their bodies on the top of pikes and lances with which they were ripping the vapor clouds over their heads. He saw the invaded temples, the yelled out proclamations calling out accusations and falsely naming crime as heroism, and abuse as justice, and the fallacious version as official. He saw flags in place of gardens and cannons where he hoped to see trees. He saw mathematical lies, cybernetic lies, philosophical lies and great television screens with the figure of the Great Beast waiting for the signal to attack earth disguised as singers, preachers, artists, politicians, journalists, scientists. He saw all the masks of goodness at the service of evil. And he realized that he had to save himself at any cost, at any price, anywhere. And he closed his eyes after that immense second where he had visions of the most profound kingdom, the one we all deny, the one that is lying under our feet, behind each insignificant lie, and he inhaled holding down the cry and scream and grief and he pronounced God's name in secret, without even noticing it then, once again, for a change of pace, with an intensity he would never regain. He was praying.

The fetidness was making him sick. A kick in the balls, the type which gets you sent off the field straightaway, the pain made him double up. Donkavian's eyes were flashing. Thy will be done: you let go of your last bit of stamina, Tito Livio.

"Stop over there," he heard.

The Seventh Cavalry? A friendly tribe? Robin Hood? Superman? The Holy Spirit? Who?

Javier Solís and the kinky-haired guy with tortoiseshell glasses. With hats, just like in Villa Alemana. Don't they ever change clothes? Sure, their glorious bodies don't get dirty or smell or weigh anything.

You've learned, Tito. You didn't let your surprise get to you. You took advantage of Donkavian's slightest distraction. It was an opening, a minimal crack in which you noticed the loss of tension of his claws in your body. He looked at the two recent arrivals and you noticed the infinitesimal letting up of his hands. You turned in the air with a movement like a gymnast which one can only attribute to a divine illumination, and you mopped the floor with him. Off guard, he went head first into the hole, without hesitation. But, careful, he slid squeezing his fingers, and he dragged you with him hanging from your right hand.

"I'm dying," you screamed.

The angels grabbed you by your legs. Donkavian floated in the middle of the pestilence of hell. The two saviors were thin but strong. It was from another force, one which definitely was not physical. They began to take you out, Rolando Donkavian was still hanging from your hand. His eyes were a mixture of desperation and rage.

"Tito, don't be disloyal. I'm not going to let go of you just like that. If I fall you'll fall with me."

Disloyal to whom? His arm was hurting. He looked at the sky. Then to the angels with hats.

"Grab me," he asked, and in the same movement he gave Donkavian's wrist a fierce bite. His scream was immediate. Tito remembered a Lino Ventura film, one of those that he saw with his mother at the Valencia: *The Gorilla's Bite*. It was working.

His fall seemed endless. After a stretched out minute there was a faraway splash, way at the bottom, which would surge up a tarry liquid, nauseating. Rolando's scream, long like a lament, was extinguished.

Tito looked at the sky again.

"Forgive me," he said.

50

God in the clams

The two archangels, that's what they were and their best trick was not to look the part (that's what those who show themselves say), were on foot.

"The Citroen conked out on us. You know, things aren't going well in the service."

"There's not much of a budget," added the whistler of boleros while they were walking towards Chacabuco Plaza. "Since the situation has been so difficult . . ."

The sun was opening a definite pathway through the clouds and Sunday was promising to be splendid, lunch under the grapevine, food on the grill, roast pork and wine with fruit slices.

Tito Livio didn't finish brushing off his clothes, very mistreated. He chose to forget it. He could give himself a good shower in his apartment where he hoped not to bump into Mina any more, he'd take a nap, clean up his hand, and without doubt he'd eat something restorative and invigorating, and then . . . Then what? Visit his mother?

Maybe. Call Anita? It's possible. He remembered that the phone would be cut off and he shrugged his shoulders. There would be a public telephone in Lo Castillo Plaza. Done.

"Everything's under control," he commented happily while they were waiting for transportation together at the great sculpted horses of the Chilean Hippodrome. The sun was hitting them straight on, surprisingly healthy.

"Thank God," muttered the shortest guy, and he meant it.

Tito smiled.

"I didn't think I'd manage it. I have to say that I was lucky."

The minivan stopped in front of them. He long had it been since he used public transportation? His daughters would not know the least thing about the pleasure of traveling in a minivan, its smell of skin, the real Chilean people, its noise with transistor radios, improvised songs and aspirin salesmen. It was evident it was Sunday by how empty the minivan was and by its slow roll towards Mapocho, along Independence Avenue.

"Where are you going?" Javier Solís said to him as his friend paid.

"I don't know, downtown. From there I'll take a taxi to my apartment."

They sat down. He and the one with the mustache together, the third man in the back seat on the other side of the aisle leaning up against the window with a melancholy air.

That's how I used to travel to school, thought Tito. He used to look at the numbers of the streets dreaming he was traveling in a time machine and that those numbers were years that were going by. I used to imagine the houses as ruins of those historic times, like an archaeologist's text coming from the future. I used to kill time, fantasizing, dreaming, a future ad man.

They barely spoke. When they were passing in front of the medical school, Tito made a comment. I lost years of my life there, something like that. The other two didn't say anything.

"We could have gotten there before," said Javier Solís suddenly. "But it took longer than we thought it would."

"What do you mean?"

"What? Didn't they tell you?"

"I don't know what you're talking about."

"Sure, if they had told you, everything probably would have failed."

Tito frowned. He supported himself on the metal chrome bar under which political slogans were displayed on the back of the front seat. Taunts against Pinochet, calling for an armed struggle, various off-color things.

"If they had told me what?"

Javier Gabriel, archangel in service, gulped.

"Look, to tell you the truth . . . in a certain way . . . everything was fake."

Now Tito was the one who felt like gagging. They were passing directly in front of his mother's apartment. He didn't even notice. She, at this moment, was opening the blinds in her solar stubbornness, thinking just as she did every Sunday about her sons and grandchildren while she was getting ready for nine o'clock mass, less sunny. With or without a parasol, she would attend.

"What?"

"Well, the one sure thing is that the whole thing about the Tetragrammaton was a fake clue."

Tito was silent. The two men were looking at him while the one with the mustache explained it to him.

"A false clue. Do you understand? We had to get the attention of his agents off track. The real thing was being played out somewhere else, with other signals and through other situations which had to go unnoticed at all costs. We needed a false target for them. On the other hand, we knew that you were halfway lettered, that you read a lot of detective novels when you were young, a lot of Borges, Lovecraft, Chesterton . . . and we set the trap."

"But . . . I thought . . ."

"You thought you were one of God's chosen ones?" The shortest guy tried to be understanding.

Rage. Once again with us, Tito Livio's fury. They made a brief out of you, they constructed an intricate plot around you. So you would do what you didn't know you were doing. Like any consumer, you thought you were the hero of the novel.

"You guys are joking."

"No, and it went real well. You shouldn't feel frustrated, you did marvelously well. We set up everything and they swallowed it hook,

313

line and sinker, absolutely all of it. It was a success. You know, they believe in appearances, in linear developments, in the spectacular, and because of that we won. We tempted the Devil, do you see?"

"We won a battle that was almost lost," added Rafael. "We were on the ropes."

"Get screwed," said a foulmouthed Tito.

"We understand your anger. You were really in danger. We're pleading with you to forgive the unpleasantness."

"The unpleasantness? My father an unpleasantness? Old Romero an unpleasantness? Old Sara an unpleasantness?"

"They knew that these things were happening and they were ready to give up all protagonistic labor. We all knew it. We'll never know the true point of equilibrium and power. It will always be unknown. Do you understand me? In the celestial project there are no primary planes. That's a typical strategy of the Devil."

"Listen, Tito, don't get upset. This whole thing seemed like a realist novel. That's exactly what they believe, that things are only like a story, they think that God functions the same way and they all become crazy because of the brilliance, the activity, the intrigue. They let the minimal escape, the simple, the casual. In order to hide the truth from the Devil there's nothing better than a beautiful lie."

"Like a novel," completed Javier Solís.

"And that's even paradoxical, listen. Then the Truth, the great one, the only one, the definite one, the Truth of Truths, does not have any other access to the human mind which is wrapped in a lie, fiction, or metaphor. It does not exist in a pure state, do you understand? But rather because of reflection, analogy, and insinuation."

"The unreal is the wardrobe of the real," completed the one with the mustache. "The lie of the truth. One with the other."

Tito began to feel sick. They continued.

"What's more, at some point the fake clue was to believe that yours was a fake clue, and in the end you did save everything believing that you were saving it, and you're going to go away convinced that you didn't do anything when in reality you did."

"Or, that is . . . we don't know anything."

Tito began to scream uncontrollably.

"I don't even know what to call this!"

314

"That's the important thing, that nobody ever finds out."

Our confused hero was trying to get out towards the aisle.

"Don't leave, we have to celebrate. It was precisely the most dangerous day and everything came out fine."

"The most dangerous day?" Tito Livio stopped.

"Yes. God rests on Sundays. He's weaker for the usual enemy aggressions. It's like catching him sleeping."

Our hero couldn't take any more. He pulled the buzzer and didn't wait for the minivan to come to a complete stop before jumping out. As soon as the doors opened, with a snort like a bull he was on the sidewalk.

"I don't want to see you any more!"

Shaking from indignation he made his way towards the Central Market. With an attitude of resignation the two archangels watched him recede. The smallest one waved a white handkerchief until he lost sight of him. Tito didn't look back. A good seafood dish would alleviate his haggard state, his cut-up body, with a good glass of wine, maybe it would get rid of his anger too.

He chose the most remote table in the Market. Cheerful survivors of the night were finishing off round shaped sea creatures, opening clams in an atmosphere filled with iodine and lemon. It was a fresh smell, healthy, from the nearby ocean.

He searched for some errant bills in his pockets and ordered the same thing as everyone else, together with the much-desired drink. He drank it in one swallow. Another, thanks. He took his time: mollusks, sea urchins, mussels. The lemon seasoned it to his taste. He ate slowly, helping himself to a hard roll which was toning down his anger.

Yes, he thought, the important thing is to not buy into the headlines in the newspapers. That was another illusion of the era: believing in the holiness of the visible and making the evident sacred. That was the origin of the poverty of spirit, that poverty which could not have happiness. Only the secret things are strong, but the perfect secret is the one you don't know you have, like his father's book would say, the one that ended up turned into dust on the Chilean Hippodrome street, next to a manhole which turned out to be the very mouth of hell.

He toasted his conclusions and comfortably savored the contents of a clamshell smothered in lemon and spicy onions. He felt put back together. He looked at Santiago beginning to snarl with Sunday traffic. The fruit, the fish, the incessant movement of commerce in the Central Market. To your health, he said to the city.

Far from there, out of view, a manhole cover began to turn without the neighbors in the area being able to understand the phenomenon, distracted in some other place by jokes about the ferocious chase in the middle of the street in the area near the Santa Laura Stadium. Rabid animals, hand to hand fighting in the middle of the street. They said that it was an old detective's quarrel with the political police, problems between them, drugs, homosexual affairs, things like that.

The cover popped up, letting out a foul odor of rot which immediately mobilized a neighbor to telephone the authorities, protesting their carelessness with a neighborhood as populous as hers; and another wrote to the newspaper, *El Mercurio*, soliciting direct intervention of the press, the fourth estate, in problems which fell upon everyone.

From the hole there appeared a muddy face, entirely covered with rubbish, which climbed out with the stumbling of a monster from a Japanese movie, onto the surface, slowly gaining its balance little by little as it walked. Children fled to tell of this apparition to their parents who didn't believe a single word. A few yards further up the monster got into the latest model Alfa Romeo, one of those rarely seen around there. With a violent fishtail it disappeared behind the open air market installed along the avenue.

Tito, for his part, interrupted his eating and asked for a telephone. Call Anita María and ask her to talk. Really talk to her sometime, now that there was nothing to hide. He dialed and waited.

"Hello?"

Anita María. He explained his plan to go out together to her. There was a pause.

"What's wrong? Anita?"

"Are you okay, Tito?"

Stupid, he had forgotten the most important thing.

"Yes, I'm fine. Everything is over. That is, at least I think it is."

There was another pause.

"Were you planning to go out with Ismael?" said Tito.

"Well, we were going to do something with the girls. You know how

316

much they like him."

Tito wrinkled his nose. Reasonable, if he had been searching for something, it was that this would happen to her.

"Okay. You know how to find me. We'll go out sometime. There's a lot to talk about. Don't you think?"

She agreed and they said goodbye. It was almost pleasant; but Tito needed another glass of white wine. It wasn't one of the best and it left a certain acidity on his palate, a bitter residue.

"The only thing that's left for me is to write a novel," he said to himself and smiled, not without a certain sadness. "A novel which no one is going to believe, one where I know how it ends, from what I already know about its destiny."

He raised his glass (his hand almost didn't hurt him) and he toasted, speaking in a loud voice faced with the indifferent look of the fishmonger.

"You don't know what this is all about," he said to him. "This is a satori."

"Listen, we don't have any of that kind of fish."

"Of course not. That isn't bought or sold. Did you know that God is in these clams, in these hakes, in those crabs? Even in this wine. Waiting for us."

"No," said the fishmonger trying to get away. Every crazy person, every drunk, every night they come in here to wander around.

"Me neither," pronounced Tito Livio without worrying now if he was talking to himself.

He raised his glass feeling relief from his wounds and a strange peace, as if recently achieved and at the same time present his whole life, which was filling his entire soul. The light which was passing through his glass seemed beautiful to him.

"To immortality," he said before drinking.

Slowly, perhaps wishing that his father could only hear him.

About the Author

Marco Antonio de la Parra, Chilean playwright, short story writer, novelist, and psychiatrist, began to establish his reputation as a writer in 1978 with his work, *Lo crudo, lo cocido y lo podrido* (The Raw, The Cooked, and The Rotten). The play caused a scandal and the Catholic University in Santiago banned its performance one day before the official debut. They considered the play to have certain elements contrary to accepted university and Catholic norms. After several months, the play was presented in the Imagen Theatre under the direction of Gustavo Mena. During this time, de la Parra had already debuted another work, *Matatangos*, which has to do with the myths surrounding Carlos Gardel, the legendary Argentinian tango singer who died in 1935. *Matatangos* was presented in October 1987 at the GALA Hispanic Theatre in Washington D.C., and was presented again in the 1988–89 season. Most recently it was presented at Joseph Papp's Festival Latino in New York in August 1990.

La secreta obscenidad de cada día (Secret Obscenities) debuted first in Chile in 1984 and then enjoyed another successful run in 1988–89. The English version was debuted at the Cleveland Play House, Cleveland, Ohio in February 1988 and ran for 14 performances. The Spanish version was produced at the GALA Hispanic Theatre during the 1988–89 season in Washington,

D.C., and at the Festival Latino in 1990. It was awarded Chile's Premio de Periodistas de Espectáculos (Newspaper Writers Award) for best play 1988. It is one of the most widely performed works of Latin American theater in recent years.

In January of 1987, de la Parra debuted another play, *El deseo de toda ciudadana* (Every Young Woman's Desire) which was directed by Ramón Griffero and was awarded Chile's Premio del Círculo de Críticos (Critic's Circle Award) for best play 1987. *Infieles* (Beds) debuted in May 1988. *Infieles* and *La secreta obscenidad de cada día* were published in 1988 by Ediciones Planeta.

Marco Antonio's recent dramatic works, *King Kong Palace* and *Dostoievski va a la Playa* (Dostoyevsky Goes to the Beach) were published together in a book in November 1990. Neither has been debuted in Chile. *King Kong Palace* has been presented in Asunción, Paraguay. His most recent play, *El padre muerto* (The Dead Father), won a prize for drama in Spain.

In addition to his work in theater, de la Parra has published a book of short stories, *Sueños eróticos/Amores impossibles* (Erotic Dreams/Impossible Loves) in 1986, and three novels. *El deseo de toda ciudadana* (Every Young Woman's Desire) was published in 1987 and won first prize in a contest judged by well-known authors and writers, including José Donoso and Ariel Dorfman. His second novel, *La secreta guerra santa de Santiago de Chile* (The Secret Holy War of Santiago de Chile) was published by Ediciones Planeta in November 1989 and enjoyed several months as the best selling novel in Chile. The third, *Cuerpos prohibidos* (Forbidden Bodies), was published in December 1991.

In August of 1988 an interview with de la Parra about his work and the future of literature in Chile appeared in an article by Mitchel Levitas in the *New York Times Book Review* entitled "Writers and Dictators." He is without doubt one of the best playwrights and novelists of the "new generation" of writers in Chile. He was honored by his country by being named Cultural Attaché to the Chilean Embassy in Madrid, Spain and remained at the post until September of 1993.